PRAISE FOR REI

"A gifted storyteller."

—*Kirkus Reviews*

"Rebecca Yarros writes words that are pure, sweet, sizzling poetry."
—Tessa Bailey, *New York Times* and *USA Today* bestselling author

"Readers will be *wowed*."

—*Publishers Weekly* (starred review), on *The Things We Leave Unfinished*

"A haunting, heartbreaking, and ultimately inspirational love story."
—*In Touch Weekly*, on *The Last Letter*

"Thanks to Yarros's beautiful, immersive writing, readers will feel every deep heartbreak and each moment of uplifting love."
—*Publishers Weekly* (starred review), on *The Last Letter*

"Rebecca never disappoints—she's an automatic one-click for me!"
—Jen McLaughlin, *New York Times* bestselling author

IN THE LIKELY EVENT

OTHER TITLES BY REBECCA YARROS

Stand-Alone Titles

Fourth Wing
The Things We Leave Unfinished
The Last Letter
Great and Precious Things
Muses and Melodies (part of the Hush Note series, written with Sarina Bowen and Devney Perry)
A Little Too Close (part of the Madigan Mountain series, written with Sarina Bowen and Devney Perry)

Flight & Glory

Full Measures
Eyes Turned Skyward
Beyond What Is Given
Hallowed Ground
The Reality of Everything

Legacy

Point of Origin
Ignite
Reason to Believe

The Renegades

Wilder
Nova
Rebel

IN THE LIKELY EVENT

A Novel

REBECCA YARROS

This is a work of fiction. Names, characters, organizations, places, events, and incidents are either products of the author's imagination or are used fictitiously. Otherwise, any resemblance to actual persons, living or dead, is purely coincidental.

Published by Montlake, Seattle

www.apub.com

Amazon, the Amazon logo, and Montlake are trademarks of Amazon.com, Inc., or its affiliates.

ISBN-13: 9781662511554 (paperback)
ISBN-13: 9781662511561 (digital)

Cover design by Shasti O'Leary Soudant
Cover image: © Angela Lumsden / Stocksy United; © Dacian Groza / Stocksy United

Printed in the United States of America

To my sister, Kate.
I'd go to war for you.
Love you, mean it.

CHAPTER ONE
NATHANIEL

Kabul, Afghanistan
August 2021

This was not the Maldives.

I closed my eyes and tipped my head back toward the blistering afternoon sun. With the breeze, I could almost pretend the moisture racing down my neck, soaking into my collar, was water from a recent swim instead of my own sweat. Almost.

Instead, I stood on the tarmac in Kabul, wondering how the hell my boots weren't melting into the concrete at this temperature. Maybe missing my trip was karma paying me back for going without her.

"You're supposed to be on leave," a familiar voice said from my right.

"Shhh. I am. See?" I opened one eye just enough to glimpse Torres standing beside me, his thick brow shaded by his multicam cap.

"See what? You standing on the flight line with your head thrown back like you're in a Coppertone commercial?"

The corners of my mouth quirked upward. "It's not the flight line. It's a little bungalow over the water in the Maldives. Can't you hear the waves?"

The rhythmic beat of distant rotors filled the air.

"I hear you losing your mind," he muttered. "Looks like they're here."

Reluctantly, I opened my eyes and searched the horizon for an aircraft on final approach, spotting the plane within seconds.

Here we go again. As much as I used to love the action that came with my job, I had to admit that it was getting old. Peace sounded so much better than constant war.

"How the hell did you let yourself get roped into this, anyway? I thought Jenkins was on this assignment," Torres asked.

"Jenkins went down with some kind of virus last night, and I didn't want to ask Ward to skip his leave. He has kids." I shifted the shoulder strap of my rifle as the C-130 touched down on the runway. "Now I'm on babysitting duty for Senator Lauren's aide."

"Well, I'm with you, like always."

"I appreciate that."

My best friend hadn't left my side since Special Forces selection. Hell, even before that.

"Hopefully by next week, Jenkins will be on the mend and I'll be on my way to the Maldives before the actual senators get here." I could almost taste those fruity umbrella drinks right now—oh wait, that was the metallic tang of jet fuel. Right.

"You know, most guys I know use their leave time to go home and see their families." Torres looked back at the rest of the team as they strode our way, straightening their patchless ACUs, like it was possible to unfuck their uniforms after four months in country.

"Well, most guys don't have my family." I shrugged. Mom had been gone for five years, and the only reason I'd willingly see my father would be to bury him.

The rest of the team reached us, falling into a line as we faced the aircraft. Graham took the spot on my other side. "Want me driving?"

"Yep," I answered. I'd already selected the guys I wanted with me until Jenkins got back. Parker and Elston were waiting at the embassy.

"Is everyone here?" Major Webb asked as he reached us, scratching his chin.

"Holy shit! I can't remember the last time I saw your actual face." Graham grinned at our commander, his bright smile contrasting with his deep-brown skin.

Webb muttered something about politicians as the plane taxied to the directions of the air traffic controllers.

There were certain perks to being the elite of Special Forces. The informal camaraderie and not having to shave were definitely two of them. Getting screwed out of leave to play security detail to the advance party of some legislators wasn't. I'd spent an hour this morning familiarizing myself with Greg Newcastle's file. My assignment was the thirty-three-year-old deputy chief of staff to Senator Lauren, and he had the polished look of a guy who'd gone straight from Harvard Law to the Hill. The group of them were coming on what they called a "fact-finding" mission so they could report back on how the US withdrawal was going. I somehow doubted they were going to be happy with what they found.

"Just to refresh . . . ," Webb said, taking a folded piece of paper from his pocket and glancing at the designated security team leads. "Maroon, your team has Baker out of Congressman Garcia's office," he began, using our designated for-public-use names for this mission. "Gold, you're on Turner from Congressman Murphy. White, you're on Holt out of Senator Liu's office. Green, you're responsible for Astor out of Senator Lauren's office—"

"I was given Greg Newcastle's file," I interrupted.

Webb glanced down at the paper. "Looks like they made a change last minute. You have Astor now. Mission is still the same. That's the office focusing on the southern provinces. The one working on bringing the girls' chess team to the States."

Astor. My stomach jumped into my throat. There was no way. None.

"Relax," Torres whispered. "It's a common last name."

Right. Besides, the last time I'd heard from her, she was working at some firm in New York, but that was three years ago.

The rain had soaked through my coat—

I clamped down on my reckless thoughts as the plane parked in front of us, guided by the ground crew. Heat radiated off the tarmac in shimmering waves, distorting my vision as the rear door lowered and the pilots powered down the engines.

Uniformed airmen descended from the C-130 first, leading a group of civilians I assumed were the congressional aides and, in one case, helping one of the suits off the ramp.

My brows lifted. *The guy can't get off the ramp by himself and thought it would be a good idea to come tour Afghanistan?*

"Are you serious?" Kellman—or Sergeant White for this mission—scoffed. "Please tell me that's not my guy."

"Here we go," Torres muttered at my side.

I blew out a long breath as I counted to ten, hoping patience would miraculously appear by the time I reached zero. It didn't. This was a waste of our time.

The airmen were all smiles as they walked toward us, obscuring their followers from view. Of course they were happy. They were here to drop off the suits. I highly doubted they'd still be all grins if they were the ones who had to escort clueless, self-important civilians to a bunch of FOBs like they were tourist destinations and not active combat zones.

Major Webb moved forward, and the airmen guided the politicians to the front of their little herd. There were six in all—

My heart. Fucking. Stopped.

I slow-blinked once, then twice as the heat shimmer dissipated with a gust of wind. There was no mistaking that honey-gold hair or that million-dollar smile. I would have bet my life there were deep-brown eyes framed by thick lashes behind those oversize sunglasses. My hands flexed, like they could still feel the curves of her body all these years later.

It was *her*.

"You okay?" Torres asked under his breath. "You look like you're about to puke up your breakfast."

No, I wasn't *okay*. I was about as far away from okay as New York was from Afghanistan. I couldn't even form words. Ten years had passed since we'd met on a very different tarmac, and the sight of her still left me speechless.

She offered her right hand to Webb to shake and shifted the strap of a familiar army-green cargo backpack higher on her shoulder with her left. She still had that thing? Sunlight caught those fingers and reflected back brighter than a signal mirror.

What. The. Hell. My heart stuttered back to life, pounding in denial so hard the thing *hurt*.

The only woman I'd ever loved was here—in a damned war zone—and she was wearing another man's ring. She was going to be another man's *wife*. I didn't even know the bastard and I already hated him, already knew he wasn't good enough for her. Not that I was either. That had always been the problem between us.

She turned toward me, her smile faltering as her mouth slackened. Her fingers trembled as she shoved her sunglasses up to the top of her head, revealing a set of wide brown eyes that looked as stunned as I felt.

A vise tightened around my chest.

In my peripherals, Webb worked his way down the line, introducing the politicians to their security details, and coming our way like a nuclear countdown as we stared at each other. A dozen feet, maybe less, separated us, and the distance was somehow simultaneously too far and way too close.

She walked forward and flinched, then captured her hair in a fist as the wind gusted, blasting every surface with sand and dirt, including the white blouse she'd rolled up her forearms. What the hell was she doing here? She didn't belong here. She belonged in a cushy corner office where nothing could touch her . . . especially me.

"Ms. Astor, meet—" Webb started.

"Nathaniel Phelan," she finished, scanning my face like she might never see it again, like she was cataloging every change, every scar I'd acquired in the last three years.

"Izzy." It was all I could manage with that billion-carat rock flashing at me from her hand like a warning beacon. Who the hell had she said yes to?

"You two know each other?" Webb's eyebrows rose as he glanced between us.

"Yes," I said.

"Not anymore," she answered simultaneously.

Shit.

"Okay?" Webb shuffled his gaze again, noting the awkward moment for what it was. "Is this going to be a problem?"

Yes. A giant problem. A million unspoken words blasted the air between us, as thick and relentless as the sand coming across the flight line.

"Look, I can reassign—" Webb started.

"No," I snapped. There was zero chance in hell I was risking her safety with anyone else. She was stuck with me, whether or not she liked it.

Webb blinked, the only sign of surprise he'd ever give, and glanced at Izzy. "Ms. Astor?"

"It will be fine. Please don't trouble yourself," she responded with an easy, polished, fake-ass smile that sent chills down my spine.

"Okay then," Webb said slowly, then pivoted toward me and mouthed *good luck* before moving on.

Izzy and I stared at each other as every emotion I'd fought to bury over the last three years clawed its way to the surface, ripping open scabs that had never quite healed to scars. Go figure we'd meet again like this. We'd always had a habit of colliding at the worst times and in the most inconvenient places. It was almost fitting that it was a battlefield this go-round.

"I thought you were in New York," I finally managed to say, my voice coming out like it had been scraped over the pavement a dozen times. *Where no one is actively trying to blow you up.*

"Yeah?" She arched a brow and hefted the slipping pack up to her shoulder. "Funny, because I thought you were dead. Guess we were both wrong."

CHAPTER TWO

IZZY

Saint Louis
November 2011

"Fifteen A. Fifteen A," I muttered, scanning the seat numbers as I muddled my way down the crowded aisle of the commuter plane, my carry-on slipping through my clammy hands with every step. Spotting my row, I sighed in relief that the overhead compartment was still empty, then cursed as I realized A was a window seat.

My stomach twisted into a knot. Had I really booked myself by the window? Where I could see every potential disaster coming our way?

Hold up. There was already a guy sitting in the window seat, his head down, only the Saint Louis Blues emblem visible on his hat. Maybe I'd read my ticket wrong.

I made it to my row, stood on my tiptoes, and shoved my carry-on up as far as my arms would extend, aiming for the overhead bin. It made contact with the edge, but the only prayer I had of getting it all the way in was to climb on the seat . . . or grow another six inches.

My hands slipped, and the bright-purple suitcase plummeted toward my face. Before I had time to gasp, a massive hand caught my unruly luggage, stopping it a few inches from my nose.

Holy crap.

"That was close," a deep voice noted from behind my carry-on. "How about I help you with that?"

"Yes, please," I answered, scrambling to adjust my hold.

I saw the Blues hat first as the guy somehow managed to twist his body, rise fully to his feet, step into the aisle, and balance my suitcase all in one smooth motion. *Impressive.*

"Here we go." He slid the carry-on into the overhead with ease.

"Thanks. I was pretty sure it was going to take me out there for a second." I smiled, turning my head slightly to look up—and up—at him.

Whuh. He was . . . hot. Like, pull-the-fire-alarm, jaw-dropping levels of hotness. A fine layer of dark scruff covered a square jawline. Even the cut and the purplish bruise that split the right half of his lower lip didn't detract from his face, because his eyes . . . wow. Just . . . *wow.* Those crystalline baby blues stole every word out of my head.

And now I was staring, and not the cute, flirty glances Serena would have given him while shamelessly asking for his number and inevitably getting it. No, this was open-mouthed awkward staring that I couldn't seem to stop.

Close your mouth.

Nope, still staring. Staring. Staring.

"Me too," he said, a corner of his mouth lifting slightly.

I blinked. *"Me too," what?* "I'm sorry?"

His brow knit in confusion. "Me too," he repeated. "I thought that thing was going to smash you in the face."

"Right." I tucked my hair behind my ears, only to remember that I'd pulled it up into a messy bun and therefore had no hair to tuck, which just continued my awkward streak. Awesome. And now my face was on fire, which meant I'd probably turned ten shades of red.

He slid back into his seat, and I realized our exchange had blocked the rest of the flight from boarding.

"Sorry," I muttered to the next passenger, and ducked into fifteen B. "Funny thing, I could have sworn my ticket said I was in the window." I lifted the strap of my purse over my head, then unzipped my jacket and wiggled the least amount possible to get out of the thing. At this rate, I'd probably jab Blue Eyes with my elbow and make an even bigger ass of myself.

"Oh shit." His head swung toward mine, and he winced. "I traded seats with a woman up in seven A so she could sit next to her kid. I bet I took yours by accident." He reached down for an army-green backpack under the seat in front of him, his shoulders so wide that they brushed my left knee as he leaned forward. "Let's switch."

"No!" I blurted.

He stilled, then turned his head slowly to look up at me. "No?"

"I mean, I hate the window. I'm actually really freaked out by flying, so it works better this way." Crap, I was babbling. "Unless you want the aisle?" I held my breath with hope that he wouldn't.

He sat back up and shook his head. "No, I'm good here. Freaked out by flying, huh?" There was no mockery in his tone.

"Yep." Relief sagged my shoulders, and I folded up my jacket, then squished it under the seat in front of me with my purse.

"Why?" he asked. "If you don't mind me asking?"

My cheeks turned up the heat a notch. "I've always been afraid of flying. There's something about it that just . . ." I shook my head. "I mean statistically, we're fine. The incident rate last year was one in 1.3 million, which was up from the year before, when it was one in 1.5 million. But, when you think about how many flights there are, I guess that's not as bad as driving, since your odds of crashing are one in 103, but still, 828 people died last year, and I don't want to be one of the 828." *You're babbling again.* I pressed my lips between my teeth and prayed my brain would cut it out.

"Huh." Two lines appeared between his eyebrows. "Never thought of it that way."

"I bet flying doesn't scare you, does it?" This guy looked like nothing in the world scared him.

"I wouldn't know. I've never flown before, but now that you went over the stats, I'm questioning my choices."

"Oh God. I'm so sorry." My hands flew to cover my mouth. "I babble when I get nervous. And I have ADHD. And I didn't take my medication this morning because I put it out on the counter next to my orange juice, but then Serena drank the juice, and I got sidetracked pouring more, and that pill is probably still sitting there—" I cringed, slamming my eyes shut. A deep breath later, I opened them and found him watching me with raised eyebrows. "Sorry. Add in the fact that I overthink just about everything, and here we are. Babbling."

A small smile crept across his face. "Don't worry about it. So why get on a plane at all?" He adjusted the airflow above his head, then shoved the black sleeves of his henley up his tan forearms. The guy was built. If his forearms looked like that, I couldn't help but wonder if the rest of his body followed suit.

"Thanksgiving." I shrugged. "My parents went on one of those around-the-world cruises after dropping me off for freshman year, and my older sister, Serena, is a junior here at Wash U—she's studying journalism. Since I'm all the way up at Syracuse, flying made the most sense since we wanted to spend the holiday together. You?"

"I'm headed to basic training at Fort Benning. I'm Nathaniel Phelan, by the way. My friends call me Nate." The stream of passengers down the aisle had trickled to just the hurried latecomers.

"Hi, Nate. I'm Izzy." I reached out my hand and he took it. "Izzy Astor." Not sure how I managed to say my full name when every ounce of my concentration was on the feel of his calloused hand engulfing mine, and the flutter that erupted in my stomach at the warmth of his touch.

I wasn't one of those people who believed in jolts of electricity at first touch like all the romance novels, but here I was, jolted to my core. His eyes flared slightly, like he'd felt it too. It wasn't a shock as much as an almost indescribable, sizzling feeling of awareness . . . connection, like the satisfying click of the final puzzle piece.

Serena would have called it fate, but she was a hopeless romantic.

I called it attraction.

"Nice to meet you, Izzy." He shook my hand slowly, then let go even slower, his fingers waking up every nerve ending in my palm as they fell away. "I'm guessing that's short for Isabelle?"

"Actually, it's Isabeau." I busied myself fastening my buckle and tightening my belt across my hips.

"Isabeau," he repeated, buckling his own.

"Yep. My mom had a thing for *Ladyhawke*." The aisle was finally empty. Guess we had everyone aboard.

"What's *Ladyhawke*?" Nate questioned, his brow furrowing slightly.

"It's this eighties movie where a couple pisses off an evil medieval bishop because they love each other so much. The bishop wants the girl, but she's in love with Navarre, so the bishop curses them. Navarre becomes a wolf during the night, and she turns into a hawk during the day, so they only catch a glimpse of the other when the sun rises and sets. Isabeau is the girl—the hawk." *Stop babbling!* God, why was I like this?

"That sounds . . . tragic."

"Ladies and gentlemen, welcome to Transcontinental Airlines Flight 826," the flight attendant said over the PA system.

"Not completely tragic. They break the curse, so it has a happy ending." I leaned forward and managed to get my cell phone out of my purse without taking the entire bag out.

Two missed text messages from Serena lit up my screen.

Serena: Txt me when u board

Serena: not kidding!

The messages were fifteen minutes apart.

"If you haven't already done so, please stow your carry-on luggage in an overhead bin or the seat in front of you. Please take your seat and fasten your seat belt," the flight attendant continued, her voice chipper but professional.

I tapped out a text to my sister.

Isabeau: boarded

Serena: u had me worried

Smiling, I shook my head. I was the only thing Serena worried about.

Isabeau: worried? Like I'd get lost between security and my gate?

Serena: i never know with u

I wasn't *that* bad.

Isabeau: I love you. Thank you for this week.

Serena: Love u more. Txt when u land

The announcement continued. "If you're seated next to an emergency exit, please read the special instructions card located in the seat back in front of you. If you do not wish to perform the functions described in the event of an emergency, please ask a flight attendant to reseat you."

I glanced up. "That's us," I said to Nate. "We're in an exit row."

He looked at the markings on the door, then reached forward for the safety card while the attendant informed the cabin that it was a nonsmoking flight. Had to admit, that only made him cuter.

Nate read while the attendant finished out her announcements and closed the door. My heart rate spiked, the anxiety hitting me right on time. I fumbled with my phone and checked my Instagram and Twitter, then put my device on airplane mode, slipped it into the front pocket of my vest, and zipped the pocket. When my throat went tight, I adjusted the air above me, putting it on max.

Nate put the safety card back into the seat in front of him and settled in, watching what activity there was to see on the ground. The fog was dense this morning, already delaying us twenty minutes.

"Don't forget your phone," I said just before the attendant said the same over the intercom. "It has to be on airplane mode."

"Don't have a phone, so I'm good there." He flashed me a smile, then winced, running his tongue over the split in his lip.

"What happened there?" I motioned to my own lip. "If you don't mind *me* asking this time."

His smile fell. "I had a slight disagreement with someone. It's a long story." He reached for the seat in front of him and took out a paperback from the pocket—*Into Thin Air*, by Jon Krakauer.

He was a reader? This guy just kept getting hotter.

I took the hint and retrieved my own book out of my purse, flipping to the bookmark in the middle of chapter eleven of Jennifer L. Armentrout's *Half-Blood.*

"Flight attendants, please prepare for gate departure," a deeper voice said over the PA.

"Is that any good?" Nate asked as the plane backed out of the gate.

"I love it. Though it looks like you might be more of a nonfiction kind of guy." I nodded toward his reading choice. "How's that one?" He looked to be about halfway through.

The plane turned to the right and rolled forward, and I took a breath in through my nose and pushed it out through my mouth.

"It's good. Really good. I found it on this list of a hundred books you're supposed to read by the time you're thirty or something. I'm just working my way down the list." He glanced over at me, and his brow puckered. "You doing okay?"

"Yep," I answered as my stomach cartwheeled. "Did you know that the most dangerous times in flying are the first three minutes after take-off and the last eight minutes before landing?"

"I didn't."

I swallowed. Hard. "I used to take sedatives. Prescribed by my doctor, of course. I'm not into the illegal stuff. Not that it's bad if you are." I cringed at my own words. Why the hell was my brain my own worst enemy?

"Not my thing. Why don't you take the sedatives anymore?" He shut his book.

"They knock me out, and I almost missed my connection in Philly once. The flight attendant had to shake me awake, and then it was a full-out run to my gate. The door was already shut and everything, but they let me on. So, no more sedatives."

The plane turned into a line of other planes, readying to taxi. *Stop looking out the window. You know that makes it worse.*

"Makes sense." He cleared his throat. "So what are you studying up at Syracuse?" His obvious attempt to distract me made the corners of my mouth curve upward.

"Public relations." I fought back a laugh. "I'm usually pretty good with people, until you stick me on a plane."

"I think you're doing just fine." He grinned, and God help me, a dimple popped in his right cheek.

"What about you? Why go into the army? Why not go to college?" I shut my own book, leaving it in my lap.

"Wasn't exactly an option. My grades were good, but not good enough to get a scholarship, and there isn't enough money for cable, let alone college. Honestly, my parents needed my help. They own a small farm just south of Shipman, Illinois." He looked away. "It's my mom's farm, really. My grandfather left it to her. Anyway, the army will pay for college, so off I go."

I nodded, but I wasn't foolish enough to think I understood. It was the complete opposite of the way I'd grown up, where the question had been *where* I was going for undergrad and not if. Mom and Dad jokingly called my tuition a *parentship*, since they were paying for my education. I'd never had to struggle with the kind of choice Nate was making. "And what do you want to do once you graduate?"

His brow knit. "I haven't gotten that far yet. Maybe teach. I like English. Something with literature. But maybe I'll like the army. Special Forces seems pretty awesome too."

"Ladies and gentlemen, this is your captain speaking. First off, I'd like to welcome you all aboard flight 826 with nonstop service to Atlanta. You may have noticed, but there's a rather thick layer of fog that's slowing everyone down this morning, and it looks like we're twenty-second in line for takeoff, which means it's going to be about forty minutes or longer before we're in the air."

A collective groan sounded from the passengers around us, me included. Forty minutes wouldn't keep me from my connection to Syracuse, but it would make it tight.

"The good news is that the weather looks good once we break free of this fog, so we'll try and make up the time in the air. Bear with us, folks, and thanks for flying with us."

There was a series of pings around us as people pressed their call buttons, no doubt stressed about their own connections.

"Are you connecting in Atlanta?" I asked Nate.

"Yeah, to Columbus, but I have a few hours before that one." He thumbed the split in his lip and shifted in his seat.

"I have some antibiotic ointment in my purse," I offered. "Tylenol, too, if it hurts."

His eyebrows rose. "You keep a first aid kit in your purse?"

My cheeks heated again. "Just the essentials. You never know when you're going to get stuck on the tarmac with a stranger who has a long story about a split lip." I smiled slowly.

His laughter was soft, barely discernible. "I'll be okay. I've had worse."

"That's not reassuring." Huh. There was a slight bump in his nose, and I couldn't help but wonder if he'd broken it at one point.

He laughed louder this time. "Trust me. It will be okay."

"That must have been some disagreement."

"Usually is." He fell quiet, and my chest tightened at the realization that I'd poked where I had no business poking. Again.

"So, what else have you read off your one hundred must-read books?" I asked.

"Hmm." He glanced upward, like he was thinking. "*The Outsiders*, by—"

"S. E. Hinton," I finished. *Shit, I interrupted him.* "Go figure. I'm pretty sure they hand that out to every prospective bad boy their freshman year of high school." I couldn't stop my smile.

"Hey now—" He drew back like he was wounded. "What about this"—he motioned down his frame—"says that I'm a bad boy? I grew up on a farm."

I laughed, forgetting that we were moving steadily forward through the takeoff line. "That body? That face? That cut on your lip? Those scraped-up knuckles?" I glanced at where his sleeve met his arm, noting the swirls of black ink. "Oh, and tattoos? Quintessential bad boy material right there. I bet you left a plethora of broken hearts in your wake."

"Who says *plethora* in a normal conversation?" His smile only made mine bigger. Bad boy or not, I knew Nate's smile must have dropped its share of panties, because if we weren't on this plane, I might have considered my first one-night stand. "I'll tell you who. Good little college girls."

"Guilty as charged." I lifted my brows at him. "You even have the hot, broody reading vibe down. Very Jess Mariano of you."

"Jess who?" He blinked in confusion.

"Jess Mariano," I managed. Those *eyes* were going to be the death of me. The shade reminded me of the Ice Lakes up by Silverton, not quite glacial. More like aqua. "You know, from *Gilmore Girls*."

"Never seen it." He shook his head.

"Well, if you ever do, just remember that you're pretty much Jess, just . . . taller and hotter." I slammed my lips shut.

"Hotter, huh?" he teased with a knowing look that sent my body temperature up another degree or two.

"Just forget I said that." I ripped my mortified gaze from his and unzipped my vest. How hot was it in here? "What else is on your reading list?"

His eyes narrowed just slightly, but he went along with the subject change. "I've already read *Fahrenheit 451*, *Lord of the Flies*, *Last of the Mohicans*—"

"Now *that* is a good movie." I sighed. "The way he tells her that he'll find her right before he jumps through the waterfall? Amazing. Total romance material."

"Watching the movie doesn't count!" He shook his head, chuckling. "And it's not a romance. It's an adventure with a little love story mixed in, but not a romance."

"How can you say it's not a romance?"

"Because the book is a little different from the movie." He shrugged.

"Different like how?"

"You really want to know?"

"Yes!" I loved that movie. It was my go-to for a broken-heart ice cream session.

"Cora dies."

My jaw dropped.

Nate winced. "I mean, you asked."

"Well, now I'm sure as hell never reading it. I'll just stick to the movie," I muttered as we moved forward in line. Glancing out the window wasn't helping me either. The visibility was utter crap.

Minutes sped by as we compared a few of the other books on his list. Some of them, like *The Great Gatsby*, I'd read in high school, but others, like *Band of Brothers*, I hadn't.

"Okay, so what would be on your one hundred books list?" he asked.

"Good question." I tilted my head in thought as we continued rolling along. "*Pride and Prejudice*, for sure. Then *East of Eden*—"

"Oh man, I had enough Steinbeck after *Grapes of Wrath*."

"*East of Eden* is way better." I nodded as if my opinion made it fact. "What else? *The Handmaid's Tale*, and *The Immortal Life of Henrietta Lacks* was really good too—oh, have you read *The Hunger Games* yet? The third book just came out last year, and it's amazing."

"I haven't. I just finished *The Adventures of Huckleberry Finn* before I picked this one up." He glanced down at his book. "Maybe I should look at a more modern list."

"Hey, *Huck Finn* is great. Nothing like sailing down the Mississippi."

"It was good," he agreed. "I won't have any reading time while I'm in basic, but I packed a couple of books just in case," he mused quietly. "A friend of mine who went through last year told me they take pretty much everything when you sign in, but I put my iPod in a labeled ziplock bag just in case."

"How old—" I pressed my lips together before the rest of that question could come out. It was none of my business how old he was, though he looked about my age.

"How old am I?" he finished.

I nodded.

"Just turned nineteen last month. You?"

"Eighteen until March. I'm only a freshman." I ran my thumb over the edge of my book to keep my hands busy. "Aren't you . . . nervous?"

"About flying?" His brow furrowed slightly.

"No, about going into the army. There are a couple of wars going on." Margo—my roommate—lost her oldest brother in Iraq a couple of years ago, but I wasn't about to say that.

Spray hit the wings as we went through the deicing process.

"Yeah, I heard something about those." Again with the dimple. He took a deep breath and looked forward as if considering his answer. "I'd be lying if I said I didn't consider the whole death-and-dying thing. But the way I see it, there are all kinds of wars. Some are just more visible than others. It won't exactly be the first time someone has swung for me, and at least this time I'll be armed. Besides, the risk is worth the reward from where I'm sitting. Think about it—if you hadn't gotten on this plane, we never would have met. Risk and reward, right?" He glanced my way, and our eyes locked and held.

Suddenly, my wish to be off this plane had nothing to do with my fear of flying and everything to do with Nathaniel. If we'd met on campus, or even back home in Denver, this conversation wouldn't have to end in a couple of hours when we reached Atlanta.

Then again, if we'd been on campus or in Denver, who knew if we would have had it in the first place. I didn't exactly make a habit of chatting up hot guys. I left that up to Margo. The quiet, accessible ones were usually more my type.

"I could send you books," I offered quietly. "If you're allowed to read and don't have enough while you're there."

"You would do that?" His eyes widened with surprise.

I nodded, and the smile he answered with sent my pulse skyrocketing.

"Flight attendants, prepare for takeoff," the pilot said over the PA system.

Guess it was our turn.

The attendant closest to us told someone a few rows ahead to put their tray table up, then strode for his seat, buckling in to face us.

I gripped both armrests as the engines revved and we hurtled forward, the momentum pushing me back into my seat. The fog had lightened just enough to see the edge of the runway as we raced past. I squeezed my eyes shut and took a steadying breath before opening them.

Nate looked my way, then stuck his hand out, offering it palm up.

"I'm okay," I said through gritted teeth, trying to remember to breathe in through my nose and out through my mouth.

"Take it. I won't bite."

Screw it.

I grasped his hand, and he laced our fingers together, warmth infusing my clammy, ice-cold skin.

"Go ahead and squeeze. You can't break me."

"You might regret it." I white-knuckled his hand, my breaths coming faster and faster as we sped toward takeoff.

"I somehow doubt that." His thumb stroked over mine. "Three minutes. Right? The first three minutes after takeoff?"

"Yep."

He crossed his left wrist to our joined hands and pushed a few buttons, starting his stopwatch. "There. When it reaches three minutes, you can relax until we land."

"You're really too sweet." The tires rumbled and the plane shimmied beneath us as we accelerated. I squeezed his hand so hard I probably cut off his blood supply, but I was too busy trying to breathe to feel an adequate amount of embarrassment.

"I've been called a lot of things, but *sweet* hasn't ever been one of them," he answered with a squeeze as we lifted off.

"Ask me something," I blurted as every worst-case scenario flashed through my mind. "Anything." My pulse skyrocketed.

"Okay." His brow furrowed in thought. "Did you ever notice that pine trees sway?"

"What?"

"Pine trees." He checked his watch. "People always talk about palm trees swaying, but pine trees do too. It's the most peaceful thing I've ever seen."

"Pine trees," I mused. "I've never noticed."

"Yep. What's your favorite movie?"

"*Titanic*," I answered automatically.

The plane pitched upward, dropping my stomach as we angled into a steep climb.

"Seriously?"

"Seriously." I nodded quickly. "I mean, there was totally room on the door, but I loved the rest of it."

He laughed softly and shook his head. "Two minutes to go."

"Two minutes," I repeated, willing my breaths to slow and the knot to untangle itself from my throat. The odds of being in a plane crash were so minuscule, and yet here I was, clutched on to a gorgeous stranger who probably thought I was a few crayons short of a box.

"What's your favorite time of day?" he asked. "Hey, I'm just distracting you."

"Sunset," I said. "You?"

"Sunrise. I like the possibilities of the day."

He glanced into the sea of gray that filled the window, and I leaned forward to chance a peek. I could see the edge of the wing through the thick fog, but everything else was still murky. Maybe it wasn't so bad if I couldn't see the ground.

The engines whined at a higher pitch.

"What the—" Nate started.

The sound of metal on metal stilled my heart.

The wing exploded in a ball of fire.

CHAPTER THREE

NATHANIEL

Kabul, Afghanistan
August 2021

"That appeared to go well." Torres's voice thickened with sarcasm as I watched Izzy walk away with the rest of the envoy. She hadn't stomped, stormed, or even glared at me before following Webb toward the armored cars at the edge of the runway. She'd simply dismissed me like we didn't have a decade of history between us.

I scoffed, but there was no stopping the corners of my mouth as they lifted in appreciation. *Well played.*

"That's her, isn't it?" Torres asked as we fell in behind the politicians. "Shit, I barely recognized her."

Politician. She hated politics—at least she used to. She'd made such a big deal about getting into the nonprofit sector, never giving in to the pressure her parents put on her to further their own agenda through her career, and yet here she was.

She'd made a choice that day after all.

When push came to shove, she was an Astor.

Anger rose, swift and hot, and I shoved it aside. Logically, I'd always known she'd chosen her parents, but seeing that choice play out cut like a dull knife.

"Sergeant Green." Graham fell into step beside me. "You want to clue me in on what that was about?"

"Nothing to clue you in on," I muttered, ripping my gaze from the sway of Izzy's hair and scanning the perimeter. I lowered my Wiley Xs to shield my eyes from the sun.

Shit, how the hell was she *here*?

"Right. Because that didn't just go down like you ran into your ex on the tarmac or anything." Sarcasm dripped from Graham's tone.

"She's not my ex." We never got to that point. "And wipe the smirk off your face."

"She's worse than your ex," Torres mumbled. "She's your what-if."

"Touchy, aren't we." Graham's grin faded. "I can't believe they turned down the Chinook."

I grunted in agreement. Earlier today, I hadn't given a shit that the politicians had refused to take the armored Chinook—or, as we called it, Embassy Air—from the airport to the US embassy. The seven-kilometer route was safe enough—for now. But that was before I knew it was Izzy we'd be transporting. I wanted her behind bulletproof everything. Hell, I wanted her out of here, period.

We reached the convoy, and the aides split between the center two of the four black SUVs. Holt—the aide Kellman was responsible for—climbed into the back of the second vehicle, Izzy following after.

Her backpack slipped off her shoulder, and I caught it by the strap before it could hit the pavement. The common olive-green fabric was soft and worn, the padding flattened by years of obvious use, but there was no mistaking the cylindrical burn mark near the zipper.

The breath punched out of my lungs, and a wry smile twisted my lips as I lifted the pack, my eyes rising to meet hers, both hidden behind our sunglasses. The lenses made it so much harder to read her. Her body language was a solid attempt at calm and collected, but her eyes had always been the best way to get a feel for what she was thinking. Was she all over the place like I was, or had three years of silence really made her that apathetic?

"*Your* bag, Ms. Astor," I said slowly as a breeze from the air-conditioning drifted over my face.

Her lips parted, and she swallowed before taking it from my hands and shifting it to her lap. "Thank you."

"Can you turn the air up?" Holt asked the driver, tugging on his tie as sweat dripped down his beet-red neck.

Graham looked back over his shoulder from behind the wheel and laughed softly. "Sorry. It's already on max. It's just that damned hot here."

Holt fell back against the seat, looking like someone had shot his puppy.

"For fuck's sake," Kellman muttered, already heading toward the tactical seats in the back row.

A quick glance told me all the luggage had been loaded into the rear vehicle, and all the aides were secure. I scanned the perimeter again, even though there were six other operators doing the same, and caught Webb's nod before he slid into the lead car.

It was time to go.

"Buckle up," I told Izzy, shutting her door before she could respond.

There. She was behind as much bulletproof glass as I had on hand.

I took the front passenger seat and shut the door. "Go." I motioned toward the rolling lead car as the manned gate opened in front of us.

The sweet scent of lemons and Chanel no. 5 hit my nose. That vise around my chest tightened another painful notch as I fought off a barrage of memories that I didn't have time for. That ring on her finger might have been new, but some things hadn't changed. She still smelled like long summer nights.

Graham put the car in drive and followed, taking us into Kabul. My senses rose to high alert, taking in every detail of the route and those who walked or drove alongside us, scanning for any possible threat.

"About how long until we reach the embassy?" Holt asked, dabbing at his neck.

Kellman had his work cut out for him with this guy. He was going to be a real pain in the ass for the next week. Not that I didn't have my own hands full.

Isabeau fucking Astor was behind me, less than two feet away for the first time since that rainy night in New York where everything had gone so massively wrong. When had she quit that firm? When had she decided to go work for a senator? I bet her parents were thrilled. They'd always been about that status-driven stuff. What else had changed in the last few years?

Focus.

"Depends on traffic and whether or not your arrival was leaked to the guys who like to make political statements with RPGs," Graham answered, his southern drawl lingering on that last word.

The back of my neck heated, and I knew if I turned around, I'd find Izzy's gaze locked on me, the same way mine would have been on her if our positions were reversed. Instead, I kept my attention on our surroundings as we passed the one-kilometer mark and traffic thickened. We'd be in the Green Zone soon.

"So is that, like . . . five minutes? Or ten?" Holt asked, squirming out of his jacket.

It took every muscle in my body not to roll my eyes.

"We'd be there by now if we'd taken the chopper," Kellman noted from the back.

"It was decided that would send the wrong message about our faith in security during the withdrawal process," Izzy stated, adjusting her backpack on her lap.

"Who the hell decided image was the most important factor in a war zone?" I glanced back over my shoulder, and her chin rose a good two inches.

"Senator Liu," Holt answered.

"Go figure, the ones who are taking armored helicopters when they get here next week are the same guys telling you to drive," Graham quipped, keeping adequate distance from the lead car. "Gotta love politicians."

We passed the two-kilometer mark; we were making good time.

"How the visit is perceived *is* important," Izzy argued.

What? Every one of my instincts wanted her on the first plane out of here, and she was concerned about the perception of it?

"The fact that you value perception over security is exactly why you shouldn't fucking be here," I snapped over my shoulder, raising my brows so she'd know I was talking right to her.

Her mouth dropped open before I looked away. *Pay attention.*

"We're just doing our jobs—" Holt started.

"As if you have a say in where I should and shouldn't be?" she fired back, her eyes narrowing into a glare.

Graham's eyebrows hit the ceiling, but he kept his attention on the road.

"You want to do this here?" Maybe it was best since I couldn't get my hands on her in the car, though I wasn't sure if I wanted to shake some common sense into her or kiss her until that damned ring fell off.

Who was he? Some trust fund baby her father approved of? Someone with the political connections and pedigree they'd always wanted for her?

"I wanted to do *this* three years ago," she challenged, leaning forward against the seat belt until I heard the click of its locking mechanism.

"Am I missing something?" Holt asked slowly, undoing the top button of his shirt.

"No!" she snapped.

"Yes," I replied at the same time.

"Huh." Holt glanced between the two of us but wisely shut his mouth.

"I've been in firefights with less tension," Graham mumbled.

"Shut up." My jaw clenched. He was right, which only pissed me off even more.

We passed the next four kilometers in silence, entering the Green Zone, but only a few ounces of the tension eased as we reached the relative safety of the embassy. The decorative glass windows that wove a chevron-like pattern on the front of the building were just that—decorative. The concrete wall right behind them was built to sustain a blast. I just wasn't sure it could sustain Izzy and me being under the same roof.

Graham put the car in park, and I got out, adjusting my weapon before opening Izzy's door to find her fighting with her seat belt.

"This. Stupid. Thing." She tugged on the belt and jammed her thumb into the release button.

The sight cooled the hottest flares of my frustration, and surprisingly, I fought a smile. It was just so . . . Izzy. If she stayed this flustered, she wouldn't only fumble; she'd also start to babble.

God, I missed her uncensored babbling.

"Let me help." I leaned in.

"I've got it." She shoved her sunglasses to the top of her head and shot me a look that didn't need four letters.

Putting my hands up, I backed out as she furiously pulled at the strap. Then I scanned the perimeter again, raising my own glasses now that we were in the shade.

Webb was already out of the lead car.

"Not. Supposed. To. Be. Here." She seethed with every yank, mocking my words.

"You're not. This is the last place on earth you belong, Iz." Did she have a death wish?

"Glad to see you're still an ass." Each time she pulled, the car bit harder into the seat belt, making it that much shorter. "What the hell is *wrong* with this thing?"

I ducked in without permission and depressed the buckle with a hard, quick push, releasing the seat belt. Her hands jerked back from the contact, scraping my palm with her ring. "At least I'm an ass who can undo the seat belt."

Our gazes clashed, and the breath of space between us charged with enough voltage to shut down the four-chambered organ known as my heart. *Too close.*

I backed the hell up, getting out of the car and sucking in a lungful of misery, giving her—and me—some space.

"Sorry, that belt sticks," Graham called back from the front seat.

"Now you tell me," Izzy muttered, her cheeks flushing pink.

"Isa, is everything okay?" Holt asked from behind me as the aides started toward the guarded door of the embassy.

"*Isa*?" My head drew back as Izzy climbed out of the car, swinging her backpack over her shoulder.

"That's me," Izzy retorted, walking right past me without another glance.

"Her name is Isab—" Holt started.

"I know her name," I said, cutting him off.

Webb stood to the side as the team filed inside with their charges, watching the exchange with a tilt to his head that said I was going to hear about this in about five minutes. It was bad enough that Izzy knew my real name—which was something I was going to have to talk to her about—but I was acting like a fool and knew it.

Worse, I couldn't seem to stop.

"You've always been Izzy." I followed her past the third row of trees that marked the front of the embassy and toward the door.

She stiffened, then spun to face me right in front of Webb. "Izzy is an eighteen-year-old girl who has to have her hand held. I'm not that girl anymore, and if you have a problem with me being here, then go ahead and assign me to someone else, because I have more important things to do than spend the next two weeks proving *anything* to you." She jabbed her finger at me, not quite making contact with my chest before turning on her heel and striding inside the embassy.

"So, I take it she's still pissed?" Torres asked.

I ignored him and the grating pain in my chest, blowing out a long, exasperated breath.

"I'm going to ask you this one more time, Sergeant Green." Webb fell into step with me as we followed them in. "Is there going to be a problem here? Because I've never seen you distracted like that. Ever."

That was because nothing distracted me like Isabeau Astor. She wasn't some bright, shiny little diversion. The woman was a meteor, a shooting star capable of granting impossible wishes or destroying life as I knew it.

And she was currently greeting the ambassador behind the glass wall of the conference room directly in front of me with the kind of practiced ease that spoke to a wealth of experience I knew nothing about. Maybe she was right, and she wasn't my Izzy anymore . . . not that she'd ever been mine. Not really.

"We have history," I admitted. *History* didn't even cut it. We were bound in ways I'd never understood.

"No shit, Sherlock. Is it going to be a liability? Because your replacement should be up and about in a few days, and you can be on your way to the Maldives."

"I'm processing." I hadn't even given my little prepaid overwater bungalow a thought since Izzy had stepped onto the tarmac.

I glanced at Torres.

"Why are you looking at me like I have anything to say that you don't already know?"

He cocked his head to the side.

My jaw clenched as Izzy smiled and shook the ambassador's hand.

"Just let me know by tonight," Webb ordered, then headed toward the conference room. "They added two stops to the itinerary, so this show is on the road tomorrow morning," he called back over his shoulder.

I slipped into an unoccupied hallway to pull my shit together.

"You going to hand her over to Jenkins?" Torres asked, leaning against the wall next to me.

"Every instinct tells me not to," I said quietly. "But at least he'd treat her as just another detail."

"Just another mission." Torres nodded. "Solid point."

Jenkins wouldn't spare a single glance for her eyes, her smile, her curves. He'd be 100 percent focused. "She'll be safer with me."

"Because you're in love with her?" Torres questioned.

I shook my head. "Because Jenkins isn't willing to die for her."

"Does it ever cross your mind that dying for someone might not be all it's cracked up to be?"

"Every single day." Remorse twisted my stomach.

"That's not what I meant. One day you're going to have to let that guilt go."

"But today is not that day."

He sighed, rubbing the bridge of his nose. "Look, talking this shit out with me isn't going to help. We both already know what you're going to do."

I nodded. I'd been protecting Izzy for too long to stop now just because it might be uncomfortable.

Graham passed the hallway and then did a double take. "Hey, boss, there you are." He waved a piece of paper. "New itinerary."

Torres and I pushed off the wall, and I took the update from Graham.

"Kunduz?" Torres read over my shoulder.

"She added two provinces in the north," Graham said. "I thought Senator Lauren was focused on the south. That girls' chess team, right?"

"Right," I said, scanning over the changes Izzy had obviously made.

Something was up.

CHAPTER FOUR

IZZY

Saint Louis
November 2011

My stomach hit the floor as we pitched sideways, the fire on the wing flowing from the engine like the tail feathers of a macabre phoenix. The engine went silent in a stream of smoke, but there were other noises to take its place.

Shrieks, both human and metal. Mechanics. The high-pitched whine as the other engine fought to carry the burden.

I couldn't breathe, couldn't think, could only hear the screams from the passengers as our roll became a dive and we careened to the left. The armrest struck my ribs. Overhead compartments burst open, raining down luggage. Something hard hit my shoulder. More screaming.

My hand white-knuckled Nathaniel's.

"We lost an engine." His grip tightened. "But we should be—"

The engine on the right sputtered and failed.

Screams erupted around us.

How was this happening? How was this real? We'd lost *both* engines. The logic in me understood. Down. We were going *down*.

I must have spoken—or cried—the words aloud, because he whipped toward me, grasping the side of my cheek with his hand and leaning in like he could somehow block out everything around us.

"Look at me," he ordered.

I dragged my focus from the apocalypse outside our window, and his blue eyes bored into mine, consuming my field of vision until he was all I could see.

"This will be okay." He was so calm, so sure.

So utterly freaking insane.

"This is not okay!" My voice was a strangled whisper as we plummeted downward, our angle only decreasing slightly as we leveled out horizontally, but not vertically.

"Stay calm!" one of the flight attendants called out as the plane shuddered, the metal vibrating around us like it would come apart at any second.

I swallowed the scream in my throat and focused on Nate.

"This is the captain," a tense voice said over the speaker. "Brace for impact."

We're going to die.

My pulse thundered so loud it became a roar in my ears, mixing with the cacophony of startled cries from the other passengers.

Nate's eyes flew wide and he released my cheek, but he kept hold of my hand as we moved to follow instructions.

"Brace! Brace! Brace!" the flight attendants yelled in cadence. "Head down! Stay down!"

I folded my body in half, resting my face near my knees and covering my head with my right hand. My left stayed firmly entwined with Nate's as we fell from the sky.

"It's okay," he promised, mirroring my position as best he could as the flight attendants repeated their commands. "Just keep looking at me. You're not alone."

"Not alone," I repeated, our hands clasped so tight we may as well have been welded as one in that moment.

"Brace! Brace! Brace! Head down! Stay down!"

There was no montage of my life flashing in front of my eyes. No outcry from my soul that I hadn't accomplished anything of any significance in my eighteen years on this planet. None of the revelations people talked about after coming out of near-death experiences. Because this wasn't near-death.

This was actual death. Period.

Serena—

"Brace!"

We hit a brick wall and I became a projectile, my seat belt punching my stomach as my limbs went limp, flinging forward without instruction.

We hurtled to the left, and pain erupted in my side. Then we were weightless for a breath of a heartbeat before ramming the earth again like a stone that had been skipped on an unforgiving lake.

Every bone in my body jarred loose.

My head bounced off the tray table.

Something heavy pressed against my back as we barreled forward through unreceptive terrain to the soundtrack of screeching metal and screams. The very ground beneath us roared and the world went dark.

We . . . stopped.

My vision blurred as I lifted my head, the seat in front of me barely discernible in the murky darkness.

Was this it? Was this death? No singing angels or waves of energy . . . just . . . this? Whatever *this* was? It felt like being rocked to sleep, rising and falling a little with each breath.

Green lights flickered, illuminating the cabin just as the darkness fell away from the windows in a wave.

I blinked, trying to force my eyes to focus.

A woman across the aisle opened her mouth, but the ringing in my ears eclipsed any sound she tried to make. There was a baby in her arms, and it, too, appeared to be caught in a soundless scream.

Warmth surrounded the side of my face as my head was turned.

Nathaniel.

He was alive . . . and so was I.

His mouth opened and closed, his eyes searching mine as a stream of blood ran down the side of his face from a source somewhere above his left eye.

"What are you trying to say?" I called out. "You're hurt!" I lifted a trembling hand to his face.

His mouth moved again, and suddenly there was another sound competing with the high-pitched roar in my ears. The intercom?

"We have to move!" Nate shouted, his voice breaking through. "Izzy! We have to move!"

As though someone had hit unmute on the TV remote, sounds of panicked cries and wailing came rushing in.

"Evacuate! Evacuate!" The command came over the intercom.

We'd somehow managed to survive, but for how long?

"Are you okay?" I asked.

"I have to get the door!" Nate gave my hand a squeeze and then unlaced our fingers, unbuckling my seat belt before unlatching his own. "Can you get yours?" he yelled across the aisle.

"I'm on it!" a voice answered.

Nate stood, his enormous back blocking the view of the emergency exit as he worked the handle.

Something ice cold rushed from the floor, chilling my feet instantaneously.

"Oh God, we're in the water," I said to myself. The river.

People stumbled into the aisles in a flurry of movement.

Nate dislodged the door, then threw it outside the plane using both hands.

"Evacuate! Evacuate!"

I fumbled under my seat, then his, grabbing the inflatable life jackets and shoving them inside my vest before yanking the zipper up. There'd be time for those later.

The baby cried as a man across the aisle cursed, grappling with his door.

"Izzy!" Nate reached back and took my hand, pulling me to my feet as the water rushed up over my ankles, my lower shins.

Someone shoved into my shoulder as the cabin-wide panic pitched higher in tone.

Nate climbed out of the emergency door, never letting go of my hand, tugging me behind him and up through the doorway, onto the icy wing.

We were in the middle of the Missouri River.

"Take that side!" I shouted at him as the water licked over the front of the wing.

His jaw clenched and he started to shake his head, but he let my hand slip from his as we each flanked a side of the doorway.

"Give me your hand!" I thrust mine toward the woman struggling at the exit, and she lifted up her hands. Nate and I each took one, lifting her onto the wing.

"Leave the damned suitcase!" Nate yelled into the cabin before helping the next guy out.

"They just got the other door open," one woman cried as she emerged, her feet slipping on the iced-over metal.

"Careful!" I shouted, steadying her.

Again and again, we lifted passenger after passenger.

"Give me the baby!" I reached for an infant cradled in another woman's arms and held the pink bundle of screaming, insulted baby girl to my chest as Nate pulled the mom out.

"Thank you!" She took the little girl and cleared the path.

The water crested over the wing, and I moved sideways to see the front of the aircraft as Nate helped another passenger out. The front exit doors were open, rafts deployed, as attendants helped passengers into the water . . . water that surged inside the doors, up to their knees as one man trudged into the rapidly filling raft.

"We're sinking."

Nate nodded.

How many passengers were there? How long did we have until the water filled the fuselage?

A man. A woman. Another man. A scared child. We pulled them all out of the cabin until the wing was full and no one else called out for help from inside.

"Is that all?" Nate yelled into the cabin.

No one answered back as the water soaked the seat cushions.

A splash turned my head, and I saw a few of the passengers jumping into the river. We were fifty yards from shore.

Nate moved across the doorway and took my hand.

"We have to swim," I said as calmly as I could manage. There would be no pretty little rescue-on-the-Hudson for us.

"Yeah."

"I can't swim!" a kid next to me cried out, burying his face in his father's jacket.

The life jackets.

"Here." I reached into my vest and pulled out a plastic packet, ripping it open with my teeth before handing it to the father.

His startled eyes met mine. "I didn't grab ours."

"Take mine. I'm fine." I gave him a reassuring smile and nod before grabbing the other packet from my vest. "I grabbed yours too," I told Nate, pushing the packet at his chest.

He blinked down at the vest and shook his head. "Put it on."

"I don't need it," I assured him. "Six years on the swim team."

He looked from me to the vest a couple of times and then looked over the passengers. "Where is the mom with the baby?" he called out.

Her hand flew up from somewhere midway down the wing.

"Give this to her," Nate instructed the dad next to us, and he passed it down the line until the woman received it.

Splotches of bright yellow filled my peripherals as a few other passengers slipped the vests on and started blowing them up.

Water covered the edges of the wing, and we all shuffled back, not that our weight was going to balance the aircraft or keep it from sinking to the riverbed.

The plane dipped, and a simultaneous cry of panic ripped through the crowded wing as two passengers slipped into the water.

"Look at me," Nate demanded, tipping my chin up with his thumb and forefingers.

Had he always been this blurry?

"Shit, your pupils are huge," he muttered, his fingers ghosting over my forehead with a wince. "And that's one hell of a goose egg. Ringing in your ears? Blurry vision?"

"Both."

"You're concussed." He looked over my head, then swung around to look at the dipping nose of the plane as the water ate up the cockpit glass and surged toward the door. "Everyone's out, there's nothing else we can do, and we're going to be underwater in minutes. We have to swim for shore. Can you do that?"

My side twinged, a subtle, cutting ache. "I can make it."

He nodded, his grip tightening on my hand. "We're going together. The water is about ten degrees above freezing this time of year."

Another splash, this time from the other side of the aircraft.

"And we don't even have a door to float on. Well, there's nothing like living out your favorite movie, right?" I forced a shaky grin.

"You've got jokes. Nice."

The plane pitched forward, nose-down, and my feet slipped as people shrieked around us, sliding into the water.

"Shit!" Nate's hand tightened like a vise as I skidded toward the edge, and he yanked me back, wrapping his arm around my side.

Pain exploded from behind my ribs, and I gasped at the intensity as it washed over me, raw and sharp.

"Got you! Now let's get off this thing!" He edged us toward the back of the wing, which rose abruptly as the plane leaned into the water, the fuselage groaning like a dying man as water devoured the front doors and started marching up the windows. "We're jumping," he said, holding my hand between us and facing the shore. "Ready?"

"Ready." I swallowed, bracing for the icy welcome of the water beneath us.

"On three." He looked at me and then our landing zone. "One."

"Two," I continued.

The plane gave a death gasp and rattled as it plunged into the river, picking up speed. "Three," Nate rushed.

We jumped.

CHAPTER FIVE

IZZY

Kabul, Afghanistan
August 2021

It had to be the altitude, right? That was why I couldn't seem to get a deep breath, to take in enough air to relieve the burning sensation growing in my chest. It had *nothing* to do with him.

Liar.

Out of the billion scenarios I'd pictured over the years when it came to seeing Nate again, this wasn't one of them. I'd imagined him showing up at my door on some rainy night, or even marching into my office in DC to tell me I couldn't marry Jeremy. Fine, that scenario was far fetched, but that didn't mean it hadn't run through my brain a time or two.

I twisted the gaudy, heavy ring around my finger with my thumb and paced the length of my suite.

Nate was here. The man I used to consider my soulmate was in the same city—the same *building*. My pulse skyrocketed, and I clamped down on every instinct that told me to hunt him down and either scream at him for what he'd put me through or hug him so tight neither of us would be able to breathe. Maybe both.

"Are you even listening to me?"

Jeremy.

Shit, he was still on the phone.

"I'm here." I shook my head and looked out the window, taking in the view of the embassy's courtyard, hoping for a glimpse of Nate . . . if he was even out there.

He'd shown me to my suite with a brusque civility that suggested he wanted to get as far away from me as possible. Not surprising, given the last three years.

"Look, I said I was sorry—"

My thoughts muffled the rest of Jeremy's excuses.

There were some things that even apologies couldn't fix.

"I said I needed some time." I sagged into the oversize armchair that flanked the seating arrangement in the living room.

"You didn't say that you were going halfway around the world for Lauren! You and I both know that was supposed to be Newcastle on that flight," he snapped. "Look, if you needed some time to . . ." There was an audible swallow on the other line. "Come to a decision, then you could have done that from DC or gone to Serena's place—"

Serena. A whole new wave of nausea washed over me, so thick I could taste its bitter coating on my tongue. "Look, Jer, being here has nothing to do with you and your choices, just me and mine. If you'd even remotely paid attention to what I'd been telling you for the past six weeks . . ." I rubbed the spot between my eyebrows and huffed out a self-deprecating laugh. "Then again, you've been juggling a few things, haven't you?" I looked around for a clock. Eight sixteen p.m. here, and the jet lag was kicking my ass. My body didn't care what time it really was as long as I let it sleep, but my brain knew I needed to adjust as quickly as possible, and an early bedtime wouldn't help.

"Look, we've both been busy with work, Isa. Just . . . let's talk this out like mature adults." His condescending tone stiffened my spine.

"I'm not ready to talk it out." Three knocks sounded at my door. "Someone's here." I stood and made my way toward the door.

"Let me guess? Ben Holt is there to soothe all your feelings?" Jeremy fired back. "We're not done with this conversation."

"We are *absolutely* done with this conversation." My voice rose, and I threw open the door with about as much grace as a drunken llama. It slammed into the doorstop and bounced back. A broad hand flew out and caught it before it could smack me in the hip . . . a hand attached to a tattooed forearm I knew as well as my own.

Nathaniel stood in my doorway, dressed head to toe in black combat gear, to include a Kevlar vest and squiggly little earpiece that probably kept him connected to the other ninjas who'd escorted us from the embassy.

First a scruffy beard and unmarked uniform, and now this? Apparently, Nate had been busy in the last three years.

"We need to talk." He nodded toward the room behind me. "Inside."

That burn in my chest transformed into a searing flame that threatened to incinerate me from the inside out. Those eyes would always be the death of me, so blue they deserved their own classification, but the warmth I'd always depended on had chilled, making the man in front of me seem more like a stranger than he had the morning we'd jumped into the Missouri River.

My anger stuttered in response to that glacial gaze.

Of course he looked like the next action star on the Hollywood screen, and I didn't even have the armor of some decent mascara.

". . . that's not what a partnership means!" Jeremy barked in my ear, finishing some tirade I hadn't really heard. "Let me come and get you. I'll take the family jet. I can be there by morning."

"Now," Nate whispered, a muscle in his jaw flexing.

"I have to go," I told Jeremy, hitting the end button before he had a chance to counter.

I backed up a step, and Nate brushed by as he walked into my suite, the scent of earth and spearmint tingling my nose. He still smelled the same. Did that come-screw-me fragrance just emanate from his pores, or was it bottled somewhere?

He didn't pause or speak as he swept through my room, checking behind the curtains before marching into my bedroom like he owned it.

Not this one, at least.

"I'm not hiding someone in my shower, Nathaniel," I called after him, perching my butt on the edge of the desk and abandoning my cell phone to its surface. Jeremy could wait. I didn't have the answers he wanted. Not yet, maybe not ever.

"Very funny," Nate called out from the bedroom.

My muscles tensed, ready for battle with this you-shouldn't-be-here version of Nate, but there was a part of my soul that seemed to settle and calm just because the asshat was in the same room.

"Just making sure there aren't any assassins hiding behind your curtains." He walked back in with that confident, efficient stride and moved to the window, nodded at whatever he saw in the courtyard below, and turned to face me.

"No one wants to assassinate me." My boss was a different story, but she wouldn't be here until next week, and her upcoming visit wasn't public knowledge anyway.

"Yeah," he said, his face deadpan as he stared me down from the other side of the room, "they do. What the hell are you doing here, Izzy?"

Izzy. So few people called me that anymore. The second I'd walked into Senator Lauren's office, I'd become Isa, plain and simple.

"I could ask you the same thing," I fired back, crossing my arms over my chest. Heat sang through my cheeks as I felt the bulk of my Georgetown hoodie behind my arms. I was dressed for bed, barefoot in pajama pants, not outfitted to confront Nate.

Nate. After three years, *this* is how it happened? Not because he'd come back, or apologized for disappearing off the face of the earth, but because once again, we'd proved to be the magnets that fate could never quit playing with?

This was bullshit.

"Nice earpiece, by the way," I continued. "At least someone here knows how to get ahold of you." I fought the knot in my throat. There were too many emotions fighting for supremacy, each choking the other out until the hurt of it all won out, turning my words sharp and acrid.

"I'm being serious."

"So am I."

His jaw flexed once. Twice. "Say it. Whatever it is you've been holding back all evening, just say it." He folded his arms across his chest, mirroring my stance, but he pulled it off way better. He had the whole "dark mercenary thing" going for him, though I knew if he was on our security detail, then he was still on the government's payroll.

"You abandoned me." The words slipped out.

He arched his brow. "Really. *I* abandoned *you*? Is that how you remember it? Twisting facts. Guess you really are a politician now, just like Daddy wanted."

"You disappeared!" I came off the desk in a flurry of years-old anger. "Not one letter! Email! Your social media? Erased. Your phone? Disconnected!" My fury carried me across the room until I was bare foot to boot with him, glaring up at the face that had haunted my dreams and a few of my nightmares. "You vanished!" The years of not knowing, of wondering if he was safe, or hurt—or worse—erupted in every word. "Do you have any idea how hard I looked for you? I went to Peru as we planned. Borneo too. By the next year, I got the point."

A flash of something—regret?—flickered across his features, but it was gone a heartbeat later. "This is getting us nowhere." He sidestepped and walked away from me, headed for the front door. "You didn't even lock the damned thing." He threw the dead bolt and turned, leaning back against the door. "You're supposed to be in some glitzy office at that law firm in New York, so I'll ask again. What are you doing here?"

"Making a difference. I believe that's what someone suggested." I padded across the soft carpet to the kitchenette and pulled out two bottles of water. "Want one?" Even as pissed as I was, my first instinct was to care about him. God, I was pathetic.

"Sure. Thank you," he answered, his voice softening. "And this"—he gestured to the suite—"was not what I had in mind when I made that suggestion." He caught the bottle I hurled his way. "But it's definitely what your parents had in mind, isn't it?"

I shrugged and opened the water. "It's where I landed." I took a drink, hoping it might dislodge the boulder in my throat. "What are you more pissed at, Nate? The fact that I'm not where you left me? Or the fact that I'm meeting the version of you that you never wanted me to see?"

"It isn't safe for you to be here." He rolled the bottle between his hands, clearly ignoring the question. "The country is unstable as hell."

I cocked my head at him. "But that's why *you're* here, right? To keep people like me safe? Is that what you do now? Where you've been for the past three years?"

His jaw ticked. "I can't tell you where I've been for the last three years. Rules of the game haven't changed—they've just gotten more restrictive." He twisted the bottle open and drank half of it down.

All these years and he still wouldn't open up. Guess his world hadn't changed that much, but mine *had*. "Fine, if you're not here to explain what happened in New York, and I'm not going to take your suggestion and leave, then why exactly are you in my room?"

"I'm not supposed to be here."

"No shit. I highly doubt Holt's security detail is in his room drinking from his minibar."

"That's not what I mean." The corners of Nate's mouth turned up, but it wasn't quite a smile, so at least I didn't have to deal with that dimple of his making an appearance.

Nothing knocked off a few IQ points like the sight of that dimple.

"Please, do stop speaking in army-guy codes." My gaze narrowed slightly. "Assuming that you're still army?" They'd told us we'd have

Special Forces as our security, but there was a black-and-white name tape on the left side of his chest that read *Green*, not *Phelan*.

No matter what name he was using, he still looked so damned good. Someone hadn't been skipping the gym.

Stop it.

What was it about being in the same room with Nathaniel Phelan that made me revert back to eighteen years old?

"Yeah, I'm still in the army. Just the part that no one talks about," he answered slowly, raising his eyebrows. "And as for my phone, my email, my social media . . . it was all sanitized."

"Okay then." A tiny kernel of something like hope took root in my stomach at the small but openly offered truth. "And that's why you don't . . . exist anymore." The days and months following his disappearance had been maddening, but part of me had always known why he'd fallen off the face of the earth. This had always been his dream.

Making his obsolete had become mine.

He nodded.

"And Green?" I motioned to his name tag. "Is that your call sign or whatever?"

"No. These"—he pointed to the name tag—"are for you guys, not us. It's what you need to call me—if I stay. I told you I'm not supposed to be here." He glanced toward the window and then back, as if meeting my eyes was something . . . painful.

"Where are you supposed to be?" Was there someone else in his life now? Someone who had the right to know if he made it home? Someone waiting? A nauseating twist of jealousy struck deep inside me, souring my stomach.

"On leave in the Maldives." He had the decency to look a little guilty.

I blinked. "You were going to the Maldives?" Indignation heated my blood. "Funny, but I thought that was an October thing." Did our pact mean absolutely nothing to him? *Of course it didn't.* He'd blatantly shown me that for the last three years.

"Yeah." He flinched. "But Sergeant Brown came down with something, so I filled in for him."

"Let me guess. *Sergeant Brown* isn't his real name either?"

"Just roll with it." He finished off his water and twisted the top back on. "Point is, you walked off that plane."

"And?" I shrugged and forced a fake smile. "You can still go to the Maldives. Just assign me to someone else." It sounded empty and fake because it was. It didn't matter how pissed I was at Nate, how wrong things had gone the last time we'd been in the same room; I couldn't bear the thought of him walking away. Not again. Not like this.

"Yeah, okay." He gave a self-deprecating laugh and sent me a pointed stare. "Because it's that easy."

My heart stumbled through its next few beats. The air thickened and charged as we stood there, our eyes locked on each other across the small, mine-laden distance between us. One wrong step and we'd both bleed out.

"I know," I admitted softly. "It's not easy. Never has been."

He nodded curtly and looked away, breaking the spell.

I sucked in a breath.

"I don't get it. You're about to spend two weeks in some of the most inhospitable areas known to man, hopping province to province, all so you can what? Feel better about how *not* stable this country is and label it *fact-finding*?"

My spine jerked ramrod stiff. "We're here to write down our observations about how the drawdown is going, and you know it."

"And you won't go home?" His eyes met mine, the plea blatant.

"No." I swallowed back the truth on the tip of my tongue. If he knew why I was really here, would he help? Or throw me out faster? "I'll do the tour Senator Lauren requested and then meet her when she arrives next week. And no one is supposed to know—"

"You're here. Yeah, I get that a lot." He raked his hand over his thick, dark hair and blew out a slow breath.

I felt his sigh in every bone of my body, until it became my own.

"Fine. Then this is how it's going to go." He pushed off the door and chucked the bottle into the trash with excellent aim. "I'm Sergeant Green to you. Not Nate. You can never call me Nate. Not out there. Not in here. Not anywhere. Got it?"

"If you insist." I had to tilt my head back to keep eye contact as he came closer—whether it was the fact that I was barefoot and he was in boots, or just being apart for three years, the guy felt *huge* next to me.

"I insist. Anonymity is a requirement in this line of work. In here, you can be as belligerent and . . ." He struggled for a word. "*Izzy* as you want, but out there"—he pointed to the door—"out there you listen to what I say, and do what I ask when I ask it."

"Nate—" I cringed. Shit, I was never going to get this right.

He arched a single brow at me. "As. Soon. As. I. Say. It."

"Have you always been a pain in the ass?" I fired back.

"That's pretty funny, coming from you."

I rolled my eyes and folded my arms across my chest.

He glanced down and winced, jerking his focus to a spot over my head as he took another deep breath. "I'll be at all your meetings, your meals, and the one who stands outside the door when you pee."

"That's graphic."

"If you need me, I will be across the hall tonight and every other night that you're in Afghanistan. If your life is at risk, press this button." He pushed a remote the size of my thumb into my hand and let its black nylon necklace hang loose. "And I will appear."

I looked down at the device and huffed a sarcastic laugh. "So this is what it takes to get your phone number? A girl has to haul herself into a war zone?"

"Izzy," he whispered, stepping back and putting a few feet of distance between us.

"Oh no." I pocketed the magic-button remote. "If I can't call you Nate, then you don't get to call me Izzy. Fair is fair."

"Well, I'm not calling you Isa, that's for damn sure," he shot back. "I'm not your father."

My father. Because he knew that had been Dad's pet name for me. He knew all sorts of things he shouldn't because he was Nate and I was Izzy, and as screwed up as this place was, facts were facts. History was history.

"Then Ms. Astor will be just fine."

"Then have a great evening, *Ms.* Astor." He gave me a mock salute and headed for the door. "I'll be here bright and early to fetch you for our first destination."

After all this time, *this* was where we were? Not quite strangers or enemies, but . . . bitter what? Acquaintances?

"So you're staying on my detail?" My voice hitched, and he heard it, pausing midstep before turning to face me.

"You won't leave, which means neither can I. Simple physics." His gaze narrowed. "But you weren't supposed to be here, either, were you? Greg Newcastle is supposed to be in this room."

I felt the blood drain from my face. "You can assign me to someone else," I offered again in a rush.

He ignored me. "So why did you get on the plane? Did Newcastle get sick too?"

I swallowed.

"Huh. Not sick, then. It was your choice." He tilted his head. "Why did you add Kunduz and Samangan to the itinerary? Those weren't on the list before you got on that plane." He stalked forward.

Shit. Shit. Shit.

"All of your little friends are sticking to the east, and Newcastle was focused on Kandahar. Something about the girls' chess team Senator Lauren has been working to get out."

"Hey, that was actually *my* project. I'm the one who's been coordinating everything. Newcastle just wanted the credit."

He stopped right in front of me, staring down like he could see right through me if he tried hard enough. "And yet you added two provinces to the north."

"Nate," I whispered, already breaking the rules.

"What aren't you telling me?"

"I . . ." I shook my head and closed my eyes. I could have lied to anyone else, but not him.

"Don't even think of lying to me." His thumb and forefinger gently lifted my chin. "What's going on?"

I opened my eyes and my heart clenched. Under all that armor, this was Nate. *My* Nate. He would help, I knew he would . . . as long as I wasn't putting myself in danger. That was where he'd draw the line. And if he thought I was already in danger just being here, there was every chance he'd tie me to the seat of the next outbound aircraft once I told him the truth.

"What's in the north, Isabeau?" My name was nothing more than a whisper.

"Serena."

CHAPTER SIX

NATHANIEL

Saint Louis
November 2011

The water was *freezing*, shocking the air from my lungs as we started the frantic swim for shore. At least I thought the shore was this way. The fog wasn't exactly doing us any favors, and neither was the current, dragging us downstream with the rest of the passengers as we fought our way toward the bank.

The reactions around us varied from stoic to downright hysterical, and I did what always worked for me when shit went down—narrowed my focus to one goal. Right now, that goal was keeping Isabeau alive.

"You okay?" I asked Izzy, only losing sight of her between the waves of the Missouri as the plane submerged fully behind us, a rush of air bubbling up from the fuselage.

Holy shit, that just happened.

"Never swam in shoes before," she answered with a teeth-chattering grunt and more of a grimace than a smile.

"It's a day for firsts." I swam closer to her, my heart thundering as we fought for every foot against the current.

Off in the distance, I heard someone cry for help, and another passenger answered. Hopefully the rafts could pick up more of us, especially the ones who couldn't swim, but I was grateful that the people around us all seemed to be forging forward.

Some of my panic eased when the shore came into view through the fog, dense with trees. "It's right there," I told Izzy, keeping up with her, stroke for steady stroke.

"Thank God." Her face contorted and she gasped, but she kept pushing forward.

"What's wrong?" My chest tightened as the vision in my left eye went red and blurry. A quick swipe of my forehead came away bloody. *Awesome.*

"Other than the whole plane-crash scenario?" She forced a sarcastic, staccato smile through the shivers. "I'm okay, just some pain in my ribs. I'm sure it's nothing. You're the one bleeding."

And she was the one with the blown pupils. I'd been knocked around enough to know the signs of a concussion.

"The blood is probably just bluster. Let's get you to shore." My stomach twisted, and I got that sinking feeling that sometimes came over me, the one that told me to pay attention, that there was more to whatever was happening on the surface of any given situation. I'd always had good instincts. They were the only reason I'd survived nineteen years under my father's roof.

Ahead of us, a few of the passengers dragged others up the bank to safety. The father and son were upstream, almost there now, but I couldn't see the mother and baby.

Just focus on Izzy.

My feet found purchase on the rocky bank, and I immediately swept my arm across Izzy's back, pulling her against me until she could reach the bottom. It was an act of God that we'd found a portion of the river with a sloped shore. Then again, just about everything about today was miraculous.

Careful of her ribs, I pulled us up the embankment, and then the two-foot rise to the wooded area. Where the hell were we?

"Help!" a kid screamed from behind us.

I looked over my shoulder to see one of the women rushing forward from shore to pull a kid in an inflatable yellow life jacket.

"Thank you." Izzy shot me a watery smile as I sat her at the base of the nearest tree. "I can help," she argued, her hand cradling the left side of her rib cage.

I hit my knees beside her, praying the bluish tinge to her lips was just cold. "Can I see?" I asked, reaching for her vest.

She nodded, water droplets streaming down her face as her head fell back against the tree.

With numb fingers, I somehow managed to unzip her vest and lift the side of her shirt. Then I muttered a curse. "There's no blood, but it's a hell of a contusion. I wouldn't be surprised if you broke the ribs."

"That would explain the pain. I think I did something to my shoulder too." She brushed her hand over my forehead and into my hair. "You have a nasty cut just beneath your hairline."

"That's okay. It will just increase my appeal. Chicks dig scars, you know." I studied her blown pupils, which were consuming way too much of those beautiful brown eyes.

"Help!" someone else shouted.

Izzy lurched forward.

"Nope. You stay right here." I leveled my best stare on her. "I mean it. Right. Here. I'll be right back."

"Just . . . don't die." She fell back against the tree.

"Not planning on it." I jumped down the bank and started helping pull others up, and I couldn't help but sigh in absolute relief when the mom and baby made it to shore. It took all of ten minutes to get everyone out of the water, with the exception of the rafts that had floated farther downstream.

By the time I made my way through the stumbling, crying crowd of passengers and got back to Izzy, my muscles shook with cold and the aftereffects of the adrenaline.

"See?" She lifted her right hand and gifted me with a wan, shivering smile. "Still right where you left me."

"Good. I'm not in any condition to chase you." I sat down beside her and pulled her under my arm, tucking her uninjured side against me. The visibility was improving, and I could even see halfway across the river now. "Let's get you warm."

"We survived a plane crash." She leaned in, resting her head in that sweet spot right above my heart.

The beat of my pulse changed, slowing, steadying.

"We survived a plane crash," I repeated, cupping the side of her face with my hand and bending my head toward hers. "Now all we have to do is wait for rescue."

"We can't be that far from the airport. They'll be here soon."

"Yeah." Other passengers sat down near us, all in various states of shock from crying softly, to crying loudly, to . . . not crying at all, just staring straight ahead.

"Just think. If this was a book, we'd be in the middle of the Alaskan wilderness, or the lone survivors, forced to share an abandoned cabin."

A laugh rumbled up through my chest, despite . . . well, everything. "Don't forget, it would be conveniently stocked with all the supplies we'd need."

What the hell was wrong with me? I'd just taken my first plane ride and survived my first plane crash, and yet here I was, making jokes with a woman I'd just met, curled up with her like we'd known each other for years.

She snorted when she laughed, which made me grin, but then she tensed, and my smile faded. "I don't . . . I don't feel well."

I dropped my hand from her face to her neck, finding her pulse, and my brow furrowed. It was going a mile a minute. Not that I had any clue what to do with that knowledge, but I figured it couldn't be good, not with the pale skin, concussion, and general plane-crash issues. "Just hold steady. They'll be here any minute." Sirens sounded in the distance. "See? I bet that's them. Let's just hope there's a road around here."

"Are you tired?" she asked, leaning into me. "I'm just really tired."

"You need to stay awake." Fear dripped down my spine, colder than my soaked clothing. What were more of those icebreaker-question things? I had to keep her talking. "If you had to choose between popcorn and M&M's, which would it be?"

"What?"

"Popcorn or M&M's?" I repeated.

"Both."

Interesting. "If you could live in any state, which one would it be?"

Her head bobbed.

"Izzy. Which state?"

"Maine."

"Maine?" I searched for the source of the sirens, but no luck.

"No one in my family lives there," she mumbled. "No expectations."

I looked over my shoulder and around the tree as the sirens approached. "They found us."

A police car came to a stop, and the officer jumped out, speaking into his radio. "We're getting help here, folks! Ambulance is four minutes out!"

The father of the little boy rushed forward to the cop, his son's arm bent at an unnatural angle, and several others took his lead.

That feeling hit again, like an anchor on my chest. "Izzy, what's your blood type?"

"O positive," she muttered. "Is that your idea of a pickup line?" Her words slurred.

"I wish," I whispered. Not that a guy like me would've ever had a chance with a girl like her. Even her babbling reeked of class. "What about allergies?"

"What?"

"What are you allergic to?"

Another set of sirens sounded like they were coming closer.

"Shellfish. What about you?"

"I'm not allergic to anything," I answered. "Is that it? Just shellfish?"

"Oh, um. Penicillin." She tilted her head back and looked up at me with glazed eyes. "Would you like my medical history too?"

"Yes." I nodded, and my heart started to race the closer the sirens sounded.

She looked at me like I was the one slurring my words. "I broke my arm once when I was seven. But that was a trampoline thing, and Serena—" Her eyes fluttered shut.

"Izzy!" I shook her gently. "Wake up."

Her eyes flew open.

"Tell me more about Serena." I stood, forcing my legs to work, and lifted Izzy into my arms as the first of two ambulances arrived. "What's she like?"

"Perfect." She sighed, her head flopping against my chest. "She's beautiful, and smart, and always knows what to say."

"Must run in the family." I didn't even bother with the first ambulance, which was already getting mobbed, and headed straight for the second.

"Nate?"

"Hmm?" I stood right in the middle of whatever path there was, forcing the ambulance to stop.

"Don't leave me, okay?" she asked, her voice barely a whisper over the blaring sirens.

"I won't." The paramedics killed the sirens and climbed out of the rig, and I locked gazes with one of them. "I need you to help her!"

She went limp in my arms, her eyes closing.

"Bring her back!" The paramedic jogged to the back of the rig as the doors burst open and someone brought down a stretcher.

"Put her here," the paramedic ordered, and I laid Izzy on the white sheets. "What's the problem?" She jumped in, pushing me out of the way to start her checks.

"She said her ribs hurt." I raked my fingers through my hair. "And she has a huge bruise there, and her pulse is—"

"Shit," the paramedic whispered, taking her pulse as another one slapped a blood pressure cuff on her.

"—racing," I finished. "She started slurring her words, and . . ." Damn it, what else had she said? "Her shoulder hurt. Her left shoulder."

"She's hypotensive," one of the paramedics noted, and the two shared a look that couldn't be considered good under any circumstance. "We have to go."

"What's her name?" one asked me as two of them strapped Izzy to the gurney and loaded her into the ambulance.

"Izzy," I answered, fighting every urge to push someone aside so I could climb in next to her. "Isabeau . . ." What was it? What the hell was it? "Astor! She's allergic to penicillin, and she's O positive."

The driver raced around me to get back to the wheel.

"Relatives only," the paramedic in back said, already hooking her up to something. "I'm assuming you're her . . ." He glanced up.

Don't leave me.

"Husband." I moved, climbing up into the rig in one step. "I'm her husband."

Ruptured spleen. That's what they told me four hours ago.

Four very long hours, in which all I did after changing into a dry set of scrubs and calling my mother to assure her I was okay was to sit in this waiting room and alternate between watching the media coverage of the crash on a national network and the second hand tick by on the large clock above the door.

Oh, and completely, utterly ignore the clipboard in front of me, because how was I supposed to know who her insurance provider was?

Because you said you were her husband.

The surgery was only supposed to take about ninety minutes, which made me start shifting my weight in the world's most uncomfortable chair about two hours ago.

What if I'd made it worse by picking her up? Or when I pulled her out of the river?

"You're sure I can't get anything else for you?" a representative from the airline asked, concern and panic in her eyes. Guess we were all a little out of our depth here. She'd taken our names when we'd first arrived—I'd given her Izzy's, and she'd hovered around the dozen or so of us who'd been sent here ever since.

According to the news, there were passengers at three of the local hospitals.

"I'm fine," I assured her. There hadn't been much more to do for me than the eleven stitches in my forehead.

"Okay." Her smile was an attempt at reassurance. "Oh, and a representative from the army said they'd send someone local to get you, but that was a few hours ago."

I tensed. I'd promised I wouldn't leave her.

"You are"—she glanced at her clipboard—"Nathaniel Phelan, right? The one who was headed to basic training?"

I nodded, flipping my sodden wallet over in my hand. "I'm sure everyone has their hands full right now."

She gave me an awkward shoulder pat and moved to the next passengers, while I watched the clock for another ten minutes.

"That's him," a nurse said, pointing to me, and my brows shot up, hoping it would be a doctor next to her, but it wasn't.

The woman was a little taller than Izzy, with light-brown hair and worried brown eyes. The family resemblance was unmistakable.

"You're Izzy's *husband*?" she said, charging my way like a bull who'd been shown red.

I stood. "You must be the sister. Serena, right?"

She nodded, swatting a single tear off her face.

"Sorry," I whispered. "I'm just the guy who was sitting next to her. We're not married."

"Obviously," she whispered back. "I think I'd know if my baby sister was married."

"I lied because I promised I wouldn't leave her, and then I may have . . . forged a document agreeing to the surgery."

Her eyes flew wide. "Surgery? All they told me when I showed up to the reunification site was that she was here. It took me about an hour to realize it was her flight, and then I've been running everywhere." She closed her eyes and took a shuddering breath, reopening them when it seemed she had some control. "Tell me what surgery."

I gestured to the chair next to mine, and we both sat. "She ruptured her spleen in the crash and broke two ribs, along with getting a concussion. She was bleeding internally."

She nodded, absorbing the information with a calm I respected. "Okay. And you signed for the surgery?"

"I didn't know what else to do." I handed her the clipboard. "I'm hoping you'll know most of that."

"I can do this." She stared at the forms like they were in a foreign language. "Do you think she'll be okay?"

"I hope so. She was conscious right up until I handed her to the paramedics." I resumed flipping my wallet in my hand and watching the clock.

"Oh God, she's allergic to—"

"Penicillin," I finished for her. "She told me. They know."

She sat back in the chair and stared at the door, the one the surgeons had been coming in and out of the last few hours. "Lucky she was sitting next to you."

"I'm not sure I'd call anything about today lucky, except that we're somehow alive."

"That's the luckiest you can be."

The door to the left swung open, and two uniformed men walked in wearing camouflage. My stomach hit the ground.

"Nathaniel Phelan?" one of them asked, scouring the room.

"That's me." I lifted a hand and stood.

"Hell of a day you're having. Are you cleared by medical to leave?" one of them asked.

I nodded. "Just needed stitches."

"Good. Let's get you out of here." He motioned to the door.

Picking up the clear bag of my personal items, I walked over to them. "Is there any way we can wait? The woman I was sitting next to is in surgery."

They shared a look, and I knew it wasn't going to go my way. "Is she your wife?"

"No." I shook my head.

"Mother? Sister? Daughter?" the other asked.

"No. I'm just worried about her."

Sympathy knit his brow. "I'm sorry, but we're tasked with getting you out of here, and if she's not next of kin or a blood relative, we really need to go. Orders are orders."

My chest tightened, and I nodded. "One second." Serena was still filling out forms when I reached her. "I have to go."

She looked up at me, her eyes a shade lighter than Izzy's. "Thank you for taking care of her."

"Just . . ." I shook my head. Fuck my *life*, I couldn't even ask her to call and tell me if she made it out all right. "Just tell her that I didn't want to go, but orders are orders."

"I will. Thank you." She reached out and took my hand, squeezing it. "Thank you. I can't say that enough."

"Nothing to thank me for." Taking a deep breath, I walked back toward the soldiers, then followed them out.

Isabeau would be okay. She had to be. I refused to believe that fate, or God, or the cosmic energy of the universe would make her go through all of that and not come out of it alive.

But I would never know.

"We can get you on another flight, or a bus if you're not . . . you know . . . keen on flying at the moment. Or I'm sure they'll give you a waiver, and let you postpone basic," one of the soldiers said as we made our way out of the hospital.

"No." I gripped my bag harder. Everything I owned was now in it, and I had absolutely nothing to go home to. "No, I'm ready now."

CHAPTER SEVEN
NATHANIEL

Kabul, Afghanistan
August 2021

"Change your mind," I ordered Izzy when she opened her door the next morning. Fine, maybe it was more plea than order. Sleeping hadn't been an issue for me in years, but I'd tossed and turned all night after she told me why she was really here.

Searching for her sister was going to get her killed. Every step Izzy took outside this embassy was a calculated risk, and we'd prepared security for her precise itinerary, not for hunting a needle in a haystack. American photojournalists made excellent propaganda targets for the enemy around here, and with the country destabilizing, the odds of finding Serena in the window of Izzy's visit were grim.

"Good morning to you too." Izzy cocked an eyebrow at me and held open her door so I could enter. "Give me about three minutes, and I'll be ready."

"Ready to change your mind?" Fuck me, she smelled good. The scent was straight out of every dream I'd had over the last decade.

"No." She buttoned what looked to be a linen blazer up to her throat and packed a scarf in her tote bag with a pair of overear headphones. "Ready to get on the helicopter. Is Mayhew ready?"

"Already downstairs." The junior aide was so much easier to deal with than Izzy, but then again, I'd never been in love with him, so that probably influenced my opinion.

"I see you're dressed for a funeral again." She eyed my all-black combat gear.

"As long as it isn't yours. Tell me something. What exactly was your plan coming here?" I leaned back against her door.

She glanced down at my M4. "You really have to carry that everywhere?"

"Yes." I didn't bother to tell her about every other weapon I had strapped to me. "Now what was your plan, Isabeau? Just show up here and start calling out Serena's name?"

A blush rose up her cheeks as she shouldered the tote and faced me, lifting that stubborn chin of hers. "Something . . . like that."

I let my head fall back against the door for a heartbeat. "I've always known you would do anything for her—you'd do anything for each other—but this is ludicrous. How long has she been in country?"

"Five months. She was offered the opportunity to end her assignment early when the rather"—she winced—"abrupt handover of Bagram indicated a larger . . ." Izzy searched for the right words.

"Shit show was about to go down?" I supplied. "Because that's what's happening."

"Withdrawal was never going to be pretty." Her chin lifted a good three inches. "I just didn't think Serena would be stubborn enough to stay, especially after the embassy staff was reduced back in April. But she's . . ." Izzy shrugged.

"Serena."

Izzy nodded. "If I can just find her, I can talk some sense into her and get her out of here."

"Do the other members of your delegation know what you're up to?"

"No." She gripped the straps of her bag so tight I half expected them to start screaming. "And I know you aren't going to tell them either."

I pushed off the door and flat out invaded her space. "And what makes you think that?"

She looked away, and her throat worked before she dragged her gaze back to meet mine. "Because you owe me."

"I. Owe. You?" My eyebrows rose. Apparently, she remembered New York a little differently than I did.

"After leaving me in—" She closed her eyes and blew out a slow breath through puckered lips that claimed every ounce of my attention.

My stomach drew tight, remembering exactly how soft those lips felt under mine, against my skin.

"You owe me," she said, straightening her shoulders, our gazes colliding. "Besides, I've already put feelers out at her paper and narrowed it to those two provinces, without, you know . . . advertising that I'd be here with a congressional delegation. She's a photojournalist for the *Times*. She can't just disappear, Nate." She winced. "I mean, Sergeant Green."

"People disappear here all the time."

"Well, not Serena." She shrugged, like her statement could somehow give her older sister a layer of impossible protection that simply didn't exist here.

"And you're willing to bet your life on it?" I wasn't. As much as I cared for Serena and everything she meant to Izzy, my priorities were clear as fucking day.

"It's not going to come to that." Izzy shook her head. "We both know that as secret as we'd like this fact-finding mission to be, it isn't. Serena will know I'm here. She'll find us, and we'll put her on the helicopter, and I'll bring her home with me."

Disbelief mixed with a heavy dose of anger raced through my veins, and I took a step backward. "You're using yourself as *bait*?"

Her eyes narrowed. "Please don't pretend that you're concerned about my welfare."

"Your welfare has been my concern for the last ten fucking years!" I snapped, immediately regretting the slip. Damn it, this woman pushed me to the edge faster than anyone on the planet.

Silence stretched between us as I fought to level my head.

"Let's go." I turned around and walked out of the room, holding the door so she could walk through first.

Tension radiated between us as we walked down the steps and into the lobby.

"Isa!" Kacey Pierce, one of Senator Lauren's junior aides, raced over from one of the glassed-in conference rooms, notebook in hand. "Is there anything else you need me on while you're gone?"

Izzy adjusted her tote bag, looking over the list that Kacey shoved at her. "I think this just about covers it."

I moved closer and leaned in, putting my lips dangerously close to her ear. "Ask her to pull the latest correspondence from any American journalists with accompanying pictures, and have them printed for when we get back."

Izzy turned her head so quickly, her gaze whipping to mine, that I barely had a millisecond to draw back before the entire lobby would have been spectators to a crossed line. "You're helping?"

"It's just a suggestion." Blatantly retreating, I waited by the door as Izzy gave her orders to the junior aide. Had to admit, leadership looked really damn good on her.

We made our way to the convoy, where my team already waited. She protested when I took her bag from her and tossed it on the floor of the armored vehicle, then drew out a Kevlar vest.

"Arms out."

"This is ridiculous." She put her arms out, and I slipped the vest over her head and the practical french braid she'd woven her blonde strands into this morning.

"So is you being here, but at least this will stop bullets." I brought the straps from the back of the vest under her arms and secured them to the front with as much professionalism as I could muster.

"It's heavy."

"Being shot is worse." I reached into the vehicle and brought out a Kevlar helmet.

She glared at me. "Seriously?"

"They're not too bad!" Mayhew, the other junior aide, called out from inside.

"No preferential treatment." I shrugged at Izzy. "Put it on, or you stay here." She wasn't getting shot in the head on my watch.

She shoved it onto her head, then climbed in next to Mayhew, and I took the front passenger seat just like yesterday, while the rest of the team filed in.

Within moments, we rolled through the embassy gates, heading toward the field just down the road where the helicopters were staged.

We passed through a barbed wire gate and onto the field, where six Blackhawks were all in various stages of run-up. Taking her into blatant danger went against every instinct I had, but I knew she'd just go without me if I refused her, which meant I got out of the car and opened her door. She'd managed the seat belt just fine by herself this time.

"Is this a . . . soccer field?" Izzy asked as she stepped out of the car.

"Yep," I answered as Graham came around the car, Torres not far behind.

"Which one is ours?" Izzy asked.

"We're taking the front two."

"Two?" She shot a confused look my way.

"Yeah." I nodded. "We travel in two in case something happens, like one getting shot down."

Her eyes flared.

"Black, Rose, and four grunts are in the second aircraft," Graham said, moving out of the way when Holt stumbled out of the car after Mayhew.

"It's so damned *hot*," Holt muttered, rolling his neck as Kellman rolled his eyes behind him.

"That works for me. We'll take the first one," I told Graham before turning to Kellman. "Good luck with that one today." I cracked a smile as Holt wiped the sweat from the back of his neck.

"I should say the same thing to you." He shot a poignant look at Izzy, who stood looking at the Blackhawks with wide eyes before cramming her sunglasses on her face. "Looks like you've got a knuckler."

Fuckity, fuck, *fuck*. What was she thinking?

I walked over to her, dust coating my boots, and took her elbow, leaning down so she could hear me over the high-pitched whine of the engines. "I'm guessing you never got over your fear of flying?"

"I'm fine." She yanked her elbow out of my grip. "I'll be . . . fine."

"They're not big, cushy planes where you can put your headphones on and pretend you're somewhere else," I warned her as we headed for the first helicopter.

"I'll manage," she shouted, glaring over her shoulder at me as she stepped up into the bird I'd led us to, walking past the door gunner.

"This should be fun," Torres said with a grin.

I rolled my eyes and climbed in.

The Blackhawk was set up to carry troops, and I took the seat directly against one of the pilot's backs, facing Izzy. The pilot twisted in her seat, handing me a headset. I nodded my thanks, fitted it around my helmet, and turned it on, but I kept the mic muted.

Izzy strapped herself in with surprising efficiency and took out her overear headphones from a shoulder bag that looked like it cost more than I made in a month, looking at them with dismay.

Yeah, those weren't going to work with her helmet, and putting her through a flight without music was . . . unfathomable to me, a torture I wasn't willing to impose on her.

She dropped the headphones into her bag and stared out the window like nothing was wrong, but her back was ramrod straight, her lips pressed between her teeth, and she white-knuckled the seat as we launched.

Her gaze met mine as we left the ground, and just like that, we weren't in the Blackhawk. We were staring into each other's eyes, our hands clinging as flight 826 plummeted into the Missouri.

She slammed her eyes shut, and I unhooked my belt, adjusted my rifle, and pulled my AirPods out of a cargo pocket on my Kevlar. Then I moved, kneeling in front of her.

A touch of her knee had her eyes flying open and locking with mine. My chest tightened at the fear in those brown depths. She blinked quickly, trying to mask it, but she'd never been able to hide anything from me.

Reaching up, I slipped my AirPods into her ears, then sat back in my seat, aware of her gaze tracking my every move as she adjusted the fit.

The aircraft was nearly full, and yet it might as well have been only the two of us as I pulled out my phone—disconnected from service, but not the music I kept downloaded—and scrolled through my library.

I tapped on "Northern Downpour," and our eyes locked as the helicopter rose above Kabul, heading toward JBAD.

Her lips parted, and the way she looked at me . . . shit, it may as well have been 2011, or 2014, or any of the other years fate had thrown us together. It was one of her favorite songs, which was one of the only things we had in common. The shaky breath she drew, her chest stuttering, nearly unraveled me.

To sit here, to see her and not touch her, not demand to know whose ring was on her finger, was a hell I wasn't sure I could live through, and yet, I'd endure it without faltering if it meant I'd get to see her one last time.

After all, she was . . . Isabeau.

She mouthed along with the lyrics, then ripped her gaze away, staring at her knees.

I leaned forward and handed her my phone so she could pick whatever she wanted to listen to, then sat back and pulled out the paperback of *The Color Purple* I'd kept in the cargo pocket of my pants for the last few weeks and began to read.

The embassy was bustling with tension and a touch of chaos when we returned later that evening.

Izzy's meeting with leadership in Jalalabad had been only an hour, maybe less, but what she'd heard hadn't eased her tension or mine. There was an atmosphere of desperation, yet resolve, and I hoped the latter won out against the former.

The news we'd received once we'd gotten back to the bird a few hours ago had only confirmed what everyone knew—the country was destabilizing. Zaranj, in the southern Nimruz Province, had fallen to the Taliban today.

Expected, yet . . . disappointing.

"And these are the last articles from American journalists in country," Kacey said after filling Izzy in on the day, shoving a manila folder at her as we trudged up the stairs to her room.

"Perfect. Thank you. I'm going to shower off the dust, and then I'll be down for dinner," Izzy said, leaving Kacey at her bedroom door before shutting it.

I nodded at Kacey and then turned my back on Izzy's door like I was standing guard.

After thirty seconds, I tried the handle, and it opened. "Damn it, Izzy, can't you lock it?" I snapped, shutting it behind me and throwing the dead bolt.

"I knew you'd follow me in," she said from her bedroom, kicking off her shoes in the doorway. "Folder is on the table."

I picked it up and thumbed through the latest articles. "They shouldn't even be here," I muttered, checking the bylines for Serena's name. "Americans have been warned to get the hell out for months."

"You know Serena," Izzy said, shrugging off her blazer and then throwing it onto her bed. Couldn't blame her for wanting it off. It had been hot as hell out there. She walked over in just her dress pants and lace-trimmed camisole.

Nope, not looking at the way her breasts rose against the fabric.

That way lay madness.

"I do know Serena." I shook my head when I reached the last of the articles. "She didn't file today, or yesterday, and last week's didn't give a precise location. We'll have to check every day until we see her name."

Izzy's eyes widened, and the corners of her mouth tilted up into a smile that made my pulse quicken. "You really are going to help me, aren't you, Nate?"

God, that smile, those eyes . . .

"Yeah. I want you out of here as fast as fucking possible," I said, gesturing to her ring. "And I bet he does too."

Her sharp inhale told me I'd crossed a line, but I didn't care. That was all we were together: one giant, crossed line that neither of us belonged on the other side of.

I put the folder on the table and got the hell out of there.

CHAPTER EIGHT

IZZY

Saint Louis
November 2011

"Okay, I managed to scrounge up Twix, Butterfinger, and one very sketchy bag of SunChips," Serena said as she walked into my dim hospital room, carrying her loot. "The vending machine is pretty slim pickings out there." She did a double take at the television and snatched the remote off my bed. "Watching that isn't going to help."

I lunged for the remote and winced when she danced out of my reach. "Crap." Falling back against the bed, I breathed through the pain that engulfed my entire left side.

"Shit, I'm sorry, Iz." Serena grimaced and handed back the remote, then sat in the armchair next to my bed that she'd occupied ever since I'd woken up this morning, though she'd told me she'd been sitting there since last night. Two broken ribs and a ruptured spleen had done a number on my blood supply, but a couple of transfusions later . . . well, at least I wasn't dead.

Thanks to him.

None of us had died in the crash, which was a miracle, considering the footage.

"I'm just hoping that watching the footage will help clear my memory up," I told her, adjusting to sit up a little straighter and immediately regretting the decision. "God, it hurts."

"Then push the little clicker thing." She leaned over and put the pain-med pump in my hand. "You just had surgery yesterday—oh, and a *plane crash*. Give yourself a little break and clickity-click."

"That's not going to help. It's only going to fog up my head more and put me to sleep." I watched yet another replay of home video footage of the crash, shot by a fisherman who'd been on the Missouri. It was . . . horrifying.

We'd come out of nowhere, a roaring missile through the mist, barely missed that man's boat, and rammed the water.

"You sure you want to remember everything?" Serena asked softly, handing me the Twix, my favorite.

I tore open the package and then sank my teeth into the sweet caramel goodness, thinking as I chewed and swallowed. "It's mostly the stuff after getting out of the river that's missing. I remember the takeoff, the moment I realized we were going to crash, and even the frenzy to get out of the plane. The water was so cold . . ." I shook my head. "I just can't remember his name."

Everything else was right there—the concern in his eyes, the feel of his hands pulling me up the bank. He'd kept me breathing and laughing, and then carried me to the ambulance, according to what the nurses had told me.

I would have bled out internally under that tree if he hadn't.

"I'm sorry." Serena sighed, tearing into the chips. "I wish I remembered, but I was in such a panic that I didn't pay attention." Her gaze darted sideways at me as I watched the coverage of our rescue—though I was long gone by the time news crews had shown up. "He was a hottie, though, I can say that much."

"I remember what he looks like." I rolled my eyes. And what he was reading, and that he'd grown up on a farm and was joining the army for college money. It was just his name that eluded me, and pretty much everything after sitting against the tree.

"And he cared enough to tell everyone he was your husband. Signed for your surgery and everything." A teasing smile turned up the corners of her mouth. "Miraculously knew your blood type and your allergies, too, which means you must have been conscious enough to tell him. And seriously." She leveled a stare on me. "The doctor said you're not supposed to be watching TV with a concussion."

My sigh rose from the bottom of my blanketed toes, but I hit the off switch just as the nurse came in to do another round of vitals. Luckily, she kept the lights dimmed, since my head felt like it was about a billion pounds of pulsing TNT.

"Is there anything else I can get you?" she asked, jotting down the numbers in the chart that hung from the end of my bed.

The chart.

"No, I'm okay, but thank you." I gave her a smile, and she headed out of the room before closing the door behind her. "Serena, grab the chart."

Two lines appeared between my sister's eyebrows. "What?"

"The chart." I waved my hand toward the end of the bed. "If he signed for the surgery, it must be in there."

"Good idea!" She bolted out of her chair, abandoning her snacks on the bedside table. "You'd think you were the one studying journalism."

Studying. Oh shit, I was going to have to get back to Syracuse, but the idea of getting on a plane was . . . there was just no freaking way. I'd have to be not only sedated, but fully unconscious with an escort, and even then I wasn't sure I could bring myself to walk down the jet bridge anyway. "How am I going to get back to school?" The rhetorical question was a whisper.

Serena lowered the side rail of my bed and then sat on the edge, depressing the mattress as she handed me the chart. "We'll figure it out. Just because they're going to release you tomorrow doesn't mean you have to go back to New York, Iz. There's no rush. I'm sure Mom and

Dad will understand if you decide to take some time off. And if you do want to go back, then I'll just blow off some classes and we'll drive." She shrugged. "No biggie. Or I'm sure Mom and Dad will be here in a few days, and they can drive you home to Colorado if that's what you want."

"Thank you." I took the chart and set it on my lap. "I just don't know how to make myself get on a plane."

Did *he*? When he'd left yesterday with the soldiers, had they immediately put him on the next flight to Fort Benning? Sure, I was scared of flying, but at least yesterday hadn't been my only experience in the air.

"Then we'll work through it," she said as the phone next to my bed rang, startling us both.

I leaned but couldn't quite reach, and the stitches in my side protested in the loudest way possible. Or maybe it was the broken ribs, or the spleen. Who knew? My entire body was pretty damn angry with me.

Serena rushed around the side of the bed and answered the phone, pushing her long hair out of the way. Even after twenty-four hours in the hospital, she still managed to look . . . perfect. If I hadn't loved her so much, I would've loathed her out of sheer jealousy.

"Hello?" she answered, and a muffled voice replied. Her eyebrows shot up. "Oh, thank God. I sent a message through the cruise lines, but I wasn't sure how long it would take to get to you. When are you coming home?" *Mom and Dad*, she mouthed, listening to whatever they were saying. "She's okay. They're releasing her tomorrow. Ruptured spleen repaired, concussion, broken ribs, and bumps and bruises, but she's past the worst of it. She's right here if you want to—" Her brow furrowed.

I held out my empty hand.

"Are you serious?" Her face tensed. "Well, you can tell her that yourself." She closed her eyes and swallowed, then handed me the phone.

Dread twisted my already nauseated stomach. "Hello?"

"Isa!" Dad answered. "Oh, honey. I'm so sorry you've been through this."

My eyes burned, but I swallowed back the tears. The same thing had happened when I'd found Serena next to my bed. It was like my emotions were simply too big for my body. "I'm okay," I forced out.

"That's what Serena says," Mom added, and I could picture them sharing the handset, leaned in so they could both be a part of the conversation. "I'm so glad she's there to take care of you for the next couple of days."

"You'll be back by then?" I held the phone between my right shoulder and ear and started flipping through my chart.

"Well." Mom sighed. "Honey, you know how long we've waited to take this trip, so if you're not in any life-or-limb danger, there's not really a reason for us to come back, is there?"

I blinked, my hands going completely still.

Serena took her place on the side of my bed, watching me with an assessing gaze that I couldn't bring myself to meet.

"I mean, we'll see you at Christmas. That's only four weeks away, and I'm sure you don't want to miss out on any classes, which is all that us coming home would accomplish, really," Mom continued.

"You're not coming home?" I had to say it, had to make sure that's what I'd actually heard them say. My parents were masters at words and every way they could be interpreted.

Serena reached for my hand and squeezed.

"If they're releasing you tomorrow, then you must be on the mend," Dad said, his tone changing to the matter-of-fact one he used at the office. "And I know you've been through a shock, Isa, but this will really be an opportunity for you to rise above the challenge and show your mettle."

An *opportunity*?

"It wasn't a *shock*," I argued as my heart crumpled in on itself. "It was a plane crash. My plane *crashed*. I had to climb out the emergency exit onto the wing and then swim for shore while bleeding internally." And still they weren't coming home.

"And we're so proud of you!" Mom sounded like I'd just earned a trophy. "Guess all those years on the swim team paid off."

Not that they'd been at a single meet.

"We know you crashed, Isa," Dad interjected. "Which is why you have full access to my credit card to book another flight back to Syracuse, of course. Don't worry about a thing—we'll cover it."

Don't worry about a thing except them being here. Got it.

"I don't know what to say."

"Don't feel like you have to thank us. Of course we'd cover your travel expenses." Dad chuckled. "And we can't wait to see the dean's list when we get back stateside."

You have to be kidding *me.*

"Of course we'll come home if you really, honestly need us to, Isabeau," Mom said, her tone softening. "I'm sure we could get refunded for the rest of the trip, and of course there's always next year if we want to finish it, right?"

"Don't baby her, Rose. Serena already told us she's being released, which means she's fine. She's an Astor. Aren't you, Isa?" Dad questioned. "Astors do what needs to be done."

They really expected me to come through this like everything else—with flying colors. What the hell was I supposed to do? Ask them to leave the only vacation Dad had taken in the last ten years where he hadn't been in constant contact with his office?

I lifted my gaze to meet Serena's and found her watching with compassion and a supportive smile.

"We'll handle it together," she whispered. "Just like we always do."

I nodded and cleared my throat, banishing the knot that threatened to close it. "I'm fine. Serena will get me back to school."

"Of course she will," Dad said, pride filling his tone. "And we'll see you at Christmas. And I know this has been horrible, but I'm glad we got to talk to you. We love you."

"We love you!" Mom declared. "And we'll get you something special at the next port."

Tell me your love language is gifts without telling me . . .

"Sounds great. Love you guys too."

Serena and I said our goodbyes, and she hung up the phone.

"I'm so sorry, Iz. I legitimately thought . . ." She sighed, plopping down in the armchair.

"No, you didn't." My voice softened. "Let's not lie to each other." The priorities in Mom and Dad's life were Dad's company, and themselves. Serena and I had always been hood ornaments, shined up and shown for status. But still, my lungs hurt when I drew my next breath.

"You have me." She leaned in. "You always have me."

"I know." I clasped her hand for a moment and then took a shuddering breath. Crying about it wasn't going to help, so I focused on the chart in my lap, flipping through the pages until I found the first documents. "There it is!"

Serena stood and leaned over the bed. "Are you sure that guy wasn't a doctor? Because his handwriting is utter shit."

"Nathaniel," I whispered, my fingers skirting over the signature, but I couldn't read the rest of it.

"How the hell did you get Nathaniel out of that chicken scratch?" She shook her head. "All I see is an *N* and . . . whatever that is."

"Nate." My lips curved into a wide grin, my first since waking up. "His friends call him Nate." That was all I could remember, and probably all I'd ever know, but at least I had a name to put to the face of the man who'd saved my life.

Two months later, I adjusted my bag on my shoulder and stomped off the snow from my boots on the entry mat of my dorm. Colorado got snow, so it wasn't like I was a stranger to the white stuff, but Syracuse got *snow*, especially in January.

It was up to my waist out there.

I walked to the mail room and spun the dial on my box as students chatted around me. My eyebrows rose at the telltale orange slip that meant I had a package to be picked up.

Mom and Dad weren't exactly the care package type, and I'd seen them just last week before coming back to New York after break, so there was absolutely no chance it was from them. Serena, maybe?

I shut my mailbox, tossed one of the weekly credit card offers in the trash, and headed to the line at the window to pick up whatever had been sent to me. There were only two people ahead of me.

"Hey, Izzy!" Margo, my roommate, called out from the lobby with a thick southern accent, trudging toward me and leaving wet boot prints all over the muddy floor.

"Hey," I answered. "How was psych?"

"Normal." She shrugged as we moved forward in line and shook the snow out of her midnight-black hair. "We're studying posttraumatic stress disorder." A meaningful gaze cut my way. "Thought any more about maybe . . . discussing yours with a therapist?"

Nice and subtle.

"I don't have PTSD. I'm scared of planes." Which was why Serena and I had driven a rental car all the way from Colorado after break, despite my father telling me that I couldn't afford to let the fear of flight hold me back.

"Resulting from a traumatic experience of a freaking plane crash," she lectured, and the line moved again.

"I was scared of flying before the crash."

"Slip?" the attendant asked, and I handed mine over. He disappeared into the mail room.

"I'm just saying that it really helped me after I lost my brother," she said softly, and I couldn't help but look over at her.

The thought of losing Serena was incomprehensible.

"So maybe it might help you to talk too," she suggested. "I live with you. I know you're not sleeping like you were before the crash. It couldn't hurt, and from what I'm studying, the earlier you talk it out with a professional, the better."

Maybe she was right. If anything, a therapist could tell me I was perfectly fine, and maybe suggest a few alternate forms of transportation. "I'll look into it."

"Good!" She hugged my side.

"Astor?" the attendant said, pushing a box across the counter. The brown box was a foot wide, about eighteen inches long, and maybe six inches tall if I had to guess.

"That's me." I reached for the clipboard he handed over and signed my name on the recipient line.

"Who's it from?" Margo asked.

"Not sure." It was surprisingly light as I picked it up off the counter and read the printed address label. "Transcontinental Airlines." My chest tightened.

"Is it a giant check for your pain and suffering?"

"No clue." What could the airline possibly have to send me? A pillow so I'd sleep better? A thousand travel vouchers I'd never bring myself to use?

We took the elevator to the third floor, and Margo used her key to open our door since my hands were full. Our furniture was simple—matching beds, desks, and mini dressers—but our decor was all Margo. Everything was hot pink and lime green, like the entire room had just stepped out of a Lilly Pulitzer ad.

I set the box down on my desk, then cut it open, taking out the letter on top of a dark-blue plastic bag.

> Ms. Astor,
> With the initial investigation into the unfortunate incident regarding flight 826 complete, we're returning the personal belongings found in your seat's floor storage. Though many paper items were water-logged

and unsalvageable due to the plane's submersion, we wanted to return what we could.

We apologize for the inconvenience of the time you've lost without your belongings,

Transcontinental Air

I snorted a laugh and read the last line out loud to Margo. "They're sorry about the inconvenience about my lost luggage."

"And the loss of your spleen?" She peeked over my shoulder.

"Hey, maybe it's my purse!" I lifted the bag with zeal. It was probably ruined after spending weeks in the Missouri River, but I was kind of ruined, too, so we were a match. My thumbs pried apart the plastic closure, and the bag fell away, revealing an olive-green army backpack.

My heart stopped, and I had to take a deep breath to get it started again.

"That doesn't look like your purse," Margo said, a laugh in her voice.

"It's not mine." I set the backpack down on the empty portion of my desk. "It's his."

Her eyebrows launched upward as she moved to my side. "*His* as in . . . the dreamy guy who saved your life like some kind of river *Baywatch* Prince Charming?"

Obviously I'd spent a fair amount of time talking about Nate and too much time thinking about him: wondering how he was doing, wishing I had some way to contact him. He deserved so much more than my thanks, and besides, I'd said I'd ship books to him if he was allowed to have them in basic training.

If he was even still in basic training. I didn't know enough about the army to even guess at how long stuff like that took.

"Yeah." The backpack had obviously been washed, and it somehow looked exactly the same as when Nate had nearly pulled it out to switch seats with me. "He was sitting in my seat."

"Open it." She leaned in.

I unzipped the bag, and found a worn, soft, Saint Louis Blues hoodie and an iPod that had been protected by a ziplock bag. It turned on when I pushed the button through the plastic bag, "Panic! at the Disco" flashing across the screen. "I guess everything else must have been ruined."

"I'm sorry it's not your purse," Margo said, turning back toward her side of our room.

"I'm not," I whispered. How was it possible to feel so . . . connected to someone I'd only known for a couple of hours? It wasn't even that he'd pulled me from the river, or that he'd carried me to an ambulance. He'd held my hand the entire way down and never looked away.

I shoved the sweatshirt back into the pack and then inhaled sharply. There, on the tag just beneath the handle on the inside of the pack, in permanent marker, was printed *N. Phelan*.

My grin stretched my cheeks. I knew his name. Wherever he was or whatever he was doing aside, I knew his *name*. I could find him, if only to return his bag.

Nathaniel Phelan.

CHAPTER NINE

IZZY

Kabul, Afghanistan
August 2021

"Sergeant Green," I said the next day. My stack of manila folders was balanced precariously between my hands, cell phone on top, as I walked toward where Nate stood guard at the doorway of the conference room our team had taken over as office space in the embassy. Guess it was fitting to call him an entirely different name, considering he felt like a completely different person.

But he'd slipped those earbuds into my ears yesterday and played "Northern Downpour" to distract me when the helicopter took off. What the hell was I supposed to do with that? It was a glimpse of who we'd been in this dusty, bleak landscape of what we'd somehow become.

"Ms. Astor." Nate nodded, his eyes trained straight ahead.

"Isa!" Ben Holt came flying through the lobby behind me, dodging the thickening crowd of Americans looking for assistance, and I half expected him to pull a cartoonish skid, but he managed to stop before barreling into me.

"Is something on fire?" I asked, adjusting the folders.

"Did you file your report with Senator Lauren when you got back last night?" Worry creased the area between his brows, and I sighed, already seeing where this was headed.

"Yep. I sent my initial impression from yesterday's trip when we got back." It had been late in the afternoon, and I'd been more than a little emotionally exhausted after clenching every muscle in my body during both flights, but work was work. "Kacey is still drafting the pretty version in there." I nodded back toward the conference room.

"Shit," he muttered, letting his head fall back for a second. "Do you always have to be so ahead of things?" There was a teasing glint in his brown eyes. "It would help the rest of us every once in a while."

"Not ahead," I reminded him as my cell phone buzzed with an incoming call. "Just on top of things. If I don't get my notes turned in, then the junior aides can't get theirs started." My cell moved across the top folder with every buzzing ring.

Jeremy's name and contact photo filled the screen.

Shit. It was his third call today.

"Let me help," Ben said, reaching for the phone a half second too late. It fell from the stack of folders, crashing into the shiny floor, bouncing on impact.

Naturally, where Ben was too slow, Nate had the reflexes of a freaking cat, and he caught the device before it could impact again.

I was acutely aware of the rise of Nate's body next to mine, and if I hadn't been staring at his face, watching for any possible reaction, I would have missed the way his brow furrowed for a second when he saw the screen. "Just hit decline," I said softly, my heart pounding at the thought that he'd answer it.

I wasn't ready for the conversation Jeremy wanted, or the very different one I needed, and I sure as hell wasn't ready for Nate to talk to him. Nope. No way was that happening.

Nate might not have known Jeremy, but Jeremy sure as hell knew who Nate was. Couldn't blame Jeremy for hating him, though. I wasn't keen on fighting a ghost for my fiancé's attention either.

Except Nate wasn't a ghost anymore. He was flesh and blood next to me, smelling like that spearmint gum he was obsessed with.

Which meant I knew exactly how he tasted right now.

"You sure?" Nate's ice-blue eyes rose to meet mine, his finger hovering over the decline button.

"Absolutely." I nodded, never as certain about anything in my life.

"Man, you're fast," Ben noted, leaning around my stack of folders to look at the phone. "Jeremy, huh?"

Nate looked at the phone for a second longer, and I knew he was memorizing every detail about Jeremy in that way he had, filing the information away for later. Then he tapped the decline button, and instead of putting my phone back on the stack in my arms, he slid it into the side pocket of my black slacks.

He didn't touch me with his hands, but damn, did it feel like he had.

"How's that going, anyway?" Ben asked like Nate wasn't even there.

"It's . . ." I swallowed, hard, and couldn't help glancing over at Nate, but he'd already stepped back, taking his interminable position at the door. The files grew heavier every second we stood here. "It is what it is."

"You know, I heard rumors." Ben rubbed the back of his neck, giving me that pitying look I'd become accustomed to over the last six weeks. "But you hadn't said anything, so I didn't want to push—"

"Which I appreciate," I said, cutting him off. "I'd just rather focus on the work we have here and leave Washington in Washington." What I had to decide wasn't for public knowledge, especially not in the gossiping fishbowl that was DC politics.

"Understandable." His voice softened. "But just in case you need someone to talk to"—he reached for my shoulder—"I'm here." With a sympathetic nod, he walked past me and into the conference room.

"Give me those." Nate moved over and took the files from my arms without waiting for me to respond, and I nearly sighed with physical relief. "Whatever he's asking you to share, don't."

"Really?" I asked, pivoting to face him.

"He's . . ." Nate's forehead crinkled, which meant he was searching for the right words. "He's too eager for the information. Just a gut feeling."

"Yeah." I fought my smile, because he was right on the money. "He asked me out our first week on the Hill, and I'm not sure he's ever really accepted that no."

Nate's brow furrowed as he glanced through the glass into the conference room. "Guys who wait for a woman to hit her lowest so they can make their move are pieces of shit."

"Noted." I pressed my lips between my teeth to keep from grinning.

"What?"

"You've always had the ability to judge someone's character within minutes of meeting them, and I've never seen you proved wrong." I shrugged, looking away quickly. "You know we don't need a guard at the door, right? We're in the embassy."

"And I told you that for the next two weeks, I won't be any more than a room away from you. Not until you're safe and snug on a plane pointed stateside." His gaze took a quick sweep of the files.

"But you'll stay here, won't you?" I whispered, my stomach sinking. Putting me on a plane would only guarantee my safety, not his. Never his.

"These names aren't on our itinerary." He arched a brow.

"They're all SIV applications," I said. "For Special Immigrant Visas."

"For people employed by us," he said. "I know what SIVs are. What are you doing with a stack of them?"

"I got the rundown on how to process them earlier and figured we could help out between meetings." Looking over my shoulder, I noted how crowded the lobby was. "I walked into the waiting room, and every chair is full. They're overwhelmed."

"They are," he agreed. "Good to see some things haven't changed," he said, turning to walk into the conference room. "You're still trying to save everyone but yourself."

Ice-cold water soaked my feet and panic seized my muscles, making my numb fingers useless as I fought with the seat belt. We were going under, and there was nothing I could do about it but sit there and drown. The screams around me filled my ears as I yanked harder and harder on the belt. The water rose to my knees, and I tried to cry out for help, but my throat wouldn't work.

The sudden silence made me look around at the other passengers, but they were gone, all evacuated through the emergency exit across the aisle.

I was alone.

They all left me.

I forced out a scream, the sound garbled as the water rushed up my thighs and the floor lighting failed. There wasn't enough air, enough time. I was going to die in here. The fuselage sank faster and faster, water rising around my chest, but the stupid belt was stuck.

Looking left, I saw the emergency exit open, but I couldn't get there.

This isn't right.

He wouldn't leave me. He never left me. Not until I—

"Izzy!" Nate jumped through the doorway, splashing into the freezing water, then unhooked my belt with one flick of his hand, but he looked different. Thicker. Older. Harder. The name tape on his Kevlar read *Green*.

This was a dream.

With a gasp, I shot up in bed, my tank top soaked through with sweat and my heart pounding as I struggled for breath. My ribs squeezed like a vise, but I forced air in and out through my lungs. That was all it ever took to escape the nightmare. I just had to realize it was one.

Falling out of bed, I hit my knees and the carpet stung my bare skin.

This was real.

"My name. Is. Isabeau Astor," I managed through the narrowing passage of my throat. "I was a passenger on flight 826." There we go. That was a full sentence. "We hit the water. I made it out." The words had been drilled into me through years of therapy, though they always took different forms, depending on the nightmare. "I swam to safety. I survived." By the time I finished, my throat had opened enough that I could take a deep breath. Then two. "We survived."

I glanced at the clock. It was four a.m.

Fresh air. I needed fresh air.

A beep alerted me that my door opened, and then it slammed shut, but the scant amount of moonlight coming in through the windows didn't give me much visibility.

"Izzy?"

"In here." My shoulders slumped in relief. There was only one person that voice could belong to.

"You screamed." His shadow filled my doorway, and I could tell his weapon was drawn.

"It's just me," I assured him, wrapping my arms around my midsection.

He walked right by me, clearing my bathroom and then the area next to the window before flicking on the light on the nightstand behind me. "Fuck."

That word was the only warning before there was a sound like him holstering his weapon. Then he lifted me into his arms, holding me close against his chest.

"I'm okay," I promised, but that didn't stop me from melting into his familiar embrace. He wasn't decked out in that thick Kevlar vest anymore, not that I expected him to be at four in the morning. There was soft black cotton and a steady heartbeat against my cheek.

"Yeah, seems like it." He walked us into the living room, then sat on the couch, holding me in his lap and clicking on the table lamp next to us. "Shit, you're soaked."

I should have moved, should have scooted to the other end of the couch, but instead, I tucked my legs up and curled into him for the simple reason that there was nowhere safer in this world.

"It's just a nightmare." I shivered as my skin chilled beneath the beads of sweat.

Nate reached over his shoulder and pulled the blanket from the back of the couch over me, then wrapped one arm around me. His other hand stroked up and down my arm in a soothing, repetitive motion. "Would a hot bath help?"

"No water." I shook my head and barely kept myself from arching my face into his neck. It should have been illegal to smell that good, all fresh soap and spearmint.

"The plane," he guessed, resting his chin on the top of my head.

"The plane."

Minutes passed in silence as my heart rate slowed to match his. That was one of the things I loved about being around Nate. We didn't have to fill every empty second with chatter.

"Do you ever get them?" I asked, knowing I should move off his lap, out of his arms, and yet unable to make myself.

"Not really anymore." He continued the slow, steady strokes up and down my arm.

"What changed?"

"It became one of the lesser traumatizing things I've seen," he said softly. "But if I do get them, they're usually that I can't get you out, or that you slip away in the current. Never gets past that, though. I'm perpetually battling to get you to shore." His hand paused, and he squeezed my shoulder. "What about you? How often do they still happen to you?"

"Depends. Usually only when I'm in the middle of something really stressful, or something that's out of my control." *Like right now.* "Feels like I went through years of therapy for nothing," I tried to joke.

"If they happen less than they used to, it's worth it."

I somehow doubted he'd acted on that sentiment in the last three years, given how opposed he'd been to it before.

Moments passed, and the impropriety of it all struck me straight in the chest. "Is this how you comfort every assignment you're given?"

"Hardly," he scoffed, shaking his head, and I knew that if I looked up, I'd see that slight smile curving his lips. The one that always made me ache to kiss him.

I couldn't stay there, curled up against him like I wasn't someone else's fiancée.

Are you really, though?

I shifted my head slightly and felt the lump under my cheek, then drew back to stare at it.

"I was in the middle of getting dressed when I heard you," he said, pulling the chain from beneath his shirt to reveal what looked like a dog tag, but it had been wrapped in black tape.

The tape was so he wouldn't make a sound when moving around, if I remembered correctly.

"Explains the bare feet," I said, shifting out of his lap and taking the blanket with me. It was odd that he was wearing dog tags if I wasn't even allowed to call him by his name. All these years later, he'd dug deeper into the same life, while I'd completely changed mine.

He cleared his throat and moved to the other end of the couch, leaving only my feet on the no-man's-land of the center cushion.

"What were you doing up at four in the morning?" I asked, tugging the blanket closer to cover the fact that I didn't exactly wear a bra to bed. Not that he hadn't already seen every inch of me naked.

"Getting back from the gym."

I dropped my gaze to his hip, where a weapon was holstered. "And the first thing you do after a shower is strap up?"

"Listen to you." He grinned, flashing that dimple, and my heart freaking clenched. "*Strap up.*"

God, it was safer against his chest, where I wasn't looking straight into those eyes. Ten years later, and they still had the same thigh-clenching effect on me. The man could have done nothing but look at me, and I bet I would have come if he stared hard enough. I gripped the edge of the blanket.

His brow knit. "You're not wearing your ring."

Heat flushed my cheeks, and I drew my hand back beneath the blanket. "I don't sleep in it," I explained. The damn thing was cumbersome and caught on the sheets, and maybe I just needed a damn break from wearing the symbol of being Jeremy's. "It's . . . not comfortable," I finished in a tone so lame even I cringed.

"I can see how a rock like that would get . . . heavy." He looked away, his jaw ticking.

Guilt sat like a rock in my stomach, and a thousand things I wanted to say tickled the tip of my tongue. Then I remembered the sight of his rain-soaked back retreating down my hallway in New York, refusing to turn when I called his name over and over, and my chest tightened. "How are we supposed to do this?"

"Do what?" He leaned forward, bracing his elbows on his knees.

"Stay this close for the next two weeks and just ignore . . . everything?" It came out as a whisper.

He shoved his dog tags back under his shirt. "It's only twelve more days," he answered quietly. "And we just have to."

"Nate." I moved to scoot closer, and he pinned me with a look that stopped me dead.

"Don't, Izzy." He shook his head. "I have one weakness on this entire planet, and you're *feet* away when you're supposed to be halfway round the globe." That mask he wore like armor fell away, and the pain in his eyes was enough to make me suck in a sharp breath. "So please, have some goddamn mercy on me for once in your life and just . . ." His eyes squeezed shut. "Just ignore it."

I studied the lines of his face, the tattoo that moved and rippled on his forearm when he curled his hands into fists. Every line of him was tight, like he was prepared to fight a battle I couldn't see. It wasn't fair to him. I was here by my choice, and he was only staying for me. "Okay," I said. "I can ignore it."

"Thank you." His posture relaxed, and he stared at the coffee table in front of us. "What is that?" He motioned to the folder.

"The latest posts by American journalists," I answered. "Kacey must have come in and put them on the table after I went to bed. I crashed early."

"She has a key?"

"Yes. She's a junior aide. She's not a threat, Nate." I rolled my eyes.

"You need to lock your dead bolt," he muttered, reaching for the folder.

"And if I had, you wouldn't have been able to get in, either, would you?" I challenged, tucking my legs underneath me as he handed me the folder.

He snorted. "Like a piece of metal is keeping me out when I hear you scream."

I didn't bother pointing out that if he could get past a dead bolt, so could anyone else. Instead, I thumbed through the articles. My breath caught when I saw her byline. "Nate," I whispered, shoving the printed article at him. "She's not in the picture, but it's Serena's article."

I bet if I check my phone right now, I'll have a Google Alert waiting in my inbox.

He took the article and studied the picture, sighing. "She's in Mez."

"What?" Against my better judgment, I moved closer so I could see it, too, my shoulder brushing his arm.

"That building. It's the Shrine of Ali, also known as the Blue Mosque." He pointed to the building in the distance of the picture. "She's either in Mazar-i-Sharif, or she was recently."

I couldn't help but smile, because she'd filed it earlier this evening, according to the post time. "But she's alive."

"She's alive."

And now we knew where she was.

CHAPTER TEN

NATHANIEL

Tybee Island, Georgia
June 2014

"Seven ball, corner pocket," I called out, flipping my ball cap backward before leaning over the pool table and making my third shot in a row.

"Damn it, Phelan," Rowell muttered, his head falling back as our friends howled with laughter, bottles lifting all around me. "You gotta run the table on me like that?"

"Hey, you were the one pushing me to play." A smirk turned up the corner of my mouth as I surveyed the table in the corner we'd commandeered at our favorite beach bar on Tybee Island. There were three other tables nearby, a dance floor that always seemed to have sand on it, and a bar that opened to the ocean breeze, a lifesaver in the Georgia summer, even at ten p.m. "Three, side pocket." I sank the shot as the beat changed in the obnoxiously loud speakers behind me, and from the resounding squeal, I could only guess that a group of women took the floor.

Couldn't argue with the music choice, though. "Miss Jackson" wasn't my favorite Panic! at the Disco song, but it was up there. The favorite? Now that was "Northern Downpour" . . . which was the last song I'd listened to before boarding flight 826.

Fuck, why had I just thought about that? Flashes of breathtaking brown eyes invaded my memory just like they had my dreams over the past two and a half years. *Isabeau.*

"There goes another twenty." Rowell leaned back against the wall, clearly resigning himself to his wallet being a little lighter after this game.

"You going to show the man a little mercy?" Torres asked, running his hand over his dark, close-cropped hair as I scanned the table. After two years in the same platoon, and one of those spent in the sandbox, he was the closest thing I'd ever had to a best friend.

"Why the hell would I do that?" I lined up another shot. "Six ball, corner pocket." And there went another one of Rowell's twenties. "Wishing you'd bet a little less?" I asked Rowell over my shoulder.

"I thought you were a farm boy from Illinois." He looked around the rest of our platoon who had come out tonight. "Did anyone else know he's a pool shark?" Everyone shook their heads.

"He's a real chatterbox." Torres laughed and threw back another swig of his beer.

"Damn," Fitz remarked, leaning his lanky frame sideways to see past me as I studied the table. I'd given it a little too much spin and left myself with a shit angle for the one ball. "Pretty sure an entire sorority just took to the floor."

Almost every head in my platoon turned, but that didn't surprise me. It was only us single guys out tonight. Most of the married men preferred to spend their last weekend before deployment with their families.

"That's a bachelorette party," Torres said, a slow smile spreading across his face as I moved to the other side of the table to line up the best shot I had. A group of women danced into view, a bunch of hot-pink tank tops surrounding one in white with a light-up veil.

Yeah, that was a bachelorette party, all right.

"You would have helped me out if you'd managed to clear a few of your balls out of the way, Rowell," I said, bending low to concentrate.

Rowell grunted in reply.

I glanced up as the closest woman on the floor spun, her arms raised and blonde hair flying as she danced to the chorus.

It was only a glimpse, but my heart stuttered and my grip slipped, causing me to miss the shot completely. The cue ball went skittering across the green felt, and I startled.

"Guess your luck had to run out sometime." Rowell laughed as I stood, scanning the dance floor with single-minded focus.

That wasn't her. A different blonde had taken the edge of the floor. Or was it the same blonde? Had my head pulled the ultimate trick on me?

Was it the music? The way it made the memory surface again?

There was no way it was her.

But the surge of adrenaline in my veins screamed that it was. I threw my pool stick at whoever was closest and *moved*.

"Phelan!" Fitz called out, but I was already in the thick of the dance floor before I even thought of replying.

The strobe light kicked on as the song changed, and faces blurred all around me as I turned left, then right, then left again, searching the features of every woman in a pink tank top who danced near me in the momentary flashes of light. There were six . . . no, seven.

And none of them were her.

Shit. Was I losing it? I'd seen some shit on deployment, and it wasn't like the plane crash hadn't screwed my head in ways I tried not to linger on, but hallucinations? I wasn't that screwed up, was I?

"You okay?" Torres asked, coming up on my left as I stood in the middle of the pulsing dance floor.

"I thought I saw someone."

That woman was brunette. That one was redheaded. Blonde. Wrong smile. Not her eyes.

"Apparently. You took off like your ass was on fire."

"Scared I'm going to clean you out now that it's my turn?" Rowell asked from my right, but there was a concerned tilt to his brow despite his shit-giving tone.

Like it was an act of fate or some other equally fortuitous force, the crowd parted for a length of a heartbeat, but that was all I needed.

Standing at the bar was Isabeau fucking Astor. She tucked her hair behind an ear, giving me a full view of her profile, and my heart jumped into my throat.

"Better things to do," I said to Rowell, barely sparing him a glance before walking through the crowd.

"Better than winning a hundred and sixty bucks?" he yelled over the music.

"I forfeit!" I shouted over my shoulder. "The money's yours!"

The crowd converged again, all jumping in rhythm to the music as I eased my way through the dancers until I'd made it to the other side of the floor.

The bride had joined Izzy near the curve of the bar, and a riot of emotions assaulted me as I took the space across the corner, where I could see her entire face. I opened my mouth once, then twice, but couldn't think of what to say.

There was every chance in the world she wouldn't remember me, not with the concussion she'd had. And as often as I'd wondered about her, dreamed about her, I'd never once let myself even imagine actually seeing her again, or what I would say if I did.

Izzy was thoroughly distracted in the opposite direction, trying to flag down the bartender, but the bride glanced my way, then hoisted her eyebrow when she noticed me staring at her friend.

Time to speak before the bride accused me of creeping, and this already had the potential for being awkward as hell.

"I must have dreamed of you a million times," I said loudly enough to be heard over the music. *Smooth, Nate. Real smooth.*

Izzy rolled her eyes without even looking my way.

"She's not interested." The bride leaned into my line of sight, blocking Izzy, and shook her head. "Trust me, she just got out of a shitty relationship, and you aren't interested either."

"Trust me, she's interested." I grinned. Had to give it to loyal friends.

Izzy scoffed and turned her head away even more, purposefully ignoring me. She was just as beautiful—even more so—as I remembered, in a bar full of frat boys on summer vacation and soldiers preparing to deploy. I couldn't even begin to imagine how many times she must have been hit on tonight.

"What could you possibly know about what interests her?" The bride glared with slightly glazed eyes. "We're having a girls' night. So just go back to whatever"—she gestured at the plain black T-shirt that stretched across my torso—"gym you crawled out of."

"I like you," I told the bride, then leaned farther onto the counter so I could see Izzy. "And I know she likes to read and hates to fly."

Izzy stiffened and her gaze shifted, but she still didn't look at me.

"Random guess," the bride huffed, crossing her arms.

"I know she's allergic to shellfish and penicillin," I continued. Izzy's eyes widened as she slowly turned my direction. "And she keeps Tylenol and antibiotic ointment in her purse."

Izzy's gaze locked with mine, her gorgeous brown eyes flaring with recognition as her lips parted. She looked as shocked as I felt.

"Oh, and her blood type is O positive." My smile somehow widened. "Am I forgetting anything?"

She sidestepped the bride, and my breath stalled as she came closer, until only a matter of inches separated us. "Nathaniel Phelan?"

"Hey, Isabeau Astor."

She cried out and jumped at me, throwing her arms around my neck. I caught her easily, splaying my hands over her back and hugging her tight. Forget awkward. This felt like coming home.

The last time I'd felt this relieved, this whole, was the moment we'd made it to shore after the crash.

"I have your bag," she said as she pulled back, studying my face like she was looking for the scar my ball cap hid.

"What?" I set her back on her feet and forced my hands to let her go.

"Your bag." She flashed a smile, and my chest constricted around my heart. Shit, I hadn't imagined that instantaneous connection I'd felt with her on the plane. It was all too real, shining brightly in my face. "The airline sent it to me because you'd been sitting in my seat."

"No way." My eyebrows hit the ceiling.

She nodded, her grin just as big as mine. "I have your hoodie and your iPod, which I can't believe you actually put in a ziplock bag, but it worked. My mouth just about hit the floor when it powered on. I don't have them with me, of course—they're all at my apartment in DC—but I'm not really sure what box they're in, since I haven't even had time to unpack between graduation, moving, and now Margo's bachelorette party," she babbled, yelling to be heard over the music.

She *still* babbled, and there was nothing better in the entire world.

"Holy shit, this is Plane Guy?" the bride—Margo—asked, staring at me like she'd seen a ghost.

"Yes!" Izzy nodded. "Can you believe it? Nate, this is Margo. Margo, this is Nate." She hooked her arm through Margo's elbow. "She was with me when I got the backpack."

"Hi, Margo." I managed to rip my gaze from Izzy long enough to nod at the bride.

"Hi, Plane Guy!" She smacked a kiss on Izzy's cheek. "If you need me, I'll be out on the floor!" Arms up, she ran back out to the other bridesmaids.

Izzy and I stood there, the beat pounding all around us, and stared at each other.

"You want to grab a drink?" I asked, suddenly remembering that she'd been at the bar for a reason.

She nodded, and we both turned back to the bar, our arms brushing as I lifted my right hand to flag the bartender. Fuck, it was like I was sixteen again—that was how quickly that innocent touch went straight through me.

"You're not drinking either?" she asked after I'd paid for our sodas.

"I've already had a couple." I shrugged. There was no chance I was going to dull a single second of seeing her again. "Want to grab a table outside?"

"Absolutely."

We made our way through the bar crowd and onto the beachfront patio, where we scored one of the two-seater high-tops at the edge.

Then we stared at each other again, this time in the relative quiet.

"It's nice out here," she said.

"You look good," I said simultaneously.

We both smiled.

"Thanks, but it's probably just the fact that I'm not bleeding out internally." She shrugged playfully.

"You were looking a little pale there for a minute." I flashed a smile and took a sip of my Coke.

"I don't remember anything after getting to the edge of the river," she said quietly, wiping the condensation from her glass.

"But . . ." My brow furrowed. "You swore your eternal love and devotion to me. You promised we'd have three kids and everything." Shit, it was hard to keep a straight face.

She didn't even try, her eyes dancing in the soft outdoor lighting. "Very funny."

I took a deep breath, sorting through my memories of that day. This was all so incredibly surreal. "We got you to a tree so you could sit down," I began, and then I told her everything I could remember.

"You saved my life," she said when I got to the part about the ambulance.

"Nah. Technically that was the paramedics."

"There you are!" Fitz called out, coming across the patio. "You disappeared." He glanced at Izzy's shirt. "With a member of the bridal party, I see."

"Izzy, this is Fitz." I took a drink.

Izzy stuck her hand out, and Fitz shook it. "Hi, Fitz. I'm Isabeau Astor. I'm Nate's wife."

I slammed my hand over my mouth to keep from spitting Coke across the table.

"His wife?" Fitz raised his brows at me. "Do Justin and Julian know about this, seeing as they're his best friends?"

Rowell and Torres definitely didn't know I'd lied my way into an ambulance for a woman.

"According to my medical records," Izzy said with a laugh that woke up every emotion in my body, even the ones I'd done my best to shut off when we'd deployed.

Somehow, I managed to swallow without making an ass out of myself. "I thought you said you didn't remember anything."

"My sister told me." She leaned back in her seat.

"Your sister had to tell you that you were married?" Fitz asked, leaning his elbows on the table. "Please, do go on. Phelan over here tells us next to nothing about himself."

"I lied to the paramedics so I could get into the ambulance with her," I explained.

"After the crash," Izzy finished. "We were sitting next to each other when the plane went down."

Fitz's head whipped in my direction. "You were in a fucking plane crash?"

I shrugged.

"How did you think he got . . ." Izzy leaned over the table, reaching for my hat, and I dipped my head so she could take it. She removed my hat with one hand and pushed the short strands of my hair up with the other, no doubt showing Fitz the scar he'd seen multiple times over the last two years. "That? I knew you'd have a scar!"

"Eleven stitches," I told her.

"You got that scar in a *plane crash*?" Fitz's voice cracked.

"Yep," Izzy said, putting my hat back before sitting down.

"I thought we were friends!" He clutched his chest.

"We are," I assured him.

"Friends tell friends when they've been in plane crashes," he lectured.

"Torres knows." I shrugged again.

"Okay, now that just hurts." He got all melodramatic, staggering like I'd wounded him. "You told Torres, but not the rest of us?"

"Maybe I was saving the story."

"For what? *This* deployment instead of the last one?"

"*This* deployment?" Izzy asked, and the worry in her eyes made my chest clench. No one worried about me except my mom.

The mood immediately changed.

"Yeah." I nodded. "We're leaving soon."

"When?" Two little lines appeared between her brows.

"Really soon." The day after tomorrow, but that wasn't public knowledge.

Fitz cleared his throat. "Well, I'm going to head back inside so I can watch Rowell beat the shit out of Torres on the table. It was nice to meet you, Mrs. Phelan."

"Technically, he's Mr. Astor," she corrected him with a smile that didn't quite reach her eyes.

"Not surprised. My man's a good guy. Always been a true feminist." Fitz clapped me on the shoulder and headed inside.

For a moment, the sound of crashing waves overtook the music from inside the bar.

"Can you tell me where you're going?" she asked.

"Afghanistan." It had been all over the news, so it wasn't like I was violating OPSEC over here.

Her face fell. "And you've already been there once?"

I nodded. "We got back a little under a year ago, but I joined the unit a little late, and left a little early, so I wasn't there the full time." An IED had ended that deployment a month early for me, but at least I was alive.

"And you're already going back?" Her eyes flared. "How is that fair?"

"*Fair* isn't a word that really plays into military life." I shifted my weight.

"That's what you're doing here, huh?" She gestured to the bar. "Letting loose before you leave?"

"Yeah. We're stationed at Hunter. It's about a half hour from here." I took the obvious opening for a subject change. "And you live in DC, but you're here for a bachelorette party?"

"I just moved to DC for law school."

I did the math, and it didn't add up. "Shouldn't you be a senior this upcoming year?"

"I graduated a year early." She shrugged like it was no big deal, but then she looked away, concentrating a second too long on her soda, and I knew it was, and not in a good way. "Anyway, Margo is from Savannah, and she wanted her bachelorette party to be close for her sisters, since the wedding is in Syracuse next month. We fly out tomorrow morning."

"And we just happen to be in the same place at the same time for all of twelve hours." I couldn't stop looking at her, taking care to memorize every detail of her beautiful face. There were subtle changes here and there, the result of two and a half years passing, but she looked exactly like I remembered her. "Talk about coincidence."

"Serendipity," she said with a smile that went straight to my dick. Any other place, any other time, I would have asked her out.

But she lived over five hundred miles away, and I was deploying.

"I didn't want to leave you." The words slipped out.

Her eyes widened.

"At the hospital," I clarified. "I wanted to stay until you were awake, to know you'd made it out okay. But the recruiters showed up for me."

"Serena told me." She sighed. "I couldn't remember your name. Everything was a little fuzzy thanks to the concussion. I made out *Nathaniel* on my hospital records—your handwriting is something else, by the way—and then your bag showed up, and under this little flap, *N. Phelan* was written. The airline wouldn't give out contact information, and you . . . you don't exist online. No social media. Nothing. I looked."

"Not a fan of random people watching a highlight reel of my life." She'd looked for me. *Me.* A guy whose parents didn't even bother to show up for my graduation from basic or ranger school, not that I blamed Mom for that.

"Did you at least get a phone?" She arched a single brow.

I shifted to the side and pulled my phone from my back pocket, sliding it across the table as proof.

She caught it and grinned, hitting the home button. It lit up her smile, and she tapped at it. "There we go." She handed it back. "I texted myself—that way I can at least get your address to return your stuff. And can we talk about your taste in music?"

"Keep the stuff. You have a problem with Panic! at the Disco?" I asked, sliding the phone back into my pocket.

"No, actually. That's one band you turned me on to, but Radiohead? Pearl Jam? Did you ever leave the nineties?" she teased.

"Hey, half the music on that iPod's from this century. I think?" My brow furrowed. "Shit, I can't remember."

"I do. I can name every single song." She sipped her drink.

"Can you, now?" Damn, it felt good to smile, and not one of those fake ones, but to really, honestly smile. This was the only thing I'd forgotten about her: how effortless it had been to talk to her in those minutes we'd been delayed on the tarmac.

She put her first finger up. "Panic! at the Disco, 'Northern Downpour.'" She put up a second finger. "Radiohead, 'Creep,'" she started, then shocked the shit out of me by naming every single song.

"And out of all those, what was your favorite?" I asked.

"'Northern Downpour.'" She smiled. "I remember you doing that too. Asking me questions to distract me."

"Maybe I was just trying to get to know you better."

"Fine. Then it goes both ways. Which out of those is *your* favorite?"

"Same, ironically. 'Northern Downpour.'"

We spent the next few hours out there, talking about music and books. She filled me in on how college had gone for her, and I told her about the classes I'd managed to take during the year we hadn't been in the sandbox.

I deflected every single question about the deployment, not because she didn't deserve reciprocity as she shared the details of her life, but because I didn't want that shitty year to claim so much as a second of the time I had with her.

The hours passed with the ease of breathing, and when everyone was ready to leave—everyone except us—we somehow managed to say goodbye.

I hugged her close, the girl I'd survived the impossible with, the girl I would have given my right arm to actually have a shot with. "Fly safe tomorrow, okay? I won't be there to haul you out through the emergency exit."

"I'll try my best." She sighed and hugged me back, fitting against me with the kind of perfection that didn't exist in my world. "Don't die over there."

"I'll try my best." I rested my chin on the top of her head and closed my eyes, breathing in the scent of salt air, lemons, and a perfume I couldn't place but would never forget.

It felt like she'd taken back the missing piece I'd found when I saw her tonight as she walked away with her girlfriends, headed toward the vacation rental she'd told me about earlier.

She was nearly out of sight when Torres and Rowell finally walked out of the bar after paying their tabs.

"Dude!" Fitz exclaimed. "You guys missed Plane Crash Girl!"

"What?" Torres took one look at my face and then tracked my line of sight.

"That was Izzy." I watched until she turned the corner.

"No shit?" Torres's eyes flared wide. "I missed meeting the one and only Isabeau? I saw you out on the patio, but I didn't want to interrupt if you were hitting on . . ." He shook his head. "That was seriously her?"

"Seriously her." I nodded.

"What fucking plane crash?" Rowell asked, and we headed to the car.

I told them the story as I designated drove half their asses back to post while Fitz took the others.

It took me hours to get to sleep that night, and once I did, I dreamed about her. No plane. No river. No ambulances. Just her.

My phone rang the next morning as I finished my run, and I didn't recognize the area code, but I answered, my chest heaving from the nine miles I'd just covered. "Hello?"

"Nate?"

The smile on my face was instantaneous. "Izzy?"

"Yeah." She laughed nervously. "Look, you're not leaving today, are you?"

"No." I stared at the stack of boxes in my barracks room, already packed for storage. "Why? Everything okay?" Juggling the phone, I stripped off my shirt and threw it in the pile of the last load of laundry I'd do tonight.

"I didn't get on the plane."

CHAPTER ELEVEN

NATHANIEL

Kabul, Afghanistan
August 2021

I had just pulled my Kevlar over my head and fastened the Velcro when three pounding knocks sounded on my bedroom door. There was a more-than-furious woman waiting for me on the other side when I opened it.

"What the hell do you mean, I'm not going with you?" Izzy yelled up at me, her hands fisted on her hips. She was dressed for another day in the office, in black linen slacks and a blouse that cut across her collarbone, but the heels made me smile. And that perfume? Swore to God, Izzy was the only woman I knew who could pull off Chanel in a fucking war zone.

"How do you even know I'm going anywhere?" I asked, bracing one hand on the doorframe and the other on the handle of the door.

She glared up at me, her eyes lingering on my combat gear, and then she hoisted a brow. "Because Orange or Blue, whatever the hell his name is supposed to be, told me that he'd be standing guard outside the conference room today while we work, and I'm more than aware that you wouldn't switch out babysitters unless you were leaving," she snapped, fire in her eyes.

"One, it was Sergeant Black. Two, we're not going to argue in the hallway like a pair of dramatic college kids."

"Fine by me." She ducked under my arm and marched into my room, folding her arms across her chest as she took in the space. It wasn't a suite like hers, just a single with a private bathroom, which was the next-best thing I had to being stateside. As accommodations came, this was the Ritz-Carlton of Afghanistan.

A sigh ripped through my lips as I recognized that there was no throwing Izzy out of my room without making a bigger scene, and I shut the door to give us privacy. "I thought you wanted to get Serena back. I pulled a shit ton of strings to make a flight happen, and I'm going to see if she's still up there, hence why I asked Sergeant Black to keep an eye on you since none of your entourage has meetings today."

We were supposed to be back on the road—or in the sky—tomorrow, but given the state of the country, I was hoping I could talk her onto a plane home instead if I brought Serena back.

"I'm going with you." She lifted her chin.

"You have zero reason to go with me." I shook my head. "It's not happening."

"You don't get to tell me where I go!"

I stalked forward until the toes of my boots touched the tips of her high heels. "That's *exactly* what I get to do as the head of your security. Remember, you agreed to listen to every order out there," I said, pointing to the door. "You only get to throw your fits in here."

Her jaw dropped. "I am *not* throwing a fit, Nathaniel Phelan."

"You are." A corner of my mouth quirked up. "Whether you like it or not, Isabeau, you're a senior congressional aide, which means unless you have a reason to put yourself in harm's way, then I'm not going to dangle you in front of the enemy like a tasty little target."

"And if I do have a reason?"

"You don't. I changed your itinerary this morning the second I read the reports that it looks like Kunduz is going to fall today." A couple of hours ago, I'd had her curled up in my lap, which was something I desperately tried to forget. It had been a slip on my part, but the second I'd seen her kneeling on that floor, shaking like a leaf, I'd acted on instinct, just like always when it came to her. "There's zero chance you're keeping that meeting."

She swallowed and nodded. "Which I appreciate, as much as I hate it." Closing her eyes, she rubbed the bridge of her nose.

"In fact, I'd feel entirely better if you all got your polished asses on a plane and abandoned this whole trip. Cut your losses, Izzy," I blatantly begged.

"We have a job to do," she retorted. "Senator Lauren is still coming next week—"

"Which is a mistake." I stepped back so I could get a break from the perfect sweetness of her perfume invading my lungs. "This country is going to fall a hell of a lot faster than forecasted."

"Reports said we have six to twelve months," she argued, but the pursing of her lips told me she knew I wasn't blowing smoke.

"Yeah, well, I trust what I'm seeing in a place I know pretty damned well more than someone's best-case-scenario analysis of it from half a world away, and what's going on out there"—I pointed to my window—"is *not* the best-case scenario."

"I'm not stupid, Nate. I know that." Panic flared in her eyes. "But Serena is up there."

"And I know what Serena looks like. I've already got feelers out in the area, so by the time I get there, hopefully someone will have tracked her down. I'll be back before dinner."

"She might not recognize you," she fired back.

"Oh, come on, that's the best argument you've got?" I cocked a brow at her, and she dropped her gaze, but it wasn't in that *You've won* way I'd seen before, or even the *Fine, I'll give in* way. No . . . that emotion beneath those furrowed brows was guilt. "What did you do, Isabeau?"

She swallowed. "Mazar-i-Sharif is still safe."

My eyes flared. "You're shitting me if you think that. Sheberghan fell to the Taliban yesterday. Intel indicates not only is Kunduz Province being overrun, but also Sar-e Pol, and Takhar. What do those all have in common, Izzy?"

"I'm not going to sit here and wait for you to see if you can find her. You might not be able to convince her to leave the country, but I will. Finding her means nothing if we can't get her on the helicopter," she argued, but that tone . . . she wasn't telling me everything.

"Those provinces are *all* in the north," I said, ignoring her reasoning. Maybe it made me an ass, but I wasn't against hog-tying Serena and throwing her over my shoulder if it meant Izzy got the hell out of this country. "If Samangan falls, that leaves Balkh Province—Mazar-i-Sharif—cut off. Do you understand that?"

"I understand that every day she stays there, she's in danger of never getting out, so I did what I had to do."

She changed the itinerary. I saw it in her frustratingly beautiful eyes. My stomach hit the floor at the same moment Webb's voice came across the radio in my ear.

"Sergeant Green."

I tapped the button to speak. "Green here."

"Your departure has been pushed back to give the aides enough time to assemble, since the itinerary just changed, and they're now meeting with leadership and a group of stranded Americans in Mez at noon."

I didn't take my eyes from Izzy's. "And we think that's safe, sir?"

"Orders are coming straight from Senator Lauren's office. Apparently, she has constituents in that group, and we're going to evac them."

"Acknowledged." Fuck. My. Life. I got off the radio and leaned into Izzy's space. "You went behind my back."

"Yes," she whispered, dragging her tongue over her lower lip nervously. "But we're saving—"

"No," I snapped. "No excuses. You go behind my back again, and I'm done." She was putting herself directly in danger, and it ate through my veins like acid. Serena would have done the same for her, but I wasn't irrevocably in love with Serena. Just Izzy. Always Izzy. "You trust me, or this doesn't work."

I wanted the words back as soon as they left my mouth, because that's exactly why it *didn't* work between us to begin with. Not that there ever had been an *us*. What Izzy and I had been was undefinable.

"I just—" she started.

"You trust me, or this doesn't work," I repeated.

She nodded. "I'm sorry."

"You'll want to ditch the heels." I opened my door and pointed to the hallway.

Two hours later, we buckled into one of four Blackhawks headed for Mez, accompanied by a Chinook.

"Won't the Chinook hold us back?" Holt yelled over the noise of whirring rotors.

"They're faster than we are," Kellman yelled back, checking his charge's belt. Naturally, three of the other aides had decided to come for the "fact-finding," once the trip had been announced. Politicians never seemed to mind sending their underlings into situations they wouldn't chance themselves.

Izzy belted herself in across from me, her movements smooth, with no hint of her fear of flying. The put-together woman in front of me looked nothing like the devastated woman I'd picked up off the floor this morning. This woman was a consummate professional, dressed in the opposite of her sleep shorts and tank top. Then she white-knuckled the seat cushions, and I saw the crack in her facade.

Leaning out of my seat, I slipped my AirPods into her ears again.

Her gaze locked with mine, and damn if my pulse didn't quicken, because that look, the same one she'd had as we'd held hands during that crash ten years ago—scared and somehow trusting—made her feel like mine again. But that ring flashing in the sun was an eviscerating reminder that she wasn't mine. If the way she'd reacted to that phone call yesterday was any indication, she belonged to someone named Jeremy. Apparently *Jeremy* was good enough for her. Stable enough for her. Rich enough to appease her parents, too, judging by the size of that rock.

I added *Jeremy* to my list of douchebag frat boy names, right up there with Chad and Blake. But douche or not, he was the one she'd chosen. I was just the one willing to fly into a combat zone for her. It didn't matter how much time had passed; I couldn't seem to let go. It wasn't her fault that I still loved her. It was mine.

I handed over my cell phone so she could pick what she wanted to listen to.

You choose, she mouthed, handing it back, reminding me too much of those sun-drenched days in Savannah. Pressure settled in my chest, and I scrolled through my playlist, picking the song that fit.

The helicopter launched as I hit play on the acoustic version of "This Is Gospel," and her eyes widened. She looked away right when the chorus would have hit, and I heard the lyrics about asking to be let go of in my own head as surely as if I'd had one of the AirPods in—that was how well I knew the song. It was another one of her favorites.

But I was the one who needed to let go.

"We can only wait another ten minutes," I told Izzy as she looked over the emptying room we'd commandeered at Mazar-i-Sharif's airport. The aching look of expectation on her face made my chest go tight.

"Ten minutes might be too long," Torres muttered as he walked by.

I wasn't going to risk taking her into the city, or farther than a two-minute run from the birds. The Americans and those who qualified for the SIVs had met here over the last three hours, discussing their evacuation needs while representatives of the leadership gave their reports to the congressional aides.

The few dozen who had their visas and wanted immediate evacuation were already loaded into the Chinook, and there were only a few stragglers left, picking up paperwork that Izzy and the others had brought to help speed up the visa process.

"And you won't let me go out looking?" Izzy asked again, hope dimming in her eyes.

"Going out there and shouting Serena's name from the rooftops isn't going to get you the reaction you want." I both hated and was grateful for her naivete. It meant I'd done my job keeping the horrors of war away from her . . . until she'd come seeking them. "According to the contacts we have here, she knows there's someone who wants to see her."

"But you didn't say it was me?" Izzy's gaze whipped from the retreating back of the civilian she'd just finished helping across the table to mine.

"You mean, did I advertise that an aide to a United States congresswoman was out here searching for a needle in a haystack? No, I did not. Because I like you alive."

She stood and glared at me, her chair squeaking against the linoleum floor, and I noted the reactions of every person in the room who wasn't part of my team or hers. There were only a few now, and they were headed for the door, since Graham had started shutting the place down.

"I'm not going to leave her here," Izzy hissed, keeping her voice low.

I shot the interpreter at her side a glance, and he backed away, giving us space, but Torres hovered. He always hovered when he sensed I was about to blow.

"You will if she's not here in ten minutes." I leaned in. "You promised you'd do as I asked out here, and I'm holding you to it. We're leaving in ten minutes, whether or not Serena is on board."

Izzy's body tensed and her eyes narrowed at me. "And spend the next . . . however long wondering if she's alive or dead? Wondering if I could have done or said something that could have brought her home? No, Na—" She grimaced but recovered quickly. "Sergeant Green, I'm not going to do that, not again."

"I don't think she's talking about her sister anymore," Torres whispered before backing away.

"Point made," I replied, and she lifted her stubborn little chin. "Ms. Astor," I started again, dropping my voice, more than aware of the people around us, "you can't control the decisions other people make, nor do you bear the blame for the consequences of their choices." The fact that we'd made it this far without having this discussion was a miracle, but I sure as hell wasn't getting into this using some code language, and this was far from the appropriate place.

"You sure about that?" She wrapped her arms around her waist, careful not to catch the printed silk scarf that covered her hair. "Because I've had a few years to think about it, and I'm pretty sure if I'd just looked at *someone* and said, 'Please come home,' maybe they would have." Her eyes searched mine, and I struggled to pick my heart up off the goddamned floor.

She'd never asked. Not outright. Then again, I'd never given her a reason to think I would have stayed.

"Hey, Isa, you ready to head out?" Holt asked as he walked over, stopping to glance between us, his perfectly groomed eyebrows rising. "Did I interrupt?"

"No," I answered.

"Yes," Izzy fired back.

"Okay, well, I'm going to head out with Baker and Turner," he said, retreating slowly.

Kellman whistled as he walked by, herding Holt out the door behind us, leaving only Graham and a couple other operators in the room. If I hadn't promised her these ten minutes, Izzy would've been buckled in on the Blackhawk by now.

"Did you ever think about me?" she questioned, her voice dropping to a whisper.

I clenched my jaw, fighting off the urge to tell her the truth. *Every fucking day.*

"That's a loaded question," I answered finally.

She blinked. "Not like that. I mean, did you ever think about what it felt like to sit there for *years* and wonder if you were out there somewhere fighting, or if you'd . . . died?" The last word came out strangled. "Do you have any idea how many times I cried myself to sleep, terrified of the possibility that you were buried somewhere? That I wouldn't even know where to visit your grave?"

Shit. My stomach dropped, and I blew out a slow breath, more than aware of my team trying to give us space. "This isn't the time."

"It's never the time," she retorted. "That was always the problem, so I guess it's nice to know some things don't change. You ask me to ignore"—she gestured between us—"*everything*, and then you go and pull that bullshit by playing that song in the helicopter? Sorry, *Sergeant Green*, but not all of us are capable of walking away without so much as looking back like you are. But you moved right on to the next assignment, didn't you?"

Graham raised his eyebrows where he stood at the middle of the room, then turned his back on us when I sent a glare his way.

"It looks like you moved on just fine," I whispered, glancing meaningfully to her ring.

She swallowed, then tucked her left hand into her elbow, hiding the ring, and she had the decency to look . . . shit, what was that? Remorseful? "Every day," she said quietly. "I searched your name on Google every goddamned day, Sergeant Green, terrified that an obituary would pop up. Don't forget that you were the first term I ever used for a Google Alert. It will *destroy* me if I have to do the same for Serena."

I looked away, my ribs squeezing my lungs painfully at the imagery she'd used. That alert had saved my sanity in the past. *She* had saved my sanity. I owed her more than I'd ever be able to repay in that department, but that didn't mean I was willing to eviscerate myself by throwing our relationship on the autopsy table. There were things I'd never be able to say to her, never revisit or rehash just so she could have some of that precious closure everyone prattled on about. But this? This I could give her.

"I never changed my next of kin form," I told her softly, lowering my voice so only she could hear, since we'd somehow gotten back to damn-near yelling.

"What?" She blinked.

"I never changed the paperwork." I shook my head. "If anything had ever happened to me, someone would have told you. Probably not the details of where, or how, or why. But they would have told you I was dead. Though it might have taken a couple days to track you down, since the last address I had for you was in New York."

Her entire expression softened, and the sorrow radiating from her eyes sliced into me with lethal precision.

"So now you'll know when you head back to your real life," I continued, my hands curling at the thought of the giant rock on her left hand. "No news is good news. Unless you want me to change it, given that your last name probably won't be Astor for long, and it might make the fiancé wonder why you're getting notified—"

"No." She shook her head vehemently. "Don't change it. I mean, unless someone comes along who needs to know more than I do, of course." She shifted her weight and glanced away before slowly dragging her gaze back to mine. "Is there someone else who should know?"

"Right through here," Elston said as he pushed through the front door, saving me the awkwardness of replying to Izzy.

"Thank you, Sergeant Rose," a female voice replied from behind him.

A voice I recognized. My head swung in the direction of the door as my pulse leapt with hope that this had actually *worked*.

Izzy took off running, and I didn't bother to stop her as she dodged the tables and blew by Graham. Elston barely got out of her way before she flung herself at the woman. "Serena!"

CHAPTER TWELVE

IZZY

Tybee Island, Georgia
June 2014

"I never would have taken you for a cookies and cream kind of guy," I said, taking a lick of my two scoops of butter pecan as Nate and I wandered Tybee aimlessly. I'd tossed my hair up into a messy bun to combat the humidity, leaving my neck and shoulders bare to the June sun.

"Never would have taken you for an 'ice cream at ten a.m.' girl, but here we are," he replied, flashing that damned dimple. And his eyes? Yeah, those were still just as heart stopping as I'd remembered.

We crossed the street, and his fingers skimmed my lower back as he switched places with me on the sidewalk, walking closer to the street. On a scale of one to ten, that was a freaking twelve on the sexiest things a guy could do that weren't sexual, which wasn't helping my pulse settle.

Something within me had shifted the second I'd recognized him last night, and as much as I wanted to go back to being who I was yesterday, I couldn't, not when I had the inexplicable, chaotic, senseless feeling that I was somehow tethered to this man.

The man I'd called from the airport two hours ago, sitting on my suitcase outside the departures door while Margo watched on, worried that I'd end up stranded.

I hadn't worried. Not for one second. He hadn't left me in that airplane or abandoned me in the river. Nate had shown me everything I needed to know about his character two and a half years ago. Which also meant I was terrified my impetuousness had wrecked his day.

"You sure I didn't ruin your plans for the day?" I looked up at him from behind my cone. "I wasn't exactly thinking rationally when I changed my flight this morning. It was just that I was standing there, watching the other girls check their bags, and I couldn't do it." Oh God, I was babbling, and there was no stopping the flow of words. "I couldn't leave if there was even the slightest chance I could spend five more minutes with you. And I know that sounds"—my nose scrunched—"creepy. And it's worse because I didn't even bother to ask if you were seeing anyone last night, and who knows? Maybe you have a girlfriend, and now I've just thrown an entire wrench into your plans—"

"Izzy," he interrupted, lifting his brows under his Saint Louis Blues ball cap and cupping my bare shoulder with his hand. Crap, his touch felt nice. "I don't have a girlfriend. If I did, I would have told you last night, and I wouldn't be here with you now." A corner of his mouth lifted into a smirk, and my thighs tightened. "Or at least I wouldn't have a girlfriend anymore."

Did that mean he felt whatever this pull was between us too? "So, I didn't ruin your plans by upending mine?"

He shook his head. "There is nothing better I could possibly imagine than spending my last day stateside with you. As long as you stop mocking my cookies and cream, considering you have the ice cream tastes of an eighty-year-old woman."

"Do not," I scoffed in defense of my favorite flavor.

Last day stateside. He was leaving tomorrow. My stomach dropped.

"It's butter pecan," he teased. "It's been around since the late eighteen hundreds. It's like the grandmother of all other ice cream flavors." He took a bite out of my own selection.

"It's a classic." I licked up the side of my cone, and his eyes flared, tracking the movement.

"I still can't believe you're here." He shook his head, looking at me the same way I bet I was looking at him—with pure awe.

"Same." I turned, and we continued to walk, meandering down the picturesque street.

"I've been here for a couple years now, so my presence isn't that much of a surprise." He took another bite. "You showing up, that's some happenstance."

Who did that? Actually *bit* their ice cream?

Someone who doesn't have time to let it melt.

Then again, my eyes had been way bigger than my stomach when I'd ordered this. I threw away the cone and spotted a bookstore up ahead. "Are you still making your way through that list of books?"

"Slowly." He took another bite, demolishing what was left. "It's hard to find time to read between college classes and people shooting at you, but I'm making a dent."

I halted, my eyes flying wide.

Nate turned, his brow furrowing. "Shit. I forget you're probably not used to hearing stuff like that."

"It's fine." I forced a smile. It wasn't. Not even close. The thought of him being shot at was . . . incomprehensible.

"It's not. Forget I said it." He tossed what was left of his ice cream in the nearby trash and scanned the street around us. "I have an idea." He held out his hand.

I took it. "Lead on."

Two hours later, we sat on the wooden double swing on North Beach, Nate gently rocking us as my feet stretched over his lap to rest on the opposite railing. The one at my back dug in a little as I scoured the pages of *Outlander*, marking my favorite lines with neon-yellow highlighter as he did the same to *Their Eyes Were Watching God*, but I didn't care.

I couldn't remember ever having spent a more perfect moment in all twenty-one years of my life.

"I can't believe that's the book you chose," he muttered, glancing my way before dragging the highlighter across one of his pages.

His idea had been . . . swoonworthy. He'd taken me into the bookstore and told me to pick one of my favorite books that I'd guess he hadn't read yet, and he'd done the same, buying both and a two-pack of yellow highlighters.

"A little romance won't hurt you." A smile curved my mouth as the ocean breeze ruffled the pages of the thick paperback. "Besides, it's being adapted right now. Comes out in August, I think. You'll thank me then."

"I'll still be deployed in August." The side of his hand skimmed my knee as he adjusted his hold on the book, and butterflies kissed the edge of my stomach. I was hyperaware of everything about him, from the subtly sexy way he curved the bill of his hat to the care he took while spraying me down with sunscreen so I wouldn't burn in my jean shorts and the bikini top I'd changed into when we thought of the beach. "And you'll be starting up classes, right?" He flipped another page, skimming the contents.

"Yep, at Georgetown," I answered, choosing only the most romantic of lines to highlight and imagining his face when he got to those parts. He'd be half a world away.

"You don't sound happy about it." His head tilted to the side as he looked at me from under his hat. "From what I know, that's a pretty stellar school."

"It is." I shielded my eyes from the sun with my hand to see his face clearer. "And it's not that I'm *not* grateful to have been accepted;

it's just . . ." A sigh deflated my shoulders, and I looked out over the Sunday families playing on the beach.

He shifted, and his hands framed my face for a heartbeat when he set his hat on my head. "For the sun."

"Thank you." I smiled at the sweet gesture, my fingers skimming the brim. "I've never worn your sweatshirt," I blurted. Shit, I should have taken my ADHD meds today, but it was a weekend, and I thought I'd just be flying, and they always killed my appetite, and sometimes I just wanted to snack for the fun of it, and now I was saying whatever came to mind.

"You should," he said. "Wear it, I mean. You've had it longer than I did now, anyway. Same with the bag and the iPod. They're pretty much yours." His dimple made an appearance, and my pulse skittered. "In fact, I'm officially giving it all to you."

"You don't want me to ship it?" It was the only reason I'd come up with to ask for his address, since I didn't think he'd be getting texts over the next year—the length of this deployment.

"No. I kind of like the idea of you wearing it. As long as it isn't all messed up from the river." He grimaced. "Is it gross?"

"No." I laughed. "It's surprisingly not gross, though the white parts aren't exactly as bright as they once may have been. But anything else you had in there must have been destroyed, because that's all that came back."

"Did you ever get your purse?"

I nodded. "It showed up a month after your bag. I think having my ID in there helped."

"I would guess so." He looked back to the book, but his highlighter hovered over the page without moving. "Are you still afraid of flying?" he asked softly. "I've always wondered if the crash . . ."

"Screwed me up even more?" I offered, highlighting a particularly racy line.

"I wasn't going to put it that way, but now that you mention it . . ." He shot me an apologetic look.

"I didn't fly for eighteen months," I admitted, skimming the next chapter to get to my favorite parts. "It took a lot of therapy. For that and the nightmares." A chill tried its best to work its way up my spine despite the climbing heat. "But I have coping mechanisms for both now."

"Coping mechanisms?"

"Well, yeah. It's not like I can actually control the panic attacks. We were actually in a plane crash. And sure, we got the best of a worst-case scenario, but I'll never be able to tell myself that the likelihood is next to zero again, because now the fear is grounded." My eyes narrowed. "You never had an issue flying after what happened?"

He lifted one shoulder in a shrug. "I was put on the next flight out of Saint Louis, so I just . . ." His throat worked as he swallowed. "Flew. I told myself that if the universe wanted me to die in a plane crash, I would have. I understand the nightmares, though. I do the whole 'You aren't there anymore; you're home' affirmations thing I saw on some therapist's YouTube."

My eyebrows shot up. "Some therapist's *YouTube*?"

"Having your file marked up by a shrink isn't exactly good in my line of work." He highlighted another line and kept going. "I do what I have to in the moment and then I move on. Like you said," he said, looking over at me. "Coping mechanism, I guess."

"Is there *anything* you're scared of? There has to be something, right?"

"Sure. Becoming anything like my father." He reached to the right and pulled something out of his backpack. "Gum?"

"No, thanks." Guess that topic wasn't up for discussion.

He popped a piece in his mouth, and we spent another hour just like that, swinging on the beach, marking up our favorite books for each other.

By the time we finished, the sun was high in the sky and my skin was sticky with sweat. "Want to get in?" I asked him, nodding toward the beach.

"Sounds good to me." We put the books in his backpack and walked toward the water, picking out a spot far from anyone else. He pulled out two towels from his bag, and I lifted my brows. "It's the last of what has to be packed," he said in answer to my unspoken question.

Then we stripped down. For me, it was a simple matter of shimmying out of my jean shorts and kicking off my sandals.

I tried to keep my eyes off his body as he pulled his shirt over his head. I failed. Miserably. But in my defense, Nathaniel Phelan had been created to be looked at, to be admired, to be flat out drooled over.

His stomach was cut out of an Abercrombie ad, roped with muscles that rippled and flexed, and the diagonal ridges that led to his board shorts had my mouth watering to trace those lines with my tongue. His chest was built, his arms strong, and every inch of his skin that I could see was tanned to a touchable bronze.

"You ready?" he asked, satisfaction curving my smile when he did a double take at me in my bikini. I wasn't in his level of shape—I had curves that spoke to just how much time I'd spent studying this year—but the way his eyes heated made me feel . . . beautiful.

I took off his hat and shook out my hair. "Ready."

We walked into the water, and I gasped as the first cold wave hit my sun-warmed stomach.

Nate laughed, then submerged completely with the confidence of someone who did this way more often than I did. When he stood, the water reached the elastic of his board shorts, and I stared, transfixed, as the water sluiced off him.

Then I blinked and stepped closer, my hand rising but not touching the silver lines that had almost faded into the upper ridges of his abs. "What happened?"

His jaw flexed, but then he quickly smiled. "I ruptured my spleen in Afghanistan last tour. Now we have matching scars."

My gaze widened by the second as waves pushed by us. "Plane crash?" I tried to joke.

"IED."

Suddenly my body was as cold as the water around us. "You were blown up?"

"The vehicle I was in was blown up." He reached out, tucking my hair behind my ears with cool fingertips. "Don't look at me like that, Izzy."

"Like what?" It was barely a whisper as the next wave hit me a little higher. "Like I'm worried?"

"My mom worries enough for every other person on the planet. You don't have to. I'm fine. See?" He put his arms out and turned slowly, but I didn't savor the sight of his bare back and torso like I had just a few minutes ago. Now I saw every place he could be hurt. Every vulnerable inch.

"Do you like it?" I asked when he faced me again. "What you do?"

"I'm good at it." He shrugged.

"That's not the same thing."

"Says the woman who doesn't seem too excited to be starting Georgetown at twenty-one years old." He lifted a dark brow.

"No one's trying to kill me," I blurted.

"Which is why I don't mind what I do." He moved closer, his hand palming my waist to steady me when a bigger wave threatened to take me back to shore. "If no one's trying to kill you here, then that means I'm doing my job over there. That's how I choose to look at it, how I *have* to look at it."

"And is that your dream?"

"I don't follow." His fingers flexed, and I fought to keep from leaning into his touch.

"Is this what you're going to do for the rest of your life? Is this your career?" *Say no. Say that you're out after three years like you said on the plane.*

"I'm really good at it, Iz," he said softly. "I'm already a ranger. I'll probably look at Special Forces selection once we get back. My friend Torres is a legacy—his dad was Delta, and I told him I'd think about going through the process with him."

If he comes back.

"You going to tell me why you're not wandering around with a megawatt smile over getting into Georgetown Law?" He changed subjects, and I got the point.

"It wasn't my dream, that's all." Stepping back, I sank beneath the water, letting the power of the insistent waves remind me just how small we both were in relation to the world around us. Then I stood and pushed my hair out of my eyes.

"Whose dream was it?" His brow knit as we waded deeper, the water resting just beneath my breasts between waves.

I looked away from that penetrating blue gaze of his.

"You don't have to tell me. I'll never push you for something you don't want to give." He ripped his hands over his hair. "It's not like I have the right to know, anyway. We've known each other for a total of what? Eighteen hours if you combine all our time together?"

That had me turning back toward him. "Two and a half years," I said, correcting him. "We've known each other two and a half years. And I didn't want to graduate early, but my boyfriend was a year older, and he said he wanted me to come with him." A sour taste filled my mouth. "And my parents were so thrilled with the idea that I might marry a Covington—"

"You were engaged?" His gaze dropped to my hand like he'd missed something. "And what the hell is a Covington?"

"No." I shook my head. "And *who* is a Covington." A bitter laugh escaped at my own foolishness. "God, I love that you don't know. Love that you can't tell me every senator that's come from his branch of the family, or what their net worth is, because believe me, my father could spit those details out like a computer. The idea of me marrying into a family like that made him practically salivate. It's everything they want for themselves, though they'd say it's for *me*, and it's why he offered to pay for Georgetown if I graduated Syracuse early and went with—"

"Dickface," Nate supplied. "I don't want to know his name. If he was stupid enough to lose you, as the term *ex* implies, then he's a dickface."

This time my laughter was anything but bitter. "Yeah, we can go with that. *Dickface* got accepted to Georgetown, too, of course, so we started planning." I sighed. "I can even admit that it felt nice to live up to my parents' expectations for once. They came to graduation and even threw a giant party. We rented an apartment close to campus, put the deposit down and everything . . ." My forehead puckered. "I should have known the second Serena told me she didn't like him. She's a freakishly good judge of character." I bobbed up and down with the next wave now that we were deeper. "Anyway, he was accepted off the wait list for Yale just before graduation, and now he's in New Haven."

"He left you for a *school*?"

"Yep." I sputtered when the next wave got the best of me, and Nate pulled me against his rock-solid torso. My heart skipped a freaking beat, but Nate's was steady under the hand that I splayed over his chest. *Concentrate.* "And I tried the whole 'let's do long distance' thing, because I'm naive. And he . . ." I searched for the right words. "He respectfully declined, seeing that there was a plethora of women who weren't *new money* to choose from at Yale."

"Dickface," Nate muttered.

"Dickface," I agreed. Yet, at that moment, with the cool water rushing around us and Nate's warm skin under my fingers, I was overwhelmed with gratitude for my newly single status. Nate was the opposite of everything *Dickface* had been. He was open, brutally honest, brave to a fault, and remarkably careful with me. "My parents haven't quite recovered from their crushing disappointment of *nearly* marrying into the Covington family. So now, I'm at Georgetown because I chased someone else's dream, and I haven't quite figured out what to do with that."

"Find a way to make it your own," he suggested, lifting me off my feet when the next wave came. "Find a way to make a difference."

Emboldened by the way he held me, I reached up and ran my fingers through his wet hair. This time tomorrow, I'd be in DC, and he'd be on his way to a war zone. "If I could make a difference, I'd find a way to keep you here."

An emotion I couldn't define but that looked a lot like longing passed over his face. "That would pretty much take an act of Congress." His gaze dropped to my mouth.

"Guess you'll have to go then. I've never been particularly interested in politics," I whispered as another wave pushed my body firmly against his.

"Me either." His arm locked around my back. "Izzy?"

"Nate?" God, I couldn't stop looking at his mouth.

"I'm going to kiss you." The certainty of his words made my skin flush.

"Oh yeah?" I ran my tongue over my lower lip, tasting salt.

"Yeah." He lowered his head slowly, giving me more than enough time to object. "So, if that's not what you want—"

"I want." I tilted my face and arched up, brushing my mouth across his. It was nothing, a ghost of a kiss, but it brought every nerve ending in my body to life, and every single one of them wanted him.

His blue eyes flared with surprise, and then he brought his mouth to mine and kissed me senseless. His lips were cool, but his tongue warm as it slipped past my parted lips to slide along mine. Spearmint and salt consumed every thought. Electricity danced along my skin.

More. I needed more.

His fingers speared into my hair, and he tilted my head to kiss me even deeper. I was no stranger to sex, but I'd never been kissed like this. He took my mouth like I was the key to his next heartbeat, with equal parts mind-blowing finesse and dizzying need.

It was the best first kiss in the history of . . . everything.

I moaned, and he lifted me so our mouths were level, never breaking the kiss.

My legs wound around his waist like they belonged there, my ankles locking at the small of his back. Kissing Nate wasn't just everything I'd dreamed of; it was *better*.

"Shit," he swore, ripping his mouth from mine once we were both panting, and resting his forehead against mine.

"Not what you expected?" My fingers laced behind his neck as another wave crested over my heated skin, but didn't even faze him.

"Just the opposite." He pressed a kiss to my jaw, then my throat, before returning to my lips. "Everything I expected and so much more. I fucking *knew* it would be like this with you."

"Chemistry," I muttered, but that wasn't the word tickling the edges of my mind. *Fate.* There was no other way to explain this, to explain us.

"It's more than that, but I don't think defining it would be fair to either one of us. Not when we only have a few hours before your flight." He studied my face like he was committing it to memory.

"Our timing is pretty awful." My thighs squeezed his waist as I feathered a kiss over his cheek.

"Our timing is shit." His hand stroked down my spine but never went for my ass.

I wished he would. I wanted him in every possible way I could have him until the sun set. "Then give me the next few hours."

Every line of his body drew tight against me, and his breaths grew ragged when I kissed a line down the side of his neck.

"Izzy," he groaned, his grip tightening in my hair to gently pull me away. The lust in his eyes dimmed the sting of rejection. "I don't want hours. I want nights. Days. Weeks. I want to haul you into a room and lock us away until I know every inch of your body, taste everywhere you like to be kissed, explore every way to make you come, and then listen as your voice goes hoarse from screaming my name. That's . . ." He shook his head.

"Yes. That's a yes." Everything he'd listed sounded fantastic.

"I was going to say madness." He grinned, and I melted at that flash of dimple. "And I might kick the shit out of myself for saying this next week, when I have every second of this moment on constant replay in my head, but I want the one thing we don't have, Izzy, and that's time."

"I know. Me too." I wanted a chance, a real, unhurried chance at what we might be. "Does that mean you're done kissing me?"

"Fuck no." He kissed me long and slow, the tempo changing into an unhurried, thorough seduction. "I'll kiss you whenever you ask, Isabeau Astor."

"Promise?" I smiled against his mouth.

"Promise." He made good on it, kissing me until our skin puckered in the water. He kissed me as we dried off, as we walked to his truck, and before and after our very late lunch.

He kissed me until my lips were swollen and I knew every line of his mouth with the same familiarity he did mine.

Then my bag was checked, the book he'd chosen was tucked into my carry-on, and my throat tightened with every step as he walked me to the security checkpoint at the airport.

What if the time we wanted never came?

What if this was all we'd have?

What if—

"Stop." He turned me in his arms and cradled my face. "Whatever you're thinking, just stop."

My eyes stung, and I knew it wasn't from salt and sun. "What if you don't come home?"

His brow knit and he leaned in slowly, pressing a kiss to my forehead. "I'll come home."

"You don't know that." The fabric of his shirt was soft in my fingers as my fists clenched against his chest.

"You don't have to worry about me. I'm ridiculously hard to kill." He hugged me tight, resting his chin on the top of my head.

"You say that like it's going to stop me from worrying every day for the next year."

"No." He gripped my shoulders and leaned back, looking at me with such intensity that my breath caught. "Don't do that either.

Don't you dare sit around and worry. Don't waste your life waiting on me, Izzy."

My lips parted, but there were no words for the way my heart teetered on the edge of his demand, ready to fall . . . or to break.

"I won't do that to you." He cradled the side of my face, stroking his thumb over my cheek. "You are worth so much more."

"And if I want to do it to myself?" Shit, was that my voice breaking?

"Don't," he begged, his voice fading to a whisper. "You just uprooted your whole life for someone. Don't wish away the months for someone else." He lifted a brow. "And don't think this has anything to do with me not wanting you, or some bullshit. God, what I would do for you if I just . . . could."

"So where does that leave us?"

"We're—" He swallowed and took a stuttered breath. "We're us. Nate and Izzy."

"Undefined," I whispered, remembering his earlier words that it wouldn't be fair to either of us to try and label the unexplainable.

"If you want to write, then I'll do the same. If you don't, then I won't pressure you. I want you to have every single opportunity you want for yourself in DC."

"Even if that opportunity means someone else?" I challenged. Maybe it was childish, but I didn't care. Not when we were about to take the gift fate had given us and squander it over him not wanting me to *wait*.

He held my gaze with steady, unwavering eyes and nodded. "Even if that means someone else. Every second I've had with you is a gift I've never deserved, and I refuse to think of you back here, missing out on . . . anything because of me."

"And in a year?" I leaned my cheek into his palm.

"Could be less—I just like to prep for the long haul."

"What happens when you're home?"

He sighed, then lowered his head and kissed me like we weren't in the middle of the airport. He kissed me like there was no one watching, and nothing waiting for us on the other side of tomorrow. "You know the best part of not defining this?"

"My begrudging freedom?" I muttered.

He laughed. "No. The possibilities, Izzy. That's what we are. Possibility."

Possibility. The same reason he loved the sunrise.

Everything in me screamed to hold on, but I let him go, because that's what he wanted and, honestly, probably what I needed. I'd just gotten out of a two-year relationship. Jumping into another when I was bound to sabotage it with my unresolved baggage was the last thing I wanted to do to Nate. If there was ever a shot to be had when it came to us, he was right—it wasn't now.

I kissed him one last time and stepped back. "Just . . . don't die." They were the last words I remembered from the crash, but they seemed to fit this occasion too. I wasn't sure what that said about us.

"Not planning on it." A corner of his mouth lifted, but it wasn't a full smile.

I blinked. "That's what you said—"

"I know." He backed away, shoving his hands into the pockets of his shorts. "I remember everything about you. Now get on that plane so I can remember this too."

"Possibilities?" My chest ached so deeply that it hurt to breathe.

"The very best of them." He gave me a grin, flashing that dimple, and disappeared into the crowd.

CHAPTER THIRTEEN

IZZY

Mazar-i-Sharif, Afghanistan
November 2021

"Serena!" I wrapped my arms around my shocked older sister, locking them above the backpack she wore, and held on tight, my heart beating so wildly I half expected it to jump out of my chest. It worked. She was here. Every string I'd pulled to take Newcastle's place had been worth it because she was *here.* It was almost too easy, too simple, but I wasn't about to curse my good luck.

I was bringing my sister home.

"Iz?" Serena tensed for a second before her arms closed slowly around me, her camera caught between us, secured by the neck strap. "Isabeau?" Her hands moved to my shoulders, and she pulled back, her brown eyes wide as she scanned my face. "What the actual hell are you doing here?" she shouted, something akin to horror etching her features, two lines appearing between her brows.

"Tell me how you really feel." There was no stopping my smile. I'd found her. Well . . . Nate had found her. She looked like she could use a solid month of sleep and might need to wash the very serviceable button-down shirt and blue headscarf I'd inadvertently pulled down by hugging her so tight, but those were all easy to remedy.

"I'm not kidding!" Her fingers dug into my shoulders, and her voice pitched higher in panic. "You shouldn't be here!"

I blinked. Thinking she might have been annoyed at my interference and actually seeing it were two different things. "But I came for you."

"You *what*?"

Okay, she was a little more than annoyed. She was pissed.

A commotion erupted behind Serena, and she whipped her gaze over her shoulder. "He's with me. He's my interpreter," she said to one of Nate's teammates. White? Gray? Brown? Whichever one it was.

The operator—to use Nate's terminology—lowered his weapon and let a lightly bearded man in. He quickly moved to Serena's side, looking between the two of us with surprise and obvious recognition I didn't share.

"Izzy, this is Taj Barech, my interpreter," Serena said. "Taj, this is the sister I've told you so much about, the one *who is supposed to be in Washington*." She bit out every single one of those words in my direction.

"It is a pleasure to meet you," he said with a nod and an energetic smile.

"Likewise," I assured him as Nate moved to my side.

Serena's eyes widened to impossible dimensions, her jaw dropping as she stared at him. "You have to be kidding me."

"Nice to see you, Serena," Nate said, one hand on the rifle that hung from his shoulder. "No pictures of me or my guys."

"I know the rules when it comes to your type." Her gaze narrowed, and her hands fell from my shoulders. "I can't believe you actually let Izzy—"

"He didn't *let* me do anything!" I snapped, backing up a step. "Trust me, if he had his way, I'd be on the first flight out of here."

"If I had my way, you wouldn't have come here in the first place," he grumbled before addressing Serena. "She took another aide's place. I didn't even know she would be in country before she stepped onto the tarmac, or I would have done something to stop it."

"Okay, well, screw you *both*." I folded my arms across my chest. "I'm a grown woman who makes her own decisions, which is something neither of you seem to understand."

"It was a bad decision, Isabeau." Serena's voice rose again. "Do you have any idea how dangerous it is here?"

"I'm sorry . . . what? I can't walk three steps outside my bedroom without Sergeant Sour here shadowing my every move." I gestured toward Nate. "So, yes, I get just how dangerous it is here. Do you? Because I don't see armed guards with *you*."

Taj glanced between the three of us and cocked his head to the side. "This seems like a family matter. I'll be . . . somewhere else." He backed away slowly, but it wasn't like there were a lot of places he could go in the nearly empty room.

"Look, as fun as it is to finally have someone on my side regarding Isabeau's field trip to Afghanistan—" Nate started.

"Assuming I'm on your side about anything is a gross error." Serena glared at Nate.

"—we have to get on the bird," he finished, completely ignoring my sister's jab. "They're waiting on us."

"So, get her out of here already," Serena countered.

"Great, then let's go," I said, turning toward the exit. "We can finish fighting at the embassy."

"Hold on. Do you think I'm going with you?" Serena asked, jogging to catch up with me and taking hold of my elbow.

I stopped in my tracks, pivoting to face her as dread settled in my stomach. "Why else do you think I would be here?"

Her anger melted, but the look of pity that replaced it wasn't much better. "Izzy, I can't leave. I have a job to do here. It hasn't been the full six months. I'm still on assignment for another thirty days."

"The country is . . ." I shook my head.

"Collapsing," Nate said, striding our way. "The country is collapsing."

"Then it's my job to cover it," Serena stated like that was the end of the discussion.

"You don't mean that." The words rushed out in a whisper.

"I do." She adjusted the straps of her backpack. "I'm here doing exactly what I'm supposed to be doing. This is the longest assignment I've ever been given. I fought for it, and I'm not about to end it early just because it's getting dangerous. I'd never be able to hold my head up at the office."

Nate lifted his hand to his earpiece and cocked his head to the side. "Working on it," he barked in the professional tone I'd grown accustomed to before facing Serena. "Serena, I hear what you're saying, but it's not safe for you to stay. You know that. I know that. Izzy knows that. Three provinces have fallen in the last twenty-four hours. I completely understand your dedication to your profession, but for the sake of your sister, I'm not above begging you to get on that helicopter."

And *that* tone? That wasn't Sergeant Green. That was my Nate. I looked up at him, and my heart clenched. Underneath all the Kevlar and the weapons, he was still the same man who'd held me after my nightmare this morning. The same man who'd pulled me from that airplane ten years ago.

"You would get my dedication to my profession, wouldn't you?" Serena said with a sigh. "Hell, your dedication to yours is the entire reason Izzy ended up in Senator Lauren's office. Are you going to end your deployment early?"

She. Did. Not. My head snapped toward Serena, but she didn't catch the panicked rise of my brows because she was looking at Nate.

"What?" Nate asked.

Serena scoffed. "You seriously thought it was a coincidence that she's spent the last three years working for the woman who's been pushing legislation to end this war? That she took off for Washington right after you . . ." Her voice trailed off.

A muscle in Nate's jaw ticked as he slowly brought his gaze to lock with mine.

My stomach dropped.

Shit. It didn't matter that the legislation had never stood a chance, or that I'd basically been beating my head against a brick wall for all the progress we'd made. I'd spent the last few years fighting fruitlessly to end the conflict that had dragged him from my arms time and again, and now he knew it.

I saw it all in those blue eyes. Shock, disbelief, denial, and an emotion too dangerous to acknowledge, let alone name. He looked at me like he used to before New York, dropping the wall he'd locked himself behind.

"Oh shit. You thought it was coincidence. You really didn't know," Serena muttered.

I couldn't look away. Couldn't speak. Couldn't confirm or deny the blatant truth Serena had laid at his feet, exposing me with nothing more than a few words. All the Kevlar in the world couldn't protect my heart from its own foolish longing to hurl itself at Nate.

"Izzy, I'm so sorry," Serena said softly.

Nate blinked and looked away. "I know. ETA five minutes." He was talking through his radio, and when he finished, he looked at Serena. "Here's the deal. I'm putting Isabeau on that helicopter in five minutes. I really hope you're on it."

She swallowed and glanced back to where Taj was talking to Sergeant Whatever Color. "Even if I wanted to go, which I don't, I can't leave him. He doesn't have his visa yet."

"Has he started his paperwork?" I asked. "Because if that's all that's keeping you here, I can—"

"It's in process." She moved forward and cupped both sides of my face. "What did I tell you the first time you asked me not to cover a war zone?"

"That ignoring a situation doesn't make it better for the people living it." My throat threatened to close, my body recognizing my defeat before my heart.

"I still feel the same way. Me leaving isn't going to help these people. The least I can do is bear witness."

"You're not coming with me, are you?" My voice broke on the last word.

She shook her head. "I've worked too hard to get where I am to quit."

I pressed my lips between my teeth and fought the immediate burning in my eyes. The very passion I'd always admired about Serena had the potential to get her killed, and I didn't know what to do about it.

"I'll give you guys a minute, but that's all we have," Nate said quietly before walking toward Taj.

"I won't be able to come back," I whispered. "I pulled every string I had to get here, and I have the feeling Nate did too."

She smiled. "Only you would come searching in the first place, and I love you for it." Leaning forward, she rested her forehead against mine. "But I can't leave. Not yet."

"And if the province falls before your thirty days are up?" I could barely get the words out. "Please tell me you'll get out before then. I can't leave you here—"

"I'll leave if the province falls."

"Promise me."

"Promise. I'm not trying to get myself killed. But I'm not leaving Taj. It would be unspeakably cruel to abandon the person who has done so much for me, and he won't be safe here anymore, not after the work he's done for me, the work he's done for our government in the last few years. You know they'll kill him the first chance they get."

Hope sprung up in my chest. "I can work on his paperwork. At least I'll do what I can to push. The State Department is overwhelmed."

"I appreciate that." Her hands fell to my shoulders. "Just remember that I'm here because I choose to be. What's happening is more important than me."

"Not to me." I winced. "And yes, I can hear exactly how self-centered that sounds."

Serena laughed and pulled me into a hug. "I've missed you. And no matter what, my assignment is up in a month. I'll be home before you know it."

Nate walked by, followed by the remaining operators, but I couldn't let her go, even when the wind gusted in, somehow hotter than the stifling, stagnant air of the room.

"Stay with Nate," Serena whispered. "That man has his faults, but there's nothing he won't do to keep you safe."

"And how would you know that?" I found the strength to pull back so I could look at my sister.

A smile curved her lips. "Because I see the way he looks at you. Guess nothing much has changed there."

I shook my head. "He's been an absolute ass from the second I got off the plane. The only reason he's looking at me is because I'm his assignment." But that wasn't the entire truth. Feeling his gaze on me, I glanced over my shoulder to see him waiting for me in the doorway, and turned back to Serena. "But there's been a minute or two that he's just been . . . Nate. We're making the best of a really awkward situation."

"Are you, now?" She retreated a couple of steps, her fingers sliding down my arms until she held both my hands. "If I had to promise that I'd leave if the province falls, then you make me one too."

"What promise do you want in return?" I gripped her hands and told myself this wouldn't be the last time I saw her. If I even thought it, I wouldn't be able to walk away.

"Promise me that you won't marry Jeremy." She nudged my ring with her finger.

I blinked. There was no way she knew. "Because he's Mom and Dad's choice, or because you've never liked him?" She'd made her opinion widely, loudly known the night Jeremy proposed at our family's very renowned, very well-attended Christmas party.

"No." Her voice lowered, and her posture softened as she grinned at me like we were back in that apartment in DC and not in the middle of a war zone. "Because I see the way you look at *him* too." She glanced meaningfully over my shoulder. "You have no business marrying one man while you're in love with another."

"I'm not—" I yanked my hands back, but she held tight.

"You are." She gave my fingers a squeeze and then let me go. "And Jeremy's never been good enough. Stop settling for less than what you deserve. Stop walking the path Mom and Dad laid for you unless it's the one *you* want." One step at a time, she backed away. "I'll see you in a month. Let's grab pizza from that little place near the old apartment. God, I miss pizza." She flashed another smile, then turned away and walked out, taking Taj with her.

Somehow, I made myself walk to Nate.

Somehow, he got me into the helicopter.

Somehow, I managed to breathe as we took off, leaving my sister behind in Mazar-i-Sharif.

Nate slipped his earbuds into my ears and played some of my favorite music on the flight back to Kabul, but it barely made a dent in the noise of my thoughts. I'd had her, hugged her, and now she was gone. Our flight back to the States was scheduled for ten days from now.

Was there any way I could convince Serena to leave by then?

How did I let this happen?

"You didn't fail," Nate said quietly as he opened my car door once we reached the embassy.

I'd been so consumed by my thoughts that I hadn't even noticed we'd arrived. "Why would you say that?" At least this seat belt didn't stick as I got out of the car.

"Because I know you, and I know how you think."

Unfortunately, he was right.

"It feels a lot like failure." The heat beat mercilessly as we walked toward the entrance.

"She made her choice." We passed the marine guards, and Nate opened the door. "Serena has always been stubborn as a mule when it comes to her work."

I nodded, but it didn't make it hurt any less. The crisp air was a relief against my face as we entered the embassy's foyer and started toward the stairs. I wanted to crawl into bed and sleep off the utter, heart-wrenching defeat. Lucky for me, none of the staff was waiting, which meant I had a chance to make it to my room without being noticed.

Nate and I walked up the steps in silence.

"Is what Serena said true?" he asked as we neared the door to my room. "About why you went to work for Senator Lauren? Why you went into politics?"

I stopped dead in my tracks.

Oh. God. I'd almost forgotten that Serena had accidentally ratted me out. I opened my mouth to answer, but someone stepped out of the next room down the hall, saving me from embarrassment.

"Damn, I've been waiting all day for you," a man said angrily, and Nate and I both looked down the hallway to see the figure striding our way with purpose, his face becoming disastrously clearer with every step.

Not just any man.

Jeremy was here.

My stomach hit the floor.

"I'm done hearing you don't want to talk." He reached for my arm and got a good grip on the upper part. "I just flew all the way—" he started, abruptly halting when Nate ripped him away. Jeremy's body slammed against the wall beside me as Nate put his forearm against Jeremy's windpipe.

"Didn't anyone teach you not to touch a lady without her consent?" Every line of Nate's body radiated threat.

Oh shit.

"No!" I put my hand on Nate's shoulder. If he hurt Jeremy, the consequences would be dire to the career he'd fought so hard for. "Don't. It's okay. I'm okay."

"Isa—" Jeremy managed to squeak out.

"You know him?" Nate asked me, his eyes narrowing with accusation.

"Yes." I nodded, trying to swallow the huge boulder in my throat. Jeremy had never grabbed me like that before.

"Of course she knows me!" Jeremy croaked, stretching his neck melodramatically.

Nate dropped his forearm and backed up a step. Through all these years, I'd never had the two men side by side to compare before, but now that I did, the differences were startling.

Jeremy was polished, from his gelled, coiffed head of dark hair to his Armani shoes. His face was flawless, and I knew he'd flash that politician's smile in a heartbeat with every certainty that it would sway someone to his side.

But he didn't know Nate. Nathaniel was taller by a couple of inches, stacked with muscle, and he wielded an aura of fuck-around-and-find-out. One of Nate's smiles had to be earned. And every scar the man carried only made him . . . more.

"I'm her fiancé!" Jeremy straightened the Hermès tie I'd given him for his birthday.

Hermès. In a freaking war zone.

The hurt that flashed through Nate's eyes cut into me with a single glance, but he quickly masked his features as he ripped his gaze from mine, assessing Jeremy in a whole new way. His eyes caught on the badge Jeremy had pinned to his suit coat.

The badge that said *Jeremy Covington*.

Nate's body managed to go even more rigid.

"I don't know who the hell you think you are," Jeremy began, all but poking Nate's chest.

Not a good idea.

"He's my security detail," I said quickly. "Let's just . . ." Shit, this was bad. So, so, *so* bad. I needed to get him away from Nate before it got even worse. "Let's just go in my room and talk." My hand trembled as I fumbled for my room key, but Nate had his out already.

He opened the door with efficiency and stood back, holding it open so Jeremy could swagger through into my suite.

I followed after, pausing to glance up at Nate, who stared ahead with professional indifference. "It's complicated."

"Seems pretty simple to me." His scoff was almost silent, but not quite. "You're marrying Dickface."

CHAPTER FOURTEEN

IZZY

Georgetown
October 2014

> I've been thinking about leave. Maybe not this year, since you'll be in the middle of classes when I'll get block leave—aka, vacation—but maybe next year we can pick a place neither of us has been and just go. Just leave everything behind for a week or two and just . . . be. And I know you've probably traveled a lot more than I have. There wasn't money for that growing up, but the only good thing about deployment is the ridiculous amount of money I've been able to save. So, if you're down, send back a list of where you'd want to go with the next letter. Let's go somewhere warm, Izzy. Somewhere with a beach. Somewhere I can XXXXX

He'd crossed that part out so many times that the pen had ripped through the paper in one place. I sighed and set the letter on the kitchen counter.

How was it possible to miss someone so much when I'd spent so little actual time with him?

"How many times have you read that one?" Serena asked as she finished up dinner on the island cooktop in front of me.

"Once or twice." Just like Nate, I could find the positives in the bad, and the one good thing that had come from *Dickface* leaving me for Yale was Serena moving into the two-bedroom apartment when she'd been hired by the *Post.* She liked to beat herself up that it wasn't the *Times*, but I was just ecstatic to have her with me.

"More like a hundred times," she muttered, flipping the grilled cheese in the pan.

"You know I'm happy to cook, right?" The exposed side was more than a little charred. "I lived with Margo that last year at Syracuse. It's not like I don't know how."

"Your job is to study." She pointed a cheese-covered spatula at me. "Study, Isabeau. Not memorize love letters from Nate."

"They're not love letters." I snatched up the paper just in case any of that cheese made a jump for it and landed on Nate's letter. "He made it clear that we're not together."

"Right." She arched a brow.

"You look like Mom when you do that," I muttered.

She scoffed, and snatched the letter out of my hands. "Take it back!" she demanded, holding the letter above the grilled cheese, which was now smoking.

"You're going to set the apartment on fire!"

"Take. It. Back." She dangled the letter just above the pan.

"Fine, I take it back!" I lunged, but she leapt out of reach and then started to read. "Serena!"

She whistled low, leaning back against the other counter. "The man is good with words."

"I know that." I grabbed the handle of the pan and moved it off the burner, then threw open the window in hopes of avoiding another encounter with the smoke alarm and our noise-sensitive neighbors in 3C.

"'Promise me that you're out there living and not just existing,'" she read from the end of the letter, blowing out a long sigh. "See, even the guy who is clearly in love with you wants you to get out more. Which is weird, but if it helps convince you, then I'm all for it."

"One, Nate is *not* in love with me. Someone who loves you doesn't turn you loose on the male population and tell you to have at it while he's gone." I understood his point, really and truly, but that didn't mean I agreed with it.

"In this case?" She waved the letter as the scent of smoke dissipated. "That's exactly what someone who loves you would tell you to do. I have to give the guy some respect. He could have locked you down in Georgia and left you pining. Instead, he thought of what would be best for *you*." She made a face. "I think you may have found the one good guy left on the planet, and I don't care what Mom and Dad say about him."

They didn't know much about Nate, but they'd made it clear they thought dating an enlisted soldier was a major step downward from a Covington. I hadn't bothered telling them we weren't dating after that comment, and honestly, whatever I *was* with Nate was a step up from Jeremy. He'd sent me an Insta DM last week I'd happily ignored. That guy had some major growing up to do.

"So why are you so keen on me getting out more?" I settled on the kitchen stool and started scrolling on my phone for takeout.

It was like we were kids again, fending for ourselves while Mom and Dad were at one gala or another, except we were adults. Kind of. Since my definition of adulting was paying all my own bills, and Dad was still covering tuition, books, and this apartment, I wasn't exactly the poster child for independence. Not in the way Nate was.

"Because there are plenty of decent ones left who aren't perpetually unavailable." She looked up at me. "And you need at least a few nights a week that you aren't wearing . . . that."

I looked down at Nate's hoodie. "What's wrong with this?"

"Nothing." She rolled her eyes. "What's going on with Paul, anyway? That was your second date a couple nights ago, right?"

"Patrick," I corrected her, finding a local restaurant that had a reasonable delivery time. "And pretty sure that's not going to work out."

"Shocker." Her eyes flared with mock surprise. "Let me guess. You're both at Georgetown Law, and that's just too much in common. He wants to go into politics, and you abhor it. He's good looking but just doesn't rev your engine. Nice, but not memorable? Oh, and the death sentence to every potential Isabeau Astor suitor—he's available."

"He's a 2L who wants to go into corporate law, and I'm pretty sure he's more attracted to his phone than me." Patrick didn't look at me like I was the answer to every question. He'd only kissed me once, and it had all the heat of three-day-old leftovers. And . . . I sighed.

He wasn't Nate.

None of them were.

"I'll trade you." I waved my phone. "Dinner for my letter back."

She cocked her head to the side and stared at the paper. "I really wish he hadn't redacted this part. I bet it was hot."

"Serena!"

"Fine. Have your non-boyfriend's letter." She gave it back to me and entered her order into my phone.

I folded it neatly and put it back in its envelope so I could store it with the others. He'd sent a package this time, complete with three newly highlighted books. I had mine ready to go back for him, too, and had started a birthday package that needed to get out in the next couple of days if it was going to have any hope of making it to him. So far it had spearmint gum, the brownies he'd revealed a secret weakness for, and a Georgetown hoodie to wear around the base, or the FOB, as he called it, on his downtime.

"You know, you should really watch the congressional race back home," Serena said, handing my phone back.

"Someone interesting?" I slid the phone into the back pocket of my jeans. "Or someone you think is interesting because you're a high-powered reporter on a mission for truth and justice?"

"Can't it be both?" She dumped the burnt sandwich in the trash can and set the pan in the sink.

"Not usually."

"She's running on a platform of ending the war in Afghanistan."

My gaze jumped to hers.

"Figured that might get your attention." She leaned toward me, bracing her elbows on the small island. "Not sure she's got the numbers to get elected, and honestly, I don't see legislation like that passing. Not with the makeup of the Hill right now. But still, I bet Dad could pull a few strings to get you an internship if she wins."

"Politics?" I shook my head. "No, thank you. Any string Dad pulls comes with more, and I'm going into the nonprofit sector." Somewhere I could make a difference.

"Dad's going to be thrilled." She grinned. "You should tell him at Christmas, just so we can watch him turn red like one of the decorations."

"He took your journalism major okay." I grabbed the closest notebook to me and opened it to the first blank page, numbering one through ten on the left side.

"Because he was still hoping you'd be his key to gaining a little political power with Covington. Dad wants a politician in the family more than he's ever wanted us."

"Isn't that the sad truth." The past few years had only made that glaringly obvious. "The least we could have done was given him one kid with an MBA for Astor Enterprises."

"I'm not working my ass off to rid myself of his leash just so he can slap a harness on me and take me for a little walk in whatever direction he sees fit. Nope." She shook her head.

"On that we agree. And let's spare the awkwardness at Christmas. I'll break the news when they come out for my birthday in March."

Serena grimaced but quickly covered it. "Look, I know you're excited that they say they're coming, but just don't . . ." She bit her bottom lip.

"Get my hopes up?" I finished the sentence she obviously didn't want to.

"Exactly."

"They'll come." I lifted my brows at her skepticism. "They will. They promised. Besides, they booked a hotel already."

"I just don't want to see you disappointed. Again. I wouldn't exactly call them reliable, which is why I think you would benefit from dating someone who actually *is*." She glanced pointedly at my paper.

"Nate has yet to let me down." I stared at the empty numbers on my list, my brain spinning with my favorite word—*possibilities*. Somewhere with a beach. Somewhere Nate could kiss me in the water. That's what I pretended was in that scratched-out portion of the letter.

"Oh, and it's Lauren," Serena said.

"Who?"

"The woman who's running for Congress. Eliana Lauren."

"I'll look her up." The least I could do was see if she was worth voting for.

I tapped my pen next to the number one, then wrote a single word.

Fiji.

By December, my collection of letters had grown exponentially, as had my stress. Law school was even harder than I'd expected. Finals left me almost no time to read, and I wasn't exactly holding up my end of the conversation with Nate.

And true to Nate, he didn't say a single word about me ghosting him for nearly a month, just kept writing, telling me how proud he was that I was conquering law school.

Christmas had been an awkward extravaganza of overpriced gifts and awkward, two-pat hugs, but January arrived, and I got my rhythm back.

Never apologize for doing what you need to. That's what Nate said when I got a letter at the end of January.

February, I managed not to screw up a relationship for all of three weeks.

By the fourth, I cut him loose. It just happened to be the same week Mom and Dad canceled their trip to DC for my birthday in favor of opening Dad's new Chicago offices.

I didn't know Nate's dad, and he'd never told me why he feared becoming like him, but I was starting to feel the same way about my own. I didn't need to be my parents' number one priority, but making the top ten would have been nice every once in a while.

"Again?" Margo asked in March on our weekly call.

"Hey, I gave it four dates," I told her, holding the phone between my shoulder and ear as I folded the last of my clean laundry and put it away. "Not all of us are happily married at twenty-two."

"You're not twenty-two," she reminded me. "Not until tomorrow."

"You get my point." I hung my favorite shirt and put Nate's hoodie in the drawer beneath my bed. "I just don't see a reason to string someone along when I know it won't work."

"It's never going to work if you don't give it an actual shot," she lectured.

I glanced at the box of letters on my desk. "Totally agree with you there."

A loud giggle sounded from the living room.

"Sounds like someone's having a good time," Margo said.

"Serena has her boyfriend over, which is why I'm hiding in my bedroom."

"And how are classes?"

"Fine, Mom." I smiled when she scoffed. "Really, I'm oddly caught up, and it's Friday night. I have the entire weekend to binge TV or—"

"Write Nate," Margo suggested in a singsong voice.

"You're starting to sound like Serena."

"Serena adores Nate. I'm . . ." She went quiet.

I tossed my empty laundry basket on the floor of my abysmally small closet. "Just say it."

"I'm withholding judgment until it's a little clearer if you guys are some destined fairy tale or if it's the initial trauma of the crash that bonded you."

"And how are *your* classes, psych major?" I asked, not that I hadn't wondered the same thing once or twice. But the way I missed him all these months later had to mean something more. Between our letters and the short bursts of time we'd had, I almost knew Nate better than I had dickface Jeremy. Letters didn't leave a lot of space for bullshitting the way empty movie dates did.

"I'm barely passing one of my classes," Margo admitted.

"Like actually barely passing?" I asked, pausing. "Or in danger of getting a C?"

"They're basically the same thing."

I grinned. "No, they're not. But seriously, is there anything I can do?"

"Besides moving back to the tundra of upstate New York and personally taking me to coffee every afternoon so I can see your pretty face?"

"Right. Besides that." The doorbell rang, but I flopped onto my bed, knowing Serena would get it.

"Nope. Just listen to me whine on our calls."

"Always happy to do so."

"Izzy!" Serena called out.

"I have to let you go; I think our dinner just got here." We said our goodbyes, and I ended the call.

"Izzy!" Serena shouted again.

"Coming!" I hoisted my soft flannel pajama pants up higher on my hips and zipped up my Georgetown hoodie over my braless boobs so I wouldn't freak out Serena's company in the two seconds it would take to snag my dinner and fade back into the cave of my room.

I opened my bedroom door to find Serena grinning at me with an eerie resemblance to the Cheshire cat. "Yes?"

"I'm getting out of here for the weekend. Luke's roommate is out of town, so we'll have his place to ourselves. He's throwing some stuff in a bag for me right now." She looked so happy that I couldn't bear to remind her that tomorrow was my birthday.

"That sounds amazing! Have a great time!" I forced a smile and prayed she didn't see through it.

She squeezed me tight. "You're going to have the best birthday. Promise me you'll actually leave the apartment."

"Will do." That was a blatant fib. I'd leave the apartment long enough to fetch coffee down the block, but that was it. I was already planning out a full binge-fest on the couch.

She pulled back and studied my face like she could detect lies. "Okay. Dinner is on the kitchen counter. I love you, Iz."

"Love you."

She squeezed my hand and then raced out, grabbing her boyfriend's hand and shutting the front door before I even made it to the living room.

"Weird, but okay," I muttered, turning toward the kitchen and the scent of freshly delivered Chinese food.

I jumped at the sight of the handsome man leaning casually against the counter, like he was *supposed* to be here and not half a world away. He was dressed in jeans and a coat he hadn't even unzipped yet, and a travel-worn camouflage backpack rested on the floor next to his feet. Despite the exhaustion in his blue eyes, he looked so damned beautiful that I could barely breathe.

"Nate?" He was here. In the States. In my kitchen.

"Hey." He smiled, flashing that dimple.

My heart took off like a racehorse, and so did I. It took less than a second for me to dart over the couch. Who cared if pillows went flying? I wasn't wasting time by going around. He caught me in his arms before I could land on the other side.

"You're here," I mumbled against the warm skin of his neck, my feet dangling as he hugged me tight.

"Happy birthday, Isabeau," he said.

Best present *ever*.

CHAPTER FIFTEEN

IZZY

Kabul, Afghanistan
August 2021

I leaned back against my closed door, my heart pounding for all the wrong reasons as I watched Jeremy survey the suite, taking in the seating arrangement and little kitchenette. Guess the conversation I'd avoided for the last six weeks was going to happen whether I was ready or not.

Anger rose swiftly, heating my skin. How *dare* he show up like this?

You could always tell Nate to throw his ass on the curb.

Except I doubted Nate was going to be speaking to me after that exchange in the hallway. No doubt he was already calling his replacement.

"You're marrying Dickface." God, the look on his face had been worse than betrayal. Nate had been . . . disappointed. Seeing that he knew my history with Jeremy, I couldn't blame him.

I was disappointed in myself for how long I'd let this go on. The weight of the ring on my finger felt like an anchor, tying me to the one person I was starting to realize had never deserved me.

"Your room is nicer than the one they gave me," Jeremy said, taking off his navy-blue suit jacket to reveal an immaculately pressed shirt. He was dressed to enter the Senate chamber, not Afghanistan. After draping the jacket across the back of the desk chair, he turned toward me, his brown eyes sweeping over me with the same assessment he gave the suite. The little crease in his forehead told me he found me as lacking as he did his own accommodations.

For the first time since we'd started dating back at Syracuse, I didn't give a shit what he thought about me, my travel-worn slacks, or my dusty blouse. I didn't need to impress him anymore.

The thought made me stand a little taller.

"What are you doing here?" I pulled my scarf off, dropped it into my bag, and crossed my arms over my chest. After failing to get Serena on the helicopter, this was the last thing I wanted to deal with.

There were no words for whatever the hell was going on, or how I felt about it. Every failure in my life was rearing its head today. I was a tangle of crossed electrical wires in danger of going up with the slightest provocation.

"Never one to beat around the bush, are you, Isa?" He walked forward, offering me one of his five practiced smiles. This one was number four, his contrite-but-boys-will-be-boys version.

Isa. Because my father had been the one to introduce us.

I held up my hand, and he stopped midway across the room, arching a groomed eyebrow. "Let me guess, you borrowed Daddy's private jet?" I cocked my head to the side. "Or is this a campaign stop?"

"As you can imagine, this little trip actually meant canceling three of my appearances." His smile faltered, and he scratched the point of his chin. "Appearances you were supposed to attend at my side."

"That wasn't going to happen, whether or not I was in the States." I shook my head and made my way to the little table behind the couch, leaving my bag on the surface and rolling my stiff shoulders. "And you shouldn't be here, Jeremy. I asked you for space, and you chasing me halfway across the world is hardly giving it to me."

"Come on, Isa." He offered me smile number three, the boyish one he used whenever he was trying to get his way, the one that had fooled me into thinking we had a shot at a real second chance. "I thought you loved all those romantic, bold moves in the books you read. I flew into a war zone for you. Doesn't that tell you how much I love you? How badly I want to make this work?"

I kept the couch between us when he came my way. "It tells me you probably already had a photo opportunity downstairs, where you were no doubt helping process visas, or talking to would-be constituents about how best to evacuate them."

Surprise flared in his eyes, and then he looked downward as he trailed his fingers across the arm of the upholstered couch. "Naturally I did what was needed to convince my father that this was a campaign expense."

"Aren't you sick of that yet? Constantly appeasing your father? God knows I am." I didn't even realize it until the words were out of my mouth. I was stuck in a perpetual cycle of trying to please the men in my life, only to have them abandon me at their convenience. Seeing Nate only made it that much clearer because unfortunately, instead of breaking the pattern, he'd become part of it.

"Come on, Isa. You know I can't get elected without my dad's support . . . we play the game. That's what we do."

"Right. Well, feel free to get right back on that plane." If I could have rolled my eyes any harder, they would have come out of my head. Politics always came first with him. It was one of the many reasons my parents loved him more than I did.

"Come with me." The pleading look he shot me was unpracticed, and it nearly disarmed me.

"If I have to listen to one more person lecture me about how unsafe it is—" I started.

"Oh no," he said, shaking his head. "I have nothing but the utmost respect for the work you're doing here. It's going to be a great bullet point on your résumé and talking point for future interviews, but . . ."

My eyes flared. Of course it was all about points with him. "But what?"

He cringed and offered me smile number three again. "But we had an agreement. You would support me on the campaign trail, and I wouldn't push you to leave your career once I was elected."

My mouth opened, then shut, then repeated the process as I struggled to find the words. "Are you so delusional that you think I would show up on your arm after I walked into your office to find Clarisse Betario splayed out on your desk like lunch?" The memory made my stomach churn, but my heart didn't ache like it was supposed to.

"That was . . . unfortunate," he admitted. "But don't act like you were heartbroken. We know each other too well to lie. You were pissed. Probably embarrassed—"

"Humiliated is more like it!" My hands curled into fists, my fingernails biting into my palms. "Everyone in that office knew what was going on, and believe me, they were more than happy to tell me it wasn't a onetime lapse in judgment. You've been having an affair for six months! The ink wasn't even dry on our engagement announcement."

He took a slow, deep breath, and his eyes shifted, a habit he had yet to control that meant he was scurrying for an answer. "I regret that you were embarrassed, Isa. Truly, I am."

I blinked. "But you don't regret cheating on me?" Of all the tactics I thought he'd use, this hadn't been one.

"We agreed never to lie to each other." He straightened his shoulders.

"Right, because that was the only way forward after what happened after Syracuse!" I'd been so incredibly stupid to trust him again.

"Are you never going to let that rest?" He raked his hands through his hair, mussing the perfect brown strands. "I thought we were past that!"

"Yeah, we moved on to you screwing your staff. Big improvement." I gave him a thumbs-up and kicked off my shoes. Thankfully I'd chosen flats for the meeting in Mazar-i-Sharif, but my feet still weren't ready to forgive me.

"Look, I thought we'd discussed having an open relationship—"

"You discussed!" I slammed my hand down on the table, the sound of the impact of my ring against the wood punctuating my disgust. "I never agreed. You knew that was never going to fly with me. I would *never* agree to that!"

"Your father wants—"

"My father doesn't make my decisions for me." I recognized just how true the words were, but only because it was dawning on me just how false they had been in the past. Even Jeremy was Dad's choice, not mine, and I'd been so hungry for his approval that I'd gone against my gut and given a second chance to a relationship that had never deserved a first. "And as much as he's desperate for political ties, he'd never expect me to accept less than I deserve, and I'm finally seeing that you, Jeremy, are *way* less."

He swallowed and glanced down at my hand. "If you're still wearing the ring, then there's still hope."

"I haven't taken it off because your actions have rendered me speechless," I replied, walking past him toward the kitchenette. "I don't know how to tell people why I'm *not* wearing it."

"So just keep wearing it," he suggested, following me.

I pulled a bottle of water from the fridge and didn't offer him one. He'd taken enough from me already. Then I twisted the top off and drank almost half of it in greedy gulps before setting the bottle on the counter. "If we're going for complete honesty, let's just lay it out," I said, bracing my palms on the counter and hopping up to sit on it. "Neither of us really honestly wants this. It's been engineered by everyone around us for optics."

"Not just for the good of my career, but for yours too." He tugged his tie loose.

"I never wanted to go into politics." I shook my head.

He laughed, and it wasn't the happy, melodious sound he'd perfected over the years. It was raw and a little ugly, but at least it was real. "Let's not pretend we both don't know exactly why you went into politics." He shoved his hands into his pockets. "Exactly why you're still *here*."

I gripped the edge of the counter, preparing myself for the scathing verbal assault that had made him such a star in the DA's office. After all, public service looked much better on his résumé than private practice.

"Don't act like there haven't been three of us in this relationship from the second I saw you again in DC two years ago." His eyes narrowed. "Or did you think I didn't recognize your bodyguard out there? Like you didn't have his picture stuck to your fridge for the first *year* of our relationship. You've never gotten over him. I may have slept with other women, but I sure as hell didn't love any of them."

Other *women*? How naive had I been?

"How were we supposed to have a devoted, committed relationship when there was never any room for me in your heart?" Jeremy continued. "You might not like it, but we both know he's been standing between us for the last two years. Of course I went looking for someone who actually wanted me, because you never really did. It didn't matter that he left you in New York. You've still been pining for him."

I sucked in a breath but didn't deny it. "Mind your words, Jeremy."

He put up his hands and backed up two steps, leaving the kitchenette. "Oh, heaven forbid I speak against the saint that is Nathaniel Phelan. Tell me, is he the reason you've been declining my calls? The reason you were so quick to take Newcastle's place on that plane? Did you know he was here? Have you been having the same kind of fun you're guilt-tripping me for?"

"I don't owe you an answer," I said, lifting my chin. "But just so you don't think I'm anything like you, no. I didn't seek Nate out. He just happened to be ordered here and assigned to me."

"Of course he was." Jeremy glared at the wall as though he could see Nate standing on the other side of it. "That's the thing with you two, right? You seem to magically appear in the other's lives."

"Your point is?" Nate and I had a connection I despised but also marveled at, and it wasn't up for discussion, not with Jeremy.

He moved quickly, reaching for my arm, and I slid out of his grasp. "Touch me again, and I'll scream. You'll be dead in seconds. Nate doesn't care who your daddy is." The threat left my mouth before I could think twice about risking Nate's career over a situation I should've been able to handle myself.

Then again, the threat worked, because Jeremy took a step back.

"Have you fucked him?" Jeremy's face turned a mottled shade of red. "I mean, this time around?"

"You're seriously going to ask me that? Like I'm the one who's been cheating in this relationship?" I slid off the counter but left my arms loose at my side, ready to reach for the panic button in my pocket if Jeremy decided that grabbing onto me wasn't enough this time.

"He put me into the wall, Isa." A corner of Jeremy's mouth quirked upward but didn't quite reach smile number two, the smirk. "Pretty passionate response, if you ask me. Pretty dangerous one, too, if you ask me."

"He's. My. Security. Detail." I bit out every word.

"Security would have held my wrist. Your man went for my throat." He blinked, and then his expression shifted, like he was calculating something. "Hold on. This can work."

"I'm sorry?" Every minute I spent in his company was convincing me of the opposite.

"As much as it chafes my pride, you'll see that I can compromise. I came here to get you back, and that's exactly what I'm going to do. You want to get back at me? Fine. Do it. You can have him, and I can continue with more . . . discretion." There it was, smile number one, the politician.

My jaw dropped.

"Don't you see?" He shrugged, the gesture disturbingly happy. "It's perfect. Our families will get what they want, our careers will flourish, and we'll both find satisfaction elsewhere. It wouldn't be the first arrangement of its kind. Half the relationships in DC are staged. Think of it as less of a marriage and more of a partnership. An alliance."

I stared in open shock as any feelings I carried for him shriveled and died. Maybe I'd always known that our relationship was remarkably convenient, but I'd still thought it was based on mutual affection and love.

But that dull ache in my heart at the memory of Jeremy's infidelity was nothing compared to the way it hurt to even breathe knowing that Nate was on the other side of the wall. *Damn it.* I'd been fooling myself for the last two years.

"This is great," Jeremy continued, nodding enthusiastically. "Everyone gets what they want."

"Except that I don't want *you*." I yanked the ring from my finger.

"No one has caught wind of what happened. We still have time to salvage this. We'll say that I flew here out of gallant concern for your safety, and the media will eat it up." He ignored me, staring off into the center of the room as he spat out how to spin it, how to control whatever fallout there might be.

"Jeremy," I said with enough force that he turned back toward me.

"What?" His brow knit almost comically.

"I made a mistake, and I'm sorry." I reached for his hand.

His face softened as our fingers brushed. "It's okay. It's all fixable. I still want to marry you."

I pushed the ring into his palm, and then curled his fingers, closing his fist around the heirloom diamond. "But I don't want to marry you. I made a mistake thinking that what I felt for you could grow if I gave it enough time. I made a mistake giving in to what my parents wanted just because it was comfortable, because I thought I'd finally earn their approval. I made a mistake in settling for someone who obviously doesn't know the meaning of love, or devotion, or exclusivity. I will never be what you want, and you will never give me what I deserve. I made a mistake when I said yes, and now I'm remedying it."

He stared down at his closed fist. "You don't mean that."

"I do." I nodded, using the opportunity his shock provided to pass by him and walk toward the desk where he'd left his jacket. I took the expensive fabric in my hand and then moved to the door, grasping the handle.

"You don't," he argued, pivoting to face me, shaking his head emphatically. "You aren't telling me no. That's not possible."

I sighed and opened the door as a wave of pity washed out whatever was left of my anger at him. "Oh, Jeremy. Someone should have told you no a long time ago."

His eyes flew wide.

"Hey," I said into the hallway, then startled. It wasn't Nate standing guard at my door. It was Sergeant Gray.

My stomach sank.

"Ms. Astor?" Sergeant Gray asked, lifting his thick brows.

"Right." I forced a smile. "Sorry. Mr. Covington was just leaving. Could you please make sure he gets back to his room?" I asked.

"Isa!" Jeremy argued.

Sergeant Gray quickly squelched a smile. "Absolutely. Mr. Covington, I believe your suite is next door."

"Fuck this." Jeremy stomped past me, snatching his jacket out of my hands. "You'll regret this, Isa, and when you do, I might not be willing to take you back."

Sergeant Gray stoically ignored the exchange.

I let Jeremy have the last word, knowing the conversation couldn't possibly end any other way. He'd just keep talking.

"Thank you," I said to Sergeant Gray. When he nodded, I shut my door, locked it, and then leaned back against the wood, sliding down slowly until my ass hit the floor.

I should've been angry about a lot of things. My father's constant political chess moves, the flippant way Jeremy treated his cheating, or my own participation in something that obviously never had a chance.

But the ire that consumed my thoughts prickled my skin because Jeremy was right about one thing.

It didn't matter who I met, who I dated, or who I tried to love.

Nate would always be in the way, even if he was never physically there.

It was impossible to give away a heart I'd never gotten back in the first place.

CHAPTER SIXTEEN

NATHANIEL

Georgetown
March 2015

"I only get two days with you, and you want to spend tonight at a bar?" Izzy shouted over the pounding beat of the bass in the club as we surveyed the grinding bodies on the crowded dance floor.

"I promised your sister I'd take you out," I replied. "That was the deal for her keeping my trip a secret." My pulse leapt at the crush of the crowd around us, its proximity, its numbers. There were too many people between us and the exit. Too many people to keep track of whose hands were where, who might be reaching for what. Too many fucking people in general.

This had been a bad idea, and yet I'd fought tooth and nail for special permission to take a weekend pass before completing reintegration training with the rest of my unit. Not like that shit helped, anyway.

"I know you must be exhausted after not sleeping last night," she started, two little lines appearing between her brows. Damn, I'd almost forgotten how long her lashes were. Pictures didn't do her justice.

"I'm okay. We're not spending your birthday worrying about me." Guess I hadn't been as stealthy as I'd thought during my sleepless hours, but at least I'd kept my personal promise to rack out on her couch and keep my hands to myself. Looking at her now, in that V-neck wrap-style blouse, and jeans that looked like they were created with the sole purpose of hugging her ass, I was pretty sure I deserved sainthood. Hell, I deserved sainthood the second she'd invited me to sleep in her bed and I had managed to decline.

There was nothing I wanted more than to pull her against me and pick up where we'd left off nine months ago, with my tongue in her mouth and her legs wrapped around my waist. But there were things she didn't know, and I had the feeling that once she did, she wasn't going to want me in her bed, even if we were only sleeping.

It didn't matter how badly I wanted Izzy, when I logically knew I could never have her. She was out of my league in every way. She would be out in the world soon enough, changing lives, and the only thing I was good at was ending them. I was turning out to be immeasurably more violent than my father was. At least he'd never killed anyone.

"Come on," I said, holding out my hand. "Let's get you the drink I promised Serena."

"One drink and we're out." She laced her fingers with mine, and just like we were back on that plane, tumbling toward uncertainty, I felt the unmistakable warmth of home.

"Agreed." I led us through the crowd, fighting the rise of my blood pressure that seemed to spike a little higher with every person who brushed against us, then claimed the only two empty barstools at the counter.

Izzy took the one closest to the door, and I sat so I faced her, casually looking back over my shoulder to see how many people were behind us. There were only a half dozen or so between the corner of the bar and the wall, so this was definitely the lesser of the evils.

But it was all still pretty fucking evil. There were people between us and every exit in this place.

"So, what's it going to be?" I asked, lowering my voice now that we weren't in the direct blast radius of the speakers. "Beer? Tequila? Cosmo?"

"Nope." She drummed her painted fingernails on the counter and looked over the shelves of liquor as the bartender approached.

"What can I get you?" the bartender asked, flashing me a smile.

A few years ago, the brunette would have been just my type.

But I'd found out over the last year that my type was now Isabeau Astor. Not just blonde. Not just brown eyes. Not only quick wits and an infectious laugh. Not just a tendency to talk about fourteen subjects at once through lips softer than silk. Only the complete package of Izzy seemed to do it for me. No one else. I'd fallen for her a little harder with every letter, every secret she shared, every time she made me laugh. And it wasn't that I hadn't had offers while we were in the sandbox, or that I'd deluded myself into thinking she was back here waiting for me, especially after I'd told her not to. It was just that no one was Izzy.

Which put me—both of us—in a damnable situation.

"A glass of champagne," Izzy ordered with a grin.

"Champagne?" the bartender asked, leaning in like she'd misheard.

"Yep," Izzy replied, reaching into her purse and handing her driver's license to the bartender. "It's my birthday."

"So it is. Happy birthday." The bartender smiled and handed back Izzy's ID. "And for you?" she asked, turning toward me and leaning in even though I hadn't spoken.

"Yuengling, please," I ordered, reaching for my wallet. "And we'll take the bottle of champagne if you don't serve by the glass."

"I've got you," the brunette said, getting to work.

"So what was your favorite part of today?" Izzy asked. "When I dragged you to my favorite pizza place? My favorite bakery for my favorite cupcakes? Or when I hauled you through campus?"

"Everything about seeing you," I answered honestly. The ability to speak my mind around her was my favorite part of our . . . whatever this was. There was no need to play games, to play coy or even flirt. I could be exactly who I was and say exactly what I was thinking when it came to Izzy.

Today had been everything I'd traveled from Savannah to give her, and I had to give Serena major credit for making it happen. The second I'd messaged her from the Instagram account Izzy had insisted I set up, telling her I wanted to surprise her sister, Serena had happily flipped her lid. She'd also slipped in the fact that their parents had bailed on Izzy as usual, and that she wasn't seeing anyone, into the brief conversation.

Not going to lie, I'd been . . . relieved—about the boyfriend situation, not her parents. Not that Izzy didn't deserve someone. She did. I was just selfishly glad that I'd get her to myself for the weekend.

Her smile was instant and heart-stoppingly beautiful. "Just wait until we get home and I make you watch *Ladyhawke*."

"Your namesake?" The corners of my mouth curved. "Can't wait." I would sit around and watch someone read a phone book if it meant I got to be with Izzy . . . I just wasn't sure I was going to last in this bar much longer without losing whatever was left of my sanity.

"If you could only watch one movie for the rest of your life, what would it be?" she asked.

"That's a tough one." My eyes met hers, and I knew what she was doing—the same thing I'd done for her on the plane, distracting me with the questions.

"Take your time."

"*Lord of the Rings: Return of the King*," I answered. "But maybe my answer will change to *Ladyhawke* after tonight. Who knows?"

She leaned in and brushed her mouth over mine, and every nerve in my body went on high alert. "Thank you for today."

I threaded my fingers through her hair and pulled her in, deepening the kiss but keeping my tongue firmly behind my teeth. The first taste of her was a rush that flooded every cell in my body. Keeping myself in check was a struggle, but I managed. I wasn't about to kiss her the way I wanted in front of all these people, so I pulled away before we headed that direction.

She smiled against my mouth as we broke apart, her hand rising to her chest. "You should feel the way my heart is pounding." Her fingers brushed over the little lock necklace I'd bought her for her birthday. The shit that came in the little blue boxes was expensive, and she'd protested, but I figured classy girls wore classy jewelry.

"Mine too." Maybe the admission wasn't smooth, but I didn't feel that kind of pressure around Izzy.

"Here you are," the bartender said as she returned, putting our orders in front of us.

Izzy leaned back, and I instantly mourned the loss of her mouth.

"Thank you." I put my debit card on the counter before Izzy could even try. "For a tab."

"We won't need a tab." Izzy shook her head as she took the slim stem of the champagne glass between her fingers. "We're only staying for one drink." She glanced my way. "And thank you."

"I'll get your check." The bartender nodded and took my card to the register.

"You sure about only one drink?" I lifted my brows at Izzy. "It's your birthday. I'm down for whatever you want."

"I don't want to be drunk on the last night I get to have you with me." She shrugged.

I would have argued, but I knew exactly how she felt. I wanted to remember every single second. "Happy birthday, Isabeau." I lifted my beer.

"Thanks, Nate." She smiled and clicked her glass against mine. "I'm so glad you came."

"Me too."

After the bartender brought my card back, Izzy and I sat there talking about her classes for the better part of a half hour while she sipped her champagne, and I barely touched my beer. Every time she tried to steer the conversation to how the deployment had gone for me, I carefully altered course right back to her. I tried to sit still, to focus only on her smile, her laugh, the light in her eyes, the overwhelming way I wanted her and didn't have a damn clue what to do about it. But the walls closed in tighter and tighter, and the people came closer, reaching around us to get to the bar, bumping into my back, reaching into their pockets for . . . wallets.

Just. Wallets.

Not weapons.

Because I was stateside, not in Afghanistan.

Fuck. It wasn't this bad last time. Then again, I hadn't spent nine straight months in hell, facing extension after extension. Rangers were supposed to have shorter, more frequent deployments, but that hadn't been our luck. I hadn't been wounded this time, but I hadn't stood in four separate formations in front of makeshift memorials of boots and rifles last time either. Hadn't—

Not here. I took as deep of a breath as my tight chest would allow and shoved all that shit back in the box where it belonged. I glanced back at Izzy to see her watching me in that way she had, like she could cut through all the bullshit with nothing but her beautiful eyes.

"If you had to pick a zombie-apocalypse partner, who would it be?" she asked, then threw up a finger. "Present company excepted. That's just an easy way out."

"Rowell, I guess." Torres would have chosen his girlfriend, and it felt wrong to deprive the man of his love life, even in a hypothetical situation. "We've fought our way out of some shit together."

"Fair answer. Now, let's get out of here," she said.

"You haven't finished your drink." There was no way I was forcing her out of her birthday celebration because I couldn't hold myself together.

She rolled her eyes, downed the last quarter of the glass, and set it on the counter. "I have officially finished the drink you promised Serena." Slipping off her barstool, she held out her hand for mine. "And I'd honestly rather spend the rest of my night at home. With you."

"Not even a dance?" I glanced toward the crowded floor, and every muscle tensed reflexively.

"Not even a dance." She wiggled her fingers, and I couldn't resist her. If she wanted to go home, I'd take her home.

Our fingers twined, and I led us back through the crowd and out of the club. The brisk March air was a godsend as it hit my face, filling my lungs as I took my first full breath since walking in.

"You okay?" she asked as we started walking down the sidewalk, heading the half-dozen blocks to her apartment.

"Okay is a relative term." I picked up her hand and pressed a kiss to the back of it. The touch was innocent enough, but the scent of her perfume had my thoughts dipping into flat-out carnal territory. I wanted to stretch her out underneath me and kiss every curve she possessed until that scent was branded on my brain, replacing every bad memory I'd gained over the last few years.

"You haven't talked about the last nine months for you," she said, her finger flexing around mine as we started to walk again. "Even in the letters."

I looked both ways before crossing the first street with her and fumbled for the right words, if they even existed. "Writing you was my escape. I wasn't exactly eager to put all of that on you."

"Even if I want to know?" She flinched. "Crap, that came out weird. I mean, even if I want to listen?"

"I know what you meant," I replied softly, pulling her closer against the bite of the cold. She'd been against bringing a coat, but I guess it gave me an excuse to hold her. "But it's not a conversation for birthdays." Or ever.

"Oh." She nodded slowly. "Right."

We passed the rest of the blocks in an awkward silence that I loathed. Everything with Izzy had always been . . . easy, and I'd just put up a barrier. It was for the best. I didn't want the ugliness of what went on over there to touch her in any way. But I felt that wall I'd erected like a tangible fence between us as we made our way into the apartment.

I followed her into the kitchen, and she dropped her purse on the counter, grabbing the box we'd carried home from the bakery earlier.

"Cupcake?" She put the box on the counter, then braced her hands and hopped up to sit next to it, her feet swinging gently. "I always like sugar with my movies." Flicking open the box top, she revealed the ten cupcakes we hadn't eaten earlier.

Taking the olive branch, I leaned in to see what we had left.

"You don't seem like a vanilla guy," she teased, looking over the contents. "Maybe a carrot cake one?"

I shook my head, a smile tugging at my mouth. "Those were always Torres's favorites. I swear, he had one every day for an entire year. I can't stand the smell of them anymore." It took me a second to realize she'd stopped breathing. "Izzy?" My gaze shot to hers.

"Torres. That's your best friend, right?" Fear widened her eyes.

"Yeah. One of them." I nodded, my brow furrowing at the look on her face.

"Oh, no. Did he . . . while you were gone . . ." She pressed her lips in a tight line, and the pieces clicked for me.

"No, Iz. No. He's not dead." I shook my head and squeezed her knee in reassurance. "He just had to give up the carrot cake cupcakes when he decided to go for Special Forces selection." He'd spent the last few months trying to talk me into it, too, since I'd been wavering during the deployment.

Her entire body relaxed. "Okay. That's a relief."

"Fitz died, though." I took the one that looked like lemon, making sure there was another just like it before lifting it from the box. Fitz would have gone for the chocolate. I breathed through the stab of pain I recognized as grief, then shoved it in the box with everything else.

"What?"

Shit. I should *not* have said that.

I paused in peeling the wrapper from the cake and found her staring at me. "Fitz. You met him—"

"On Tybee. I remember," she whispered. "He . . . died?"

I nodded. "About a month in. There was a firefight—" My mouth snapped shut. Those were the things I deliberately kept separate, and here I was, shattering the only peace I had.

"Nate, I'm so sorry," she whispered, lifting her hand to my shoulder.

"Don't be." I continued peeling the wrapper, concentrating on the sight of the cake and blinking away the memory of the blood pumping out of Fitz's body. "You didn't kill him." The subject had to change immediately. "Which flavor is your favorite?"

Silence stretched between us.

I looked up and found her watching me with a look I'd never seen before. She looked like she didn't know what to say or how to act, like I'd destroyed the ease between us for the second time that night. "Which is your favorite?" I asked again. "Movie time, remember?"

"Red velvet," she answered, slowly taking one of those.

I put my cupcake down and then helped her off the counter, even though I knew she didn't need it. Her curves slid against me as I lowered her to the ground, setting my body on fire, but the way her eyes darkened was even hotter.

We stood there for a long moment, my hands on her waist as she stared up at me, color rising in her cheeks, her chest rising and falling a little faster.

"Movie," I reminded her—reminded myself.

"Right." She drew her tongue across her bottom lip, and I bit back a groan. "Prepare for greatness," she said and led me to the couch. She rested her head on my shoulder, and I savored the absolute peace.

I hadn't ruined everything by keeping her out.

Two hours later, she looked up at me with expectation as the credits rolled. "What did you think?"

"I think it's bullshit that they only got to see each other at dawn and sunset." I glared at the screen.

"They win in the end," she replied with a laugh, tucking one leg under her and turning to face me on the couch, her knee brushing my thigh.

"Doesn't mean the years they spent like that weren't bullshit." I shook my head.

"Aw, Nate." She grinned, taking my face in her hands and pulling my attention from the credits. "You're a romantic at heart."

I scoffed. "I've been accused of a lot of things, Isabeau. Being romantic isn't one of them." There were only two people in the world I even remotely softened for. She just happened to be one of them.

Her gazed dropped to my mouth, and I fisted the cushion by her side to keep my hands from reaching for her. "You know what I've decided?"

"What?" My palms itched to feel the curves of her body.

She leaned into my space until her lips were only a matter of inches from mine.

Fuck, I was going to *break*. I could already taste her, already hear the little gasps she made between kisses. The memory of her had been my constant companion these last nine months.

"Fiji," she whispered against my lips.

"I'm sorry?" The blood had definitely fled my brain.

"Fiji." Her smile was contagious as she swung one knee over and settled into my lap, straddling me. "That's where we should go for vacation. It's warm. It has sandy beaches. It's remote, so you won't worry about crowds."

"I like beaches." The last time I'd been on one had been with her. My hands rose to her hips as arousal hummed through me.

"Good. Then Fiji it is." She ran her fingers through my hair, and I leaned into her touch. Her lips ghosted across mine. "You can kiss me in the water."

Yep. I was done for. The strands of my good intentions were unraveling by the second. It was all I could do to keep from flipping her back to the couch.

"Nate?" Her lips blatantly teased mine.

"Hmm?"

"I'm going to kiss you now."

They were the same words I'd said to her back in Georgia, but fuck me if they didn't sound a million times sexier coming out of her mouth.

I kissed her first and groaned when she opened for me. She was so damned sweet, her tongue rubbing against mine as I relearned every line of her mouth. Kissing her was just as explosive as I remembered, and a thousand times more addictive.

My fingers speared through her hair as I tilted our heads for the perfect angle, the kiss spinning out of control. Her breasts pressed against my chest. Her hips rocked over mine. Her breath became my own. This was exactly where I belonged, wherever she was.

The connection between us was as undefinable as it was undeniable.

"I'd almost forgotten how good at this we are," she said between kisses.

"I thought about it every single day." I angled her hips and rolled mine so she could feel exactly what I was thinking right now.

"I missed you." She kissed my jaw, my neck, as her hands swept down my arms, then my torso. "And I know I shouldn't have. That it's completely illogical—"

I fisted my hand in her hair and brought her mouth back to mine, using my lips and tongue to tell her that I felt the exact same way. My fingers drifted from her hip to the small of her back, slipping under her shirt to stroke the hollow of her spine.

She gasped at the light touch, and I swallowed the sound.

"I bet you're sensitive like this everywhere, aren't you?" I asked, trailing my fingers up and down the smooth skin of her back.

"Why don't you find out?" Her hands worked at her waist and her blouse fell open to the sides, revealing a pale-blue lace bra that cupped her breasts with an expertise that made my mouth water.

"Fuck." The word escaped as a guttural groan. "You are so goddamn perfect, Isabeau."

"Touch me."

She didn't have to tell me twice. My hands stroked up her sides, caressing the dip of her waist, and then up and over her ribs before cupping her breasts over the lace. She was more than enough to fill my hands. "See? Perfect."

She laughed, then kissed me, and I lost myself—and every good intention I'd had—in the taste of her mouth, the sound of her little moans, the feel of her nipples hardening beneath the fabric under the stroke of my thumbs.

I licked and sucked a path down her throat and across her collarbone, then grasped her ass with one hand and lifted her slightly so my teeth could test the buds of her nipples. The lace was too thick for what I needed, what I craved. I tugged one cup down and savored the sound of her soft cry as I sucked the peak into my mouth.

"Nate!" Her fingernails bit into my shoulders.

My dick strained at my zipper, but I was thankful for the barrier. It kept me in check as I moved to the other breast, exposing it so I could give it the same treatment. "So sensitive," I said against her skin as she shuddered.

"Or maybe I only respond like this for you," she replied, her voice all breathy and sexy as hell.

I didn't want anyone else touching her like this.

Mine. Fate, God, whatever energy ruled the universe had brought her to me. And she. Was. Mine.

Except she wasn't. There was a reason we shouldn't be doing this, but I couldn't remember what it was.

I shoved that thought aside, kissing her deep, then banding my arm around her back and flipping us so she was underneath me. Bad idea. My hips settled into the cradle of hers like they'd been created to fit mine.

Her hands stroked down my back, then tugged up my shirt and took the same path along my bare skin. My common sense fled as I rocked against her, eliciting the sweetest moan I'd ever heard.

"Again," she demanded, sliding her hands to my ass.

I pressed a hot kiss to her throat and gave her what we both wanted. White-hot need raced down my spine. Kissing her felt like I was sixteen again, with no control, no experience, just blind, primal want.

"Tell me what you need," I said between kisses as I moved down her neck to her breasts, flicking my tongue over the peaks one at a time.

"I want you to touch me," she said, arching up for my mouth as I rolled my hips against hers again. There was too much space between us. Too many clothes. Which was a good thing . . . if I could just remember *why*.

"Tell me how." I wanted the words as I pressed my mouth to the sensitive skin beneath her breasts and then the hollow just under her ribs, where her stomach planed, kissing every line of the scars from the plane crash.

"Or you could tell me how you *want* to touch me," she challenged, smiling even as her back bowed the closer I got to the button of her jeans.

I lifted my head and met her gaze. "I want to unzip your pants and slide my fingers between these sweet thighs to see just how wet you are for me."

Her lips parted and her eyes glazed.

"And then I want to dip those fingers inside you so I can stroke and tease." My hand moved across the waistband of her jeans, and I watched her for any sign of hesitation. "But I'm going to need you to tell me that's what you want." Her dilated pupils and stuttered breaths weren't enough.

I wasn't going to screw this up over a lack of clear communication or push her further than she wanted to go.

"That's exactly what I want," she said, covering my hand with hers and putting it right over the button.

Fuck yes.

Eyes locked with hers, I flicked open the button and drew the zipper down.

She nodded, tugging her lower lip between her teeth.

The motion snapped my self-control, and I rose up over her, sucking the tender curve free, then kissing her breathless. She sucked my tongue into her mouth as my fingers slid under the lace of her underwear, and I groaned.

She felt like heaven, hot, slick, and softer than satin.

"You're so fucking wet that you could take all of me in a single thrust." I circled her clit with my middle finger, and her back bowed again.

"Nate!" She pushed her hips against my hand.

The sound of my name like that on her lips made my dick throb.

Make her do it again.

"So hot," I whispered with another kiss, sliding a finger inside her. "I bet you'd burn me alive." It would be a hell of a way to go.

I trembled like a teenager at the feel of her heat, the way her muscles clamped down tight around my finger as I stroked in and out as I watched her, cataloging exactly what made her gasp, and what made her hips swivel for more.

"Oh my God," she moaned, her fingers digging into my back with a bite of pleasure when I pumped a second finger into her, wishing it was my cock.

I wasn't a stranger to lust, but this was something else entirely. I'd never lived for the sound of a woman's gasp, never had my next breath depend on hers, never been so focused on her pleasure that mine didn't matter. My world narrowed to Izzy. I didn't just want her to come; I *needed* her to.

My thumb stroked her clit, working her relentlessly as my fingers curled after every thrust, hitting over and over at the spot that made her hips jerk upward and her breath catch.

"Beautiful, Isabeau." I kissed her softly as her thighs locked, then quivered. "You're so beautiful." It only took a little more pressure from my thumb, and she danced to the edge of her orgasm. I felt it in her quick inhales, the squeeze of her inner muscles around my fingers, and the tightening of her body under mine.

"Nate . . ." She rocked back into my fingers, riding my hand, seeking out what she needed, and I pressed my dick into her thigh to keep from stripping off what clothes she had left and taking her.

I couldn't take her.

She'd never forgive me because she didn't know—

Her back bowed and she cried out as she came, her walls fluttering against my fingers, her back arching over and over.

Watching her come undone and knowing I'd been the one to take her there was the highlight of my entire fucking life.

I buried my face in her neck, kissing her soft skin and inhaling the sweet scent of her perfume as I eased her down. Only when she fell limp underneath me did I slide my fingers from the warmth of her body and kiss her mouth one last time before sitting up.

I'd remembered exactly why going any further would make me an asshole.

She looked at me through hazy eyes and sat up with me, reaching for my jeans.

"We can't." I flew off the couch like it was on fire and nearly tripped over the coffee table. *Smooth.*

"Why not?" She arched a brow and glanced meaningfully at my dick. "I'm not blind, and you clearly want to."

"Trust me, I want to. That's not the problem." I shook my head. The knowledge that I was about to disappoint her was all that held me back. She deserved so much more than someone who flew in and out of her life like a hurricane. She deserved someone who could give her everything.

"Is it because I suggested Fiji?" she asked, and it took every ounce of self-control I'd ever had, or ever would have, to keep my eyes on her face, and not her bare breasts rising above her bra.

"No. I would love to go to Fiji with you." Damn it, I could still taste her skin, and I was pretty sure that for the rest of my life, I'd be instantly hard the second I smelled her perfume.

"Okay, then what's wrong?"

I looked into those big, brown eyes and debated lying, preserving the tiny breath of happiness that existed in this moment, but I just couldn't. "I can't go until 2017."

She clutched the sides of her shirt and tied it, covering her incredible body. "Because you don't have time? Do you need to go home instead? Because I get it if you need to see your mom."

"No." I shook my head. "She actually flew out when I got home a couple days ago." Besides, Mom knew that as much as I loved her, I wasn't ever going back there while he could still breathe. "We can't do this because as much as I would love for now to be the right time for us, it isn't."

"It isn't?" She drew her knees to her chest, and my stomach twisted.

"It can't be. I'm on orders to a new post. Three months from now, I'll be stationed at Joint Base Lewis-McChord. It's in Washington State."

"That's not the Washington I was hoping for." Her shoulders slumped, and she tucked her long blonde hair behind her ears.

"Yeah." I swallowed. "I wasn't going to tell you on your birthday, not that . . ." Fuck. What was I trying to say? "Not that it should bother you—"

"Of course it bothers me that you're being sent across the damned country." She stood, wrapping her arms around her waist. "And I know that I don't have a right to expect anything—you were really clear in Savannah that we're not together—but I was hoping . . ." Her eyes closed, and she blew out a long, frustrated sigh. "I don't know what I was hoping."

"I do." I moved toward her and cradled her face with my hands. "I was hoping I'd be a hell of a lot closer to you than twenty-eight hundred miles. I'd hoped that we could actually be more than a possibility."

She lifted her hand to my chest. "Me too."

There it was. Everything that needed to be said and everything we couldn't.

"How long will you be there?" she asked.

"Probably three years," I said as softly as possible.

Her breath caught, and the war of emotions that waged in her eyes was enough to crumple my chest. "Three years."

"And that's not all." Shit. I'd avoided this since I'd walked through that door, and yet here I was, walking right into it. "The unit I'm headed to is already on the patch chart for rotation in a few months. Another deployment." I could barely get the words out when it looked like each one sliced her to the quick.

"You're . . ." Her lower lip trembled. "You're going back?"

I ran my thumb across her lips and tried to ignore the crushing feeling in the center of my chest. "I'm always going back, Isabeau. They're just shorter, more frequent deployments, as long as we don't get extended. You're in law school. You have more important things to focus on than someone who can barely get within three thousand miles of you on a regular basis."

"And we agreed not to start something long distance." A sad smile lifted the corners of her mouth. "We've already covered that topic once."

"Right. I won't do that to you. Even when I'll be in the States, I'll probably be at some school or another for professional development. All we'd ever have are weekends." Weekends I would live for, but I wouldn't accept the same for her.

"Maybe I could do weekends." Her hand fisted in my shirt.

"Until you couldn't. Until we couldn't. Until it got to be something that broke us both. The last nine months felt like an eternity. I missed you every single second of every single day, Izzy, and we weren't even in a relationship. Imagine what three *years* would feel like." I leaned down, putting my forehead against hers. "We'd kill the possibility of us before we even had a shot at succeeding. I don't want to waste our shot by taking it before we're ready."

"So why even come here?" she asked quietly, her eyes searching mine.

"Because I couldn't stay away." The truth of it was simple, and yet it complicated everything.

"And is this what you want for us?" One of her hands slid up to hold the back of my neck. "To be what? Pen pals? Friends? You want me to date other guys while you date other girls?"

My jaw ticked. "Of course that's not what I want," I somehow managed to say. She'd told me all about the guys she'd dated while I was gone. All law students. All here. All infinitely more capable of making her happy. "But that's where we are. I want you to live, Izzy. I want you to go to class and get excited for your Friday nights. I want you to smile and laugh and not spend your months locked away in your room, waiting for me. It would kill me to watch you waste your life like that. I want us to get the shot we deserve, which means we both have to agree the timing is right, and it's just . . . not. Not yet."

"Have you thought about getting out?" The question was barely a whisper and only words away from a request.

"And do what?" I lifted my head.

"Oh, I don't know." She shrugged, her smile anything but happy. "You said on the plane that you wanted to teach."

That dream felt a lifetime away.

"We could move someplace where we could watch pine trees sway," she continued. "Like a ski resort. Or one of those towers where you watch the wilderness for fires."

"Because that's a good use of your education," I teased.

"Come on. Play along." She tugged at my shirt and looked at me with pleading eyes. "Just pretend with me for a minute."

I dropped my hands to her waist and tugged her against me, then ignored the pulsing of my dick, which hadn't given up hope that I'd change my mind. I wouldn't.

She meant more to me than a single night, and I was in this for the long haul. The far-distant long haul.

"We could open a restaurant." I grinned.

"Can you cook?" she asked.

"No." My shoulders shook with wry laughter.

"I can make a mean grilled cheese."

I kissed her forehead. "Then there you go. We'll open a grilled cheese restaurant."

She laughed, shaking her head. "Come on. Let's go to bed."

Going to sleep meant we'd be hours closer to me leaving.

"I'm so sorry to ruin your birthday," I whispered. "That was never my intention."

She gestured at the clock on the wall. "It's eleven thirty, which means it's still salvageable if you agree to come to bed with me. Even if it's just to sleep."

"Just to sleep," I repeated, knowing that lying next to her was only going to result in a sleepless night where I imagined acting out every fantasy I'd had over the last nine months. It sounded like the most exquisite form of torture, and I was down for it.

She backed away slowly.

I followed.

CHAPTER SEVENTEEN

NATHANIEL

Kabul, Afghanistan
August 2021

"You going to hide in here all morning?" Torres asked, leaning against the door with one ankle crossed over the other.

"It's only seven a.m., and I'm not hiding." I turned the page in my book and ignored him, leaning back against my headboard, my legs stretched out in front of me.

"Looks like hiding to me."

I wasn't hiding. I was already dressed, armed, and ready. I just wasn't on shift. Graham was, and he was fully capable of handling a little shadowing while Izzy and Dickface ate breakfast.

"Don't you have something better to do?" I asked Torres, picking up the highlighter from my nightstand and marking a line, pausing halfway through. Not that I was ever going to give the book to Izzy. There were at least a few dozen of these already, all marked up and boxed. *Old habits die hard and whatnot.*

"Hey, I'm only in here because apparently you can't get your shit together." He shrugged. "Otherwise, you'd already be out there, trying to talk her out of going to Kandahar."

"My shit is just fine." I read the same paragraph twice before I gave up and closed the book. "And I'm realizing that it's not my job to talk her out of anything. She has someone for that."

Dickface. She was marrying *Dickface*. After everything he'd put her through, she'd still said yes to him, still put his ring on her left hand.

I rubbed my chest, right above my sternum, and felt my little good luck charm shift on the chain against my skin. It was far past time that I left it at home, that I recognized it for the bad omen it really was, but every time I took it off, I put the thing right back on.

"Yeah. Looks like you're squared away." Torres rolled his eyes. "Swear to God, nothing fucks you up more than that woman."

"She's not fucking me up." I turned the page with more force than necessary.

"Maybe that's the problem, then." He pushed away from the door and walked across the room. "When's the last time you two were in the same space and didn't wind up in bed?"

I put my book down on the nightstand, since reading was futile when Torres got into my head like this. "New York."

"Yeah, that's what I thought." He rubbed the back of his neck. "Do you need to bring Jenkins in to take over?"

"No." As pissed as I was, as disappointed as I was that Izzy had *settled*, that didn't mean I wasn't going to see the mission through, or put her in a position where she could be hurt.

Someone pounded on my door.

I muttered a curse and swung my legs off the bed as I rose to answer it. When I pulled the door open, Graham stood on the other side.

Torres slid out, walking into the hallway. "Good, now he can deal with your moody ass."

"There's new intel," Graham said, his face tight. "We're briefing."

"Let's go." I slung my rifle over my shoulder and closed the door behind me. Guess it was time to face reality and Dickface.

Maybe I *had* been hiding.

A half hour later, we were briefed, and I stopped avoiding Izzy and sought her out instead. Under any other circumstances, I wouldn't blink over being in a rapidly deteriorating country where my only mission was to get out as many Americans as possible.

But these weren't normal circumstances. I had Izzy to think about.

I walked through the crowded foyer of the embassy and stepped into the conference room the congressional teams had commandeered, passing by Parker, who stood guard at the door. It took me all of two seconds to find Izzy in the organized chaos of the room.

She stood in the far corner, a telephone held between her shoulder and ear as the assistants moved files at the edge of the long table. One of them nearly knocked a laptop off the surface. Guess we weren't the only ones on edge.

After making a quick sweep to make sure Dickface wasn't on premises, I headed toward Izzy. She was dressed in navy-blue slacks and a blouse that was a lighter shade, her hair in a low bun that looked like it might survive a helmet.

Because wearing a helmet was the only way I was letting her out of this building.

"Of course it's no bother," she said into the phone, double taking when she saw me approaching. "You're the one up in the middle of the night."

Her eyes were slightly red, and not the I-stayed-up-all-night-being-brought-to-orgasm-again-and-again variety of red I was achingly familiar with when it came to her. She'd done a good job with her makeup, too, but the skin beneath the brown orbs was swollen. She'd been crying. She tilted her chin and held my gaze, as if she was daring me to say something about it.

"Absolutely, Senator Lauren," she continued.

"We have to talk," I said, keeping my voice low so the senator wouldn't hear.

Izzy sighed. "I think there may be some security concerns," she said into the phone. "The head of our detail needs a word with me."

I nodded.

"I'll ask." She covered the microphone. "Is today's mission at direct risk?"

"You being in this country is a risk. Three more provinces fell yesterday."

Her eyes widened, and her knuckles whitened on the phone.

"Not Balkh Province," I reassured her. "Mazar-i-Sharif is still standing."

She let out a breath of relief and uncovered the microphone. "Senator, we seem to have an issue. If you don't mind holding, we'll get to somewhere more private."

Izzy motioned toward the door, and I nodded, leading her out of the conference room and into a nearby empty office. I cleared the room with a quick look, then locked the door behind us as Izzy set her phone on the cluttered desk, tapping the speakerphone button.

"We have you on speakerphone, Senator Lauren, but it's just Sergeant Green and me in this room," Izzy said, folding her arms across her chest. Something was off about the motion, but I couldn't put my finger on it.

"Sergeant Green, I understand that you're my team's security lead?" the senator asked, her voice surprisingly alert for it being nearly midnight in DC.

"I am, ma'am."

"What can you tell me about the safety of Isa's planned trip to Kandahar today?" she asked.

For a split second, I pretended that the woman in front of me wasn't Izzy, that she was just another aide on just another mission. But she wasn't. "Kandahar is concerning. The city's been under siege for months, and hasn't fallen *yet*, but all civilians were asked to evacuate six days ago, and the airport is under constant threat. I'm not in favor of taking Ms. Astor into that kind of environment. The team's visas are here, and as far as I know, the plan is for them to be evac'd tomorrow by the Afghan Air Force. I see no reason for the trip, honestly. Yes, it would be a great photo op, but she can take the photo tomorrow, once they arrive in Kabul. Delivering the visas in person places Ms. Astor in unnecessary danger."

Izzy shifted her weight and leaned against the cleanest edge of the desk. "I don't mind the danger."

"I certainly do," the senator replied. "And it complicates what I need to tell you."

I tensed at the tone in the senator's voice.

"We received a call this evening from the coach, and it seems they're not comfortable with the evacuation plan."

Izzy's brow knit. "They're not?"

"No. They're saying that given the status of the city, they don't trust any of the men claiming to be Afghan Air Force, who are, of course, coordinating the trip."

"Fuck," I muttered under my breath, rubbing the bridge of my nose.

Izzy chastised me with a single look. "I see."

"Newcastle asked them what would make them comfortable enough to leave and mentioned that you're in country, thinking it would give them some reassurance," the senator continued.

I stopped myself from cursing again, knowing exactly where this conversation was bound to lead.

"They said they'll only trust you, Isa."

Damn it. I hated it when I was right.

"Oh." Izzy gripped the edge of the desk. "Because they don't trust the air force?"

"They don't trust them to be who they say they are," I said. "Unfortunately, that's a common problem. I assume the team is in hiding in case the city falls?"

"They are," Izzy replied. "They were supposed to be moved—"

"To the airport today to evac tomorrow," I finished. "That's why they were meeting you there for visas."

Izzy nodded.

My mind went to work. "If I can get a female operator to take Ms. Astor's place, would that be sufficient?"

Izzy shook her head even as Senator Lauren said, "No, I'm afraid not."

"We had Skype calls as part of the planning," Izzy said. "They know what I look like."

Silence filled the office.

"Isa, I'm not going to ask you to put yourself in danger to get those girls—" the senator started.

"We can't just leave them there," Izzy interrupted, her gaze locking with mine.

"Can it be done safely . . . I'm sorry, I don't know your first name," the senator said.

"That's intentional, ma'am." I glanced at the framed map of Afghanistan on the wall, thinking about the security briefing, the threat assessments, and the girls whose only crimes would be their intelligence and education. "There are six of them?"

"And their parents," Izzy supplied. "A few siblings too."

I nodded. "The Kandahar airport is currently being held by Afghan special ops. If we can get the team to the airport and luck out with a secure landing zone—understanding we'd spend as little time as possible on the ground—it can be done." I'd hate every minute of it, but we could do it.

"With minimal danger to Ms. Astor and American lives?" the senator asked.

"Respectfully, ma'am, there's no such thing as minimal danger in this country right now, but those girls will be in considerable danger if they stay where they are."

"Isa? I'd never demand you risk your life."

"I know." Izzy swallowed and moved to tuck her hair behind her ears, even though the strands were already secured in a bun. She was nervous.

"Today is the only day," I said. "The rate this country is falling, Kabul is going to fall within the next month—if not faster—and I honestly don't know how much longer Kandahar has."

"Intelligence reports said we had six to twelve months," Senator Lauren said softly.

"Things change, ma'am."

"We'll go today." Izzy straightened her shoulders. "I'll call Coach Niaz. I have her number." After exchanging a few more pleasantries and well wishes, she ended the call.

"You have an hour to say your goodbyes to Dickface, and then we need to leave," I said, walking out of the office and leaving Izzy behind.

Guess we were going to Kandahar.

We left every other member of Izzy's delegation and flew out three hours later with the three operators on my team and four others, since none of the other congressional aides were leaving the embassy today. Our fleet of four Blackhawks launched, and I still wished we had more firepower.

Izzy sat across from me just like every other flight, looking out the window, and I handed over my earbuds and phone, but didn't put them into her ears like before. I took out my book and blatantly looked away before Izzy could reject my offer.

After seeing Covington in the hallway last night, I wasn't sure how I'd react if Izzy once again reminded me that whatever I had wasn't good enough.

She'd been able to get ahold of Coach Niaz, and the chess team was currently en route to the airport. They were just as skittish as the senator had implied, and I couldn't blame them. With any luck, we'd be on the ground for less than an hour, and out again before the Taliban knew we were even around to mortar.

That didn't stop my pulse from rising the closer we got to Kandahar.

I stowed my book as we landed and slung my rucksack over my shoulders, tucking my phone and earbuds into one of the pockets of my uniform when Izzy handed them back. The distance between us was palpable, painful, and necessary. Dickface's arrival had been a much-needed reminder that the ring on her finger meant something.

The helicopters ran down as we all filed out.

This wasn't the first time I'd been to Kandahar's airport, but it very well might have been the last. The destruction from the reported shelling was obvious in the broken decorative arches and piles of rubble lined against the barbed wire fence. The runway was damaged too.

The sun beat into my bare forearms as we moved as a team, walking quickly toward the terminal, where our liaison from the Afghan army would meet us. I kept Izzy at my side and my eyes moving, taking in every detail of our surroundings, and Graham covering our six.

An Afghan officer waited at the end of the walkway connecting the tarmac to the terminal, escorted by six of his own soldiers. They looked like they'd been through hell and dragged back again.

"Twelve inches," I said to Izzy once the noise of the rotors had faded enough to hear myself.

"Not quite," she shot back quietly, clutching the strap of her messenger bag.

"Smart-ass," I muttered. "Twelve inches is the maximum distance you're allowed to be from me while we're here."

"You don't trust the Afghan forces?" she asked quietly.

"Some of them, absolutely." I kept my hands on my rifle. "But I didn't live this long by trusting anyone I don't personally know." And I wasn't trusting *anyone* with her.

"Noted." She glanced at me once we were halfway down the path. "And what if I have to pee? Does your twelve-inches rule apply then?"

"I'll be happy to hand you the toilet paper."

"Graphic." Her nose crinkled.

"You're the one that went there. We'll only be here for an hour, remember? Hold it."

We made it to our liaison, and I shook the young captain's hand while the others kept their hands on their weapons. "Are the evacuees ready?"

"They arrived about thirty minutes ago," he said, leading us into the terminal. Two of our operators hung back to secure the entrance and recon. "We might be losing the edges of the city, but we still hold the airport road."

"That's good to hear." If they lost that, there would be no evacuation route for anyone in the city. We were officially surrounded.

The air-conditioning was still working, which was a welcome relief. The floor and chairs were covered with dust, and two of the windows in my line of sight had been boarded up.

Izzy lifted her hand to the strap under her chin.

"Leave it on."

"It might scare the girls if I walk in dressed like we might be bombed at any moment," she whispered.

"I highly doubt they'd expect anything different." We passed by gathered groups of both military and civilians waiting for evacuation. "You might be forgetting that children here aren't strangers to war like American kids. The helmet stays on."

"Are you going to be this pleasant the entire trip?" She arched a brow but kept up with me step for step.

"Yes."

"This looks good," Graham said, motioning to an area on the right.

I looked at his recommendation—rows of chairs that formed what had been an exclusive-looking waiting area. No boarded-up windows. Glass that could be blasted open if we needed out. A direct line to the tarmac and our birds. It was exposed for a quick exit, but defensible, and we could control the environment. "This will do," I told the Afghan officer. "Please bring the evacuees here."

"We have them waiting—"

"Here," I said in a tone that didn't leave any room for argument.

He glanced out the window, toward our helicopters, and nodded, then, in Pashto, ordered two of his soldiers to escort the chess team to us.

The other operators spread out for an efficient perimeter.

"They'll be here momentarily," the captain said in English. "Is there anything else we can do?"

"No, thank you," I replied. "I'm sure you have way more important things to be doing."

"Indeed, I do." He shook my hand again and walked off, leaving two of his soldiers behind with us.

Izzy and I stood in the middle of the waiting area. "He sent the soldiers to go get them? You're sure?"

I nodded. "I speak Pashto."

"Of course you do." She shook her head. "Is that another new development?"

"No." I scanned our surroundings, not entirely at ease. I knew we should be safe here, but Izzy would be a fantastic and expensive trophy for our enemies.

"Just something else you didn't tell me." Her tone was low but cutting.

"The number of languages I speak didn't seem like worthwhile space in a letter, and I never wanted to waste your time. But apparently you—" I locked my jaw to still my words. This wasn't the time or the place to get into it with her.

She glanced up at me, her eyes narrowing. "Just say it."

I shook my head.

"I know you're pissed about Jeremy. I saw the disappointment in your eyes. I know you well enough to read your emotions, Sergeant Green. At least I used to." She crossed her arms over her chest and drummed her fingers on her arm.

"You have no idea what I think about Dickface."

"Like the nickname isn't a dead giveaway." Her fingers moved faster.

Anger welled up, overruling my common sense. "He fucking left you at Georgetown," I said as quietly as possible.

"He did."

"He forced you to graduate early, leave your friends, and enroll at a school that wasn't even your first choice, and then he *left you*." I spared a WTF look in her direction.

Torres cocked an eyebrow at me from where he stood at the nearby wall, obviously able to hear us.

"I remember. I was there."

"Yeah, well, I was too." I glanced at the rest of the squad, who were all doing exactly what they were supposed to be. I was the only one engaging in high school behavior and arguing with a woman who wasn't even my ex.

"Get off your high horse. Jeremy's not the only one who disappeared on me at one time."

I ignored the dig because it was true. But she'd obviously forgiven him, and I'd gotten the opposite treatment. "When did you two get back together? Before New York?" It would have explained everything.

"No!" she hissed. "Not until I went to DC. My parents took me out to lunch, and he was there with his family . . ." She sighed. "I don't owe you an explanation."

"You don't," I agreed. "And no explanation he could give would be sufficient. You deserve so much . . . more."

Her head whipped toward mine, and three things happened at once.

I finally figured out what was bothering me about the way she'd been holding her hands all day. It wasn't her hands. It was what *wasn't* on her hand—her engagement ring.

The chess team came down the corridor, escorted by the Afghan soldiers.

And the runway exploded.

CHAPTER EIGHTEEN

IZZY

Georgetown
December 2016

If it was nine a.m. here, then it was six thirty p.m. in Afghanistan, which meant maybe I was actually eating at the same time Nate was. Of course, he'd be having dinner, and I was fiddling around with a stack of pancakes, but still, it was kind of like we were eating together.

"Which is why she's specializing in charity work. Aren't you, Izzy?" Serena's tone demanded my attention.

I blinked, looking up from my breakfast plate, and found Serena arching an eyebrow at me from across the diner table.

"Right. Yes. Exactly," I agreed. This was supposed to be a double date, and I wasn't holding up my end of the deal. I glanced from Serena's current boyfriend, Ramon, to the friend he'd brought for me.

Shit. What was his name? Sam? Sandy? Shane? Something with an *S*. It wasn't that he wasn't cute. He had nice brown eyes, smooth bronzed skin, and a handsome smile. It was just . . .

I was hopeless.

"I love that you're focused on charity," he said, offering me a toothy smile.

"And you?" See? I could keep the conversation going.

His dark brows knit. "I'm in tech, remember?"

Serena kicked me under the table.

"Of course!" I shot my sister a glare. "I just meant where you saw yourself taking your career in that particular industry."

"Oh." He smiled again. "I'm really focusing on the financial market, and how to make banking more accessible in remote locations . . ."

Remote locations like where Nate was. My thoughts drowned out his monologue.

God, what was wrong with me? It had been months since I'd been able to maintain a relationship, and here I was again, choosing the *thought* of Nate over an actual guy. Maybe that was what had gone wrong with Nate's last relationship too. He'd been seeing someone for a couple of months there, and for a minute, I'd wondered if we'd actually take the trip we'd booked to Fiji in June. And fine, I'd been jealous too. Super healthy.

Our letters had shifted to emails in the eighteen months it had been since I'd seen him, and even those had been less frequent since he'd deployed yet again. I'd lost track of which number this was.

My phone buzzed on the table, and Serena tilted her head at me as I picked it up to check for a text. Nope, just an email. I had Google Alerts set up to send once a week, and it was just this week's articles.

But it wasn't. My heart stumbled at the subject line.

Nathaniel Phelan.

I stopped breathing and stabbed at the smooth surface of the phone like it would make the application open faster. He was fine. He had to be fine. Him not being fine wasn't an option. And yet I couldn't breathe.

As I clicked the link, a dull roar filled my ears as an obituary site loaded.

No.

My world couldn't exist without him in it somewhere.

I blinked as the article appeared. *Alice Marie Phelan.* I skimmed the obituary, my stomach lurching three-quarters through. *Survived by her husband David and only son, Nathaniel.*

Nate's mom died. According to the obituary, her funeral, a graveside service, was at four p.m. today.

He was going to be devastated.

"I have to go." I grabbed a twenty out of my purse and threw it on the table, already running for the door before Serena could even call my name.

At 3:44 p.m. that afternoon, I stumbled out of the car I'd rented at the smallest airport I'd ever seen and popped open the umbrella I'd brought with me. I'd only had an hour to get changed in the only available hotel room in town—which had also been the most expensive—but at least I'd had a black dress in my closet ready to pack in my carry-on. Getting a flight out? Now that had been . . . tricky. But I'd made it.

I would have thought that December in Illinois meant snow, but freezing-cold rain pelted the umbrella as I rounded the front of the sedan and stepped into the cemetery. My heart pounded as I headed for the small crowd gathered nearby, my heels sticking into the brown grass with every step.

My phone buzzed in my pocket, and I fumbled getting it out of my jacket. A text previewed on the screen.

MOM: Serena said you ran out of breakfast this morning?

She chose *now* to be concerned?

I shook my head and shoved my phone back into my pocket.

People moved forward, and I followed the sea of umbrellas, eventually reaching the back row of what looked to be a split configuration of about three dozen folding chairs set up at the edge of the last row of tombstones.

I glimpsed brightly colored wreaths and an elevated closed casket under a wide green canopy ahead of the chairs as the crowd continued to shuffle its way down the aisle, some taking seats on either side and some continuing on, only to turn at the end and loop back around.

They were paying their respects to the family.

My stomach churned with nausea, and I strangled the umbrella handle as I considered for the first time that I might have made a mistake. I'd been so concerned with trying to get here in time that I hadn't considered that maybe I *shouldn't* be here.

There was every chance Nate wouldn't want me here, every chance that he already *had* someone here. It wasn't like he'd called me.

Or maybe Nate himself wouldn't be here, and I was walking into a crowd of complete strangers.

Either way, I wasn't sure I'd be welcome.

Maybe just picking a seat was my best option.

My pocket buzzed again, and I yanked my phone free. Another text came across the home screen.

MOM: ISABEAU ASTOR, you'd better answer me NOW.

MOM: Do not make me send people to look for you!

I typed out a quick response.

ISABEAU: My friend Nate's mom died. I'm at the funeral. TTYL.

I shoved the phone back into my pocket and hoped that would be enough to keep her from freaking out.

"Damn shame," a woman behind me said. "Alice really was an angel."

"That curve has always been dangerous. Carl told me the tire tracks showed the Marshall boy was on her side of the road," another added, her voice lowering as we passed the third row of water-covered seats. "Hit her head on."

She'd been killed in a car accident.

"Look at those two," the first woman said with a sigh. "They can't even stand next to each other up there."

I glanced over my shoulder as discreetly as possible and saw a woman with a lone streak of gray in her auburn hair leaning to the right and looking past me.

"You and I both know that boy hasn't been home since he left for the army," the friend responded. "Always was a wild one."

"Can you blame him after the way David . . ." She trailed off. "Well, none of us really did anything for him, did we?"

I leaned to the right, searching past the half-dozen people ahead of me.

And I saw him.

My chest threatened to cave in, but I forced myself to breathe. Nate stood stoically at the edge of the canopy at the end of the aisle, rain falling ceaselessly, soaking into his hair and black trench coat. He nodded at something the woman in front of him said, then shook the next man's hand as she moved on, turning to the left to do the same with someone I couldn't see.

I couldn't take my eyes off his profile as the line moved steadily onward. He showed no emotion as he greeted each person with the same robotic motions, his head forward, and the vacant expression on his face physically hurt my heart.

The older man ahead of me turned to Nate. "I'm sorry for your loss, son. Your mother was a gem."

"Thank you," Nate answered, shaking the man's hand, but there was no intonation in his voice, no life.

The man turned across the aisle, and I stepped forward into the place he'd vacated, tilting my umbrella backward as I looked up to Nate.

"Isabeau?" His red-rimmed eyes flared as they locked with mine.

"I'm so sorry about your mom, Nate." I lifted my umbrella to cover both of us.

He stared at me in silence for the span of a lengthy heartbeat, then reached for me and tugged me close. His arms banded around my back, and I felt the strain in every tense line of his body as my cheek rested against the chilled, wet lapel of his coat.

"I came as soon as I knew," I whispered.

He must have dipped down, because I felt his chin bob against the top of my head, in front of where I'd pinned my french twist into place. "Thank you."

"I'll see you after," I promised.

"Stay." His arms loosened, and when I moved to step back, he caught my free hand and pulled me to his left side, clasping his frozen fingers with mine before greeting the next mourner.

I held the umbrella over him the best I could. There were only a few people left, but I offered them each what I hoped was an appropriate nod of thanks as they offered condolences for a woman I'd never met.

A woman Nate had loved wholeheartedly.

The last of the crowd passed through as the minister took his place under the canopy, and I faced a man I didn't need to meet in order to know he was Nate's father.

Nate was a few inches taller, but they had the same nose, the same facial structure, and even though his eyes were darker than Nate's, they were infinitely colder as his gaze narrowed on me.

"If we could all be seated," the minister said. "We'll start in just a few minutes."

Nate put himself between his father and me, then took the aisle seat, cringing when I sat on the metal chair next to his. "I'm sorry. You have to be freezing."

"Don't worry about me. I'll be fine." Water soaked into my wool coat as I shuffled the umbrella, trying to keep him covered. He reached across my lap for my hand, and I gave it, holding him tight.

"They only had one canopy," he said, facing the minister. "And I thought she should be the one covered."

"You did great." I rubbed my thumb over his frigid skin, wishing I had another way to warm him.

"How did you know?" He glanced my way.

"I set up a Google Alert for your name," I admitted. "But I set it for weekly. I should have set it to daily, and then I would have known sooner. I would have been here sooner."

"I'm just glad you're here." He squeezed my hand. "And if I'd been able to think about . . . anything for the past week, I probably would have called you, but I don't think I realized how much I wanted you here until I saw you." His gaze shifted forward to the casket. "She was in a car accident and died instantly." His throat worked as he swallowed. "So it's good that she wasn't in pain."

"It is," I agreed, unsure of what to say, or why the chairs beside me were empty. "But I'm still sorry you lost her."

"I can't talk about her. Not up there. Not anywhere. I just can't."

"So don't."

He nodded, and the service began.

It felt short, but I only had my grandparents' to compare it to. Nate's aunts spoke, and his father recited a verse, but Nate shook his head when the minister looked his way. The wind picked up, numbing my face as the service drew to its conclusion.

I stood when Nate did.

Moved when he did.

Went wherever he did.

It was just us and the people I assumed were immediate family by the time the grounds crew was ready to lower Nate's mom into the ground.

Nate's body stiffened as his father approached us next to the casket.

"We're going to have to talk about the farm." His father planted his feet in front of Nate and leaned in. "No more avoiding me, boy."

His tone told me everything I needed to know about their relationship.

"Is there anything you're scared of? There has to be something, right?"

"Sure. Becoming anything like my father."

Wasn't that what Nate had said that day on the beach?

Nate let go of my hand and lifted his arm in front of me, gently pushing me backward.

"Now isn't the time, David," one of the aunts said, the older woman snapping her umbrella closed now that the rain had passed. Her hair was black like Nate's, and the set of her shoulders told me she wasn't a fan of Nate's dad.

I lowered my umbrella, too, pressing the button to close it as the tension thickened.

"When else are we supposed to talk about it?" Nate's dad snapped. "He hasn't said a single word to me since he got home, and we all know he's headed back to Afghanistan tomorrow. Are we going to talk then?"

Tomorrow? My heart sank.

"It's no secret that she left the farm to him," his other aunt said, coming to stand next to her sister. "We've all seen the will."

"It should be mine," his father argued, but Nate didn't move a muscle. "I was her husband." When he couldn't provoke a reaction from Nate, he turned to me. "Maybe your pretty little girlfr—"

"Don't fucking talk to her." Nate took a step forward, simultaneously urging me farther back.

Oh shit. In all my years of knowing Nate, I'd never seen him angry.

"He speaks!" His father threw his hands up like he was thanking God. "You ready to talk about the farm now? It's been my home far longer than yours."

"I have nothing else to say to you." Nate backed up, his arm still extended in front of me, keeping a barrier between his dad and me.

"Or you could just run away like you always do!"

"David!" one of the aunts chided.

"Just stop into the goddamn lawyer's office and sign the deed over to me," his dad commanded, his voice icier than the weather. "It's the least you can do after not bothering to come home and visit her for the last five years."

I gasped.

"Izzy, I'm going to need you to step back," Nate warned, in a low, lethal tone I'd never heard before.

"Nate?" There had to be a way to postpone whatever confrontation was looming until they buried his mother, wasn't there?

"Please." He didn't take his eyes off his father.

I did as he asked, retreating a handful of steps for that very reason. If Nate wouldn't look away from his father, it meant he'd been given grounds not to in the past.

"So nice to everyone but your own damned family." His father glared at Nate. "Just sign the deed and go back to your new and better life. We both know you don't want it, and you sure as hell can't run it."

"You're right. I don't want it. But I'm not signing the farm over to you," Nate replied, his arms loose at his sides.

"So you're just going to kick me out?"

Nate shook his head. "Not yet."

"What the hell is that supposed to mean?" Color flushed his father's cheeks.

"It means that you can live in it for now." Nate shrugged.

"For now?" His brow furrowed, and his hands curled into fists.

My pulse jumped.

"For months. For years. Who knows. But one day I'll sell it." Nate's voice lowered, and even the groundskeepers stopped what they were doing to watch. "And I won't tell you, won't warn you." He shook his head. "No, I want you scared. I want you to wake up every single day and wonder, worry, if today is the day that what you did to her comes back to haunt you. I want you just as anxious as she was every single night, waiting to see what kind of mood you'd be in when you got home, waiting to see if she'd be your punching bag or if you'd reach for me."

My stomach fell to the ground. Nate had boarded our flight with a split lip four years ago. What had he said about the wound? About the split knuckles?

It won't exactly be the first time someone has swung for me, and at least this time I'll be armed. He'd been talking about his father.

"And my biggest regret isn't that I didn't come home to visit," Nate continued. "She knew I'd sworn to never breathe the same air as you ever again. My biggest regret is that I couldn't get her to leave, too, no matter how hard I tried."

"You little shit." His father lunged, and before I could shout, Nate caught the fist swinging in his direction.

"It's going to take a lot more than that to hit me now." Nate's knuckles turned white, and his father yelped, yanking his fist out of Nate's grip. "I'm not a scrawny teenager anymore. I've spent *years* ending bullies just like you. You can't scare me anymore."

His father's eyes widened as he cradled his hand, backing away from Nate slowly. "You'll regret that." The frost in his voice made me shiver.

"I doubt it."

"You want to swing on me, don't you, boy?" A corner of his mouth twisted.

"Yes." Nate's arms fell to his sides. "But I'm not going to. That's the difference between you and me."

"You keep telling yourself that." Nate's father spat on the ground, then turned and stalked away, heading for a blue F-150 parked along the curb.

Holy shit. This was how Nate grew up, and somehow he'd turned out like . . . Nate.

He pivoted slowly to face me, and for a second, I didn't recognize him. This man wasn't the Nathaniel I knew. I had no doubt that the man in front of me had been to war, that he'd seen things, done things, I'd never fully understand.

And yet, I wasn't scared of him.

"I'll walk you to your car," he said, leaving no room for argument.

I nodded, and his hand gentled as he set it on the small of my back. We walked silently to the sedan I'd rented, because for once, I was at a loss for words. There was a tension in him, a restlessness I didn't know what to do with. I was out of my depth.

My phone buzzed rhythmically, and I reached for it out of habit, but my fingers were stiff with cold, and I accidentally answered and managed to hit the speakerphone instead of end. "Mom, I'll call you—"

"Tell me you did not leave a date with a promising tech developer to chase after that soldier, Isa, or so help me—"

I stabbed at the screen, taking the call off speaker, and I lifted the phone to my ear. "Mom! I will call you later." My cheeks heated with embarrassment. Nate *heard* that.

"You're showing a serious lack of judgment with your choices."

"They're my choices to make. I'll call you when I'm back in DC." I hit the end button with more aggression than necessary and chanced a look up at Nate. "I'm so sorry. She's . . . my mother."

His jaw flexed. "Nothing to be sorry for. She didn't say anything about me that isn't true."

"She doesn't even know you," I argued as we reached the car and I traded my phone for the car keys.

"Where are you staying?" he asked, then scoffed. "I don't know why I asked. There's only one hotel in town."

"I'm in the presidential suite," I answered, opening the door I hadn't bothered to lock. "It was all they had left."

His tan jaw flexed as he nodded.

God, my entire body, as cold and waterlogged as it was, hurt for him. "I can stay."

He looked back at the grave site. "No. I'm thankful you're here. Really, I am. But I just want to be alone with her for a little while." His mouth twisted in a grimace. "If I can get my aunts to leave."

"Okay."

"I hate that you saw that." He wouldn't look at me.

"I hate that you went through it." His coat was soaked through as I reached for his forearm, desperate to touch him, to comfort him in any way I could. "Tell me what you need, Nate."

"If I figure it out, I'll let you know, Izzy." He walked away, and I let him.

I tied the belt on my robe, then ran my brush through my wet hair as I walked back into the bedroom of my hotel suite, finally warm enough to feel my toes.

Serena had already called to apologize for accidentally telling Mom about my hasty exit at breakfast, but I wasn't mad at her. My mother? That was a whole other story. It felt like she'd kicked Nate when he was already down, though I knew she'd been aiming for me.

There were no words for the way my chest ached for everything Nate had been through today, and my utter, complete uselessness to save him from *any* of it. Not the loss of his mother. Not the cruelty of his father.

I sat on the edge of the bed and checked my phone, hoping for a text or a missed call, some sign that he wasn't going to spend tonight alone, when his emotions had obviously been flayed open and left bleeding. A sigh ripped through my lips at the blank screen, and I swallowed the knot in my throat that instantly formed at the idea of him spending the night with another woman.

Get over yourself. He wasn't mine. Not like that. And I could hardly begrudge him any measure of comfort he could find. I put my brush on the nightstand, next to my ADHD medication, then picked up what was left of my room service tray from the polished expanse of the dining table. I'd devoured the cheeseburger the second my meds wore off about two hours ago. Opening my door, I set the tray down in the hallway and moved quickly to get back into my room so I wasn't seen out in just the thigh-high robe, but the ding of the elevator down the hall caught my attention.

Nate stepped out of the elevator into the hallway, shoving his hands through his wet hair, still dressed in his suit from the funeral.

Our eyes met and held as he came my way, his strides eating up the distance between us with single-minded focus. My pulse jumped into a thundering beat. The hours we'd been apart hadn't done anything to quell the restlessness in him. He still walked that dangerous edge between whoever he'd been when he lived here, and whoever he was now . . . whoever the constant deployments were turning him into.

And in the seconds it took for him to reach me, I realized it didn't matter which version of him I was getting. I was inextricably linked to every single one of them. The guy he'd been when he lived here had been the one who'd pulled me from the plane crash. The one he'd grown into had knocked me off my feet in Georgia. And the man he was now . . . the one who made my heart simultaneously race and yearn for him—

Oh, *God.*

That feeling in my chest . . .

I was in love with him.

And he was going back to Afghanistan tomorrow.

My feet shuffled backward into my room, but I held the door open for him, and he followed me in, smelling like rain and the faint remains of his cologne.

"I need . . ." He turned toward me as I closed the door, and the turmoil in his crystal-blue eyes nearly brought me to my knees. "I just need you."

"Okay." I nodded.

"Izzy." It was both a plea and a warning as he scanned the length of my body and shifted his weight. The heat in his eyes was unmistakable; it was the same way he'd looked at me on my birthday last year. "I don't think you understand—"

"I know what you're saying," I whispered.

Our eyes locked, and a second later, my back was against the door, and Nate's mouth fused with mine.

He tasted the same, but the kiss was nothing like the ones we'd shared before. It was a clash of tongues and teeth, like every problem he faced could be forgotten if he simply lost himself within me. I kissed him back just as hard, showing him I could take whatever he wanted—needed—to give.

He'd never hurt me, nor would he ever push me any further than I already wanted to go.

And I wanted him.

His lips were chilled but his tongue warm as it twined with mine. All of him was cold and wet, his clothes no doubt soaked all the way through to his skin. His hands skimmed the outside of my robe, and then he gripped the backs of my thighs, lifting me against the door so our mouths were level.

I wrapped my legs around his waist and held on, winding my arms around his neck as he kissed me harder, deeper. Rainwater dripped from his hair and down his cheeks, but that didn't stop us. My teeth scraped his lower lip, and when he moved to draw back, I sucked his tongue back into my mouth and relished in the groan that rumbled through his chest.

Need raced through my veins like lava, flushing and heating my skin—even my thighs, which took the brunt of the cold from his sodden suit.

He shifted, carrying me without breaking the kiss as he crossed the suite. But he didn't take me to the bedroom. My ass hit the dining room table as I fought with the wet fabric of his tie, finally loosening the knot enough to get it over his head. I shoved the wet jacket from his shoulders next, and it hit the floor with a thwack.

"Drop your legs," he ordered between deep, drugging kisses.

I unhooked my ankles and let my legs dangle over the edge of the table.

"Perfect." His hands stroked up my thighs, under the cloth of my robe, and my stomach fluttered. I knew exactly what he could do with those hands, those very talented fingers, and I was more than ready.

But the touch I so sorely wanted didn't come.

I unbuttoned his shirt with fumbling fingers, too eager to keep my mouth on his to bother looking at what I was doing. After finally undoing the last one, I tugged the shirt free from his pants and somehow managed to unfasten the buttons at his wrists while his hands kneaded my thighs. He kissed my mouth, my cheeks, my neck, while I tugged the reluctant, clinging fabric of his shirt from his body.

Then I pulled back and looked at him.

"Nate," I whispered, awestruck by the body he'd honed to utter perfection. He'd put on muscle over the last eighteen months, his torso still carved, his abs still ridged to mouthwatering magnificence, but now there was simply *more* of him. The deep fuck-me lines that ran down the edges of his stomach begged to be traced by my tongue. I jerked my gaze up to his. "You're incredible."

"You're all I want." He cupped the back of my neck. "It doesn't matter how far I go or how long I'm away. I dream about you. Even when I know you're with someone else—"

"I'm not," I assured him, shaking my head.

"Or when *I'm* with someone else—" he continued, and my heart stuttered.

"Are you?" I leaned away, bracing my palms against the table as I waited for my heart to beat regularly again. He wasn't mine. I wasn't his. That was the agreement we'd made.

And yet he was always mine.

I was always his.

"No. Not in over six months." He looked at me, and for a heartbeat, I cursed this bond between us, the irrational jealousy that had gripped my stomach when I'd read that particular letter about the woman he'd been seeing. "But even then, as much as it makes me an asshole to admit it, you were all I wanted, Izzy."

"I know." I nodded. "It's the same for me."

He crushed my mouth to his, the kiss softer than before, but just as deep, just as powerful. It robbed me of my breath, my thoughts, and any inhibitions that might have lingered.

Then he leaned over me, lowering me until my back rested on the table.

"I want to see you," he said before kissing me again.

My hands found the belt of my robe, and I tugged, letting it fall open, just like the first time he'd put his hands on me.

He lifted his head, and his gaze roamed my naked body, lingering on the parts he'd never seen before. "Holy shit are you just . . . perfect."

"You said that last time." I grinned and tried not to fidget under the heat of his gaze.

"Nothing's changed." His eyes met mine, and the need I saw there made me melt, relaxing completely on the table. "I'm going to kiss you, Isabeau Astor."

I smiled even wider. "You've said that before too."

"Yeah. I know." He flashed a smile, and his dimple appeared for a second before he grasped my shins, then bent my knees as he put my feet on the edge of the table and spread my thighs wide enough for his shoulders to—

Oh *God.*

I sucked in a breath as he set his mouth on me, skimming his tongue over my entrance and up to my clit. It felt so damned good that all I could do was cry out, my hands grasping at his head to pull him closer.

"You taste like heaven," he said, and I lifted my head long enough to lock eyes with him as he lowered his mouth again, sending a bolt of pure pleasure spiraling through me.

He was the hottest man I'd ever seen, and he was mine to touch tonight.

My head fell back as sensation ruled my body. Every lick of his tongue made my back arch. Every time he sucked my clit between his lips, I trembled. When his fingers slid inside me, first one, then two, I couldn't help but rock back against him, seeking more, demanding it with my moans.

He pinned my hips to the table with his forearm so I could only take what he wanted to give, and then he drove me toward madness. He teased when I wanted him to take. He flicked when I wanted him to linger. He took me to the edge of orgasm, when I could almost taste how sweet that release would be, only to lessen the pressure before I tumbled over.

"Nate!" I tugged on his head as the delicious torture began again.

"What do you need, Izzy?" he asked, blowing softly against my heated skin.

I gasped, my back bowing. "I need you!" In every way possible. It was the closest I could come to letting him know how I felt.

"Like you'll scream if you can't have me?" He flicked his tongue over my clit.

"Yes!"

"Like you'll die if you have to take one more breath without me inside you?" He looked up at me, his eyes holding me as a willing prisoner.

"Yes." It was a whisper.

He nodded. "Good. Because that's exactly how I need you." He lowered his head between my thighs, and the world around us disappeared. There was only his mouth, his tongue, his fingers, building my pleasure with expert care, coiling that exquisite pressure in my stomach until my entire body went taut.

Then I snapped, release rushing through me with so much power that I screamed. It could have been words. Maybe his name. Maybe just a cry. Noises were a dull roar around me as wave after wave arched my back, and before I realized what was happening, that pressure coiled again as he worked me right to the brink of a second.

"You!" I demanded, my nails raking through his hair. "I want you, Nate."

He dragged my body to the very edge of the table. I vaguely heard the sound of a buckle, the rip of foil, and then the thick head of him was right there at my entrance.

His hand braced his weight beside my head, and he rose over me, his beautiful face hovering just above mine. "Tell me this is what you really want."

"I already said I do." I cradled his cheeks, memorized everything about the way he looked right now. His blue eyes were crystal clear, his pupils near blown, his cheeks flush with color. And he was right . . . I would die if I had to take another breath without feeling him inside me.

"Say it again." His jaw flexed, and his hand gripped my hip.

"I want you, Nathaniel," I whispered, leaning up to kiss him. "So take me."

He held my gaze as if there was any chance I'd change my mind, and then he pushed in, and in, and in, consuming every inch of my body, and then demanding more, until there was no me. No him. Only us.

He stretched me to my limit, and we both moaned.

He didn't ask if I was okay. He didn't need to, not when I rocked my hips against his and kissed him. I was more than okay. I was fucking fabulous.

His hips withdrew until he was almost entirely out of me, and then he drove back in, and I cried out, my arms wrapping around him as he started a brutal, perfect rhythm of slow, hard thrusts.

"We. Should. Move. To. The. Bed." His words were punctuated with each swing of his hips.

"Bed later. Harder now." It was all I could say. He'd robbed me of all the other words that weren't his name.

"We can do this again, right?" he asked against my mouth. "Not just on the table."

"As many times as you can take." How he could string together a coherent thought was beyond me. I locked my ankles around the small of his back and rocked up, meeting every thrust.

"Challenge accepted." He grinned, and his dimple appeared.

My heart jolted with how much I loved this man.

He kissed me deep, his tongue rubbing against mine with the same rhythm as his body took mine, driving me toward another release. We strained and gasped. We came together again, and again, and again, and somehow each time he slid home was better than the last, until my body teetered on the edge of an abyss, strung so tight that my breath came in little keening pants against his lips.

"Fuck, you feel so damned good," he said, his breathing just as ragged as mine. "I'm never going to get enough of you. The way you squeeze me. The way your skin feels against mine. The way your eyes darken. Yes, just. Like. That."

He reached between our bodies and gave me exactly what I needed, sending me hurtling into oblivion with the next thrust.

I came apart, unraveled, and was remade all within the same breath, with his name on my lips and his back beneath my fingers. The high was incomprehensible, unfathomable, indescribable, and all I could do was ride the waves as his hips swung wildly, chasing his own release as I found mine.

He shuddered above me and came with a shout of his own, catching his weight before he even had the chance to crush me once it was over.

We stared at each other, neither of us able to catch our breaths. Both watching the other as though they held the key to the very universe. Slowly, I fell back into my body and let my ankles fall from his back.

"As many times as I can take," he said, his mouth curving into the most beautiful smile I'd ever seen. "That's what you said, right?"

I nodded.

"All we have is tonight." His brow furrowed, and I knew what he was saying.

This didn't change things. Our timing still wasn't right. He was going back to his unit tomorrow, and I was flying back to DC.

"Then we'd better make it count." I stroked my fingers over his cheek.

We did.

But I still cried when I boarded my flight the next day.

CHAPTER NINETEEN
IZZY

Kandahar, Afghanistan
August 2021

One second I was fighting with Nate, and the next, he took me to the ground, covering me with his body as glass shattered. My heart beat into my throat, and my entire body locked.

The sound of another blast mingled with the screams of the girls and their parents.

"Rockets!" one of the operators behind us shouted, but I couldn't see which one.

"Fuck," Nate swore. Then his arms swept around me, and I was against his chest as he stood and moved with what felt like inhuman speed, quickly carrying me behind a nearby wall. Once my feet were on the ground, we crouched and he tucked me under his arm. Then he motioned to the chess team, saying something to them in a language I didn't speak.

They all scurried toward us as another blast sounded, and a flurry of Afghan soldiers ran by. Three more explosions sounded in quick succession.

Fear tasted like metal in my mouth. I would never forgive myself if I got these girls killed—if by coming here, I cost *Nate* his life.

"I know. You're sitting ducks out there," Nate said, and I noted the button in his hand. He was using his radio. "Go. Bring the gunships back with you."

The next explosion made the wall shudder, and Nate held me tighter.

"We can't do anything," he explained, even though I didn't ask. "The rockets are probably being fired from miles away. All we can do is wait."

I nodded, trying to force a reassuring smile for the girl closest to me—Kaameh. I recognized her from the hours I'd spent on their paperwork. Her mother sheltered her the best she could.

The others were covered by their parents and, in one case, an Afghan soldier.

The sound of rotors grew dimmer and dimmer through the shattered window. The helicopters were leaving.

I jolted when another round of explosions sounded, and Nate didn't even flinch as he surveyed everything around us. He'd always been vigilant whenever we'd been together in the past, always looking, always watching everyone else, and now I understood why. Those reactions I worried about for all those years were the ones that kept him alive over here.

A minute passed, and then another, without anything blowing up.

"I think it's over," Sergeant Gray said from the other side of the waiting area, his back pressed to the opposite wall.

"Agreed," another called out.

"Helos are gone. Nothing left for them to care about," someone else added.

Nate's hand cradled my cheek as he tipped my chin up. "Are you hurt?"

I shook my head, unable to make my tongue work.

He pulled back and looked me over for himself as the other operators moved in, checking on the chess team and their parents. "You're all right."

I started nodding and couldn't stop.

"It's okay, Izzy." He tugged me against him. "It's just shock and adrenaline. It will pass. Just take deep breaths."

I forced air through my lungs one breath at a time until my galloping heart slowed to a canter, then a trot, and finally a steady walk.

"There you go," he said softly, gently rubbing his hand up and down my back. "Gray, get me a situation report."

Gray took off.

"If you could have any superpower in the world, what would it be?" he asked.

I blinked.

"Come on, Iz. Play along."

"Running really fast so I'd never have to fly again," I managed to get out. Shifting my head, I looked up at Nate. Other than the worry in his gaze as he met mine, he seemed completely unfazed. "I always thought I'd be calm and collected if anything like that happened," I whispered. "I froze."

"You telling me that Isabeau Astor might actually be human? She's not perfect?" He flashed a grin, and that dimple appeared, rendering me speechless again.

"You know every flaw I have."

"Including your horrendous taste in men," he teased.

I scoffed.

"There she is." He ran his thumb over my cheek and stood, helping me to my feet. He took stock of everyone around us doing the same. "Hate to break it to you, but it's about to be a long night."

"Because the helicopters are gone." I nodded. "We're stranded."

"Stranded and surrounded," he said. "But don't worry, our ride will come back armed to the teeth. Until then, we'll make sure we're safe here." A corner of his mouth lifted. "And in the meantime, the twelve-inch rule still applies."

I rolled my eyes and pulled myself together, and all playfulness left Nate as we went to greet the people we'd been working for months to get out.

Later that night, we sat around one half of the VIP lounge we'd taken over on the second floor to give the operators a higher vantage point. They all took shifts, some patrolling, some sitting, others sleeping.

Everyone except Nate, who'd stuck to my side, only breaking the twelve-inch rule when I told him he would not, in fact, be handing me the toilet paper. At least he'd let me take off the helmet once they'd made sure the airport grounds were clear. The actual fighting was miles away.

Darkness settled around the airport, and the lights in the lounge were dim as most of the squad finally settled in to eat. Turned out that they traveled with their own food, which they'd split with the families who were now mostly asleep a couple of rows over, stretched out on the chairs like they were just on an extended layover.

"That's not what happened," Sergeant Rose said, pointing his finger at Gray as the others laughed.

Nate shook his head, but a smile curved his mouth as his friends told stories. At least, I assumed they were his friends. I could tell he was close to a couple of them, though they didn't have names on their uniforms. Seeing Nate smile, even briefly, was intoxicating. I found myself watching him to see if he'd do it again.

"What?" he asked, catching me staring.

"Just thinking that it's been a while since I've seen you really smile. Go figure we're in an airport."

"Fucking airports." His dimple appeared again. "You should eat," he said, handing me an opened, heated packet of something. "It's spaghetti, and trust me, it's the best of the options." He glanced at his watch. "I'm guessing your meds are wearing off, so you'll be ravenous any minute."

My lips parted as I took the packet. "You remember that."

He nodded.

"Okay, since it's just us," Gray said, leaning back in his chair across from us. The radio unit was next to him, which I guess made him the comms guy. "Tell us about Sergeant Green here, would you?"

Every other operator, even the guy sitting at the window, turned to look at me.

"No." Nate shook his head as I took my first bite.

It wasn't gourmet, but it would stop my stomach from growling.

"Come on," Gray groaned. "It's more than obvious she knows you." He grinned at me and lifted his eyebrows. "You do, don't you? I bet you know tons of stories he won't tell us."

I folded my legs under me so I sat crisscross in the wide seat and glanced Nate's way.

"Just because you guys are a bunch of narcissists who talk about yourselves all the time." He glared at Gray.

"As opposed to you, who says absolutely *nothing*," Black countered. At least I thought the blond guy was Black. Pretty sure the guy with the dark beard in the corner was Lilac or something ridiculous.

"You have to give us something." Gray leaned forward, putting his hands together. "Please. We'll never get this opportunity again."

I took another bite and looked at Nate.

We locked eyes for a second, and he rolled his eyes. "Fine. Just . . ." He sighed. "I'm trusting you."

I nodded, understanding what he was saying. If he didn't share the personal details of his life, there was a reason for it. He'd barely shared the details with me. "What do you guys want to know?"

Gray whooped and sat on the floor like it was story time. "How long have you known our boy here?"

"Almost ten years." Innocuous enough.

"Did he hatch from an egg? Arrive in a spaceship?" Lilac asked. "Grow up like George of the Jungle?"

"No." I laughed. "He grew up on a farm." *The farm.* I glanced at Nate, wondering if his father still lived there, or if he'd sold it like he'd threatened.

We locked eyes, and his expression softened.

"A farm?" Gray's eyes widened. "Really?" he asked Nate.

"Really." Nate nodded, looking away with a slight smile.

I took another bite.

"What else do you have, Ms. Astor?" Black asked, rubbing his hands together.

"He likes cookies and cream ice cream." I grinned.

"Traitor," Nate accused, his eyes lighting up.

For a second, I forgot we were in Afghanistan. No, we were on a street on Tybee Island, laughing and flirting behind ice-cream cones. I could almost taste the butter pecan. It was a lifetime ago, and yesterday, all in the same breath.

That's what Nate was to me. As far away as a lifetime and as close as yesterday, as near as twelve inches.

"This is so good." Gray glanced between the two of us. "Has he ever been married?"

I nearly choked on my spaghetti but forced it down my throat. Had Nate found someone and married her in the almost three years it had been since New York? If he had, surely these guys would have known, since they were a part of his present. Why did the thought cut like a damn knife? I'd worn Jeremy's ring until last night. I was hardly in a position to judge.

But apparently, I was in the perfect position to be jealous as hell of a woman I'd never met and would never know. She'd have his heart, his laughter, his smile, his arms around her at night, his body, his kids . . .

And I hated her.

"So is that a no?" Gray asked.

But he'd never changed his next of kin form.

"Only once," I answered, ignoring the way Nate gaped at me.

"Really?" Lilac's eyebrows rose.

"Really." I grinned. "At least that's what he told the nurses so he wouldn't get kicked out of the waiting room when I was in surgery."

Nate snorted. "Never living that one down."

Gray laughed. "This is amazing. Okay, what's with the taped-up tag he carries around?"

My brow puckered, and I looked to Nate.

He went rigid.

"I honestly don't know," I answered, doing my best to cover whatever reaction he was having to the question. "But I can tell you I know why he carries this scar." His hand was warm as I picked it up, turning it toward Gray so he could see the scar across the back of it.

"Tell me it was something undeniably stupid," Brown pled. "You have to give us something."

I grinned. "Coral in Fiji. My necklace fell off, and he swam down to get it, cutting his hand up." My touch lingered before I let his hand go, and our eyes met.

"Must have been some necklace," Gray said. "Coral cuts like a knife."

"It was," I said without looking away from Nate, remembering the way he'd made love to me when we'd gotten back from snorkeling that afternoon. My body heated at the memory, and given the way his eyes darkened, I wondered if he was reliving those hours too. "It's still one of my favorite pieces of jewelry, considering you gave it to me twice, first on my birthday and then after you found it."

"It always looked good on you," he said softly. "Took me hours to pick out the right one."

The block of ice I'd kept around my heart when it came to Nate didn't just thaw; it melted. Whatever had bound us together in the first place was still there, as tangible as ever. We'd buried it, ignored it, burned it to the ground, but never managed to sever it. At least not on my end.

It would always be there.

The radio made a noise, and Gray's attention shifted as he lifted the handset, answering what appeared to be a call.

"Do you have any embarrassing stories for us? Anything we can use against him?" Rose asked. At least I thought it was Rose. Lilac was a real possibility.

Nate lifted a single brow.

I shook my head. "No." Ripping my gaze from Nate's, I managed a smile at Rose. "Sorry to disappoint."

"Green," Gray said, lifting the handset.

Nate stood and crossed the aisle, breaking the twelve-inch rule.

"Is he scared of anything?" Gray asked, sliding into Nate's seat. "Spiders? Bats? Cucumbers?"

I laughed at the cucumber question and shook my head as Nate picked up the receiver. I knew exactly what Nate was afraid of, but that wasn't my secret to share. And from what I'd seen, he wasn't anywhere close to becoming his father.

"This is Navarre," he said so quietly that I barely heard it above the ridiculous suggestions being tossed my way. Cats. Hugs. Snakes. He wasn't afraid of any of them, so I didn't respond.

"Navarre?" I whispered, watching Nate's shoulders straighten as he nodded at whatever was being said, but his reply was lost in the hum of voices around me.

"His call sign," Gray answered quietly. "The color thing is so you don't know who we are. Our call signs are so we know who's actually on the other end of the call."

Navarre. Gravity shifted beneath my feet.

Isabeau's lover, cursed to only see her at dawn and dusk. Doomed to love her but never touch her. Never hold her. Never make a real life together.

"You okay?" Gray asked.

I nodded.

Guess Nate hadn't managed to sever the connection between us either.

CHAPTER TWENTY

NATHANIEL

Tacoma, Washington
June 2017

"I know you're not trying to talk me out of going three hours before my flight," I grumbled from the passenger seat of Torres's truck as we sped toward the airport.

Sped because he'd talked me into one last workout before leaving.

"Of course not." He shot me a look before passing an SUV and cutting across three lanes of traffic. "I saw how much you paid for those tickets." His dark brows furrowed.

"Go ahead and say the *but*, because I know one is coming." My weight shifted as he took the off-ramp. I was starting to wish I'd driven myself and just paid to park my truck at the airport.

"Do you even realize how lucky we are to both have passed selection?" He hit the brakes hard at the stoplight.

The fact that I passed psych was a miracle, but I'd gotten pretty good at giving the answers they wanted to hear.

"I do." We'd spent nine weeks in North Carolina proving ourselves for Special Forces Assessment and Selection, and both Torres and I had made it, along with Rowell and another guy from our unit, Pierson, which made sense since the four of us had spent the last eighteen months training both on and off deployment.

It had been hell, but it had been worth it.

Pierson was thrilled to make it, but I knew this was just a stepping stone for Torres and Rowell . . . and for me. That long-ago thought I'd had on the plane with Izzy, that it would be cool to make Special Forces, was now a very real, very actualized dream. I was damn good at what I did, and I had to admit: I wanted to be the best.

"And you're just going to jet off to Fiji, knowing that we'll only have a couple weeks to get ready to PCS to Bragg." The light changed, and he turned toward the airport.

"I've been talking about this trip with Izzy for *years*," I said, recognizing how defensive that sounded. "And it's not like a vacation is going to get extended. I'll be back in time to leave for Bragg." I hadn't seen her since Mom's funeral six months ago, and the terms we'd left on hadn't exactly been clear. We'd spent that night together, never talking about Mom, or our lack of a future, or anything that mattered outside that room. I'd left her asleep and sated, the sheets tangled in her long, beautiful legs, choosing to let her sleep instead of waking her for what was bound to be an awkward goodbye.

That night lived in my dreams.

Her mother snapping that she was chasing after a soldier . . . that lived in my nightmares. Knowing Izzy was out of my league and hearing it directly from her mother were two different things.

"You'd better be back. We said we were doing this together." Torres glanced sideways at me.

"Yeah, yeah." I shook my head. He was my best friend, and there was no one I'd want to go through it with, but he was a little intense these days. Or maybe my focus was just on getting to Izzy. "I know. Get through Q Course, and then it's all about Delta."

"It's going to be awesome." He grinned. "My old man is going to flip that I'm following in those boots."

I couldn't help but smile at how happy he was.

"Does your non-girlfriend know?" he asked as we pulled up in front of the departures drop-off point.

My stomach sank as I climbed out of the cab, shutting the front door, only to open the back one for my bags.

"You've told her, right?" The look on his face was equal parts judgment and worry. "Because from what I know about Izzy, she's going to want some path forward, considering she just graduated law school."

"I'll tell her." I shouldered my backpack and hefted my suitcase to the sidewalk.

"Where the hell does she think you've been for the past few months?"

A grimace crossed my face. "I didn't really explain it."

"But you've told her that you're back."

"I . . . sent her an email a couple weeks ago to make sure we were still on for the trip." Everything I had to say to her needed to be said in person, which wasn't an opportunity we'd had.

"You're seriously going to get on that plane, hope she shows up at LAX, and then what . . . pray she didn't get a boyfriend who can actually be around in the last six months?"

"Pretty much." She'd said she was coming, but the email had been short, which I'd expected given the timing of her finals. Didn't mean my stomach wasn't in knots that she might have changed her mind. We'd both bought tickets in January, and I'd covered the resort, but the financial cost would be nothing compared to the blow of knowing I'd messed up our entire relationship because I hadn't been able to keep my hands to myself six months ago.

"Right." He pulled his sunglasses down and looked over the rims. "That whole we-live-in-a-gray-area thing you have going on is eventually biting you in the ass."

"I know." I sighed. "But until it does, I'm not messing with the only good thing I have in my life."

"Don't forget that you passed selection for Special Forces. That's a pretty badass thing you have going for you." He grinned back at me.

"Truth. We are pretty badass. Thanks for the ride." I pulled my Saint Louis Blues cap down and shut his door.

Five hours later, I waited at the gate in Los Angeles for flight 4482 to Nandi, tapping my foot with more than a little nervous energy as the minutes counted down. I checked the boarding pass again and made sure I was at the right gate. I was.

Izzy wasn't here.

I picked up my phone and debated calling, but knowing she wasn't coming now as opposed to fifteen minutes from now wasn't going to change anything. At least that was the lie I told myself. Fear turned my blood to ice.

Our emails had been shorter and shorter over the last few months.

Our phone calls had been nonexistent between the deployment and selection.

She had every right to change her mind, to date, to fall in love with someone else. God knew if she was mine, really, honestly *mine*, there was no way in hell I'd be comfortable with her flying off to Fiji with another man for a week.

Minutes ticked by, and the attendant told the people around me in their vacation clothes, an overabundance of flowered shirts and cargo shorts, to prepare to board.

They called passengers to preboard, and I stood, shifting my backpack to my shoulder as I surveyed everyone around me, looking for a flash of blonde hair and sparkling brown eyes.

Then the attendant called our group to board.

Holy fucking shit. This was actually happening.

There was still time, though, and Izzy wasn't the kind of woman to stand someone up. She would have called. Written. Sent a carrier pigeon to tell me she was pissed or not coming.

I moved into line, scanned my ticket at the entrance to the gateway, and then walked down the jet bridge, my heart pounding with every step. By the time I found my seat, and hers empty next to it, the pounding had become a dull roar in my ears.

I took the seat next to the window because she'd never been comfortable there after the crash, and then I did the only thing I could—wait. Raising the shade on the window, I looked out over the tarmac and tried to find anything out there worth distracting myself with. When that didn't work, I pulled out my copy of *Catch-22* and a highlighter.

Was I supposed to get off? Go by myself? Fly straight to DC and beg her to talk to me?

The scent of Chanel wrapped around me like a lover, and I smiled.

"That was close," she said, and my head whipped toward her. Those were the first words I'd ever spoken to her in a plane considerably smaller than this one. Izzy's eyes were a little red and puffy, like she'd been crying but had stopped hours ago, and her smile was bright as she sank into her seat. "My flight was delayed out of DC."

"Hey, Izzy." My gaze devoured her, taking in the loose sweep of her hair up to the bun she wore, a few strands of the honey blonde falling around her face, and the curve of her soft lips. I needed to lean across the small barrier between our seats and kiss the shit out of her. I'd missed her more than I'd let myself realize.

"Hey, Nate," she said softly, scanning over my features like she was looking for new scars, new injuries to catalog. There were none where she could see.

"You've been crying." My stomach tightened.

She nodded.

"Want to talk about it?" All she had to do was tell me who to kill, and they'd be dead.

"I broke up with someone I liked." She shrugged. "This trip wouldn't have been fair to him. I don't regret it. It was the right choice." She fastened her seat belt and reached for my hand, locking our fingers.

It was hard to breathe under the weight of guilt of knowing I was the reason she was hurting, but with the simple touch of her hand in mine, I was home.

"Izzy," I whispered, unable to put my feelings to words as pain settled in my chest. There was nothing I wouldn't do to keep her from pain, even if it meant I wasn't her choice. "You didn't have to. And you don't have to come now. You can walk off this plane, and there will be no hard feelings."

"But I did have to break up with him." She sighed, leaning back and turning so her cheek rested against the seat as she looked at me. "Because it didn't matter how much I liked him. I would rather spend a week with you than a lifetime with him. That wasn't fair to either of us, you know?"

I thought about the relationships I'd ended because I knew I'd be seeing Izzy soon, or because I'd realized that nothing compared to the way I felt around her.

"Yeah. I know." The pain in my chest expanded, and I picked up her hand, pressing a kiss to the soft skin of the back of it. I would make it up to her. I had to.

The water lapped at our feet twenty-four hours later as we walked down the deserted beach. We'd flown, then flown again, then passed out side by side once we'd reached our overwater bungalow that had cost me more than I even wanted to think about.

I slept my first full night in what felt like years, and waking up beside her, watching the rhythmic rise and fall of her chest, was the closest I'd ever been to heaven.

Or maybe that was right now, watching her smile down at the water, the sun kissing her bare shoulders in her sundress.

"So, what are you thinking for next year?" she asked.

"We haven't even been here a full day and you're asking about next year?" I slipped my hand into my pocket, fumbling with the little box I'd brought along. "I'm still thinking about renting those WaveRunners or going for a hike later."

She tucked her hair behind her ear and grinned up at me. "It gives me something to look forward to. I mean, it took us two years just to get here, so who knows how long it will take us to get another trip."

"Solid point." I glanced around at the beauty of the island, the lush vegetation, pale sand, and aqua waters that no picture could capture. "I'm still surprised we made it here."

"Me too." She glanced down my torso, her gaze heating in a look that made me wish we'd stayed in the bungalow. Not that I was making any assumptions. I'd happily keep my hands in my pockets if that meant I'd have a week with her. Her brow furrowed, and she stepped in front of me, stopping me in my tracks. "What's that?" She trailed a fingertip down a scar barely visible in the sleeve of my tattoo.

Of course she'd noticed. I couldn't get anything by Izzy. Whether or not she chose to ask, to open topics I didn't want to discuss, to poke for answers, she noticed.

"Nothing to worry about," I assured her.

She shot an arched brow at me.

"It was a piece of shrapnel." I shrugged. "Right around when I went back after Mom's—" I swallowed, and her gaze jumped to meet mine. "It was really nothing. Four stitches and some antibiotics."

Her lips pursed, and her grip on my arm shifted so she could run her thumb over it. "I feel like you have more of these every time I see you."

"That's because I do."

"And you're okay with that?" Her hand fell away, and her face fell.

"It's my job." And if what I did over there made it even slightly safer for her to sleep at night, then it was worth it.

She looked away, and my stomach lurched. "How many years do you have to serve for the military to pay for college, anyway?"

"Oh, I'm way past that." I regretted the words the second they left my mouth. "Speaking of passing things . . ." I brought out the small box from my pocket. "I'm not sure I've said congratulations for graduating law school yet."

Her eyes widened as I held out the velvet box. "Nate . . ."

"Take it. It's not going to bite you, Iz." I grinned.

"Don't do that." She glared at me, then stared at the box.

"Do what? Buy you gifts?" I shook the little box right in front of her pert nose. "What else am I going to do with the massive amounts of hazard pay I'm racking up?"

"Flash that little dimple of yours like it's going to distract me." Two cute little lines appeared in her forehead.

"My dimple distracts you?" Shit, I needed to use that to my advantage more often, which would require actually being able to see her more often.

"Stop changing the subject. What is that?" She pointed to the box.

"You could open it and find out." I couldn't stop grinning now.

"Nate." She sucked in a breath. "It's just that it's a small box. A really small *velvet* box, and you and I have never defined whatever this is, and that's been okay with me, but I really need to be prepared if that box is *the* box, and normally I'd just laugh it off, but we're in Fiji, on the beach and—"

I laughed. "Relax, Izzy. It's not a ring. I wouldn't do that to you."

"Oh good." Her shoulders sagged. "Wait." She jerked her head back up to look at me. "What do you mean do that *to* me?"

I cocked my head to the side and tried to smother my smile. "Is it always this difficult for you to accept a gift? I mean, the last thing I'd ever do is shove a ring at you and ask you to give up everything you've worked for without giving us a chance to build something first. That wouldn't be fair to you." And I wasn't sure she'd say yes, anyway. She'd probably never admit it, but she craved her parents' approval on a level I wasn't sure she even realized, and I was far from their ideal husband for their daughter. No trust fund. No political connections.

"Oh." That *oh* sounded entirely different from the first one, but I couldn't decide if it was in a good way or a bad way.

"Present, Izzy. Present." I shook the box.

"Thank you." She plucked the box from my hand, and I memorized the moment. The excitement in her eyes, the soft bite of her teeth into her lower lip, the way she bounced slightly on the balls of her bare feet.

Feelings I couldn't comprehend exploded in my chest. How could I need this woman so much and see her so little? How could she mean everything and yet exist in a completely different world from the one I lived in?

She opened the box and gasped, her shocked gaze leaping to mine. "Nate, you shouldn't have."

And there I went, grinning again. I never smiled as much as I did when I was with Izzy. "I absolutely should have. I'm incredibly proud of you."

"They must have cost you a fortune." She looked at the diamond stud earrings I'd ordered from the store with the blue boxes. "Can you hold it?" She handed the box back.

I nodded and took the box while she changed out the earrings she was already wearing, putting the current ones in the box. "I can carry it," I told her, and put the box back in my pocket.

"How do they look?" She turned her head, letting the sun catch the stones.

"Not as beautiful as you are, but they'll do." I took out my phone and turned on the camera app, flipping it to selfie mode so she could see how gorgeous she was.

"Take a picture with me." She tugged on my arm, and I went, snapping a quick series of selfies and kissing her cheek on the last one. "They're amazing. Thank you."

"You're welcome." I kissed her forehead and let her go. If she was fresh off a breakup, the last thing she'd want or need was me pawing on her.

"I was thinking Palau." She turned, walking backward to face me, her smile brighter than the sun.

"Palau?" Damn, she was gorgeous.

"For next year."

"Right." I swallowed through the growing tightness in my throat. "And maybe Peru the year after that. We could hike up to Machu Picchu." If I could get leave. If we weren't on deployment. If we weren't headed for assessment for Delta.

"That sounds like fun." She held out her hand, and I took it. "I'll have to ask for time off, though. Going in October would give me more than a year at my new firm—assuming I pass the bar. I'm sitting for it soon. Hard to believe I'm finally out of school."

"You've done great."

We walked in silence for a few moments. "So I have a few interviews lined up at some really great firms. At least the ones that will talk to me before the bar."

"Tell me about them." I could've listened to her talk forever.

"One is in Boston, and there's one in New York I like and another that I really, really like." She looked up at me beneath her lashes, and her cheeks flushed. "Two in Seattle, and one in Tacoma. They all have reciprocity, so as long as I pass the bar in DC, I should be good."

I blinked, pausing, then turning toward her. "Tacoma and Seattle."

She nodded, and her breath caught as she searched my eyes for an answer I didn't have to give her. "I was thinking, which is always dangerous, but I can't seem to stop myself, which is why I broke up with Luke—"

Luke. Didn't know him and already fucking loathed him.

"Not just because of this trip, but because we've been dancing around each other for years, Nate. *Years*. And we keep saying that the time isn't right, and that we owe ourselves a real, true shot and not some half-assed long-distance tragedy, right?" She moved toward me, gripping my biceps. "I'm realizing that it doesn't matter who I date. They're all just placeholders because I'm waiting for you. Waiting for *us*."

"Izzy." I cradled the side of her face, soaking in every single word and rejecting them at the same time.

"I've graduated now, Nate. I can go anywhere. Do anything. You could get out if you wanted to." Her grip tightened, and the intensity in her eyes, her tone, made my heart clench. "We could be together. Not just send emails and letters and highlighted books, but actually be together. We could wake up next to each other if we wanted to, or even just *date*. I can move to Tacoma if you want me to—"

"I won't be in Tacoma," I said softly.

"What?" Her brow knit.

"I can't get out, and I won't be in Tacoma." I slid my thumb over the high rise of her cheekbone, relishing how soft her skin was. "I'll be at Fort Bragg."

"Fort Bragg?"

"North Carolina." I nodded slowly, like it might soften the blow. "I haven't told you where I've been the last few months. Why my emails weren't as frequent."

"I figured you were deployed." She drew back.

"No. I was at selection. It's like . . ." How the hell did I describe it? "Tryouts for Special Forces."

"You went with Torres," she said. "That's what he always wanted to do, right?"

"Right." I always knew she read my letters, but damn did she pay attention too. "Four of us went. Rowell—he's my other best friend—"

"Justin and Julian. I remember."

"Pierson too. We all made it."

"Of course you made it." She forced a smile, but it didn't reach her eyes as she stepped back, out of my reach. "You're not getting out. You're getting in deeper."

I nodded again, like I was a plastic bobblehead. "Yeah. It'll be about a year of training, and then . . ." The words wouldn't come. "And then we'll see where I go after that."

"Then we'll see." She tugged her hair behind her ears, and the ocean breeze blew the strands loose again.

"I highly doubt they have the kinds of law firms you're looking at in Fayetteville." I shoved my hands into my pockets. "You're probably interviewing at all the glitzy firms, right? The high-paying, high-rise, high-clout ones."

"Yes. I'm looking at the firms that make the most impact, the places I can make the biggest difference, but . . . I don't have to." She took another step backward, and then another, until the waves lapped over her feet.

"Yeah, you do. I'm never going to be the guy who holds you back, Izzy. Never going to be that asshole that demands you give up everything for what he wants." I kept my feet firmly planted in the sand and didn't reach for her. "It would be so easy to tell you yes, to move to Fayetteville and get in with a practice there for a year. And then easy to tell you to pack up and move with me again to wherever they'll send me next. Easy to be with you, easy to make this thing between us . . ." I looked down at the sand.

"Why is it that I always have too many words and you never have enough?"

A sad smile tugged at my mouth as I slowly raised my eyes to meet hers. "Because we balance each other out. And that means I'm not going to watch that light in your eyes turn to resentment when you realize I'm the reason you don't achieve everything you've worked for. I won't be able to live with myself if I'm always holding you back."

"So this is all we get?" She threw her arms out. "Moments that we have to carve out, never actually able to share our lives?"

"The sky is cloudless. That water is crystal clear. And you are the most beautiful woman I've ever seen, Isabeau. If this is all we get, then it's pretty great."

She took a shaky breath. "I know I told you that I'd rather spend a week with you than forever with him."

I held my breath.

"But I'm not going to wait around forever, Nate. There's going to come a moment where we either have to take our shot or we let each other go."

"I know." That knowledge haunted me more than the nightmares.

"Because it's not like you and I could ever be just friends."

"I know."

"Maybe you could," she said, kicking at the ankle-deep water. "But I can't. Not now that I know what it feels like to have you. I'll never be able to look at you and not want you."

Even the small amount of distance between us now was killing me. "It's the same for me."

Her shoulders dipped, and she threw her head back at the sky. "Why is our timing always shit?"

"Because nothing worth having is easy."

"Just . . . promise me you'll think about it while we're here, okay?" She looked back at me. "Think about what it could be like if we became more than a possibility."

"Yeah. I can do that." I thought about it more than she knew and always came to the same conclusion, but it was impossible to deny her request.

Her answering smile was worth it. "We have the week. So get over here and kiss me in the water like I've been dreaming about, Nathaniel Phelan."

She didn't have to tell me twice.

CHAPTER TWENTY-ONE

IZZY

Kandahar, Afghanistan
August 2021

I shifted in my sleep, rolling to my back. The pillow beneath my head was warm, but the fabric of the pillowcase abraded the base of my neck. But the scent—metal and spearmint mixed with something warmer—made me sigh with recognition.

My mind acknowledged the dream—it always did—but I clung to it, willing myself to fall more deeply asleep so I wouldn't lose it.

Fingers gently stroked down my cheek, and I leaned into the caress.

"Wake up, Isabeau." His voice wrapped around me like velvet, just like it did every morning in Fiji when he'd woken me with his hands and mouth, rousing my body to a fever pitch before sliding into me and bringing us both home.

"I don't want to," I mumbled. Waking would mean he'd be gone, that I'd have to face another day of wondering where he was.

"You have to," he said softly. "It's almost time to go."

"You're always going." I angled my head more comfortably and let my breathing deepen again, slipping back into sleep. "Ever considered staying?"

"Too many times to count." Fingers brushed through my hair. "But we can't stay here. We have to go."

This wasn't what I wanted to dream. I wanted to go back to my apartment in New York. Wanted to open the door and find him standing there. Wanted to take back everything I'd said and do it all differently.

"Izzy." His voice was still soft, but more insistent.

I forced my eyes open and was rewarded by the sight of him looking down at me. God, there was nothing better than waking up to those eyes, that mouth, even if it was set in a firm line. "Not all of us prefer the sunrise, Nathaniel."

A corner of his mouth lifted into a smirk, and my pulse jumped, bringing me fully awake. I wanted to kiss that mouth, to lose myself in him, to feel that sweet oblivion that only Nate brought me. "You might not like the sunrise, but I doubt you want to spend another night on the airport floor if we miss our extraction."

I blinked, and it all came rushing back.

We were in Kandahar, and that scratchy fabric was the material of Nate's camouflage pants. Either I'd fallen asleep with my head in his lap, or he'd moved me here, where he'd sat back against the wall. Every beat of my heart begged me to stay put, to soak in every moment that he looked at me without the cool aloof apathy he'd dished out for the last week. Without the armor of my own anger, I couldn't blame him for keeping me at a distance. It wasn't in Nate's nature to let anyone in, and when push came to shove, I'd let him down when he'd needed me most. We both bore our share of the responsibility for what happened in New York. "Do you know that this is the longest amount of time we've spent together?"

His brow knit. "Almost. Fiji was nine days with the flights. We're only on day eight."

"I liked Fiji better. No one was shooting at us."

"That's what happens when you haul yourself into a war zone, Iz. People shoot at you." He held out his hand, and I took it, sitting up against the protests of my sore muscles.

"Did you get any sleep?" I asked, rubbing the back of my neck and rolling my shoulders.

"Enough." He stood, stretching his arms, making the sleeve of his tattoo ripple. "The birds are in the air. We've got about forty-five minutes before they arrive. Let's get you out of here."

He waived the twelve-inch rule while we both used the bathroom, and then kept me close as I checked in with the chess team and their parents, who'd already been briefed on our departure.

Hopefully it would go more smoothly than our arrival yesterday.

The air thickened with anxiety with each passing second, and fear trickled down my spine, but I forced a smile for the girls. The six of them were just as I remembered from our short Skype sessions, inquisitive and funny. They also spoke immaculate English, which made me wish I'd chosen something other than French in high school so I could have reciprocated in kind.

"All the visas are in this envelope," I told Coach Niaz, handing her the large sealed manila folder as everyone gathered their things. "I didn't want to chance losing them."

"Thank you. I'll hand them out to the families just in case we get separated," she said, the shorter woman adjusting her bag over her shoulder and smiling at me with watery brown eyes that crinkled at their corners. "I'll never be able to thank you enough. I'm sorry you had to come all this way, but—"

"You don't have to explain." My throat threatened to close as emotion rose, swift and overwhelming. I'd never been a part of something as important as this, never done anything in my twenty-eight years that qualified as . . . meaningful. "I'm just grateful to be in a position to help," I managed to say, squeezing her hands.

Gray approached and leaned in at Nate's shoulder. "They're five minutes out."

Nate glanced my way, and I nodded.

"It's time," Nate said, his voice filling the waiting area. "Twelve inches," he reminded me as the other operators took charge of the family units they'd been assigned, leaving one outside watching the door.

He handed me the Kevlar helmet, and I put it on over the sleep-mussed strands of my bun, then did the same with the tactical vest. At least he'd let me sleep without it.

We passed a pile of MREs on our way out of the room, heading into the hallway and down the stairs. "Did you mean to leave those there?"

He nodded, his expression more than alert as he surveyed the area around us. "They don't have enough food here. They're basically cut off."

"And we're just going to leave them?" I glanced up at him, but he was in work mode. There were no cheek-grazing touches or smiles. This was the version of Nate I didn't see stateside.

"Not everyone wants to be saved, Izzy." He gripped his rifle as we started down the length of the terminal.

"This is our home," the Afghan soldier on my right said. "We'll defend it to the death."

I didn't know what to say, so I simply nodded, clutching my messenger bag tighter the closer we got to the exit. We passed the gate we'd taken shelter at yesterday. The windows that had been blown out had already been boarded up.

"Try to breathe," Nate said as we moved toward the door, which was guarded by Black and two other Afghan soldiers.

"And if they start firing rockets at us again?" I kept my voice down, well aware of the girls behind us, moving in the groups they'd been assigned for their specific helicopters.

"They brought Apaches," Nate reminded me. "If they start firing rockets, they'll give away their position, and then they'll get repaid tenfold." His jaw flexed as we reached the door and paused.

"Right, because warfare is logical." Panic stuttered my heartbeat. Fine, I wasn't cut out for this. I could admit that to myself.

"Just stay with me," Nate ordered, softly. "I'll get you on that helicopter."

I didn't doubt that. I also knew how lucky we'd been yesterday to have already made it inside before the explosions started.

"If it's between me or one of the girls—"

Nate pivoted toward me, took my chin between thumb and forefinger, and tilted my face toward his. "I'm not that guy." He said it so softly that I barely heard him, so I knew the family behind us couldn't.

"What guy?"

"Thirty seconds," Gray called out from the end of our group.

"The guy who does the honorable thing," Nate said, his eyes searching mine. "Not when it comes to you."

"Yes, you are," I argued.

He shook his head. "There's a difference between you and me, Iz. There always has been. If you knew the world had twenty-four hours before some calamity struck, where would you go?"

I blinked. It was the oddest question he'd ever asked me in the name of distraction. "Serena would probably be reporting, and my parents aren't exactly the comforting type, so I guess I'd go to wherever I could do the most good."

A wry smile twisted his lips. His gaze dropped to my mouth, and he let go of my chin. "Yeah. That's the difference between us."

I didn't have time to ask what he meant. The sound of rotors filled the air, and I looked through the glass to see four helicopters land on the tarmac, and two more fly by.

"Go!" Nate said over his shoulder, and the doors burst open. We were ushered through by another operator and the Afghan soldiers.

My heart raced as we quickly made our way down the same walkway we'd entered on yesterday. It looked different now. Longer. The arches we walked under were somehow less beautiful and more . . .

exposed. Or maybe it was simply the way I looked at them that had changed.

Once we hit the open air of the runway, my heart threatened to jump ship. We passed a crater in the concrete that definitely hadn't been there yesterday, and my blood rushed, pounding through my ears. Nate led me across the cool tarmac, not yet heated from the sun at this early hour, and to the farthest helicopter.

The door gunner waved us in, and Nate all but lifted me into the Blackhawk, forcing me in first. I didn't waste time by arguing. I found my usual seat and got myself out of his way.

But he didn't follow.

My head whipped toward the door. Nate waited on the tarmac, looking back toward the terminal. I held my breath. If the last twenty-four hours had taught me anything, it was that seconds counted.

And my heart noted every single one of them as he stood out there, completely exposed.

Lilac appeared, escorted by a pair of Afghan soldiers, one of whom was carrying Kaameh. He set her down just inside the door and let her go, and then the rest of the family shuffled into the helicopter. They took the seats directly across from me, their chests heaving and their eyes wide. I leaned forward and buckled Kaameh into the seat by the window, where Nate usually sat, as her mother and father juggled her little brother so they could each fasten their own.

Nate and Lilac climbed in, and once Nate's thigh touched mine, I took a full breath, then another, and another, until they came too fast. He was fine. We were fine.

The helicopter launched, and the ground fell away.

Nate reached onto my lap and took my hand, lacing my fingers with his, holding tight as we flew out of Kandahar. My breathing steadied with every mile we flew. I knew the moment wouldn't last, that he wouldn't keep hold of me forever, and he didn't.

His hand slid free, and I couldn't help but mourn the loss immediately.

But he didn't know that my left hand was bare for a reason.

And I had yet to decide if I was going to tell him, yet to figure out if he'd even want to know.

When we landed, the girls hugged me, and then were immediately put into SUVs with their families to head to the airport. It was short. Anticlimactic. Perfect.

"Look at you, making a difference," Nate said as he led me to our own SUV.

"Feels good," I admitted, sliding into the car. "It's probably the best thing I'll ever do." If that was the culmination of all my time in Washington, it would have been worth it.

Nate closed my door and climbed in front. I smiled the entire way to the embassy.

But I stopped smiling when we walked into the chaotic lobby and I saw through the anxious crowd that the glass-front conference room we'd taken over was empty.

"You need to find Dickface and tell him you're okay?" Nate asked, his voice trailing off as he followed my line of sight.

His major walked forward, his mouth set in a firm line. "Good job getting the team out."

"Where's *my* team?" I asked, my stomach sinking.

"State Department has ordered a partial evacuation of the embassy." The major looked at Nate, then me. "Sorry to tell you this, but the others on your team left a few hours ago with the congressional candidate . . . the one who wasn't scheduled to be here. Covington."

I wobbled, and Nate steadied me with a hand on my lower back.

"What do you mean they *left*?" he practically growled.

"The senators called off their trip, and they got on the plane," the major explained, his voice gentling as he studied my face. "You might want to give your boss a call."

I'd been left behind.

CHAPTER TWENTY-TWO
IZZY

Fiji
June 2017

There was nothing quite as beautiful as watching the reflection of the moon ripple on the water off the deck of our overwater bungalow. I glanced over my shoulder, back through the open double doors, and took in the expanse of Nate's naked back as he lay asleep on what had become his side of the bed in the last five days we'd been here. The top of the sheet rested at the small of his back, just above the delectable curve of his ass, and the dim light from the bedside table caught on every line of muscle, now lying dormant.

Fine, maybe there was one thing in this world more beautiful than the moon.

The breeze fluttered the silk of my spaghetti-strapped, thigh-high nightgown, and I turned away from Nate to face the water again. It was the middle of the night, and our deck was sheltered from any prying eyes—if there was even anyone awake in the bungalows beside us—but though Nate had no problem walking around gorgeously, mouthwateringly naked, I wasn't quite that confident.

I also couldn't sleep. He'd worn my body out into a blissful state of euphoric exhaustion, but my mind had spun long after his eyes had drifted shut.

We only had two days left.

Two days, and then we'd head back to the States. Back to reality. Back to a life where we never knew where we stood with each other, or when we'd see the other again. Back to a life where I pushed away every man who got too close for the simple reason that he wasn't Nate.

When I'd broken things off with Luke, I hadn't cried out of heartbreak. I'd cried because I'd spent months with him and only fallen into *like*, a like I'd been shamefully willing to toss aside.

Love? That word belonged to one man in my life, and I couldn't have him. Not really.

I was hopelessly, inexorably in love with Nathaniel, and only Nathaniel.

And he wouldn't let me in. I was forever kept in his orbit, allowed to glimpse the damage I knew lingered beneath his surface, but condemned to watch helplessly from afar as he collected scars.

Maybe it was because he'd saved me all those years ago. Maybe it was the ease I seemed to feel only around him, the way I could be me, just me, and it was more than enough. Maybe it was the way he'd looked at me at his mom's funeral, like I was the lone boat in an ocean trying its best to drown him. Or maybe it was the way he erased every logical thought with a single touch.

Whatever it was about him that held my heart, it only existed with Nate.

And we only had two more days.

How was I supposed to sleep even an hour of that away?

I wrapped my arms around my middle and stared up at the moon like it might deliver the answers I needed. Was I supposed to move to North Carolina? Give up the kind of work I wanted to do in order to be with him on the few days of the year he'd actually be home, when that clearly wasn't what he wanted?

A noise made me turn back toward the bed.

Nate's body jerked.

I moved toward him, walking soundlessly so I wouldn't wake him, watching to see if anything was wrong. After about a minute, I sat carefully on my side of the bed, then slowly pulled my legs up so I wouldn't jostle the bed too much.

He jolted again, letting out a shout that startled me.

He was having a nightmare.

"Nate." I leaned over to him, gently touching his shoulder. "Nate, wake—"

He moved so fast that my heart stopped.

My back hit the mattress in the same second that Nate appeared above me. His eyes were wide and intense, and his forearm—

It was pressed to my collarbone as his other hand batted for something on the bed.

"Nate!" I cried out as my stomach lurched into my throat.

Horror streaked across his face, and he jumped backward, removing his weight in less than a heartbeat and scrambling for the edge of the bed. "Oh shit." The blood ran from his face. "Izzy. God. *Izzy.*"

I moved back against the headboard, my mind trying like hell to catch up to what just happened.

"I'm so sorry." He lifted his hand like he was going to reach for me, then set it back down. "Did I hurt you?"

"No." The stricken look on his face broke my heart. "I'm okay," I promised.

He dropped his head into his hands. "I'm so sorry."

"I'm fine, Nate. Startled, but fine." My pulse raced, but it was nothing compared to the way my chest tightened at the misery in his voice. "Nate, look at me."

He slowly lifted his head, his eyes rising to meet mine.

"You didn't hurt me." I shook my head, logic cutting through the shock. "You were having a nightmare, and I startled you. I never should have touched you. I know enough about PTSD to know that, and I just . . . forgot. I'm the one who's sorry."

"Don't you dare apologize to *me*." He drew his knees to his chest.

I scooted closer but stopped midway across the bed, giving him space. "You didn't choke me. You didn't cut off my airway. You didn't throw me to the ground. You. Didn't. Hurt. Me."

He slid off the bed and pulled on a pair of dry swim trunks. "And I'm not going to."

"What is that supposed to mean?" My stomach sank as he walked through the doors and out onto the deck. "Nate!"

"Get some sleep, Izzy." He turned to face me but continued to walk backward. "You have no idea how sorry I am."

"I think I do," I started, but Nate pivoted and dove off the deck into the water below. I rushed to the banister, but even the moonlight didn't reveal where he'd popped up. "Nate!" I whispered as loudly as I could, trying not to wake up anyone around us.

But he didn't appear.

I waited on the deck for twenty minutes.

Then I waited in bed for another fifteen. Or maybe it was twenty. Then I closed my eyes just for a second.

I woke slowly and stretched my arms above my head, then brought my hands down to skim Nate's body.

But he wasn't there.

My eyes flew open and I sat up, staring at the empty side of the bed.

"I'm here," Nate said from my left.

I looked left and found Nate sitting on the sofa in the corner, already dressed for the day. Shadows hung under his eyes.

"Were you up all night?" I slid out of bed and took the opposite side of the couch.

"I couldn't sleep after I . . ." His voice trailed off, and he jerked his gaze from mine, then leaned over the coffee table and handed me a sheet of paper. "Anyway, I made a list. It's everywhere we've talked about over the last few days."

I took the list from him and read over it. "Palau next year, Peru the year after that, then Borneo, the Canary Islands, and the Maldives."

"Did I miss anything?" He leaned forward, resting his elbows on his knees.

"Seychelles," I said.

"Right." He handed me a pen. "Write it in."

I glanced from him to the pen, then took it slowly and wrote *Seychelles* in the empty space at the bottom, pushing a little too hard and sending the pen through the paper. "Shit."

"I already booked flights for next year. You wanted Palau, right?" he asked, putting his cell phone on the table.

My pulse leapt. What the hell was I supposed to do with that? "You did?"

He nodded. "I made them for October next year, but we can move the dates, depending on which firm you go with, or if I'm . . . not around."

In other words, deployed.

I put the paper and pen next to the phone and sat back, curling my legs underneath me. Nate's eyes heated as he glanced down my body, and I did my best to ignore the answering hum of desire that look ignited. "Where did you buy the tickets from? What cities?"

He took a deep breath. "I bought mine from North Carolina, and yours from New York."

My lips parted.

"I texted Serena, since the time difference helped me out, and she said that's where the firm you want is. The one that you've been talking about for the last year."

He didn't want me to even consider moving to North Carolina to be with him. He wanted to keep us just like this, the once-a-year fling that consumed my life, my heart.

"Is this about last night?"

"I just wanted to make sure that we followed through." He swallowed. "We spent years talking about doing this, and it took . . . years. Now we know we'll get to see each other."

"Even if it's just for a week?"

"A week is better than nothing," he said.

"And how long is nothing supposed to be our baseline?" I stood, needing a little distance from him. "How long are we supposed to try and steal a weekend here, a week there?"

"As long as we have to." He watched me pace, his body calm and still but his eyes assessing every move I made.

"That's not an answer!"

"It's the only one I have." So. Damned. Calm.

How long did he plan to stay in the military? Couldn't he see what it was doing to him? I could. It was clear as day.

"Are we even going to talk about last night?"

"There's no point in us talking about a nightmare," he said, his eyes tracking my movements. "I get them. You probably get them."

"Yeah, well, I go to therapy too." I sat on the edge of the bed. "Please tell me you're seeing someone." I held up my hand. "And before you ask, no, you didn't hurt me. I'm not mad about last night. I know you'd cut your hand off before you'd use it against me."

His jaw locked and he looked away, focusing on the scenery outside the open double doors. "I passed the psych eval for selection, so apparently I'm just fine. I can't control what I dream about, Izzy. And the second I go talking to some shrink about nightmares, I can forget all about getting through the Q Course for Special Forces. They'll kick me out."

"What were you looking for last night?" I asked. "When you had me underneath you, your hand was searching for something."

He blew out a slow breath and raked his hands through his short hair. "I usually keep a weapon under my pillow when I'm deployed, and I was dreaming—" He shook his head. "It doesn't matter. And honestly, things like what happened last night just add to the many reasons that you and I work the way we do."

"But we don't!" I pushed off the bed, unable to sit still. I felt like I was going to come out of my skin, like my body couldn't possibly hold the intense emotions coursing through me. "This isn't a real relationship if we keep doing it this way, Nate."

"I never said it was." He stood, but didn't move closer to me, just watched me prowl back and forth across our room. "We agreed not to blow our shot, remember? We agreed—"

"A lot changes in three years," I countered. "That's how long I've been waiting, Nate. Three years, constantly comparing whomever I happen to be dating to you. Constantly wondering where you are, *how* you are. Wondering if you're ever going to let me in, tell me what happens to you when you deploy."

"You don't want to know any of that." He slid his hands into his pockets, the picture of cool and collected.

"Yes, I do! How am I supposed to know you if you won't really let me?"

"You know me better than anyone—"

"No, I know what you let me *see* better than anyone." I pivoted on the hardwood floor, my back to the door as I faced him.

"What do you want me to tell you, Iz?" He cocked his head to the side, and that mask I saw from time to time—the one he'd worn at his mom's funeral—appeared. "Who I am over there isn't who I am when I'm with you. I really don't want you getting to know that guy."

"What is that supposed to mean?" I hated how unruffled he seemed, like he wasn't struggling with the constant distance between us—the ever-moving goal line of when we'd be able to have a real relationship.

"It means that I'm . . ." He sighed. "I'm an effective compartmentalizer. I've learned how to separate the shit that happens over there from my life stateside. It's one of those coping mechanisms you talked about years ago, remember?"

I did.

"And if I want to know all of you?"

"You don't." He shook his head with certainty.

"I do," I argued.

"No. You. Don't. The fact that I can keep that shit under a lid isn't to lock you out, Iz, it's to protect you. You shouldn't have to deal with . . . everything."

"Because you don't trust me to be there for you?" I took two steps closer to him. "I was there for your mom's funeral. I showed up when you needed me."

"You did, and I know I never thanked you enough for that—"

"You don't have to thank me, Nate. I want to be there! God, don't you get it? Don't you understand that there's no way I can stay away if I know you're suffering?"

"Which is *exactly* why I haven't told you." His voice rose. "You wouldn't want to know the things I've done, the things I'll do. You'd never look at me the same way. You think getting startled out of a nightmare is bad? It's not. Not to mention that you *can't* know any more, now that I'm going into Special Forces. It's mostly classified. Izzy, you're the one good, untainted thing in my life. You are the only peace I know. Why would I drag you into a shitstorm if I don't have to?"

"So, I'll never know what you go through? How to help you?" My chest clenched along with my fists.

"Why would you want to?"

"Because I'm in love with you!" I shouted, then gasped, covering my mouth with both hands. Shit, that was *not* supposed to come out.

His eyes flared. "Isabeau, no."

My cheeks stung with heat as I backed my way out of the bungalow and onto the deck. If I dove off the end right now and started swimming, I could reach the next island over by the afternoon. I could avoid the rest of this conversation.

"You can't love me," he said, shaking his head as he followed me out. The look on his face was pure devastation.

"And you can't tell me how to feel!" Once my back hit the railing, there was nowhere else to go. "Can't we just ignore that I said it?"

"No." He stalked forward, only stopping when he had me caged, one hand gripping the railing on either side of me.

"Why not? You're asking me to ignore everything that happens when we're not together. You're asking me to live off an existence of what you deign to tell me through letters and emails." I lifted my chin and tried to glare at him, but the concern, the apprehension in his eyes chipped at my anger.

"Because everything that happens when we're not together is the bullshit," he said. "This is real." He picked up my hand and put it on his chest. "This is the reality I live for."

His heart beat erratically under my fingers. "And yet you won't let me love you."

He shook his head. "You can't, Iz. You just can't. I'm not good enough for you, not yet. Look at what happened last night. One nightmare, and I've got my arm at your—" He swallowed hard. "Look, I'm not just scared—I'm terrified of ruining the only shot we'll get. You want real? That's how I feel. I can't lose you." His eyes searched mine, and I felt a crack in my chest that I tried to ignore, knowing that if I looked too closely, I'd find a fault line in my heart.

"But you won't really have me either," I whispered. That's when it hit me. He'd chosen his path, and he wouldn't allow me to follow. He would always be at war in some way or another, and my fate, if I chose it, would be to watch him slowly change from the boy I met on that plane six years ago into whatever years and years of combat would turn him into.

That crack in my heart expanded with a painful jolt.

"I'll have whatever you'll let me." He cradled my face between his hands and looked into my soul. "And *we* will have whatever we can give each other." Lowering his head slowly, he pressed his against mine.

"I can only give you what I have, Izzy. I know it's not enough, but it's all I have."

His lips brushed over mine, and I melted.

I was screwed. That was all it took—one touch of his mouth, and I was his. Because as wrong as it might be, I loved him so much that I was willing to take whatever I could get when it came to Nate.

So, I took everything he'd give me for the next two days, and then I went home to DC, packed for the job I was offered in New York, and counted down the days until I'd see him in Palau.

CHAPTER TWENTY-THREE

NATHANIEL

Kabul, Afghanistan
August 2021

To put it as mildly as possible, the country was falling the fuck apart.

And Isabeau refused to leave.

She was about to lose that choice.

We'd been back in Kabul twenty-four hours, and the embassy had descended into what could only be called chaos. For every person within its walls, seeking shelter, or a way out of the country, there were ten outside the gates demanding entrance. I could only imagine what the temporary site being established at the airport looked like.

We were at the center of a mountain of stockpiled powder kegs, just watching the flickering flame of the lit fuse race toward us. Destruction was imminent. It was only a question of when.

"Herat," Webb said, gesturing to the surveillance picture of the fallen province projected onto the wall of the conference room we'd commandeered in the basement of the embassy. All but one of us had been gathered for the noon briefing. Graham was sticking to Izzy on my orders. Webb clicked, and the next picture appeared showing the same scene in a different province. "Lashkar Gah, which as you know, means the entirety of Helmand is now in Taliban hands."

My jaw clenched.

The already-tense atmosphere around the conference table went up a notch, but no one said a word. We'd all spent enough time in country to know that the initial estimates of how long the government would remain in control were way too generous, but to watch it fall apart on our watch was beyond words.

"Add Kandahar to the list," he said, clicking again. More of the same flooded the screen. Two of Afghanistan's three largest cities were now in the hands of the Taliban.

The special ops guys at the airport—

"Unit 03?" Parker asked, voicing my exact thoughts as he leaned forward in his seat across from me. The twitch of his black mustache was the only sign of his agitation.

"Holding the airport for now," Webb replied. "But it's not looking good. They're cut off, and air is the only evac route. They're low on food and ammunition."

"So basically, fucked," Black said. "They're fucked."

"Afghan Special Forces is working on something," Webb replied. "If our orders change, I'll let you know."

Which meant we weren't going to be allowed to do shit. My jaw clenched. They were pinned down, surrounded, and starving.

"Moving on . . ." Webb clicked for the next picture, showing just how many provinces had fallen, and I took any feelings I had about the Kandahar situation and shoved them where they belonged—out of my head. Every province the Taliban had reclaimed was highlighted in red, and there was a shit ton of red.

"There's a lot of red between us and a certain photojournalist," Torres mumbled from behind me.

Like I needed to be reminded.

"As of last night, three thousand of our troops are on the way, and all civilians, Afghan allies, and diplomats are under instruction to leave." He glanced my way and I nodded, catching his meaning. "Our information indicates that an additional thousand boots of the Eighty-Second Airborne are going to be authorized today. Keeping the airport secure is the primary objective."

The next picture appeared, showing the growing crowds outside the airport.

Yeah, that fuse was headed our way, all right.

"In the last two days, forty-six flights have gotten out, and as you can see, demand is considerably higher than supply," Webb continued.

"Fucking Saigon," Elston muttered, rubbing his hand down his beard.

I reached for my water bottle and drank, refusing to let that knot of anxiety in my throat grow any bigger. Izzy had to get out. Once she was on a plane, I could concentrate on what needed to be done.

"And last but not least." Webb clicked the next picture, an overhead shot of Kabul taken by drone, showing the congested roadways leading into the city, and marking the checkpoints already captured by the Taliban on the outer rim of the small province. "The enemy is approaching the gates. I think it's safe to say that President Ghani is no longer in control."

We were about to be put into the same position as Kandahar.

Chairs squeaked as bodies shifted weight around me.

"Mazar-i-Sharif?" I asked.

"Holding," Webb replied. "But we're not sure for how long."

Seemed to be the general consensus about everything around here.

"Now that most of the congressional teams have evacuated, our mission will be shifting," Webb said as he handed out orders. The unit split into squads of four, which was nothing new to us, some assigned to high-value individuals for evacuation, and others to various tasks.

The briefing ended and everyone rose.

"Green," Webb said as I pushed my chair in, and I nodded, hanging back as the others filed out of the room. The door shut before he spoke again. "Regarding Ms. Astor."

"I'll get her on the first plane."

"Senator Lauren received her request to remain and be of use to the ambassador." He cocked an eyebrow.

"I'm going to kill her." I rubbed the bridge of my nose.

"Senator Lauren found the request . . . noble . . . and agreed, only insofar as we can get Ms. Astor out safely when the time comes, and I think we can both agree that the time is coming rapidly. Oh, and if we could make sure to get a photographer to catch a couple shots of her aide working diligently, since we didn't take the obvious opportunity presented to us with the girls' chess team."

"Right." Fucking politicians with their fucking PR.

He shut his laptop, and the projection turned to a blank blue screen. "Is there anything I should know about why your charge would request to stay in a country that is obviously disintegrating?"

"Her sister is a photojournalist on assignment in Mazar-i-Sharif." I scratched the four-day growth of beard I had going. "Ms. Astor is loath to leave until her sister, also Ms. Astor, has, and stubbornness seems to be a genetic trait in that family, and Serena's interpreter's visa isn't approved yet."

"Hmm." His eyes narrowed slightly, which I knew from experience meant he was taking in the information and calculating how it affected the mission. "I'm not in the mood to deal with a pissed-off senator or hand the Taliban a new source of YouTube material."

"Me either." That wasn't going to happen to her.

He nodded. "Keep your usual team with you. It would be nice to get both sisters out, especially given their high profile, but our priority is the younger."

"Noted." My chest tightened. I cared about Serena and didn't want to leave her behind, but I wouldn't sacrifice Izzy for her. The problem was that Izzy wouldn't agree.

I left Webb behind and headed out, finding Torres leaned up against the wall outside the door, waiting for me.

"How you doing?" he asked, keeping step with me down the dimly lit hallway.

"Fine. Can't you tell?"

"I've seen air traffic controllers with less anxiety wafting off them, but if you want to go with fine . . ." He shrugged.

"I do," I grumbled, climbing the stairs into the crowded lobby, then continuing up to Izzy's suite. Her conference room had been taken over by embassy staff, all doing their best to process as many interviews as they could to complete visas.

Graham stood guard outside her door, and his dark brows shot up when he caught sight of me walking his way.

"You might want to check with Webb, but I think you get twice the imminent danger pay for walking in there," Graham said, glancing sideways at Izzy's door.

"And I'm telling you to look again!" she shouted, her voice carrying through the door.

"See? Pretty sure she's firing live rounds."

"She doesn't scare me," I lied, a corner of my mouth lifting. "Get the others up here. We're still on Astor duty," I ordered.

"On it." He took off.

I took a deep breath and walked into the suite. Izzy had dragged the landline telephone over to where she sat on the couch, files spread out on the table in front of her.

"And I'm telling you that form was submitted, so look again," Izzy snapped, not even bothering to look up at me. "Taj. T-A-J Barech. He submitted his application in April."

Serena's interpreter.

I sat back on the windowsill to her left, where I could see both her and anyone coming for her through the door.

"Yes, I know you have eighteen thousand applicants in the pipeline." Izzy white-knuckled the receiver with a still-ringless hand and yanked on her hair, dragging it over one shoulder to get it out of the way.

That little strip of skin she'd just revealed on her neck had my instant attention.

She'd loved it when I'd kissed her neck.

What the hell had happened between her and Dickface that he'd flown off without his fiancée? Or did that term no longer apply to them? I'd promised myself I wouldn't ask, wouldn't pry into shit that wasn't my business, but this was Izzy.

"And I understand that," she continued, drumming the fingers of her right hand on the edge of the couch. "But as difficult as it is for you to process these as quickly as possible, I can promise you it's infinitely more difficult to be an interpreter who publicly worked with US forces sitting in Afghanistan right now, praying your visa gets processed in time to evacuate."

Damn, she was beautiful when she was angry. I was just glad the anger wasn't directed at me. Yet.

"No, I will not relax, and I'm not calling you from my cushy office in DC. I'm in the embassy in Kabul." She yanked the receiver away from her ear and closed her eyes, breathing in deeply.

"Need me to take over?" I offered. "I'm the trained killer in the room, remember? Not that you're not doing an admirable job of slaughtering the State Department."

She shot me a glare and put the phone back to her head. "Oh, you found it. Good. Can you tell me what the holdup is? Because I'm holding his completed file." Her eyes flew wide. "You're missing what?" She thumbed through the file on the table. "His record of military service is here. Twelve years translating for various units—" Her shoulders fell.

I pushed off the windowsill and moved to her side, reading the file over her shoulder.

"His letter of recommendation." She sighed, searching the papers again. "It's not here either. How hard can it be to get one of those?"

My stomach twisted. Hard enough.

"You're going to want to put that call on speakerphone," I said softly.

"Because you think you can—"

"You need a general or a flag officer," I replied. "Know any of those?"

Her mouth snapped shut, and she poked the speakerphone button, setting the receiver down.

"—and until we have that letter, our process is at a standstill, Ms. Astor." The man's superior tone lifted my hackles. "And we have thousands ahead of him who have their paperwork complete. Even if you could get the letter of recommendation submitted, moving him to the top of the list would be unfair, and given the shortage of interview appointments—"

"I can figure out the damned interview," Izzy interrupted, color rising in her cheeks.

"If I can get that letter of recommendation over to you within the next few hours, can you process his file or not?" I asked.

"I'm sorry, but who am I talking to?" the man asked.

"Sergeant First Class Green," I replied. "I'm with the Joint Special Operations Command."

Izzy's gaze jumped to mine.

"Could you process the file within twenty-four hours if you had the letter?" I asked, folding my arms across my chest.

"I'm sorry, are you implying you can even get a letter here within twenty-four hours?" His voice dripped with sarcasm. "Because we're a little overwhelmed here at the moment, and I don't have time to keep a file on the back burner just waiting to see if a letter magically appears."

"I can have it to you within—" I checked my watch and did the time-difference calculations. "Two hours. Can you process the file to interview status or not?"

"If it arrives." If eye-rolling was verbal, that would have been one. "I'll make a note in the file that you're sending it. What unit did you say you were with?"

"Thirty-Third Logistics Group out of Bragg."

Izzy's mouth dropped open.

"Logistics, huh?" The sound of typing came through the speaker.

"Yeah, you know us. We're always the ones getting shit done."

"Right. And who can I expect this letter to be coming from?"

"Someone way above your pay grade," I answered. "You get his email?" I asked Izzy.

She nodded.

"Good, then we're done here." I hit the button and ended the call.

"What are you going to do?" Izzy asked as I closed Barech's file and picked it up.

"I'm going to solve the one problem I can." I carried the file to the door and opened it, finding Graham, Parker, and Elston already waiting. "Get this to Apex," I told Elston, referring to Webb's call sign as I handed the redhead the file, "and tell him that we need him to wake up the general for a letter of recommend."

"Will do." He took the file and disappeared down the hallway.

"Sergeant Black." I looked at our medic. "I need the status of every checkpoint between here and Mazar-i-Sharif, and which ones are going to let an American photojournalist through without needing . . . convincing."

"On it." He nodded once and took off in the same direction Elston had taken.

"Sergeant Gray, find someone who can get a dependable cell phone into Serena Astor's hands." It was worth a try.

"You got it." He went the opposite direction, leaving the hallway empty despite the mayhem going on below us.

Awareness skittered up my arms as I backed into Izzy's room and shut the door.

"What's wrong?" Izzy asked, smoothing the lines of her wrap-style blouse as she stood. It was emerald green and brought out the depth in her eyes, but I kept that observation to myself.

"This five minutes?" We were on day nine. We were officially tied for the most consecutive days we'd spent together. "Nothing."

"And that's worrisome to you." She walked barefoot to the kitchenette and pulled two bottles of water from the fridge, then threw one at me. I caught it. Had to admit, I kind of loved it that she always thought of me, even when she was pissed at me. "I can tell, because you have that pinched look right here." She touched the spot between her brows. "It's your tell."

"I don't have a tell. They beat it out of me years ago." I twisted the top and took a drink to keep my eyes off the sight of her throat working. What was it about her neck that had me nearly feral?

"Hmm." She set her bottle down on the counter. "Well, I guess I know you better than *they* do. Now what's wrong? You know, besides the obvious."

"You mean the fact that you seem to have chosen Kabul as your place of residence during a military overthrow of the government?" I put my own bottle down and walked into the center of the suite so I wouldn't do something stupid like lift her to that counter and kiss her until she remembered that she'd loved me at one time.

"Yeah. Other than that." She perched her ass on the arm of the sofa.

"I have a feeling." I shrugged.

"Oh, we've moved on to discussing feelings? Look how much we've matured." A smirk tugged at her lips.

The remark, though clearly teasing, hit a nerve. "From what I remember, I was the one completely open with my feelings the last time we met."

"And from what I remember, you were the one who asked me to ignore our history so we could both get our jobs done here." She stretched her legs out and crossed her ankles.

"Yeah, well, that's getting more difficult by the hour," I admitted, refusing to look at the way her pants hugged her hips, her thighs. "We're in the calm before the storm," I told her as I crossed the room to look through the windows into the courtyard below. There was nothing peaceful or artistic about it now. It had been turned into a corral, another waiting room, with a winding line of desperate people.

I turned to face her, preparing myself for the coming fight. "This place is about to blow, Iz. You can't stay."

"I don't see you leaving," she said casually over her shoulder.

"We are not the same."

"Well aware." She looked away.

"The senator has given permission for you to stay insofar that we can assure your safety and get you out." I moved, putting myself in her line of sight. The glare she gave me made me wish I were wearing my Kevlar. "Iz, it's getting uncomfortably close to pushing that limit. I've seen the maps. By tomorrow, Kabul is going to be the only exit point from this country."

She took a shaky breath and straightened her shoulders. "Then it's a good thing we're already here, isn't it? I'm not leaving without my sister."

My jaw flexed. "I'm doing everything I can to get Serena out, but my orders are for *you*. And when the time comes, I will put your ass on a plane whether or not you tell me you're ready to leave."

"What are you going to do, Nate?" She stood, folding her arms. "Throw me over your shoulder and carry me kicking and screaming?"

I moved forward, consuming her space, until we stood toe to toe and she was forced to lean back in order to keep glaring at me. "If I have to, yes. You have no idea the lengths I will go to in order to keep you safe."

"Because I'm your assignment." The statement was an accusation.

"Because that's all I've done since I met you, Isabeau." My hands curled with the need to touch her, to pull her against me and beg her to leave.

"She's all I have, Nate." She held her ground as the air between us charged just like it always did. "I'm a trophy to my parents, and a memory to you, and . . ." She rubbed the empty finger on her left hand. "Serena is the only person in this world who's been there for me unconditionally, the only person who's never deserted me, and I'll be damned if I leave her to die. If I go, there's no one left here who cares about her. We both know what will happen to her."

"You'd prefer to die with her? Because that's a very real possibility. There are over four hundred miles of hostile territory for her to get through, and that's if she agrees to leave. Every air resource we have is committed. I can't just call her an Uber and send for her, and we can't wait. You can't wait."

Her lower lip trembled, and I muttered a curse.

"I deserve a day," she finally said.

"A day?" I repeated.

"For all the years I spent waiting for you, the least you can give me is a damned day to see if she'll leave. Twenty-four hours."

I straightened and retreated a step like she'd slapped me.

"I'm sorry." Her eyes flew wide, and she covered her mouth with a hand. "Nate, I'm sorry. That was wrong."

"And if she's not here in twenty-four hours, will you agree to stop being a general pain in the ass and fighting me about leaving?"

"Will your team be leaving with me?" Her eyes shifted into a pleading expression so familiar that I had déjà vu.

"You know I can't."

And there it was. The look I'd always put on her face eventually. Disappointment and misery. "You'll stay while this place implodes."

"Careful, Iz. You say that like you care what happens to me." I put some space between us.

She followed after me. "I have *always* cared what happened to you!"

Except when she didn't.

"That's something you're going to have to get over." I forced a shrug. "If I wasn't here, I'd be in Iraq, or a dozen other places you'd never even know about. I heard what Serena said, that you went to work for Lauren because she was pushing legislation to end the war." My heart swelled and broke at the same time. "And I'm not arrogant enough to think that had anything to do with me, but just in case it did, just in case you're living your life chasing that goal, then Izzy, you have to stop.

Even you aren't powerful enough to end every war. There will always be a need for guys like me to do the things that make it possible for you to sleep at night."

Even if she was sleeping next to a man who didn't deserve a single hair on her head.

"You deserve a life." She tucked her hair behind her ears and looked at me like the last three years hadn't happened. Like we were still fighting for weekends and every chance to see each other, denying that we were in a relationship when we'd both known we were.

"I have a life." One she wanted no part of.

"A real life, Nate." She moved forward, lifting her hand and then resting it lightly above my heart. "A home. A future with . . ." She bit into her lower lip and then sighed. "With whomever you choose."

The walls of my defenses cracked, and pain came flooding through, drowning my self-made promises to keep my distance and my mouth shut when it came to her love life.

"And is that what you have with Covington? A future? A home? Because I fail to see the allure."

So much for professionalism.

"The allure?" She jerked her hand away. "He was *there*."

CHAPTER TWENTY-FOUR
IZZY

New York
October 2018

The one thing no one ever bothered to tell me about New York was that I'd never be able to afford anything bigger than a shoebox in Manhattan on an associate's pay. Or maybe everyone assumed I'd permanently live off Mom and Dad.

In Brooklyn, however, I could manage a small one-bedroom apartment on my own. It was a second-story walk-up in Dumbo with an actual closet, and the best part was the scent of freedom. Freedom from my parents' expectations and their constant badgering that I use my law degree to do what I could to further their business.

"I can actually see the water from here if I stand on the couch!" Serena said from her precarious perch on the arm of the sofa. She'd been here all of an hour and was already climbing up the walls. My sister had never been good at sitting still.

"I'd be careful if I were you. That's not the sturdiest piece of furniture." I threw my suit jacket over a dining room chair and went back to organizing the grocery order that had just been delivered.

"Are you telling me you put it together with a butter knife?" she asked, jumping to the hardwood floor.

"Hardly." A corner of my mouth lifted. "Nate put it together when he came to visit about . . ." I did the mental math. "Eight months ago."

"And you don't trust his construction abilities?" She wedged herself between my body and the opposite counter in the U-shaped kitchen and grabbed the coffee creamer, then put it into the refrigerator.

"I do. But I also know what that thing looked like coming out of the box." I rose on my bare toes and put the boxed stuff on the highest shelf.

"Eight months seems like a pretty long time," Serena said, leaning back against the counter. "Have you seen him since then?"

"Nope." My chest clamped down like a vise. "He's been gone more than he's been home, according to his texts and letters." I put the fruits and vegetables away. "If he's not at some training or school, he's . . ." I shrugged because I honestly had no clue.

"Is that normal for Special Forces, or whatever he's doing?"

"How would I know?" I handed her a box of coffee. "Behind you." Truth was, I'd barely heard from him in the past seven months, and what I had heard had been vague and short.

She leaned sideways and put the coffee away without getting off the counter. "But you've heard from him, right?"

"Yeah." I finished the last of the order and leaned back against the counter. "I mean, not in the last month, but he told me that he was going to be busy." There was some kind of test he was taking, but he hadn't gone into detail, which meant I wasn't supposed to mention it.

"Busy?" Serena cocked an eyebrow as Tybee, my six-month-old Maine coon kitten, jumped onto the counter.

"You're not supposed to be up here, are you?" I asked him, scratching under his chin before I set him back on the floor. Not that he'd listen. Tybee had taught me that cats did whatever the hell they wanted whenever the hell they wanted to. I envied them their give-no-fucks attitude. I shrugged. "He texted and said he wouldn't be able to talk this month, but he'd meet me at O'Hare."

Serena blinked. "So you're just going to fly off to Palau tomorrow and hope he meets you at O'Hare?"

"It worked last time." I shrugged again. It wasn't like I needed to worry. Nate was one of the only people in my life who always did what they said they were going to do. "No news is good news with Nate. If something had gone awry, he would have told me. We planned out our trips for the next four years while he was here over Valentine's Day. We couldn't buy our tickets or book most of the resorts, so Nate hired a travel agent and dumped more money than I care to even think about so they'd make the arrangements when the dates became available." It had been overwhelmingly, sweetly romantic, and yet had told me he was still planning on this being the way we lived for the next four years. He'd gone so far as to tell me that even the wives weren't getting much face time. Hell, I wasn't even a girlfriend. "Assuming we don't have to move dates for deployments, which he said we undoubtably would. I'll just have to cross my fingers and pray I can get time off when he has leave."

Her eyes narrowed. "And it doesn't bother you that you don't know where he is half the time or what he's doing?"

"Of course it does." I lifted my shoulders and let them fall. "But I don't exactly have the right to know."

"What if something . . ." She struggled with her words. "Happened to him?"

"Then hopefully someone—probably one of his friends—would tell me."

Her head tilted to the side as she studied me. "He could have an entire family, a wife and kids, down there in North Carolina and you wouldn't know." She pointed her finger at me. "And don't you dare shrug at me again."

I locked my posture. "He doesn't. I might not know where he's sent, but he's always honest with me when he's dating someone, the same as I am with him."

"And how long has it been since you've dated someone?"

"Two months." Hugh had been a massive mistake, an attempt to fill the void, an attempt to see if I could live without Nate. I pushed off the counter and walked out of the kitchen and into the dining room, connected to the living room. "And I thought you were taking this week as vacation? Stop interviewing me like I'm your latest story."

"I'm not!" She hopped off the counter and followed me into the bedroom. "I just worry about you."

That made two of us, but I couldn't say that to her. I walked into my closet and stripped off the remains of my suit, opting for drawstring pajama pants and the hoodie Nate had given me for Christmas with some logo that represented his unit. "Thank you for taking the week to watch Tybee, by the way."

"No problem. I legitimately had nothing better to do."

I came out to find her lying across the expanse of my bed, staring up at the ceiling. "You don't have to patronize me. I know how hard you're working at that new paper."

"Apparently not hard enough." She sighed.

I lay down next to her. "Spill."

"I didn't get the assignment I wanted. They're sending a more senior photojournalist." Her voice lifted in an imitation of her boss. "But not to worry, I can keep covering the Hill until my time comes."

"I'm sorry." I kept my eyes on the blades of the ceiling fan above us so she wouldn't see the lie in my eyes. That country had a death grip on the man I loved, and I wasn't exactly chomping at the bit for it to get its hands on my sister too. "I know how badly you wanted to go."

"I just want to cover something meaningful." She laced her fingers over her rib cage.

"Afghanistan isn't the only place to do that," I said softly. "I'm sure lots of meaningful things happen on the Hill. It's the seat of our government." It was all I could think to say, and I knew it fell short of what she needed.

"You'd be amazed at how much there *isn't*." She turned her head toward me. "Senator Lauren's bill failed again. It didn't even get out of committee."

My brow furrowed. "Remind me which one that is?"

"The one trying to set a withdrawal date from Afghanistan."

"Oh." I lifted my hand to cover my heart, like I could somehow rub the ache out of it. "That's a shame."

"Speaking of shame." She rolled to face me, bracing her head on her hand. "How are Mom and Dad handling your choice of corporate law?"

"Hey!" I rolled my eyes. "I spend at least half my day handling the contracts for the nonprofits—"

"That the richest companies in New York have for tax purposes?" She laughed, then pressed her lips between her teeth when she caught my glare. "Okay, okay."

"It's only for a couple years. Just long enough to pay back Mom and Dad for law school."

"Because you're feeling guilty that you grew up privileged?" She cocked an eyebrow at me.

"Because I can't take the constant guilt trips about not working in the best interest of the family," I answered honestly.

"You know, Isa," she said, slipping into her impression of our father, and I grinned. "You could do so much good for the family if you'd simply devote your entire life to making it legal for us to pay less taxes."

"Something like that," I laughed. "I just can't take it anymore."

"I get that. I'm barely covering that apartment in DC now that you're gone, but I refuse to go to them for money." She wiggled her finger toward my nose. "You could always move back to DC just for me, you know. Forget Mom and Dad. There are tons of corporate jobs there. You don't have to take the political ones. Your room is so lonely without you."

I scoffed. "Then get a roommate."

"Valid point." She glanced past me. "Any chance that your inability to see a relationship through has to do with the fact that you keep that picture on your nightstand?"

I didn't need to look to know it was the picture of Nate kissing my cheek in Fiji. "I think it has to do with the fact that I pretty much keep *him* on the nightstand."

She slowly brought her gaze back to mine. "I know that what you two share is . . . undefinable, but Izzy, how long can it go on like this? You here and him . . . everywhere?"

A boulder lodged itself in my throat. "Nate has his reasons." That night in Fiji had scared him more than it had me, just not enough for him to go talk to someone about it. "And it doesn't matter that I don't agree with them. He won't let me choose between my career and him. I can't force him to choose between me and his career either. I don't know how to let him go, Serena."

She brushed my hair back. "I know. I just hate to watch you living your life like a first-time driver with a stick shift, jolting forward and stalling over and over again."

"I love him." There was no other way to explain my actions.

"Yeah." She offered me a sad smile. "But does he feel the same way about you?"

Weight settled in my stomach, immovable and nauseating. "I don't know. But I'm determined not to come back from Palau until I know the answer. I'm done being the person with the most to lose here."

Nate wouldn't let me down. I knew that in the very depths of my soul. I just had to make it clear that the time for our shot was *now*.

The next day, my stomach twisted into knots when my group was called to board at Chicago O'Hare. Was this how Nate felt when my flight had been delayed on our way to Fiji?

Guilt sagged my shoulders as I stood, lifting my bag to my shoulder. I should have found time to text him on that trip, to put him out of his misery.

Guess this was payback.

I looked around at the other passengers as I moved into the boarding line, hoping that one head would stand above the others, that a pair of crystal-blue eyes would already be looking my way. He wasn't here yet.

But he would be. Nate had never let me down in my life. Had he canceled plans on me because he was going to be spending his weekend "cleaning the pool"—his favorite phrase for telling me he was deploying over the phone? Sure. Absolutely. But he had never *not* called.

I checked my phone as the line moved forward, then opened the flight app for my boarding pass. The desk attendant reminded everyone at the gate that the flight was sold out as I scanned my ticket and boarded the flight.

Shaking my head that Nate had gone overboard with the first-class tickets, I slid into my seat, keeping my bag between my feet. I'd brought four new novels, complete with highlights for him, and didn't want to have to haul the bag back out to give him his pick when he got here.

"Can I get you anything before takeoff?" the flight attendant asked with a polite smile.

"No, thank you. Do you know if everyone has checked in for first class? I haven't seen my travel companion."

"I don't, I'm sorry." He glanced at the empty seat. "Don't worry. We still have about forty minutes before we close the doors. It takes a while to get everyone seated on a plane this big."

"Thank you." I sat back as he moved on to the next seats, and I kicked myself in the heart for what I'd obviously put Nate through on our way to Fiji. I pulled my phone from my purse and typed out a text.

Izzy: This seat next to me looks awfully empty.

I hit send and then watched the screen for the three scrolling dots that would tell me he was replying, but none appeared. After opening the airline's app, I searched for the flight our paperwork told me he was on.

It landed five minutes ago.

That explained it. He probably hadn't switched his phone off airplane mode while sprinting from a gate on the opposite side of the airport. He'd better be running. My heart jumped, my pulse accelerating at the thought of seeing him in just a few minutes.

But those minutes ticked by.

The flight attendant gave me a sympathetic look when he asked if he could help stow my carry-on for takeoff.

I buckled in, then shamelessly leaned into the aisle, looking above the seat's partitions to watch the door I'd boarded through. My stomach sank when the attendant moved toward the door, and I nearly fumbled my phone, dialing Nate's number.

It didn't even ring before it sent me to voice mail, which meant it was off. "Nate, I think they're closing the doors, and I'm really worried. It looks like your flight was delayed, and I don't even know if I can get off at this point, so I guess I'll catch up to you at the next layover in Hawaii? I can't wait to see you." I hung up.

He missed the flight.

He missed the next one too.

Bleary eyed, I checked into the resort the next day. "Isabeau Astor, but it might be under—"

"I have you here," the concierge replied with a smile that I was too exhausted to return fullheartedly. "We'll see you to your bungalow."

"Can you tell me if Nathaniel Phelan has checked in?"

"You're the first, ma'am."

I nodded in thanks and followed the bellhop, my steps robotic and my heart growing heavier by the hour.

"Here you are." The bellhop opened the bungalow and set my luggage inside. "Is there anything we can help you with?"

Not unless he could tell me where the hell Nate was.

"No, thank you." I tipped him, and then I was alone with my jet lag and worried heart. I sat on the king-size bed, the one that Nate was supposed to be in with me, and took out my phone, cursing that I hadn't paid for international service because I'd wanted to be left completely alone with Nate.

But I had Wi-Fi. I checked my email, then my social media accounts, but there was nothing from Nate.

Then I checked his. The last post had been from five weeks ago, when he, Torres, and Rowell went fishing. They both had *J* first names, but I couldn't remember which one was Justin and which was Julian since Nate mostly referred to them by last name. I'd never met the man with the smiling brown eyes, or the tall smirking blond, and their pages were private, just like Nate's. They'd both entered Special Forces with Nate, but the fourth friend he'd mentioned was never pictured anymore. Nate had called me after he'd gotten back from that fishing trip, then disappeared yet again.

I looked around the sumptuous bungalow. Even leaving my feelings out of the equation, this place must have cost him a fortune. There was no way he wasn't coming. Nate had always shown up for me. Always.

But doubt crept in. We hadn't been speaking as frequently these last eight months. I'd been consumed with the hours a new associate had to put in, and he'd been off doing whatever it was he did.

Lying back on the bed, I fought off exhaustion with every blink of my eyes, scared I'd miss the moment he burst through the door and kissed me.

When I opened my eyes, it was light out, but the sun shone from a different direction.

I scrambled from the bed, my body stiff from sleeping in my clothes for what had obviously been about eleven hours. "Nate?" I called out, searching the bathroom first.

If he'd gotten in and found me sleeping, he wouldn't have woken me. He was annoyingly selfless that way.

The bathroom was empty, so I unlocked the sliding glass door and stepped out onto the deck. "Nate?" My voice was swallowed by the sound of wind and waves.

Wait. The door was locked. He hadn't unlocked it. Dread skittered like ice along my spine, and I went back into the room, picked up the phone on my nightstand, and dialed for the front desk. "Hi, can you please tell me if Nathaniel Phelan checked in?" I asked.

"One moment." I heard the sound of clicking keys. "No, I'm sorry, ma'am."

My stomach hit the floor.

"Thank you," I whispered, then put the phone back on the receiver.

Nate wasn't here.

I swiped open my phone and texted the required phrases to accept the fees for international service, but the only text was from Serena, wishing me a happy trip.

This was . . . impossible. I hit Nate's button in my contacts, and it rang twice again. Yesterday—or had it been the day before—I'd been certain that meant it was off, but what if he sent me to voice mail?

"This is Nate. Leave a message." So curt and to the point, just like he was.

"I don't know what to do," I said after the beep. "I'm here, but you aren't. You haven't texted, or called, and I'm starting to freak out that maybe something has happened to you, because I know you wouldn't stand me up like this. Just . . ." I swallowed the lump in my throat. "Just call me, Nate. Even if something has come up, please tell me you're okay."

I ended the call.

I ate alone that night, holding out hope that he'd been held up and would walk in at any second.

The next morning, I sat on the sun-warmed deck, my feet dangling over the edge as I clutched my phone like the lifeline it was.

Pain filled the space between heartbeats. I knew this feeling. It had consumed me every time I looked for my parents in the stands at swim meets, only to find empty seats. It had eviscerated me when Jeremy chose to wife-shop at Yale over moving to Georgetown with me after I'd changed *everything* about my life for him. It had raced through my veins like ice, numbing me when Mom and Dad chose to keep cruising instead of coming home after the plane crash. I'd been in this position too many times to count—left waiting for someone I loved, only to realize I was never their priority.

I fought it, my aching heart promising my cynical head that Nate wouldn't do this, but as the hours passed, the truth sank in.

He wasn't coming.

I bit the bullet and called Serena.

"What are you doing calling me on your lovey-dovey vacation?" she asked. "Tybee says hello, by the way."

"He's not here." My voice came out just as flat as I felt.

"Nate?"

"He's not here," I repeated, forcing myself through the words. "Has anyone come by? Anyone . . . in uniform?" My tongue tripped over the words. It was the only other explanation I could think of.

"No, Izzy. No one's been here," she said, her voice softening. "Are you okay?"

"No." My eyes watered and my nose stung as I blinked back the torrent of tears. "Maybe he's deployed? But I mean, he's always slipped me some coded warning in a text or a call. And I don't know any of his friends. I can't think of a single person I could call and ask." I knew so little about his actual life that it was embarrassing. Serena was right. He could have an entire family that I knew nothing about. He'd kept me on the fringes of his life, never letting me in.

But no one had batted an eye when I'd stood at his side at the funeral.

A new girlfriend maybe? A new . . . wife?

"Oh, honey. I'm so sorry."

"What am I supposed to do? Staying makes me foolish, and leaving means . . ." I couldn't bring myself to say it out loud.

"Come home or stay and soak up what sunshine you can." So sensible. So Serena.

"I don't want to be here without him."

"Then you have your answer."

I started crying and didn't stop. I worried the resort staff as I checked out, and then frightened the attendants when the tears kept coming on the flights I'd changed. The tears came and came and came as I crossed time zones, date lines, and what felt like years. People stared and offered tissues, which only made me cry harder.

My eyes were nearly swollen shut, hot and scratchy, by the time I walked into my apartment, and when I saw Serena, the waterworks started again. It was like I had an unending supply of tears.

She held me tight and rocked me like we were little again. "It's okay," she whispered as I sobbed on her shoulder.

"I have to let him go, don't I?" The words were stuttered and broken. "It doesn't matter if he did it on accident or on purpose—I can't keep living like this, Serena. I have to let him go."

"I'm so sorry." Her arms tightened around me.

Nate and I had waited so long to take our shot that we'd missed it.

CHAPTER TWENTY-FIVE

IZZY

Kabul, Afghanistan
August 2021

How dare he.

He didn't see the *allure* of marrying someone who was at least present?

"And *there* has become the baseline for your standards?" The bewilderment on Nate's face was almost laughable.

"You're kidding me, right?" It was a damn good thing I didn't have anything in my hands or I might have thrown it at him. "I wonder who set that baseline?" I cocked my head to the side. "If you think my standard of showing up is low, then you only have to look in the mirror to see why that is. Out of everyone in my life, *you* were the one person I trusted to show up when needed, and you *vanished*."

He put up his hands and backed away slowly. "I think I should leave before we get into shit we have no business dragging up."

That extraordinary talent he had for compartmentalization, for remaining calm and cool when I was ready to throw down, was the one thing I both envied and loathed about him.

"'Dragging up'?" I shook my head. "It's hard to drag something up that never got buried." Emotions I couldn't handle welled up with the force of a tidal wave, devouring every shred of self-control I'd clung to in one all-consuming wave of love and grief and everything that had been left to die between us. "And you lost the right to know anything about my love life *years* ago."

"You don't think I know that?" He turned away from me and walked to the water he'd left on the counter, then slammed back the whole thing like it was a bottle of vodka. He crushed it in his fist before turning back to me, his customary composure slipping. "You think it didn't kill me not to ask who you'd actually deemed worthy of marrying you the second I saw that hunk of ice on your hand?"

"Well, it doesn't matter anymore, does it?" I lifted my left hand, showing its obvious bare state. "He's not my fiancé anymore. Does that make you happy?"

"The better question is if it makes *you* happy." He wasn't even shocked that the ring was gone. Of course he'd noticed at some point. Nate noticed *everything*. But he hadn't asked why. Because he didn't want to know? Or because he didn't think he had a right to?

I opened my mouth and shut it again. "It's complicated."

"Would you like to elaborate?" He leaned against the end of the counter, taking up more space than he should have. Everything about Nate still felt larger than life, and though I thought I'd grown accustomed to seeing him in their version of an unmarked combat uniform, I really hadn't.

He was inconveniently breathtaking and infuriating at the same time.

"Not really." I dropped my hand.

"Okay." He stared at me in that quiet, patient way he had, which only got my ire up.

"Stop doing that."

"Stop doing what?" He scratched the scruff of his beard. "Stop doing everything I can to keep you alive? Stop pulling strings to get your sister's interpreter's papers pushed? Stop putting my body between you and whatever's trying to kill you at the moment? Or did you want me to stop putting your needs above common sense? You're going to have to be more specific."

"That," I sputtered, pointing at his face. "Stop looking at me like that."

"I'm capable of a lot of things, but unfortunately for my own sanity, I seem to be incapable of *not* looking at you." He shrugged. "Whether or not you want to tell me why you're no longer marrying Dickface has nothing to do with my inability to ignore you."

"He cheated on me, okay?" *Ugh.* That was *not* supposed to come out.

Nate's body tensed, but he didn't speak.

"Did you hear me?" I shook my head and fought to get a grip. I was supposed to be helping with those files on the coffee table, not spending precious time fighting with Nate.

"Oh, I heard you." Nate's voice dropped. "I'm just trying to make that statement compute."

"What is there to compute?" I tugged my hair back behind my ears. Pulling it up would have been a much more sensible option today. "He thought it was perfectly acceptable to have an open relationship. I wasn't enough for him."

"Then he's a fucking fool." He said it with so much conviction that I almost believed him.

My heart stuttered. "Don't say things like that. You don't know . . ." Heat rushed to my face.

"I know." The way his gaze heated made my breath catch. "And if you weren't enough for him, then he's going to spend his life totally and completely miserable, because there's no one in this world who measures up to you. If he cheated, then my guess would be that it wasn't because you weren't enough—it was because he wasn't."

I covered my fluttering stomach with a hand. Why hadn't I ever felt this way with Jeremy? Why was all my desire, my driving, insatiable need, reserved for Nate? Not that sex with Jeremy hadn't been good. It had. But he didn't make the rest of the world disappear with a single touch, or brand my soul with a kiss.

I only felt that way with Nate. Hadn't that always been the problem?

An irrational laugh bubbled up through my lips. "And yet he was just my type, wasn't he?"

"I don't follow."

"Unavailable in every way that mattered." I shrugged, stroking my thumb over my naked finger and reveling in the lightness there. "I didn't even realize just how heavy that obnoxious ring was until I gave it back. How much everything about it weighed me down."

He took a deep breath and pushed off the counter, walking past me toward the door. "We should both get back to work."

"You know it wasn't the infidelity that made me break it off with him."

He jerked to a stop.

"I mean, if we're going to get it all out in the open, then let's get it out," I said to his back.

"You don't want to go there with me."

"I do."

Slowly, he turned to face me, and my pulse leapt. It wasn't Sergeant Green staring back at me. No, the war raging in his eyes belonged to *my* Nate. The Nate I'd had at Georgetown, in Illinois, in Tybee.

"It wasn't the infidelity," I repeated, my voice softening. "I knew about it for six weeks before I took Newcastle's place, and I didn't do a damn thing. I smiled for the cameras at his campaign rallies and I kicked him out of my bed, but I didn't break it off. Ask me why I broke it off, Nate."

He shook his head.

"Ask me."

"Why?" The word came out strangled.

“Because I didn’t love him in the way I know I’m capable of.” I swallowed as my heart thundered in my ears. “I knew it the second I saw you again.”

His jaw flexed and his shoulders rose as he struggled to maintain his temper, but I didn’t retreat. Nate would never hurt me, and we’d put this off for nine days too long.

“Say it.” I moved toward him, and he backed away, keeping the distance between us as he walked into the kitchenette. “Whatever you’re thinking, just say it.” Hadn’t he demanded the same that first night at the embassy?

“If you knew that you didn’t love him enough, then why did you say yes in the first place?” His tone rose, bordering on a shout as his legendary self-control finally slipped. “You know what? No. Forget I asked. I don’t want to know why. God!” His hands slammed down on the counter, and he hung his head. “Three fucking years, and we’re right back here.”

“I never left *here*!” My chest squeezed down like a vise as I tapped above my heart. “I’m stuck, Nate. I’m eternally twenty-five years old, frozen in place, in time, standing in that hallway, waiting for you to come back.”

“That’s bullshit and we both know it.” He lifted his head, and the pain I saw etched into every line of his face somehow compounded with the agony I felt. “You never wanted us. Not really. Not when push came to shove. You may have been the one arguing for us to take our shot back in Fiji, but when I pulled the trigger, you didn’t. Fucking. Want. Me.” Hurt dripped from every word.

“That’s *not* what happened in New York. How can you even say that?” My mouth hung open in shock.

“How can *I* say that?” He yanked the knife out of the sheath at his thigh with one hand and pulled his necklace from under his shirt with the other, revealing the taped silver tag. He glanced down as he made a clean slice through the tape, and then sheathed the knife before prying something from beneath the tape. "This is how I can say that." A click sounded as he set something on the counter between us.

He shoved the remains of the tag beneath his shirt and withdrew his hand from the counter.

Revealing a diamond ring.

The diamond ring.

Oh God. I couldn't breathe. There wasn't enough air in the world to fill my lungs, to oxygenate the blood that my heart refused to pump.

"I'm the one who carried you with me every goddamned day."

CHAPTER TWENTY-SIX

NATHANIEL

New York
October 2018

I barely felt the rain as I walked down the sidewalk of the Brooklyn neighborhood known as Dumbo, my fist clenching the most important box I'd ever carried.

Or maybe that had been the one I'd carried earlier this morning.

Was it this morning? The days had been a seamless blur. It was evening, and I'd driven all afternoon, so I was pretty sure it was the same day.

I slipped through the crowd, my strides quickening like a New Yorker's, blending in like I'd been trained to for the last year. Finally finding the right building, I caught the door as one of the residents was leaving and headed inside, avoiding the buzzer.

God only knew if she'd let me in.

I climbed the stairs, my fingers flexing around the box. No matter what I did, I couldn't get my mind to stop spinning, stop replaying the way things should have gone, stop forecasting every way these next few minutes could go.

She'd know what to do. She was the only person in this world who loved me unconditionally, the only person I'd been able to count on since Mom died. She'd know which path we should choose.

2214. Her apartment.

I pushed the doorbell and bounced back on my heels. When she didn't immediately appear, I started pacing. If I stopped moving, I wasn't sure I'd start again.

There was no gravity. Nothing keeping my feet anchored. My reality was every possibility and none all at the same time, and whichever path I'd take depended solely on what she said, what she chose.

The sound of sliding dead bolts made me pause in front of her door.

The door opened, revealing an older man with gelled salt-and-pepper hair and a three-piece-suit that looked like it cost more than a year's rent. His critical gaze swept over me once, and his dark eyes hardened with recognition. *Izzy's eyes.* I'd seen the pictures in her apartment—this was her dad. "Can I help you?"

"I'm looking for—"

"Oh, I'm well aware of who you're looking for. I'm asking what *I* can do for you," he sneered. "Because you're not going to see Isa. She's kept this"—he gestured at me—"arrangement you two have for too many years as it is, and yes, before you ask, yes, I recognize you. Do you have any idea how bad you are for her?"

My hand gripped the box tighter. I couldn't lose my temper on Izzy's dad. I had to hold my shit together, even when it felt like the world was spinning beneath me at a rate I couldn't keep up with.

"It's going to cost thousands to break her lease here and finally get her to where her family needs her." He somehow managed to look down on me even when I was a good four inches taller. "A family she finally sees can't include you."

"Dad?" Izzy's voice from within the apartment halted any reply I could have made. "Who is it?"

"I've got it, Isa. Nothing worth your worry." He said every word at me. "You aren't, you know," he said softer. "All you've ever done is waste her time."

"Dad, who are you—" Her words faltered as she appeared at his side, dressed in plaid pajama pants and an oversize hoodie, and looked at me like I was the absolute scum of the earth. Her beautiful eyes were so puffy they didn't even qualify as swollen anymore, and guilt seized my heart. I suspected I was the reason she'd been crying.

"Go back inside, Isa."

"Give us five minutes," she replied, looking up at him.

His expression softened slightly. "Five minutes. But don't forget our deal." He shot me a withering glance and disappeared into the apartment, leaving Izzy in the doorway.

"Good to know you're ali—" The rest of the word seemed to die on her tongue as she looked me over, stepping into the hallway and pulling her door shut behind her. "Nate?" She said my name like she wasn't sure I was really me, which fit, since I wasn't really sure anymore either.

I returned her gaze with hollow, empty eyes that devoured the sight of her. She was the meaning in all this. The sun that would warm me or incinerate me.

She was everything. She always had been.

I struggled to shove my thoughts into coherent words. "I had this all planned out in my head," I blurted. "Driving six hours will give you time to practice what you're going to say, you know?"

"You drove six hours?" Her brow knit.

"What else was I supposed to do?" Fuck, I couldn't keep my thoughts straight. "But now I'm here, and your dad says you're moving, and you're looking at me like I'm the last person you want to see—"

"You abandoned me!" she snapped, hurt radiating through her tone. "No, worse than that—you didn't bother to show up! I spent two days in Palau before I realized you weren't coming. Why would you do that to me? You're the only person who's never . . ." She took a deep breath. "What the hell happened to you? I called. I texted. I—"

"That's what I'm trying to tell you." My words ran together. What I had to tell her was so much bigger than a missed vacation, and if I didn't use the right words, the perfect words, then it was all for nothing.

"Okay, then tell." A shiver raced across her skin, and she wrapped her arms around her waist.

"I just . . . I can't think straight, and admitting that, seeing me like this would probably get me kicked out before I even start, which is just ironic because I'm always the levelheaded one in our group. That's why it didn't surprise me when Pierson washed out the second week. His land-nav skills are solid, but the second the cadre started in on him, questioning his choices, he got all indecisive, and then he was gone."

"Nate, I don't understand what you're saying." She shook her head.

A hysterical laugh bubbled past my lips. "Of course you don't, because I'm not making any sense. But I don't know what the line is anymore, not today at least. Am I allowed to not have my shit together when I buried Julian today? Or am I supposed to hold it together and just pretend his mother wasn't sobbing in the pew ahead of me?"

"Oh God, Nate." Her face fell and she reached for me, but I stepped back.

"Don't. If you touch me, I know I won't be able to hold it together, and as you can see, I'm already walking that line." I rubbed my empty hand over my rain-soaked face, wiping the water away. "And the worst part is that I never really thought of him as Julian, you know? Sure, that was his name, but we never called him that. But his mother wouldn't stop saying it, wouldn't stop crying, and now that's all I hear in my head."

"What happened?" she asked, her voice going soft. "Is that why you didn't show up? Because Julian died?"

"The trip. Right." I nodded, trying to focus my thoughts. I needed to pick a path. I needed *her* to pick our path. Once I had my feet under me again, I'd be able to move forward.

I'd never felt so unmoored in my life.

"The trip," she said again, slowly, and I realized I'd drifted into my own thoughts.

"I was supposed to be there." I nodded like I was answering one of the interview questions, like the interrogation had never stopped. "The dates worked out so perfectly that it was like fate decreed it. Like it was always supposed to be this way."

"What way?"

"Once we all passed selection, I'd have those ten days to spend with you, to figure out what you wanted, before moving on to OTC."

"I don't know what that means."

"Of course you don't. You're not really supposed to. Damn, I did such a good job of keeping my mouth shut, didn't I? Keeping you out of it all." I rubbed at my forehead with the back of my clenched fist, closed my eyes, and took a deep breath, shutting out all the noise, everything that happened today, and focused on the woman standing in front of me. "I'm messing this up."

"Since I don't know what *this* is, you're doing just fine. But you definitely have me worried." Concern etched two lines between her eyebrows. There was so much anger in her eyes, so much heartbreak, but there was love, too, right? I hadn't killed everything she felt for me, had I?

"We were blacked out," I said, grabbing hold of my focus with mental fists. "That's why I couldn't call you. Julian's parents were on vacation, and they couldn't find them to notify them, and since they had our cell phones, they kept them so someone didn't run their mouth before they could be told through official channels." The little blue box in my hand shifted, the edges giving way, and I eased my grip. "At first, I didn't believe them, the cadre, I mean. I thought it was all part of the final interview, seeing how I'd cope with that kind of news. I mean, I'd just seen him and he'd been . . . him. But then a couple days passed, and they didn't release us, even the washouts. And that's when I realized it was all my fault."

"Nate," she whispered, glancing back over her shoulder at the closed door. "Why don't we go somewhere?"

Because she didn't want me in there with her father.

"I can't. I have to get this out now. There are people waiting for me, and I have to know what you want, so that I'll know what to choose, Izzy." It all made sense in my head—at least that part—but it was coming out so jumbled.

The box. Right. The box would ask the question for me.

I opened my right hand, flicked the top of the box open with my thumb, and turned it toward her.

"Oh my God." Her hand rose to cover her mouth.

"I know it's probably not what you were expecting. I picked it out about a year ago, and then I second-guessed it about fourteen times. You come from money, and I know you would probably have wanted something bigger—"

"Nate, is that what I think it is?" Her wide eyes jumped from the ring to my face.

"It's an engagement ring."

Her mouth opened, shut, and then repeated. "You can't seriously be proposing right now."

"I am." I nodded, my stomach twisting into a series of knots that had my head swimming.

"No. You're not." She shook her head. "I know that you're not because you promised me you'd never do this, never *shove a ring at me and ask me to give up everything I've worked for without giving us a chance to build something first*. Weren't those your words on that beach?"

"Don't you see? It's the only way we can be together. I've fought it for so many years, thinking this life wouldn't be fair to you, that you deserved so much better—and you still do, but I love you, Isabeau. I've only loved you. I'll only ever love *you*. And I was supposed to do this in the water, or maybe even the plane—kind of circle back to how we met, you know?"

"I know," she whispered, her hand falling to the rise of her chest as she stared at me with shock. At least I thought it was shock. It could have been horror or even fear.

"But then Julian . . . died, and I realized that it just as easily could have been me. It *should* have been me. And I knew that I'd wasted too much time protecting you when I should have been giving you a choice, and I'm so sorry."

"Nate, I don't think you're thinking clearly. You seriously want us to get married when I've never so much as seen where you live? We've never spent more than a week together at a time—"

"Nine days," I argued.

"I don't even know where you are half the time, or what you're being *selected* for. Listen to yourself."

"Exactly." Shit, I was doing this wrong. "But you love me, and I just need you to choose, Iz. I'll do whatever you want. I'll let you all the way in. I'll tell you what I can, and we'll go back to North Carolina together. Or I'll get out if that's what you want."

"What?" Her eyebrows hit the ceiling. "You don't want to get out. You've never wanted that."

"But I would if it meant keeping you. I'm in, Iz. I made it. And I know you don't really know what that means, but say the word and I'll walk away. We'll walk away. Just tell me what you want me to do, and I'll do it," I begged. The choice was hers. I was hers.

"You can't ask me to make a choice like that for you, Nate." She shook her head. "That's not fair. And the worst part is that you've shut me out for so long that I don't even know enough to help you make that kind of choice."

Her door opened. "Isa—"

Izzy reached back and yanked the door shut, closing it on her father.

Her father. I blinked as the pieces clicked. "He said you're breaking your lease. Moving?"

"Yes." War waged in her eyes. "No. I don't . . . I don't know. I don't really want to, but it would finally make them happy, and I think they've really done some soul-searching and . . . changed. I mean, they actually came when I needed them."

"Don't do that. Don't give up what you want just because they've finally decided to show up for you."

Her eyebrows shot up. "Isn't that what *you're* doing?"

"No. I'm asking if you want *me* to give everything up for *you*." Couldn't she see that?

Her mouth opened and shut.

Fear clawed up my spine. Of all the outcomes I'd pictured—me moving to New York, her moving to North Carolina, us being *anywhere* together—I'd never contemplated her not wanting me. This whole scene was wrong.

"It's because I'm doing it wrong, isn't it?" I dropped down to one knee and held the box up. "Marry me, Isabeau Astor." We were supposed to end up together. It was just a matter of timing. That was the foundation I'd built my life on ever since Tybee.

"Nate . . . ," she whispered, staring at me as a thousand emotions crossed her features.

"Please," I said softly. "Please choose me, Izzy. Choose us. Choose us over whatever life your parents want you to lead. Choose us despite the fact that I'm asking when we haven't had time to build a life. Choose to give us that time. Choose our future. I'll do whatever you want. Just marry me." Every muscle in my body tensed, hanging on her answer.

Her shoulders fell and took my hope with them. "I can't, Nate. Not like this."

My chest tightened, clamping down like it was trying to contain the carnage of my heart as it shattered behind my ribs. "You're saying no," I said, enunciating every word just so we were clear, and I slowly rose to my feet.

"I'm saying this isn't right." She shook her head.

But she was the only thing right in my entire life.

I snapped the box shut and crammed it into the front pocket of my jacket as my mind scrambled for purchase, for a direction. Army, no army. Delta, no Delta. None of it mattered without Izzy, and she wasn't choosing me. She didn't want me.

All you've ever done is waste her time. Her father was right.

I was fine for vacations and weekends, but not good enough to marry.

"I'm sorry to have wasted your time," I said, taking one last look at her deep-brown eyes. Eyes I'd caused to cry far too many times. I'd wasted years of her life.

Time to stop.

"You didn't waste—" she started, but I was already moving, logic centering me with each step now that I knew which route my life was going to take. "Nate!" she called after me.

I had to get out of here before I fell apart.

I threw open the front door and walked into the rain. I'd be fine. I'd gotten back on a plane hours after the previous one had crashed, and this would be no different. What had Izzy said about going to therapy? It had given her coping mechanisms. I had a career most people would kill for. I was among the best of the best. That was all the coping mechanism I needed.

Or maybe it wasn't.

Melting into the crowd, I walked down the block to where I'd somehow managed to find a parking spot.

I opened the door and slid behind the wheel, then started the ignition. "Fuck!" I shouted at no one and everyone. "What would you do?" I asked Torres. "If you were me, what would you do?" I closed my eyes, wishing I could block out the world as I waited for him to answer.

"Guess that didn't go the way you wanted it to," he said from the passenger seat, cracking an eye open like he'd been napping while I'd been pouring my heart out. "What am I saying? Of course it didn't, or you wouldn't be back so soon."

"What would you do?" I repeated.

"You don't need to ask. You already know the answer."

"And yet here I am, asking."

"You need me to say it? Fine, I'll be the one to say it. Only eight were selected out of our class." Of course he'd use logic. That was his strong suit.

"I know that."

"You can wash out and be like the majority of our class, or we can drive back to Bragg and be part of those eight. To me, the latter sounds a shit ton better than the former."

He was right. He usually was.

"Bragg it is." I twisted the knob next to the steering wheel, and the windshield wipers swept away the rain and what was left of my indecision.

I put the truck in drive and pulled into traffic.

CHAPTER TWENTY-SEVEN

NATHANIEL

Kabul, Afghanistan
August 2021

"Nate," Izzy whispered, staring at the ring I'd carried with me for nearly three years.

"You didn't want me. You didn't really love me. Maybe the idea of me, but not who I actually am." It was the simple truth I'd told myself every time I put the chain on or laced it into my boot on missions that didn't require being sanitized. I said it to remind me why it was okay that I gave my life in service to my country, why it was necessary that I not show up on Izzy's doorstep between deployments and beg her to reconsider.

Beg her to love me again.

"That's not true." She ripped her stunned gaze away from the ring and lifted it to meet mine.

"You said no." I had enough practice saying the phrase that it didn't eviscerate me anymore. Instead, the words were more like a piece of sandpaper over a raw wound that refused to heal.

"I didn't say no!" She reached for me, and I sidestepped past her.

If she touched me, all bets were off. I was at the edge of my self-control, torn between doing whatever it took to push her away and pulling her close. She wasn't engaged to Dickface anymore. She wasn't his. But she'd still given him the yes I'd never received.

"You said, *I can't*," I reminded her. "And I might not have a Georgetown Law education, but I'm pretty sure *I can't* and *no* are pretty fucking synonymous."

"But they don't mean the same thing!"

"We're seriously going to argue semantics?" I walked to the window and checked the courtyard again. Somehow it looked like there were even more people in it now.

"About this? Absolutely," she retorted.

I turned to face her. "Okay, even if you want to debate the meaning of *I can't*, then we're still left with me telling you that you were the only woman I had ever loved or would love, proposing to you, and then what were your other phrases?" Glancing at the ceiling, I recited them all from memory. "*This isn't right.* That one hurt, but let's not forget my personal favorite, *You can't seriously be proposing right now.*"

Her mouth snapped shut.

"Yeah, I remember every single word you said while you blatantly told me that I wasn't what you wanted. I wasn't what you chose." Ugly, gut-twisting feelings beat at me, demanding to be let out of the box I'd kept them in for three years. "Was it because I did it wrong? What did Covington do right? Did he make some grand public gesture? Take you to some exclusive restaurant where everyone notable could watch, or some jumbotron where his commitment was blasted to the world to see?"

"No, Nate." She shook her head and looked at me like she had *any* right to act like the injured party.

"Was it the bigger ring?" I studied every nuance of her expression, looking for a lie. "The bigger bank account? The bigger family connections? The fact that your parents actually approved of him? Or the fact that he had a family jet to come rescue you in?"

"How could you even think that?" Her cheeks flushed again, turning the tips of her ears red. "You know me better than that!"

"I *thought* I knew you better than that," I admitted. "But then I'm standing on a tarmac, told that it's my job to keep you alive, and you're wearing a ring that could signal a plane from thirty-two thousand feet, doing a job you swore you'd never do." How had it only been nine days since that moment? "And I could have lived with it if he'd been a decent guy, but Dickface?"

"Oh. My. God. Will you shut up for half a second?" Her voice pitched upward.

"Sure. I mean, whatever you have to say to me can't be worse than what you already have."

Her eyes narrowed into a glare. "I never said no."

"And we're back to this again." I folded my arms across my chest.

"And I sure as hell never said that I didn't love you." She walked forward slowly. "I know, because I've never lied to you. Not once. Can you honestly say the same?"

I winced. "I've told you what I can."

"In our lives, we've spent what? Twenty days together?" She swallowed.

"Twenty-seven, actually, and if you even start to tell me that proposing marriage after those days was too much, then I'll remind you it had been seven years of knowing you and four years of loving you."

Her lips parted. "That wasn't what I was going to say. We'd spent less than twenty days together, and I was so in love with you that I couldn't fathom what my life would look like without you in it."

"You loved me, but you turned me down?" I stared at her and waited for whatever excuse she had teed up.

"Telling you that I couldn't accept your proposal had nothing to do with not loving you, Nate. That was never an issue. Not for me." Her brow furrowed.

"Was it because I stood you up in Palau? Because I wouldn't let you in when you asked when we were in Fiji?" My chest constricted. Why the hell was I poking her for answers now? Why had I opened the box marked *Isabeau Astor* in my heart?

"No—it didn't have anything to do with that." She took a single step. "Did I want you to let me in? Absolutely. That's all I've ever wanted, but it didn't—"

"You want in? Fine. I killed one of my best friends, Izzy. How's that for letting you in?" I threw up my hands.

Her lips parted, and she stopped short.

"Bet you're regretting wanting in now, huh?" My arms fell to my sides.

"I don't understand," she said, confusion puckering her forehead. "Are you talking about Ju—"

"Yes!" I interrupted. "It's my fault that he's dead. He yanked me out of the way when a timber rattlesnake struck after we'd both finished our forty-mile ruck march during selection, and it bit him instead." It was the first time I'd said the words out loud.

She blinked. "Nate, that's not your fault."

"Yeah? Well, when I told him we had to tell someone, he refused and said he hadn't come this far to get med-boarded before the interview portion, which was the final part of selection. Getting through the first courses—" I set my hands on top of my head and closed my eyes. "It was the hardest thing I'd ever done. The hardest thing *any* of us had done." It took two deep breaths to steady me before I could continue. "So, I told him fine. I wouldn't tell as long as he agreed to get help as soon as the interview was over." And he'd *grinned* at me, so certain we'd both make it. "I let him walk into his interview with a venomous snakebite, and when it was my turn for the interview, when they told me one of my best friends had just died due to anaphylactic shock in the next room, I rolled with it, thinking it was part of the fucking interrogation. That they'd want a calm, cool, collected soldier in the unit, so that's what I gave them. Figured we'd both get a laugh out of it afterward, except he really was dead." There. I'd said it.

Someone knocked on the door.

"Oh God. Nate, you didn't kill him." Sadness filled her eyes, and I didn't deserve an ounce of her pity.

"Yes, I did. If I'd told, gotten him help sooner, he'd be alive. Instead, I'm the one in the unit and he's the one in the ground. How is that for letting you in, Izzy?"

Another knock sounded.

"That's why you were so distraught. It wasn't just that he died." She came toward me, her face crumpling in a way that made me want to take every word back and just hold her. "I knew something was wrong with you. I was so worried that I stood there for a half hour, soaking wet—"

"You were inside when I proposed."

"I came after you!"

"You . . . what?" The wires in my brain must have crossed because it felt like I was short-circuiting.

The knock turned to a pound. "I hate to interrupt you guys, but I need to talk to you *now*," Graham shouted through the door.

"I came after you," she repeated in a whisper, desperation clogging her voice as she grabbed hold of my uniform.

"Come in," I managed to call out.

The door opened, and Graham walked in, his face tight.

"What's up?" My stomach tensed, bracing for bad news.

"I'm sorry to tell you, but Mazar-i-Sharif is falling."

CHAPTER TWENTY-EIGHT

IZZY

New York
October 2018

"You what?" Serena shouted, wrapping the towel tightly around her body and staring at me like I'd lost my mind.

I'd all but hauled her out of the shower in my hysteria, ignoring Mom and Dad as they stood in the living room, waiting for answers I didn't have. "You heard me!"

"And you just let him go?" Serena's eyes flew wide.

"It wasn't like I had the power to stop him!" God, he'd been so . . . lost. My heart ached, demanding I chase him down and give him whatever he needed. "What was I supposed to do? Hold him down?"

"I was thinking you'd say yes, seeing that you're obviously miserable without him, and it seems he had a pretty good reason for not showing up on your vacation."

"Say yes? That wasn't *him*. He wasn't really asking me to marry him, Serena! He was reacting out of trauma after burying Julian today."

"Wait. He buried his friend *today*? You left that out." Her brow knit. "Which one is Julian?"

The tall blond guy with the smirk came to mind. "I think his last name was Rowell. He was one of the guys he went into Special Forces with. One of his best friends." I rubbed my hands over my face. "He was so hurt. I *hurt* him. But how could I accept his proposal when he clearly wasn't in a clear state of mind? I kept trying to poke holes in his argument to get him to see that he was acting irrationally. The Nate I know would never have proposed like that, and when I said that . . ." My throat started to close, thinking of his face. "He needs a good night's sleep, or help—not an engagement."

If he'd asked me, really honestly asked me, I would have thrown myself into his arms and never let go.

"And you think he's going to race from here to a therapist's couch?" She gripped my shoulders. "Do you love him?"

"More than my own life." It didn't matter what I did; I couldn't turn the emotion off.

"Then go find him and haul him back here so he can get whatever help he needs. Go, Izzy."

I nodded and took off, skidding into the hallway in my slippered feet and then through the living room.

"I know you are not running after that man!" Mom shouted.

"I know you're not acting like you actually know anything about him!" I snapped back. They'd be pissed. Oh well. Life wasn't worth it without Nate, and if they couldn't accept that, then they'd never really loved me anyway.

I didn't bother closing my door as I ran out of my apartment and raced down the steps of my building. "Nate!" I shouted as I threw open the heavy glass door and ran out onto the sidewalk.

There were dozens of people out here.

None of them were Nate.

I shoved my hand into the center pocket of my hoodie and grabbed my phone, then hit Nate's info on the contact page. "Pick up, pick up, pick up," I said as it rang.

He sent me to voice mail. Or his phone was off. But my bets were on the first option.

I climbed the stairs to the entrance of my building for a better vantage point and searched the streets as I tried his phone again. He didn't pick up.

My chest crumpled like a discarded ball of paper. I'd sent him away when he'd needed me to pull him closer. I'd failed him at the first real test.

Serena joined me, holding an umbrella over my head as we stood there for a half hour, looking at every single person who walked by, my heart refusing to accept what my mind already had.

He was gone.

CHAPTER TWENTY-NINE

IZZY

Kabul, Afghanistan
August 2021

I sat on the couch, watching the coverage from Mazar-i-Sharif in a language I couldn't understand as Nate's team buzzed around us.

"You hungry, Izzy?" Sergeant Rose asked. They'd dropped the *Ms. Astor* title over an hour ago.

I shook my head without looking away from the television. Serena was in there somewhere.

"And these are all processed and need to go back down to the clerk," Nate told Sergeant Black, handing him a stack of files he'd personally called on in the last hour.

"I don't even know what they're saying," I whispered, holding a throw pillow to my chest.

"Oh." Sergeant Rose leaned in. "They're speaking Dari. I'm stronger in Pashto." He looked over his shoulder. "Green!"

"Nate speaks Pashto," I whispered, wincing when I realized I hadn't used *Green*.

"Yeah, and Dari, and Farsi, and French, and whatever else he's working on. Guy never slows down." He glanced my way. "And don't stress. We all know his real name."

Nate sat on my left, and I held myself rigid so I wouldn't lean into him. We hadn't exactly come to a conclusion in our argument. We'd just . . . stopped.

"What are they saying?" I asked.

"The Taliban took control of the city less than an hour after breaching the front lines at the city limits," Nate recited. "When that happened, the government forces and the militias fled without a fight."

Sergeant Rose cursed.

"That leaves only Kabul and Jalalabad under Afghan government control." Nate looked my way. "You shouldn't be watching this."

"Why not? She's experiencing it. She told me once that ignoring a situation doesn't make it better for the people living it." I squeezed the pillow tighter. "She's living it."

The door opened, and Sergeant Black walked back in, heading toward the dining area where Sergeant Gray was set up doing whatever the comms guy did.

"I failed," I whispered.

Sergeant Rose glanced over my head at Nate, then stood and joined the others.

"You didn't," Nate assured me. "Serena made her choice. We're all allowed to make our own choices. You got that girls' team out."

I scoffed. "*You* got that girls' team out. I did the paperwork." Defeat settled into my stomach like an anchor. "All I've done since I got here was fail to convince Serena to leave and waste your team's time when you're clearly needed elsewhere." I'd also lost a fiancé, but I was counting that in the plus column. I didn't even care that I'd have to explain it to my parents. There was a reason I hadn't spoken to them in weeks.

"Newcastle would have been in Kandahar too," Nate said. "He would have missed Covington's Hail Mary return flight home too. I would still be in this room." A smile curved his perfect mouth. "I just wouldn't have let him sleep with his head in my lap. I have boundaries, you know."

"Just not with me?"

"Never with you," he said softly. "I know it doesn't count for much right now, but I'm sorry for losing my temper earlier."

I sent a dose of side-eye his way. "You didn't."

"I did. You just didn't know it."

"Green," Sergeant Gray called out. "I've got something."

Nate stood, and I went back to staring at the television.

"Izzy," Nate said a minute later.

I looked over my shoulder and saw him holding up a clunky-looking phone.

"It's Serena."

I scrambled off the couch and nearly tripped on the end table to get there. "Serena?" I said into the phone after taking it from Nate.

"I'm on my way, Izzy," she said. "I don't know who your man knows, but I'm in a car with this snazzy phone and Taj."

"You're okay?" I covered my face and ducked my head as my eyes watered.

"I'm okay. But it's four hundred miles and a hell of a lot of checkpoints to Kabul. My credentials should get us there, but you can't wait for me."

My stomach twisted. "I can't leave without you."

"You can and you will. I'll be on the first plane I can get on, but you have to get out of here. Promise me."

"I don't even know if I can get out before you get here, so it might be a moot argument," I tried, lifting my head to see Nate shaking his head.

"I want to conserve the battery on this thing, so I need to go. But Iz, promise me you'll go."

"I promise," I whispered. "I love you."

"I love you too."

I handed the phone back to Nate, who lifted it to his ear. "I found a flight for her for tomorrow night." He locked eyes with me. "I will personally throw her over my shoulder and strap her into the seat myself."

My eyes narrowed at him.

He flashed a dimple.

Ugh.

"Serena, don't get yourself killed. Izzy would never recover from the guilt of you not putting your ass on the helicopter when you had the chance." He ended the call and handed the handset back to Gray.

"Thank you," I said to Nate. "Whatever you did. Thank you." It didn't even come close to what he deserved to hear, but it was all I could get out.

He nodded once. "I meant what I said. I will strap you onto that flight myself tomorrow night."

Which meant I only had twenty-four hours left with him.

I rolled over and stared at the clock just like I had every hour since I'd come to bed a little after midnight. Once the State Department had gone home for the day, there was no point continuing to call and follow up on visas, but in a few hours I could be useful helping with the interviews until Nate decided it was time to leave for the airport.

Four a.m. meant he was probably just waking up.

I flopped to my back and stared up at the ceiling, letting my thoughts run haywire.

Nate thought I'd turned his proposal down because I didn't love him, and then he'd taped my engagement ring to a dog tag and carried it with him everywhere. What was I supposed to do with that?

Staying here, wasting the only hours I might have with him, wasn't going to get me—or us—anywhere.

My heart pounded as I swung my feet over the side of the bed and then walked into the living room of my suite, turning on the lamp with the switch as moonlight poured in through the windows.

I turned near the kitchen area and folded my arms across my tank top as I stared at the ring. It was perfect. Simple. Exactly what I would have picked out if I'd been at the jewelry store with him. And he'd bought it after Fiji. After I'd resigned myself to living for the moments I had with him. He'd seen a future for us.

It took me three attempts before I actually managed to pick it up. It was slightly sticky from the tape's residue, and all the more perfect for it. My heart *hurt* at the life it represented, the life we could have had.

I grabbed my key and walked out of my room before I could think twice and then stop myself.

Sergeant Rose blinked at me from where he stood next to Nate's door. "Everything okay, Ms. Astor?"

Well. Shit. It wasn't like I could storm across the hall and knock on Nate's door now.

"You're on babysitting duty." I wrapped my arms across my chest, more than a little self-conscious that I didn't exactly sleep in a bra.

"I'm on guard, yes." He smothered a smile behind his beard.

"Right. So I'm just going to . . ." *Go back into my room and pretend this never happened.*

"You know what?" he said, whipping out a room key from his front pocket. "I'm in the mood to stir a little shit this morning. Why not." He shrugged and tapped the key against Nate's lock.

The light above the handle turned green, and I didn't hesitate. "Thank you." Flashing him a smile, I grabbed the door handle, turning it quickly so it didn't lock again.

"Just don't tell him it was me."

I nodded and opened Nate's door, stepping inside and closing it behind me before I lost the nerve. Light poured out of the bathroom, and I heard the shower running, but the rest of the room was dark.

"Nate?" I called out softly, not wanting to startle him, seeing how well that had gone last time I'd made that mistake, but he obviously couldn't hear me over the sound of the water running.

My lips parted. He was in there. Naked. Heat rushed through me, and I used my key card to fan myself before putting it on his dresser when the shower finally stopped. But I held on to the ring like it was the key to breaking through to him.

I was still wholeheartedly in love with him, and this was worth the fight.

"Nate?" I said gently, standing between his bed and the desk.

"Izzy?" I heard the sound of fabric rustling, and he walked out of the bathroom in a towel.

A *towel.*

A singular, lonely towel wrapped around his lean waist. He hadn't even dried off. Nope, there were still water droplets sliding down the same lines of his body that I had traced with my tongue. Like that one, right there . . . the one that slipped down his pec, gathering other drops, and then falling into the canyons of his abs before finding its way to the fuck-me lines that carved the deep V—

"Izzy."

My gaze snapped upward to Nate's face, and damn if my entire body didn't flush. "Hi."

His brows rose. "Hi? It's—" He glanced at his clock. "Four in the morning and you just popped by to say hi? The girl who sleeps until ten if she can?"

"You're in a towel." Was that really the best I could come up with?

"I was in the shower. That's a natural progression of events. Shower. Towel. Clothes. And how the hell did you even get—" He sighed. "Never mind, I already know who let you in."

"Don't be mad." The ring bit into my palm, but I kept my fist closed.

"I'm not mad. Confused, but not mad."

"I couldn't sleep. Not when I know I only have a few hours left with you." The last bit tumbled out.

His expression went blank. He was retreating behind those mile-high walls where I wouldn't be able to reach him, and I couldn't let that happen. Not tonight.

"I thought you were proposing out of shock," I blurted with as much grace as I'd had the day we met. *Good to see we're growing over here.*

"We don't have to do this."

"We do." I closed the distance between us but didn't reach for him. "I was still reeling from you no-showing Palau, and my parents were there, being all . . . parental for once, and then you showed up, clearly distraught over losing your friend, asking me to choose if you were going to stay in the military or not, and you weren't . . . you. Your words ran together, your eyes were wild, and you just kept telling me that you needed me to choose what you were supposed to do, despite every argument I threw at you to show that you weren't acting like yourself. And looking back, I didn't have my head on straight, either, but Nate, I didn't think it was real."

"I got down on one knee," he whispered.

"Trust me, I remember." I took that last step and cupped his bearded cheek with my free hand. "All I could think was that this was everything I'd ever wanted, and yet, if I'd said yes, I would have been taking advantage of you at your worst moment. You would have woken up and regretted asking."

"You chose your parents."

"I didn't." I shook my head. "Sure, I used Dad's connections to get into Lauren's office, but it was only to help that legislation that never passed anyway. Serena told you the truth. I didn't go to DC for my parents. I went for you."

His brow furrowed slightly, just enough to tell me I was getting through.

I swallowed the fear and forged ahead. "You asked me why I told Jeremy yes."

He closed his eyes. "I can't, Izzy. You have me so close to breaking that I can barely look at myself in the mirror, so if you're about to list my faults—"

"I said yes to him because he was familiar, and comfortable, and I'd already made the biggest mistake of my life by saying no to the right man."

His eyes flew open.

"And I've lived every single day with that regret." I opened my other palm, revealing the ring. "You may have carried this with you, but I carried you here." I slid my hand over my heart. "I should have said yes and then held on to you for dear life, damn the consequences, and if I'd known that you were going to disappear minutes later, I would have. I should have said yes. I never stopped loving you, Nate. Not for one second."

His eyes flared for a second before he grasped the nape of my neck and pulled my mouth to his.

Finally.

The kiss felt like coming home.

His tongue swept past my lips and I melted against him as desire flared to life, spreading through my veins in a rush of fire, waking up every shiver of need that had lain dormant since the last time he'd touched me. How had I lived for nearly four years without his kiss? His arms?

He tasted the same, like spearmint and Nate, and I couldn't get close enough. When he retreated, I followed, flicking my tongue along the sensitive ridge behind his teeth and reveling in the catch of his breath, the way his grip tightened as he moved us sideways.

I dropped the ring on the nightstand as he sat on the side of his bed, tugging me between his thighs, and then I kissed him like it might be the last time I'd ever feel his mouth on mine. If this was all I had, one more priceless moment where he was mine to kiss, to touch, then I wanted everything.

His hand slid to my ass, and he grabbed hold, pulling me tight against him. Water soaked into the thin material of my tank top as our mouths moved in a rhythm I'd all but forgotten. It was hunger and need and still achingly sweet.

"Say it again," he demanded against my mouth, his hands sliding beneath the fabric of my pajama pants to cup my bare ass.

"Which part?" I teased, nipping at his lower lip. God, I'd missed this. Missed everything about how right it felt to be in his arms.

"You know which part." He drew back to look into my eyes, and my heart raced.

"I've always loved you. I am in love with you, Nathaniel Phelan." I lifted my hands, running them through his wet hair. "And you love me too."

"Do I?" A corner of his mouth lifted.

"You do." My fingers trailed down his neck and across his shoulders. "Your call sign wouldn't be Navarre if you didn't."

He captured my mouth again, the kiss spinning beyond control with the first few strokes of his tongue. This was what I wanted, what I needed, and not just for the few minutes we had, but for the rest of my life. I never wanted to go another day without being in his arms.

"I need you." I'd never spoken a single sentence with so many meanings, and they were all true. I needed him in every way possible.

"I know. God, I know." His hand shifted between us, his fingers dancing tantalizingly on my skin beneath my waistband. "I feel the same way." He kissed my chin, my jaw, and the spot just beneath my ear before skimming his lips down my neck, sending a shudder of pure want down my spine and adding to the gathering need between my thighs.

My head fell back as his mouth worked down my chest, then covered the peak of my breast through the fabric, testing my nipple gently with his teeth.

"I've wanted to touch you from the second you stepped off that plane," he said, tugging my tank top down to bare my breasts and sucking at each tip.

I moaned, my fingers digging into his bare shoulders, my body leaning into his.

"It took everything I had not to grab ahold of you and kiss you until you threw that goddamned ring off your finger and remembered what we felt like together." He raked his teeth over me and dipped his fingers down the plane of my stomach. "There hasn't been a day I haven't thought of you, haven't missed you, wanted you, loved you."

My knees weakened.

"Please tell me I can have you." The tips of his fingers grazed the top of my thong.

"I'm yours."

He lifted his head and kissed me hard and deep at the same moment his fingers found me, and I whimpered into his mouth. Banding his arm around the back of my thighs, he held me upright as he pumped two fingers inside me with the same rhythm of his tongue.

Oh *God*. Need and lust swirled within me, overruling every thought that wasn't *closer*, *more*, and *now*. Nate had always known how to play my body, had spent hours edging my orgasms, building them until I couldn't take it anymore, but I wasn't going to be able to wait. Not this time.

I hooked my thumbs in the elastic of my pajama pants and my underwear and pushed them down my legs, stepping out and kicking them free.

"Izzy," he groaned against my mouth, then broke the kiss to tug my shirt off with his free hand. "You feel so fucking good."

"Don't stop," I begged as he added his thumb, working me in the exact way I liked, the way he knew I needed. I touched him every place I could reach, stroking my hands down his arms, his chest, around to the irresistible expanse of his back.

"No chance." Years of pent-up desire built and coiled, stringing my body tight. Every kiss took me higher, every plunge of his fingers brought the pleasure further to the point of pain.

But I didn't want to come like this, not after all this time.

I tugged the towel from his hips and wrapped my hand around him. He hissed as I stroked the hard length of him, swirling my thumb over the blunt tip.

"I want you inside me."

"Good, because that's exactly where I want to be." His eyes locked with mine as I straddled his lap, rising on my knees so he fit perfectly against my entrance. "I love you, Isabeau Astor."

The words filled my chest, and I kissed him as I lowered myself inch by glorious inch, my muscles gripping tight as he thrust upward and took me to the hilt.

We both groaned.

This was what I'd been missing. Not just his body, but *him*. The way he looked at me, touched me, made me feel like there was nothing in this world that mattered more than the fit of our bodies, the combined rhythm of our hearts.

"Fuck, Izzy." He gripped my hips and lifted me, his biceps flexing, before he slammed back up into me. "You feel better than every dream I've ever had. Every memory. Every fantasy. So goddamn hot."

"Again," I demanded, winding my arms around his neck and rocking back into his hips when he gave me what I asked for. Every stroke of him radiated through my body, my fingers and toes tingling with the sweetest hum of pure, unadulterated pleasure.

Then he stilled, all but freezing beneath me.

"Nate?" I asked, pulling back just enough to see his face in the dim light.

"We can't." He lifted my hips again, agonizingly slow, and the strain of the action showed on every line of his face, as if he was fighting his own instincts.

I took his face in my hands. "Yes. We can." Swinging my hips, I took him all the way and bit my lower lip at how phenomenal he felt inside me.

"I don't have a condom." He bit out every word. "I wasn't exactly planning on this."

"Oh." My hips swiveled of their own accord, as if my body was more than willing to take what I tried to withhold. "That's okay."

His brows shot up, and his fingers bit into my hips.

"I'm on birth control." I ghosted a kiss over his lips. "And I've never had unprotected sex, so we're in the clear." Not to mention I'd had the whole battery of tests after I'd found out about Jeremy's extracurricular activities.

"Me either," he admitted, his thighs tensing underneath me. "You sure?"

"Not sure I could stop even if I wanted to, which I don't." I lifted up on my knees and slid down again, biting back a moan.

"No wonder you feel even better than I remember, and believe me, I have an excellent memory of just how perfect it was between us." His hand moved to my ass, and he kissed me deep as he drove up into me, setting a pace that I met with equal fervor.

The coil of tension deep within me built and built until I knew I'd break soon, and I pushed it back.

Last. This had to last.

Our bodies moved in complete unison, partners in a dance too long denied, and never forgotten. He kissed me like I was the very breath he needed to survive and took me like each thrust only left him hungrier for the next.

"There's nothing like this in the entire world," he said between kisses. "Nothing compares to the heat, the fit, the feel of you, Izzy." Wrapping an arm around my back, he spun me to my back on the bed, then drove in, hard and deep. "I want you in every possible way."

I moaned in frustration when he pulled out, but heat flushed every inch of my skin when he flipped me to my stomach and then pulled my hips so I was up on my knees. Hell yes. "Now."

Every second I had to wait was torture.

He fit himself between my thighs and thrust forward, taking me so deep that lights flashed behind my eyes. "Nate!"

"Grab the headboard." His breath was just as choppy as mine, his questing hands just as ravenous as the clawing need within me as he stroked every inch of my skin.

I gripped the wooden frame of the headboard, then pushed back against him with the next thrust. It was beyond anything I could describe. Every time he moved, I burned brighter, spun tighter.

"So damned good." His hand stroked down my spine as he kept a rhythm that had me keening. "God, I've missed this. Missed *you*."

There were no words, only jolts of pleasure that pushed me right to the edge of reason. My orgasm was so close I felt the first waves rise within me, threatening to break at any second. "Not yet," I whimpered, my muscles tensing. "Nate, I don't want it to end yet."

"It's not going to," he promised, his fingers rolling my nipples. "Let go for me."

I came apart, bliss flooding my body in wave after wave. I screamed into his pillow, my hands falling from the headboard as I went limp beneath him. Heaven. He was heaven, and I wanted more.

As soon as I could move, of course.

"Fuck," he groaned, his hands sliding to my hips as he stroked into me slowly, coaxing that glowing ember of desire into another flame, this one hotter than the last. "You're not close enough. I can never get close enough."

He slipped his hands up over my breasts and lifted, pulling my back against his chest as he took me over and over and over.

I reached back, cupping the nape of his neck, and turned my head for his kiss. It was open mouthed, desperate, and messy as our sweat-slick bodies met again and again.

"You feel so right inside me." My nails scraped the back of his neck.

"God, I love you." He pushed deeper and I moaned. "I need to see you."

He was only out of me for a matter of seconds before I found myself on my back, Nate hovering over me like the god of every fantasy I'd ever had. Bracing his weight on an elbow, he pushed back in, and I gasped at the fit, lifting my knees for an even better angle.

"There you are." He cupped my face, staring into my eyes as he picked up the pace. "My Isabeau."

I nodded, words escaping me as I arched for him, pressure building low within me again with every push and drag of his hips.

He was everything I'd ever wanted. "I love you," I whispered, wrapping my arms around him.

The words seemed to snap whatever control he'd had, because his eyes darkened and the snaps of his hips came faster and his rhythm slipped into a frenzy. His muscles tensed beneath my fingers, and his hand fell from my face to reach between us.

He was close, the harsh lines of his face so very beautiful, that I couldn't look away as he fought his climax.

"Your turn to let go," I told him.

"You first." His fingers stroked my clit and my body exploded, the second orgasm sweeping through me without warning, making me arch and writhe as he found his own release, shuddering above me as he thrust three more times, his eyes widening with that last one.

He fell against me, immediately rolling to his side and pulling me with him, holding me close and looking at me with what seemed like a mix of wonder and . . . resolve.

"Are you okay?" I asked, stroking my hand over his face as my breathing finally slowed.

"I'm supposed to be the one asking that." He smiled.

Not a grin. Not a smirk. A real, heart-stopping *smile.*

"I couldn't be better." Leaning over, I kissed him softly, tears pricking my eyes. In a few hours I'd be on a plane back to the States. "I don't know how to live without you, Nate. And I know that's not what you want to hear right now. I tried. I really did. But existing isn't the same as living."

"I know." He stopped my words with his mouth. "Fuck, do I know."

I swallowed the knot in my throat. "What are we going to do?"

He tunneled his hand through my hair. "We're going to get in the shower, and then I'm going to make you come a few more times, and then we're going to face this day."

No promises. No sweet vows. No plans past the sunset. After ten years, we'd walked right back into familiar territory.

He did exactly as he'd planned, making me come against his mouth in the shower, and then again with my back sliding across the water-slick tile as he buried himself inside me, taking me like he could hold us in this moment if he just fought hard enough for it.

But we'd barely wrapped towels around our bodies when someone pounded three times on the door.

"Stay in here," Nate said, kissing my swollen lips quickly before walking out of the bathroom, then closing the door behind him.

I wiped the steam off the mirror and stared at the woman I found there.

Her cheeks were flushed, her eyes bright, and her neck slightly red with whisker burn. She looked like the version of me I liked best, the one who only existed when I was with Nate.

The bathroom door opened, and I tensed at the serious set of Nate's mouth.

"What is it?" I spun toward him, fearing the worst. "Serena?"

He shook his head. "Get dressed. They're at the city gates."

My lips parted. "At Jalalabad?"

His jaw clenched. "No. They surrendered Jalalabad last night while we were sleeping. They're here in Kabul."

Oh *shit.*

CHAPTER THIRTY
NATHANIEL

Kabul, Afghanistan
August 2021

"That makes three hundred," Elston said, closing the roof-access door behind us as the Chinook took off with another fifty evacuees from the embassy.

The city was in chaos beyond the defenses of the Green Zone, and we weren't faring too much better in here either. Panicked people were dangerous people, and though the evacuation was going pretty steadily, who knew how anyone within would react to the sight of one of those white-flagged pickup trucks.

"Only a few thousand to go," I said as we descended the stairs in full combat gear. "How long do you think we have?"

"Before the president negotiates a surrender, the Taliban decides to kick up their heels in the Green Zone, or you actually convince Ms. Astor to get the fuck out?" he asked, our boots the only other sound in the stairwell.

"I bet they're in the Green Zone before dinner," Torres said, catching up to us.

"They've been in negotiations for a couple hours now, so I'm sure that part is going to happen quickly. We're just lucky their forces are still outside the gates, and as for Ms. Astor . . ." I sighed as we passed the third floor and headed toward the second. "I've already told her that we're out of here at five, whether or not she's willing to go."

She'd been holed up with embassy staff all morning, processing any last-minute visas possible and gathering blank passports to burn. Graham was under strict orders not to leave her side, though if he pulled the twelve-inches rule, I was going to kick his ass.

The noise grew the lower we went in the embassy, and I had no doubt that mayhem ruled the lobby. This moment had come quicker than any intelligence had speculated, though the inevitability of it stung like a bitch.

"You sure you don't want her on an earlier helicopter?" Elston asked as we entered the second floor. Izzy's door was wide open, with Parker standing guard and a line of civilians forming down the other side of the hallway.

"It's a good question," Torres added.

"You see the gridlock on those streets?" I asked.

"Pretty sure you can see the gridlock from the International Space Station," he replied, his gaze sweeping the hallway. "Nothing's moving out there."

"All those people fleeing their cars are headed to the airport. Apex already has two teams there and said it's a fucking nightmare. The place is pure havoc. Her flight is at ten, and I don't want her in that circus any longer than she has to be. At least we're in a controlled environment here."

"For the moment," Elston said as we walked into Izzy's suite, passing Parker at the door.

"For the moment," I conceded. The second that changed, she was on the next helicopter, and I didn't give a shit who I had to throw off to make room for her.

The part of me I'd never wanted Izzy to see was in full force, and she might not like my methods, but she'd be alive, and that was enough for me.

I found her immediately, sitting on one side of her small dining table, nodding at whatever the civilian across from her was saying. Go figure the woman had had herself declared a consular officer so she could help process as many interviews as possible.

"She's been interviewing people nonstop for the past two hours," Graham said quietly, coming to stand with us.

"Did she eat lunch?" I asked, not taking my eyes off her. The red my beard had left on the skin of her neck had faded to a light rose in the hours it had been since I'd seen her. Though she was all business in a cream-colored blouse and dark pants, her hair wound in an efficient low bun, I couldn't shake the vision of her beneath me, her hair falling around her naked body as she told me she loved me.

She. Loved. Me.

"She did."

I nodded. Good. Who the hell knew what the food situation would be like at the airport.

"She flying out military or civilian?" Graham asked, concern furrowing his brow.

"Civilian." My jaw flexed. "Up until a few hours ago, they were taking off the most frequently."

"Hmm." Graham watched as the civilian woman across from Izzy rose and shook her hand.

"You getting attached to Ms. Astor there, Sergeant Gray?" Elston asked, his beard twitching as he smirked.

"I'm more attached to Green over here keeping his shit together." He cocked his head to the side as the civilian passed by, carrying her file. "Plus, I like her. She's nice."

I moved forward as Izzy stood, rolling her shoulders.

"You doing okay?" I asked, forcing myself to keep my hands at my sides. I couldn't kiss her. Not here. Not unless we were alone.

"Just trying to get as many people through as I can," she said, smiling softly at me.

Fuck, I'd missed that particular smile. It was the one she gave me when she wasn't just happy or laughing, but content. "You're remarkably calm for someone at the epicenter of a war zone."

"Sergeant Gray got ahold of Serena for me." She grinned. "She's halfway here."

"Checkpoints?" I asked.

"They've made it through every one so far, and I may have . . ." She scrunched her nose.

"May have what?" My stomach tightened.

"May have convinced the ambassador to accept Taj's interview over the phone in return for my services." She winced. "I mean, my interview services, not . . . other services."

"I would hope not." The corner of my mouth tilted upward. "So Taj's visa is good to go?"

She pivoted and leaned over the table.

I didn't look at her ass.

But if I had, that would have been okay, since she loved me, right?

"Right here." She waved the paperwork. "I need to put it in my bag."

I took it from her and stored it in one of my pockets. "I'll carry it. If shit goes south fast, there's no telling if you'll get to take your bag, but you can bet your life that you'll be taking me."

Her gaze dropped to my lips. "I like the idea of you coming with me."

My stomach twisted. "As far as the airport." It had to be said. I'd have new orders the second I delivered her to safety.

"I know." Her smile turned sad, and I debated kicking myself for having to say it. She glanced past me. "Next one is here."

"I'll leave you to it." My hand curled, but I didn't lift it to brush against her cheek the way I wanted to. "Stay close to Sergeant Gray. I have to get the next group to the roof." She nodded, and I turned away from her. "Don't let her out of your sight," I ordered Graham.

"She's not leaving the room until it's time to fly," he agreed.

Making my way into the hallway, I found Torres nodding toward my room.

I glanced back at Elston. "Five minutes."

He agreed, and I walked into my room, Torres on my heels, before I closed the door. "The city is going to shit," I said to him, throwing the rest of my stuff in my pack so I was ready to go.

"Seems like it." He grimaced, sitting on the edge of the small desk.

"What's up?" I adjusted the chain around my neck so it sat more comfortably under my Kevlar.

"Checking on you."

My eyes narrowed in his direction as the faint scent of smoke reached my nose. They'd started burning sensitive documents.

"Hey." He put his hands up like he was under arrest. "If your focus isn't just on Izzy, but wrapped *up* in Izzy, then you're not doing anybody any good out there."

"I'm not distracted if that's what you're implying." I headed to the bathroom and took care of that while I had the chance.

"I think it's a safe assumption," he said over the sound of the flushing toilet.

I washed my hands and shook my head. "I'm fine."

"You're leaving her in a matter of hours, and speaking from experience, you're always a little fucked up after you say goodbye to her."

Yanking open the door, I full-on glared at my best friend. "I'm not always—"

He arched a dark brow.

I relented. "Fine. It's . . ." I searched for the right word that wouldn't get me thrown at a shrink and off the mission. "It's *concerning* to find Izzy again, come within inches of actually having her in my life, and then send her back, not just to the States, but into the same cycle we've been stuck in for ten years."

"Right." He nodded, and I started to pace.

"I mean, is this really the best we can do?" I let the frustration out of the box I'd tucked it into, and it consumed me. "Ten years, and I'm going to what? Say it was amazing to see you again, and I'll see if I have a weekend in six months?"

"It's always worked for you before."

"It's never worked for us before. That's the damned problem. She wants more, and I can't give it to her. She wants the life, the house, the dream—"

"So do you." He shrugged.

I halted in my steps. "I don't have time for this."

"Oh, fuck off. Those are the same things you've always wanted. The military was just supposed to be what got you there, remember? Because I do. You got your degree in English specifically so you could go teach once you were done with the army." He folded his arms across his chest. "Did it ever occur to you that you're unhappy because you're living a life you never wanted?"

"No." I shook my head and glanced at the clock. The helo would be back in twenty minutes, and we had to get the next group of evacuees to the roof.

"You've been lying to yourself for so long that it's become the truth." Torres sighed and rubbed his hands over his face. "You carry that ring around because it gives you hope that one day you'll put it on her finger. One day you'll be done with this life. You live for the day you can take your shot."

"Maybe there's no shot to take." I kept my voice as even as possible, even though my chest was threatening to cave in on my heart. "Maybe she deserves better."

"Fine. You show me one guy on this planet who can love her more than you do, and we can have that conversation." His shoulders drooped. "It's time to make her the promise."

"What promise is that?" I scratched my beard. A couple more days and it would get past the itchy stage.

"The promise that you're getting out this time." He said it like it was that simple.

"You think I should leave the unit." The thought of it was . . . shit, I couldn't even examine my feelings there, or I might not like what I found.

"I think doing this"—he gestured around us—"was never really your dream. It was always mine, and I'm not denying that you carried me this far, but man, you are going to lose that woman once and for all if you don't let it go."

And this conversation was done. I turned and walked through the door into the hallway, Torres following after with a lighter step.

Elston's brows rose. "Everything okay?"

"No," Torres muttered.

"Absolutely. Let's get the next group."

Three hours later, the atmosphere had more than shifted; it had thickened with the scent of panic and the sound of gunfire. The news that the Afghan government had surrendered the city ripped through the embassy like wildfire.

Literally.

The burn buckets had been filled and torched, sending plumes of black smoke into the air, and the helo was due any moment.

It was time to go.

"I can still get a few of their interviews done," Izzy argued in her suite as I slipped the Kevlar vest onto her and fastened the sides. Her suite was empty.

"You can't. Everyone who can turn those interviews into visas has left." Helo after helo had arrived, evacuating the essential personnel, and we were going to be on the next one. I didn't give a shit who got left behind for the next flight as long as it wasn't her.

"There are still thousands of people here!"

"And there's every chance they'll die here. You're not going to be one of them." I cupped her face and kissed her hard and quick, then set her helmet on her head.

"I can do that myself."

"But maybe I like to." I ran the backs of my fingers down her cheek. "Grab your backpack."

"Your backpack," she muttered, slinging the pack over her shoulders.

"I gave it to you way too long ago to ever be considered mine again. You have your passport?" I needed her on that plane and out of here.

She shot me a look. "I *have* traveled without you, Nate."

"Fair point." I led her to the door, aware of the noise coming from the hallway. "Twelve inches, Izzy."

"I know." Her breathing picked up, and fear dilated her pupils.

"Let's get out of here." I held out my left hand and she took it, lacing our fingers. There was zero chance I was going to get separated from her in the mayhem beyond these doors. I opened the door to find most of my team waiting, blocking Izzy's door.

Elston was already on the roof, backing up the team of snipers.

"Go," I said.

They surrounded us and we moved, cutting through the crowd that ran past intermittently.

"We're leaving so many people behind," Izzy said, her head turning to watch a man sprint in the opposite direction.

"This isn't the last helicopter," I told her.

"It's packed," Graham said over his shoulder as he opened the door to the stairwell.

"They'll move," I answered, leaving no room for interpretation in my tone. I kept my dominant hand on my rifle as it hung from my shoulder. No need to scare the shit out of people unless the situation warranted it.

He nodded, and we pushed forward.

Graham cut our way through the crowd as we climbed the steps, the scent of smoke thicker the higher we climbed. There were burns going in almost every building of the embassy's compound. One blank passport in the wrong hands could lead to an enemy on US soil, and that was an unacceptable risk.

I tugged Izzy close, my heartbeat rising in an unusual way as I studied the crowd around us, looking for anyone who didn't belong, even though I damn well knew everyone here had been allowed entrance to the embassy at some point. The guards still stood outside.

We climbed story after story until we reached the roof access, bypassing every single person waiting on the inbound Chinook. Maybe it made me a callous asshole, but I had exactly one priority, and the hundreds of people left waiting in the stairwell weren't it.

Not now.

Izzy startled at the sound of gunfire as we stood in the doorway.

"It's probably just celebratory," I told her.

"Which is why you have your hand on your rifle," she muttered, glancing at the team around us. "Why you *all* have your weapons out."

"Well, that's just in case it's *not* celebratory," Torres said, bringing up the rear next to Parker.

"It's just a precaution," Parker said. "Nothing to worry about."

"Right. Just your run-of-the-mill evacuation." Izzy squeezed my hand, and I stroked my thumb over the racing pulse in her wrist.

The sound of rotors filled the air as the Chinook approached.

"Looks like our ride," I told her.

The bird landed on the roof, wind blasting us as the back door lowered.

"I think I liked it better when we took off from the soccer field," Izzy said.

"Me too." I squeezed her hand once and let it go. "Stay right behind me. Twelve inches."

She nodded, and I lifted my rifle with both hands.

We walked onto the exposed rooftop, and I swept the buildings around me. Getting to the bird meant walking closer to the edge of the building, and I knew if I could see the parade of Taliban vehicles with their white flags and mounted fifty-cals in the truck beds, that meant Izzy could too.

The Green Zone had been breached, and they were headed in the direction of the Arg, the presidential palace. The embassy might be US property, but we were firmly within enemy territory now.

I put my body between hers and the edge, and kept my rifle trained on the ground below, scanning for legitimate threats. Elston joined us as we boarded, climbing up the door and into the Chinook.

Keeping us near the edge of the exit while the others loaded, I sat us down once we hit max capacity, pulling Izzy close against the hard metal of the aircraft as the back door rose. I'd been in plenty of helicopters with plenty of bullets flying around, but I'd never had the kind of anxiety that crept up my throat at this moment.

Torres gave me a knowing look through the dim lighting as we launched, and I refrained from flipping him the bird.

We both knew exactly what my problem was.

I had Izzy to worry about.

The airport was a hellscape. Crying children, stunned men, and worried women filled the terminal, and they were the lucky ones.

The ones outside the fence, screaming to be let in? Not so lucky.

When we got to Izzy's gate, my stomach twisted.

Her flight had been canceled.

There weren't enough swear words in the world to narrate my thoughts, but Izzy simply took a deep breath and lifted her chin. "Then I guess we should find the temporary embassy here."

"Solid plan," Elston agreed.

I nodded, and we set off through the ever-growing panic of a crowd policed by US and NATO soldiers. Gate after gate said the same thing, with precious few getting their flights out.

"Oh my God," Izzy said, stopping dead in the middle of the walkway and turning toward the television.

The presidential palace was no longer in the Afghan government's hands.

"Shit's deteriorating fast," Graham said

"Fuck deteriorating, shit's *gone*," Parker corrected. "According to that news site, the airport and the embassy are the only places we hold."

And who knew how long we'd have either.

"Let's go." I took Izzy's hand, giving exactly zero cares about whoever saw, and led us through the airport, using Webb's directions to get us to the temporary embassy site.

We went from a crowd that bordered on hysteria to administrative hell. Cutting through the lines of desperate civilians, we passed through the small barricade and were met with the embassy staff who'd already been evacuated.

"Guess I'll see who I can help," Izzy said, flashing me an uncertain smile and caressing the palm of my hand with her thumb before letting me go.

"Don't leave this area," I told her. "I'll see what I can find out about flights."

She nodded, making sure her clipped badge was visible before she headed off toward the first clerk.

"Find out about her sister," I ordered Graham.

He nodded, and I got to work finding Izzy a ride out of this place.

Usually I loved sunrises and the possibilities they brought, but today's seemed more like a new variant of lighting on the same damned day.

We'd been here thirty-six hours, while the city had fallen into bedlam around us. The reports coming in were harrowing. There were over a hundred thousand people in need of evacuation, and not a single airplane could get them out. While a couple of flights had managed to depart the night we'd arrived at the airport, every flight had been halted yesterday.

Izzy had worked herself to the bone and was currently racked out on the floor, using her backpack for a pillow in what I felt was the safest corner of the temporary embassy.

"Did you find our girl a flight?" Graham asked from my right, keeping his voice down as I watched her sleep from a dozen feet away.

"Kind of." I wanted to replace that backpack with my chest, to hold her for the last few minutes I had. Our briefing with Webb an hour ago had gone exactly as I'd predicted . . . and dreaded.

"That's a bullshit answer," Graham fired back, his brow knitting.

"It's a bullshit situation." That was putting it lightly. "They're hoping to get clearance today, but until they open the runways and clear them of people, there's almost no chance of anyone getting out."

"Almost?" He glanced sideways at me.

"We're not exactly the only US *company* here." I folded my arms across my chest and memorized her face all over again, taking note of the purple shadows beneath her eyes.

"Ahh." Graham nodded, catching my meaning. "Gotcha. Does she know about her sister?"

I shook my head, my stomach sinking. "No. And she's not going to."

"You're not going to tell her about the checkpoints? About the bullet holes in reporters?" Graham lifted his brows, his dark eyes flaring.

"No." I swallowed the lump in my throat that seemed to have taken up residence there since Izzy arrived in country. "She'll never get on the plane if she knows that there's a high chance Serena won't."

And as of an hour ago, I couldn't even strap Izzy into her seat. I just had to pray and trust that she'd walk onto the plane.

We'd been reassigned.

Izzy shifted, her eyes fluttering open and finding mine within seconds. She'd always had an uncanny sense of where I was. My ribs felt so tight I half expected them to break from the ache in my chest.

She sat up slowly, her loose braid sliding over her shoulder, but she didn't smile. Whatever was on my face had given me away, and she knew something was up.

How the fuck was I supposed to do this?

"Five minutes?" Graham asked.

"Ten," Torres said from behind us.

"Ten," I agreed. Ten would never be enough, but it was all we had.

Graham slapped me on the back and walked away, headed toward our assembly area.

I stood there, my eyes locked with hers, struggling to find the words. *Wrong.* Leaving her felt wrong in every cell of my body, and yet there was exactly jack and shit I could do about it. Orders were orders.

I was getting sick of being put into a position where she could never be mine, when she already was in every way that mattered.

I walked toward Izzy as she stood, her face solemn.

"What's wrong?" she asked.

Putting my hand on her lower back, I guided her to the corner, where I could block her body from the view of embassy workers in hopes of just a few minutes of privacy.

"I have to go." Every word shredded part of my soul.

Her lips parted. "Okay. When will you be back?"

"I won't."

Her deep-brown eyes flew wide.

"We've been reassigned. There are—" I swallowed. "There are places we need to be and things we need to be doing." Even if I could tell her what I was about to head into, I wouldn't. The worry would kill her.

Everything about the next few hours could alter the rest of Izzy's life.

"Oh." Her shoulders fell. "That's understandable. I'm as safe as I can be, and your skills are definitely wasted by hanging out in the airport." She looked up at me, forcing a smile I'd seen far too many times over the last decade. She gave it to me every time I had to leave.

"Listen to me carefully." I took her shoulders in my hands. "At three o'clock, someone is going to come get you. He's got a medium build, gray beard, and he'll know how we met. He's not going to have my charming wit, but he is going to put you on a plane out of here."

Her brow knit. "Nate, no planes are getting out of here."

"Even if that's true, this one will. Company planes tend to go wherever they want whenever they want. He'll get you stateside." My hand slid to cup the side of her neck. Her skin was so soft.

She blinked. "And they have room for me?"

"You're a congressional aide. Trust me, they have a vested interest in you getting home as quietly as possible." Izzy was a PR nightmare just waiting to happen.

"And Serena?" The hope in her eyes gutted me.

"He has a seat for Serena. Taj too." It had taken calling in every favor I'd ever earned, but her safety was all that mattered. "If your sister isn't back by three o'clock, you have to get on the plane anyway." I looked deep into her eyes, willing her to agree, to be pliable for once in her damned life.

Her chin drew back as she opened her mouth, and I slid my hand across her chin, running my thumb across her soft lips.

"Please, Izzy. You have to go. It's going to be the hardest thing you'll ever do. But you have to get on the plane." I leaned down so our faces were only inches apart and cradled the back of her head. "Eventually the airport will be surrendered, and I won't be here for you. You have to get out of here. I *need* you to get out of here."

"I can't leave her," she whispered, her voice breaking.

"You can. You will. It's what she would want." If she was still alive to want.

"I can't leave you." She shook her head.

"You don't have to when I'm the one always going."

"I can wait another day," she protested, hands gripping my arms.

"You can't." I touched my forehead to hers and breathed deeply. "Do you remember when I asked, if you knew the world had twenty-four hours before some calamity struck, where would you go? And you said that you'd go wherever you could be the most help?"

"This is not the time for the trivia game, Nate." She pulled me closer, tears filling her eyes.

"Do you remember?"

"Yes." She nodded. "It was when we were leaving Kandahar."

"Ask me."

Her lower lip trembled. "If you knew the world had twenty-four hours before some calamity struck, where would you go?"

"I would go wherever you are. I knew it that night in Tybee. Hell, I probably knew it the second you reached for my hand in that plane. There is no force on earth that would keep me from you." I kissed her softly. "That's why you have to get on the plane, Izzy. I won't be able to think, to focus, to walk so much as twelve feet away from you if I don't know you're headed to safety."

"We're magnets, right?" She wound her arms around my neck. "Always finding each other."

"And we will find each other again, I promise." One of my hands fell to the gentle slope of her waist as I fought the emotions threatening to pull me under. "We haven't had our shot yet."

Surging up on her toes, she kissed me.

I slanted my mouth over hers and took it like it could be the last time, leaving us both breathing hard when I finally found the fortitude to lift my head. "I love you, Isabeau Astor. Promise me you'll get on the plane. I know you want to stay for Serena, but I need you to leave for me."

"Promise me you'll come home."

"I promise I will come home. I will find you. We will have our shot." My chest burned with how much I loved her, how hard it was to walk away from her in any situation, let alone in this place.

"I love you." She held me even tighter, and I pressed a hard kiss to her forehead, trying like hell to breathe deeply enough to minimize the burn in my eyes.

"I love you," I whispered.

Then I let her go, and her arms fell away as I stepped back, taking one last look at her before turning around and forcing my feet to move, my legs to carry me away from her.

"I'm sorry," Torres said, pushing off the wall as I walked past him. "I know what she is to you."

Everything. She was everything. "If I asked you to go with her, would you?"

"If I could, then you know I would." He shot me a look so full of remorse that I had to look away. "But I can't, Nate, and you know why."

"Yeah." I grabbed the pack I'd left near the entrance to the temporary embassy and slung it over my shoulders, boxing up every emotion I possibly could. Now wasn't the time to lose it over Izzy. Now was the time to act *for* Izzy. "Unfortunately, I do."

CHAPTER THIRTY-ONE
IZZY

Kabul, Afghanistan
August 2021

I watched the clock tick away the minutes after Nate left, then the hours, pulling myself together so I could help wherever possible.

There were too many people and not enough helpers.

The panic was palpable, and as flights began to take off again, that energy transformed into pure desperation. Desperation to find missing family members. Desperation to obtain a visa long since submitted for. Desperation to get a seat on any plane that was going anywhere but here.

I looked up every possible minute, searching for my sister in a sea of faces but never finding her. Nate was gone. Serena was God knew where, and there was nothing I could do to help either of them.

After telling the twelfth—or maybe it was more, I lost count—previous military interpreter that I couldn't do anything to speed up his paperwork, I felt defeated in every way.

Three o'clock came before I was ready, and before I could motion to the next person in line, a man appeared at my left.

A man with a salt-and-pepper beard, dressed in cargo pants with a weapon in a thigh holster, a black shirt, and a Kevlar vest.

"Isabeau Astor?" he asked.

"Sergeant Green sent you," I guessed, a fissure cracking in my heart.

"We both know his name isn't Sergeant Green, but sure." He nodded with a tight smile. "Said he met you during a plane crash."

I nodded. "It's time to go, isn't it?"

"It is." There was a healthy dose of compassion in his eyes. "I'm guessing your sister didn't show?"

I stared out over the crowd of waiting people and shook my head.

"I'm sorry, but we can't wait."

"I understand." It was on the tip of my tongue to turn him down, to stay and do what I could for as long as I could, but the look on Nate's face flashed across my mind.

I won't be able to think, to focus, to walk so much as twelve feet away from you if I don't know you're headed to safety.

He'd spent the last eleven days risking his life to protect me.

Maybe I'd failed to bring Serena home, to help her interpreter, to help . . . any of these people. But I could make it so Nate wouldn't fail.

"Okay." I nodded, then took Taj's visa and gave it to the embassy officer at the station next to me. Pulling my backpack on, I looked up at the man Nate had sent for me. The man he'd entrusted me to. "I'm ready."

I wasn't, but I would go. I would do it for Nate.

Because he loved me. Because he'd carried my ring for three years. Because he'd pulled me from that plane. Because I hadn't held on to him when I should have, and I'd regretted that choice ever since.

I followed the nameless man through the airport and didn't look away from the suffering, the fear etched into every face. I bore witness, letting each person's expression touch me, mark me, because Serena wasn't here to do so.

"I don't suppose that if I wanted to give my seat to someone else, you'd let me do that?" I asked as he led me out onto the tarmac.

"I promised your man I'd tie you into the seat myself if that's what it took to get you on the plane." A corner of his mouth rose. "And you'll find I'm not quite as moralistic as he is. I'll do it."

We walked across the scalding-hot concrete, and I looked through the shimmering waves of heat at the mountains I'd thought were so beautiful when we'd landed here eleven days ago.

Eleven days was all it had taken for my world to be shaken like a snow globe. Now all I could do was sit back and watch to see where the flurries landed and hope I recognized the landscape.

We walked silently toward a tall metal fence covered with a wind guard, and I wished like hell I'd developed Nate's incredible skill of compartmentalizing. Instead, I felt an acute sense of loss with every step I took away from my sister, from Nate. How could I leave the two people I loved most in the world?

The man nodded to a guard, who swung open the left side of a massive gate to allow us passage.

An unmarked silver plane waited beyond the fence.

"It's an adapted Hercules," the man explained to me, even though I hadn't asked.

"It's lovely," I answered, unsure of what to say.

He laughed. "You certainly are a politician, aren't you?"

"Not really." Even when I had been, I'd done it for all the wrong reasons.

He led me up the stairs and into the plane, which had been outfitted with not only air-conditioning but also a series of seats, three on each side, stretching back for a dozen rows. Almost every seat was already full.

"You're there." He pointed to the front row on the right side of the plane, where two seats remained open.

"Thank you."

"Don't mention it." His brows lifted. "And I mean that. Don't mention it."

I nodded. I wasn't so naive that I didn't understand the repeated use of *company* when Nate told me about the flight.

The window seat was open, so I took it, just to prove to myself that I could. I'd flown all over this country looking out the window of a Blackhawk helicopter. Surely I could make it out of here sitting at the window.

I fit the seat belt over my hips and tried not to think about the fact that Nate and Serena were still out there. But there was an empty seat . . .

My heart screamed with longing. I'd been on too many planes with an empty seat over the last four years, constantly waiting for Nate to appear.

This time I knew there was no chance of that, and it somehow hurt even worse.

Unzipping my backpack for my headphones, I blinked at the book that had been shoved inside. It was Nate's copy of *The Color Purple*, the one he'd been reading when I first arrived. I clutched the book to my chest and tried my best to smother a sob as someone closed the door on the right.

A minute or two later, the plane began to roll forward slowly, and my throat closed so tight it was hard to breathe.

"Forgive me," I whispered, but I wasn't sure who I was begging. Nate? Serena? Everyone I'd left behind who didn't have a seat on a secret plane?

Then the movement stopped, and I looked out the window, but there was no line for takeoff or anything. Someone walked back out of the cockpit and worked the door, opening it with quick efficiency and lowering the steps.

"Let's go!" the pilot shouted, leaning out the door.

He backed up a moment later as two figures burst through the door and into the plane.

Taj and Serena.

Thank you, God.

She had a black eye and the sleeve of her blue shirt was bloody, but she was here, moving toward me with a watery smile. Taj was in far worse shape as he walked back through the center aisle to the empty seat a few rows back.

She collapsed into the empty seat beside me, dropping her bag between her knees before turning toward me and yanking me close.

"You made it," I whispered, dropping the book to my lap and holding her tight as the pilot closed the door.

"Thanks to Nate and his team," she answered, pulling back long enough to look me over, like I was the one who'd clearly been beaten.

"What?"

"Nate's team came out to the checkpoint they were holding us at," she explained. "They're the only reason we're here." She stroked my hair back. "Well, Nate and you pushing Taj's visa through."

The plane started to roll again, and Serena leaned forward, opening her bag and taking something out. She pressed it into my open palm and looked me in the eye. "He said to tell you that he loves you, and that he'll be in touch when it's time to take your shot."

My heart jolted, and I looked down at my hand.

It was the chain and the taped tag.

I fell back against my seat and let the tears come as the plane headed down the runway, Serena holding my other hand as we launched into the air, leaving Nate behind.

"He'll be okay," Serena promised.

"I love him."

"Anyone in the same room as you two knows that," she said. "What's the necklace, anyway?" she asked, leaning to retrieve her camera from her bag. She was lucky to have made it out, let alone with her equipment.

I gently peeled back the layers of the tape until my ring appeared. "It's our shot."

"That is gorgeous." She blinked, then openly gawked through the eye that wasn't swollen shut.

"Yeah, it is."

Her brow furrowed. "Is that a dog tag?"

"Not sure," I said, forcing the tape from the rest of the metal. "Nate told me he only took the ring on missions that didn't have to be sanitized, but—" I slipped my engagement ring onto my right hand to keep it safe, then wiped the name clean of the sticky residue. "It's not his."

"It's not?" She glanced my way, clicking through the pictures on her view screen.

"No." I hadn't been the only person Nate had been carrying with him.

The tag read TORRES, JULIAN.

"I was wrong," I whispered. I'd always assumed that Julian was Rowell, which went to show just how little I knew about the time Nate and I had spent apart all these years.

"Look what I got about an hour ago." She angled the camera's screen toward me.

It was a profile shot of Nate. My heart clenched at the stubborn set of his jaw, the perfect sculpture of his lips.

"You know," Serena said quietly, "I could publish this, and he'd be out of the unit."

My gaze jumped to hers. One simple action would change . . . everything. We'd actually have a chance at being together. But at what cost?

"He'd probably be pissed—"

"No." I shook my head, my fingers curling around the dog tag. "If Nate gets out, that has to be his choice." I wouldn't make that decision for him in New York, and I wouldn't make it now. I would take him however he chose to come to me.

"And until that magical day?" Serena asked.

"I'll wait."

CHAPTER THIRTY-TWO

NATHANIEL

Fort Bragg, North Carolina
September 2021

I took a deep breath as I stood in the empty hallway, facing the door I'd been scheduled to walk through for the past two weeks. Foolishly, I'd thought making the initial call would be the hardest, but it wasn't. Standing here, staring at the clinical letters beside the door, deciding whether or not to turn the handle, was infinitely harder.

The clinic didn't have that oversanitized smell that came with hospitals, but we'd never been seen by typical doctors either.

"You can do it," Torres said from my left.

"If I do, it's over," I replied, keeping my voice low. "You know they'll kick me out of the unit."

"Yeah. And then maybe you'll start living for you. Get some help for those nightmares, too, so you're not terrified to sleep next to your girl. You're not your dad. You're never going to be your dad. But still . . .

you need the help. You should probably figure out what to do with that farm of yours."

I glanced over at him, my hand reaching for the doorknob.

"You gotta let go, Nate," he said, offering me a smile. "You've carried shit that isn't yours for too long. That guilt? Not yours. The career you're not actually that fond of? Not yours. But Izzy? She's the one who's yours. So if you won't walk through that door for yourself, consider doing it for her."

Izzy.

It had been six weeks since I'd left her at the Kabul airport so I could give her the one thing I knew she needed—Serena. I missed her with every breath, and yet I knew it wasn't time yet.

If we had one shot, then I couldn't blow it.

I took one last look at Torres and then I opened the door and walked through.

Dr. Williamson looked up from his desk with a professional smile and motioned to the chairs in front of his desk. "How's it going, Phelan?"

Usually I would have told him I was fine. That I was sleeping, eating, and relaxing just like I was supposed to.

But lying hadn't gotten me anywhere, so maybe it was time that I told the truth.

I sank into the chair and looked the doctor in the eye. "I've been talking to my best friend as a coping mechanism for the stress, the deployments, the . . . everything."

He nodded, leaning back in his chair. "That sounds pretty normal."

"Yeah, except he's been dead for four years. Think you can help me?" I gripped my knees and waited for his answer.

"Yes," he said. "I think I can help you."

CHAPTER THIRTY-THREE

IZZY

Washington, DC
October 2021

I settled into my seat and stored my bag, then clicked my seat belt as my fellow passengers boarded around me.

For the first time since Palau, I'd packed a full suitcase. Swimsuits, cover-ups, sundresses, all of it. I hadn't heard from Nate since leaving Kabul, and sure, my pulse skyrocketed when I thought of the minute possibility of him actually meeting me at the layover stop. But even if he didn't—which was more than likely—I was going to check into our bungalow in the Maldives, sleep until noon, lie out in the sun, and dream about him.

Because that's what he would have wanted me to do.

I was pretty damn sure he was still deployed, given the state of the world, and as he'd told me, there would always be somewhere they were needed.

Somewhere in the last six weeks, between watching my phone for a call that didn't come and staring at my door when my darkest thoughts got the best of me, I'd come to a conclusion. If I wanted to be with Nate, really honestly *be* with him, then I needed two things: strength and patience.

Strength to know that he loved me, and he'd come to me when he could, and patience to wait for those days.

Oh, and a little more freedom from the job I actually abhorred when push came to shove.

I took out the novel I'd picked up in the airport bookstore and cracked open a fresh highlighter as the couple across the aisle took their seats. By the time Nate got home, I'd have a full library of marked-up books for him to devour.

Whenever Nate got home.

The sun shone through the clouds for a moment, streaming in the window beside me and making the diamond on my right hand sparkle. A ring like that wasn't meant to be covered by electrical tape and hidden away. It was made to shine, which it would do from my right hand until Nate either took it back or slid it to my left.

I crossed my legs and leaned back, reading the first page.

"Excuse me, but may I walk past?" His deep voice slid over me like the softest silk, and my heart jolted as I slowly lowered the book and looked up.

It wasn't him. It couldn't be him.

But it was.

"I have the window seat." He smiled, flashing that dimple at me, and my jaw dropped as he slid right past me to sink into the seat on my right.

"You . . ." My breaths came erratically as I looked into my favorite pair of blue eyes. "You're not supposed to meet me until Boston."

"I switched flights." His shoulders rose and fell in a shrug. "Figured if we were going to spend a week in the Maldives, we should get as much travel time together as possible."

I nodded, because of course that made sense . . . in a world where Nate wasn't constantly deployed. A world where he actually showed up on the flights he scheduled.

"There are a few things I need to tell you." The smile fell away from his face.

"Well, it appears that we have time." I closed the book and turned toward him. "There are a few things I should tell you too."

"Oh?" He reached over and took my hand. The simple contact was absolute heaven.

"I really hate being in politics." I scrunched my nose.

"That's not news." His thumb moved in small, reassuring circles on my skin.

"I may have quit my job." It came out a rushed whisper.

He grinned. "Funny you should mention that. I may have quit mine too."

My lips parted as I looked for words. Any words.

"It was time." He lifted his hand to my face and cupped my cheek. "I am wildly in love with you, and I don't want to be your possibility anymore. I'm not leaving us up to fate."

I leaned into his palm and stared at him, terrified to close my eyes, scared that this would all be a dream and I'd wake alone in my bed, reaching for a figment of my imagination.

"I think it's about time we took our shot. What do you say?" His gaze dropped to my mouth. "I mean, you should probably know that I'm going through some therapy, and that might not be something you want to stick around through—"

"Yes." I nodded, my heart pumping so wildly I half expected it to burst out of my chest. "I say yes. Let's take our shot. Let's go slow or move fast. Let's do everything we talked about and dream up new stuff. I don't care where we live or what we do, as long as I get to do it with you. I love you."

"Izzy?" He leaned across the armrest as the plane rolled backward, leaving the gate.

"Nate?" I moved closer.

"I'm going to kiss you now."

I smiled as his mouth met mine, then sighed when he deepened the kiss and kept going all through takeoff. By the time we lifted our heads, we were far above the clouds.

I didn't know what this new future looked like, but I knew it was ours.

And that was everything.

EPILOGUE

NATHANIEL

Maine
Five years later

The September sun came through the pine trees in splotches as they swayed above us, rustling gently in the breeze as we sat beneath them on a thick blanket.

My legs were stretched out in front of me, Izzy's head in my lap.

It was my favorite way to catch up on our work.

Fall in Maine was my favorite time of year. It had been the perfect place for us to start our forever. Pine trees, enough room from both our families to breathe, and each other. I knew Izzy missed Serena, but she spent most of her time out on assignment, and they always made time to see each other when Serena was actually in the US.

I marked a student's paper, commenting on the unique twist she'd used in her analysis of *Macbeth*, while Izzy read through what looked to be a briefing she was filing on behalf of a local nonprofit.

Peace. The feeling coursing through me was exactly what I'd been searching for my entire life, and it existed wherever Izzy was.

Finishing that particular paper, I took a moment to brush back her hair. It didn't matter how many days I had with her. She always seemed more beautiful every time I saw her.

She put her briefing down, the sun catching on the diamond and gold band on her left hand, and she smiled up at me. "Almost done?"

"Three more. You?"

She flipped the document over, glancing at the length. "Probably ten minutes."

"Any plans for your afternoon?" I trailed my fingers down her bare arm. Touching her never got old either. It was my favorite thing to do. Well, except talking to her. Or kissing her. Basically anything that involved Izzy, I was down for.

"Nothing comes to mind." She slipped a hand under my shirt, and my stomach tightened. "Why? Anything you feel like doing?"

"I was thinking about carrying you back to bed and spending the rest of the day worshipping your body."

Her lips parted, and she scrambled to her feet. "Yep. That sounds like a plan."

"Can't wait another ten minutes?" I laughed, already grabbing my pile of papers and the blanket we'd been sitting on.

"Nope." She backed away with an irresistible grin, heading toward the back door of our house. "Work can wait."

"I've never agreed more." I chased her up to the house and, once I caught her, lifted her into my arms, tangling her up with the blanket.

The papers hit the floor with the briefing once we made it in the door.

Then my hands were full of Izzy.

She was right. Work could wait.

We finally had forever.

ACKNOWLEDGMENTS

First and foremost, thank you to my Heavenly Father for blessing me beyond my wildest dreams.

Thank you to my husband, Jason, for handling our life when I disappear into the writing cave. Writing this put me right back in the feels of those long years you spent in Afghanistan and Iraq. I'm immeasurably grateful for each of the twenty-two years you spent in uniform, but even more thankful for the days we have together now that you're retired. Thank you to my children, who don't bat an eye when I'm on deadline and always inspire me. Thank you to my sister, Kate—growing up as a military brat is way easier with a friend like you. Thank you to the one and only Emily Byer, because you always call.

Thank you to Lauren Plude, Lindsey Faber, and the team at Montlake for making this all happen. You guys are a dream to work with! To my phenomenal agent, Louise Fury, who makes my life easier simply by standing at my back.

Thank you to my wifeys, our unholy trinity, Gina L. Maxwell and Cindi Madsen, who always answer when I call. Thank you to Shelby and Cassie for putting up with my unicorn brain and being the best hype girls I could ever ask for. Thank you to K. P. Simmon for showing up not only in business but as a friend. To every blogger and reader who has taken a chance on me over the years—you make this industry what it is. To my reader group, the Flygirls, for giving me a safe space in the Wild West of the internet.

Lastly, because you're my beginning and end, thank you again to my Jason. None of this would be possible without your love and support. I know the helicopter pilots in this one don't have any lines, but there's a little of you in every hero I write.

ABOUT THE AUTHOR

Photo © 2022 Katie Marie Seniors

Rebecca Yarros is a hopeless romantic and coffee addict. She is the *Wall Street Journal* and *USA Today* bestselling author of over fifteen novels, including *The Last Letter* and *The Things We Leave Unfinished*. She's also the recipient of the Colorado Romance Writers Award of Excellence for *Eyes Turned Skyward*. Rebecca loves military heroes and has been blissfully married to hers for over twenty years. A mother of six, she is currently surviving the teenage years with all four of her hockey-playing sons.

Seriously. All four are teenagers. Send wine.

When she's not writing, she's at the hockey rink or sneaking in some guitar time. She lives in Colorado with her family, their English bulldogs, Maine coon cat, and feisty chinchillas who love to chase the bulldogs. Having fostered then adopted their youngest daughter, Rebecca is passionate about helping foster children through her non-profit, One October.

Want to know about Rebecca's next release? Check her out online at www.rebeccayarros.com.